NARCO ASSASSINS

JASON KASPER

Severn River
PUBLISHING

NARCO ASSASSINS

Severn River Publishing
www.SevernRiverBooks.com

ISBN: 978-1-64875-283-4 (Paperback)
ISBN: 978-1-64875-284-1 (Hardcover)

ALSO BY JASON KASPER

American Mercenary Series

Greatest Enemy

Offer of Revenge

Dark Redemption

Vengeance Calling

The Suicide Cartel

Terminal Objective

Shadow Strike Series

The Enemies of My Country

Last Target Standing

Covert Kill

Narco Assassins

Beast Three Six

Spider Heist Thrillers

The Spider Heist

The Sky Thieves

The Manhattan Job

The Fifth Bandit

Standalone Thriller

Her Dark Silence

To find out more about Jason Kasper and his books, visit severnriverbooks.com/authors/jason-kasper

To the citizens of Ukraine

Slava Ukraini

See, if you look at the drug war from a purely economic point of view, the role of the government is to protect the drug cartel. That's literally true.

-Milton Friedman

Avenge me, Cancer. Avenge me!

-Reilly

1

Medellín, Colombia

I proceeded up the sloping flagstone walkway, glancing sideways at Ian beside me.

He did a better job of playing a tourist than I did—his phone was in hand, a video recording in progress as he scanned for any signs of pursuit before we committed to the meeting ahead.

"Beautiful," he said, "just beautiful."

"Yeah," I replied, taking in the view that expanded with each step of our ascent.

Palm trees dotted the walkway, rising from planters brimming with tropical bushes. To either side of the path was Medellín in all its glory: tree-lined city streets weaving between apartment buildings and skyscrapers, the verdant mountainsides beyond dotted with sprawling barrios. Just as appealing was the weather: clear blue skies, light breeze, and temperatures hovering in the mid-seventies just as they did most of the year. Situated at 5,000 feet in a valley within the Andes, Medellín's climate had earned it the nickname "City of Eternal Spring."

That was, of course, far from its only designation.

In the bygone days of Pablo Escobar, Medellín was alternately dubbed murder capital of the world, or the most dangerous city on earth. Neither title was inaccurate, per se, but the present era had far outpaced that dark past. Medellín was now a vibrant modern city, teeming with culture and tourism. In the three days we'd been here, I'd chatted with many friendly street vendors, seen countless American hipsters on vacation, and encountered exactly zero gun-wielding sicarios.

And while that should have been a source of comfort, there was something unsettling about a public exchange with an intelligence asset, particularly one we'd never met. Because while Ian and I had spent the better part of two hours performing a surveillance detection route before arriving at the meet, there was no telling whether the asset had been disciplined enough to do the same, or if he'd be able to spot a tail in the first place. And considering our tourist attire didn't provide much in the way of concealment, if things went bad it would be us versus the world with nothing more than the Glock 26 pistols concealed in our waistbands.

I directed my attention to our destination, a tall, trapezoidal building looming at the walkway's end. The sign declared it to be *Museo Casa de la Memoria*, the House of Memory Museum, which would serve our purposes nicely. It was, after all, a centrally located tourist destination where two gringos wouldn't appear out of place, and filled with secluded exhibits to allow a hasty meeting before both parties went their separate ways amidst the normal flow of foot traffic.

An unarmed security guard stood beside the door, nodding at us as we entered the lobby and were greeted by a female receptionist. She addressed us in English, directing us to register ourselves in an open ledger on the desk before her. I scanned the page to find the pseudonym Arturo García, indicating that our asset was here; now we just had to find him at the appointed meeting place. Then I scrawled a fake name—as long as it wasn't David Rivers, it didn't really matter what I wrote—and handed the pen to Ian.

The first exhibit was disorienting, to say the least. An array of chairs, window frames, doors, and nightstands hung from the ceiling, dangling in a random array that was, according to the translated sign, an artistic tribute to the millions of Colombians displaced by violence.

We made our way into the next room, pausing respectfully at the various exhibits as I glanced at our fellow visitors. To my surprise, most appeared to be native Colombians: a man and woman with teenage children, a couple in their twenties, and an older gentleman who appeared intently focused on the map detailing refugee numbers by geographic area. Nothing out of the ordinary, but then again, none of them were wearing the red Puma shirt and ballcap that would mark our asset.

Ian and I passed beneath another exhibit dangling from wires and headed into the adjoining corridor, where touchscreens displayed interactive maps with news reports of various massacres, sieges, and political assassinations. A lone woman scanned a wall displaying a timeline of the violence from 1964 to present. Since I didn't speak Spanish beyond a few conversational pleasantries and some basic survival terms, the text was lost on me—but select titles plastered across the timeline weren't.

Amidst various cartel names I saw acronyms like M-19, AUC, FARC, ELN, and EPL, a veritable alphabet soup of deadly organizations. Each had played their part in the sixty-year conflict that continued to rage far from tourist centers like Medellín, with a death toll far exceeding that of the Hiroshima and Nagasaki bombings combined. The vast majority of victims were innocent civilians. In retrospect, I thought dryly, the Colombian government should have funded a bigger museum to commemorate their fallen.

We slipped past the woman, and I caught sight of our asset in the shadowy confines of the next exhibit hall. He was facing the far end, wearing the designated clothing as he watched a video monitor with both hands folded across his front. As long as he hadn't been followed here, he was being a model informant: waiting in the right place at the right time, performing the right action. All we had to do now was exchange bonafides and find out what had been so urgent to require a face-to-face meeting.

But first we had to cross the long room to reach him, reminding me why we'd selected this massive exhibit hall for the initial contact.

Six-foot-high video screens were situated at oblique angles across the floor, each projecting a full-body view of a Colombian man, woman, or child speaking Spanish. The combined effect was of slipping through a dinner party where every attendee relayed their personal tale of surviving their village's massacre, or fleeing across the country with their families and whatever they could carry, in an endlessly looping monologue. Together with the low lighting, the overlapping audio provided a nearly ideal setting to exchange information without being surveilled.

My first indication that something was wrong was a woman's scream, coming not from a video monitor to my front but rather the room we'd just departed.

"Take the twelve," I said, instructing Ian to pull security in our direction of movement as I drew my pistol, catching a fleeting glimpse of our asset darting behind a video display as I spun in place. There was one way in and one way out of this large exhibit, and we'd need to control both doors to protect the asset, let alone ourselves.

That thought had barely occurred to me before the woman appeared in the doorway, now trying desperately to flee some unknown threat. She spotted me and came up short, causing me to lower my pistol and shout, "*Vámonos!*" Relief and gratitude flashed across her face as she resumed her run, now trying to get behind me. But the woman had only taken three steps when her torso blossomed with a trio of exit wounds, and she fell dead.

Her body hadn't yet struck the ground when her killer appeared in the doorway, a young, goateed man clutching an MP5 submachine gun with suppressor. I had him in my sights before he could register my location in the darkened exhibit, firing a controlled pair of 9mm jacketed hollow points into his sternum. And while my accuracy wasn't a problem—both rounds found their mark, and I was transitioning to a follow-up headshot even as he toppled forward—the fact that he'd come with backup was.

The second shooter had seen his comrade's fate and removed guesswork from the equation; my first indication of his presence was the hissing *whiffs* of a suppressor blasting a fully automatic burst from the doorway.

Incoming rounds thwacked into the wall beside me as I scrambled behind one of the video displays, shouting the word "incoming" for Ian's benefit before dropping to a knee and taking aim from the opposite side.

The doorway was empty; the shooter had made it into the room.

I heard Ian firing behind me—at least, I hoped it was Ian—a loud double bang of pistol shots followed by a second pair, before I shouted, "One got in."

To my horror, Ian responded with the last two words I wanted to hear.

"Same here."

Suddenly the vacationing hipsters didn't seem so bad, I thought as I surveyed the room from my kneeling position, hearing the faint metallic clank of a magazine hitting the ground as one of the shooters reloaded.

Determining his location from sound alone was impossible: all around me, the faint murmuring monologues of the video displays continued to play. My hearing was merely adequate on my best day, courtesy of a brief stint in the US Army that included trips to Afghanistan and Iraq, to say nothing of my subsequent career. And while Ian covered my backside, that was of little consolation given that he was an intelligence operative, blooded on previous missions but far from a career shooter. I'd chosen to keep him by my side because this foray was supposed to be an asset interview, and my remaining teammates were no more suited to facilitate that than Ian was to repel the current attack.

And in the meantime, no less than two killers were in the large exhibit hall with us, seeking me and Ian in the interests of finishing the job they'd clearly come here for. Because while Medellín certainly wasn't crime free, no alternate universe existed in which Ian and I hadn't just become the ultimate targets. Assassins being targeted by assassins, I thought bitterly, a uniquely Colombian proposition.

Panning my aim across the room, I continued kneeling behind the video display, whose glare would keep me relatively hidden in the shadows. When my second scan ended without sighting a bad guy, I realized that the remaining two assassins were doing the same thing I was.

Leveling my pistol at the waist level of a farmer speaking on the far left screen, I fired a single round, using the recoil to drive my aim right to the video projection of an elderly woman before shooting again.

One by one, the screens flashed to black in the wake of my gunshots. My hope was to achieve a hit to the chest or pelvis, depending on whether the killers were standing or kneeling, and when my fourth gunshot shattered a display with a yelp of pain from the other side, I followed it with three more shots.

A man in a navy jumpsuit stumbled out from behind the screen in a half crouch, clutching his stomach with one hand and jabbing his submachine gun toward me with the other. I attempted to shoot twice, the first round hitting but not killing him before my second trigger squeeze resulted in an impotent click. My slide was locked to the rear, pistol empty.

I was in the process of diving left when the man opened fire, spraying wildly as I hit the ground and scrambled for the concealment of the nearest screen display. It wouldn't provide cover from bullets, as this shooter had just learned the hard way. At best I could break his line of sight for the time it took me to reload my sole remaining magazine, this one designed for a full-size Glock with a corresponding 17-round capacity.

Incoming bullets popped into the wall and glass fragments showered down as I completed my desperate crawl, a white-hot pinprick of pain lacing into my left shoulder—some kind of debris, not a bullet. By the time I rolled to my side to fumble for the magazine on my belt, I heard a momentary pause in the suppressed gunfire as my attacker moved forward to find me.

Shifting onto my back, I ejected the empty mag and slammed the new one into place at the exact moment not one but two shooters appeared to my front, one to either side of the screen. This was the kind of hellish split-second decision making where no conscious thought entered into my mind; while either man could easily kill me, and probably would in the coming seconds, I felt my arms extending into a firing position toward my left even as I thumbed the slide release.

No sooner had my pistol chambered a round than I began firing as fast as I could squeeze the trigger, pumping bullets into the uninjured shooter I'd instinctively prioritized. I discharged three or four rounds in one blazing streak before swinging my pistol right, toward the gut-shot assassin whose MP5 suppressor was arcing upward to my face. Too late, I knew, and at best I'd have time to mortally wound him while getting shot to death.

But before he or I could open fire, he jolted forward and the submachine gun fell from his grasp. It took me a moment to register the sound of Ian's gunfire behind him, and by the time that occurred, the assassin dropped to his knees, a gold crucifix on a chain swinging as I delivered a pair of bullets to his chest. He fell forward, convulsing in a spastic post-mortem twitch before going still.

Only then did I see Ian completing a semicircle sweep of the carnage around us with his Glock at the ready. The sound of running footsteps behind me caused me to roll onto my stomach, assuming a prone aiming position toward the doorway with whatever rounds I had left.

The final man to the scene was a clean-cut, muscular Colombian who deftly slipped inside the room with a master's grip on his CZ 75 pistol.

"You're late," I said.

Maximo didn't respond, at least not verbally; instead he swept through the room with surprising grace, looking for survivors as I struggled to my feet. The previously sterile museum air now reeked of hot metal and gunpowder, and while the security guard at the entrance hadn't responded —hell, for all I knew he could have reported us to the shooters the moment we entered—the cops would be arriving in short order, regardless of whether they'd been paid to temporarily turn a blind eye.

Which, given that this was Colombia, certainly wasn't outside the realm of possibility.

But that was only my second concern at present: Maximo's asset had just been exposed in a confrontation with two gringos who could reasonably be presumed to be affiliated with the CIA, to say nothing of his Colombian handler.

It was going to suck, but there was no choice—we had to recover the asset to my team's safehouse, then debrief him before arranging his emergency departure from the country.

I said, "We've got to find your asset."

"I already have." Maximo gestured to the far corner with a thrust of his chin.

Clearing the shattered screen to my front, I saw a dead man at the far door, a MAC-11 machine pistol just outside his grasp. Ian must have felled him with an opening salvo.

Beside that corpse, however, was the man we were supposed to meet. He had sustained two gunshot wounds to the head, one tearing across the gumline of his lower jaw with predictable results, the other impacting squarely within his left eye. It was a horrifying disfigurement that caused me to cringe in disgust.

Maximo holstered his pistol, then turned to Ian and me.

"Get their wallets, cell phones, and photos of their faces. If we're lucky, we can find their *patrón*."

2

Cancer ended the call on his cell phone and spun away from the window and its seventh-story view of Medellín's El Poblado neighborhood. He'd scarcely begun moving toward the desk when he heard keys jangling outside the apartment's main door. Unholstering the Glock from beneath his shirt, Cancer jogged to the wall, stopping beside the door and taking aim by the time the deadbolt unlocked.

Then the door swung open and a man strode into the apartment—stout, with auburn hair, and most definitely white.

"Got some more street treats for Reilly," he announced in a Georgia twang. "I wonder how long we can keep this up."

Glancing sideways, he caught sight of Cancer, eyes dropping to the pistol.

Worthy raised the paper bags in each hand, holding them aloft in mock surrender. "Whoa, easy, buddy. I come in peace."

Cancer sidestepped to check the hallway, then closed and locked the door.

"Where's Reilly?"

"Still on the supply run with the 7th Group guys."

"Call him back. Meet went bad."

Worthy set his bags atop the counter and pulled out his cell phone. "How bad?"

"Four bad guys dead, one civilian, plus the asset. I gotta call it in."

"Shit. Our boys okay?"

"They're fine."

Worthy left to dial Reilly, leaving Cancer alone in the living room that wasn't really a living room at all—at least, not anymore. The upside to working in a country where the CIA had been meddling for the better part of a half-century with the host government's full permission, he thought, was the lodging.

To call this a safehouse would have been an insult; it was a well-furnished, multi-bedroom apartment, one of several that the Agency maintained in this building alone. It came complete with hookups for encrypted internet and satellite communications, the latter of which concerned him now.

He approached the central desk, dropping into a seat and lifting a radio hand mic from beside the computer, one of six available for planning in the retrofitted operations center. What an ass-backward mission this was turning out to be, he thought. Team leader and intel guy got to do the shooting, while Cancer—who was nothing if not a shooter—was left to run communications.

Keying the mic, he transmitted, "Raptor Nine One, this is Cancer."

A woman replied, "*This is Raptor Nine One, send it.*"

This was another idiosyncrasy of the current assignment, Cancer mused. During his days in the military, even as a mercenary, he was reporting up the chain of command to someone who'd experienced their fair share of ground combat. Now, he had to appease a former CIA station chief with the literal callsign of "Duchess" who was pulling the strings from Langley, a woman who had probably never heard a shot fired in anger much less killed anyone.

Keying the transmit button, he said, "I just got off the phone with Suicide Actual. The meeting with Maximo's source resulted in enemy contact. Shooters converged on the room, two from the front and two from the back. All four EKIA. One female civilian killed, along with the asset."

Duchess replied, "*Who killed the civilian?*"

A surge of anger welled in his chest. "Who do you think?"

"*I think*," she responded hotly, "*that I have to report this event to the ambassador before we get thrown out of the country. So give me something to work with.*"

Cancer shook his head. "Bad guys killed her, along with the asset. Enemy weapons were left on scene so forensics will confirm. Our guys are fine, in case you were wondering, on their way back now. Suicide will give you a full report once he's in. They recovered whatever intel they could from the shooters, so you'll have a data dump coming your way."

"*Copy all, I've got to forward the report before this gets out of hand. Anything else?*"

"Yeah." Cancer paused for a moment. "Maximo was late to the meet."

"*How late?*"

"Sounds like he showed right after the hit failed. I think we need to reconsider how much we trust this guy."

Now it was Duchess's turn to pause, and Cancer felt his jaw clench before she responded.

"*Understood. I'll have some people dive back into the vetting, see if there's any new info.*"

"Cancer out."

"*Raptor Nine One, out.*"

He tossed the mic down, not envying Duchess's role in the aftermath of the failed meet. The tactical stuff came more or less naturally to him: shoot, move, communicate. Infil, exfil, clean weapons, and re-cock for the next mission. As for diplomacy and damage control, well, Cancer would rather hang up his spurs than have to deal with that mess.

Plucking his pack from the desk, Cancer withdrew a cigarette and sparked it. He was mid-exhale on his first plume of smoke when he heard Worthy's drawl.

"No smoking in here."

Cancer turned to face him. "Everyone keeps saying that. Grab me an ashtray, would you?"

Worthy grabbed an empty soda can from the kitchen countertop, then handed it to Cancer before pulling up a chair and sitting down.

"So what do you think?"

"I think," Cancer said, taking another drag, "that Maximo could be a rat. He was late to the meet, and showed up as soon as the shooting stopped. I've seen enough mob movies to know what that means."

"Did you have a bad feeling about him before?"

"No, but that doesn't mean he's on our side. I'm not questioning his experience, but everyone's got their price. And ordering that hit would be as good as pulling the trigger on the asset himself."

Worthy folded his arms, considering the comment. "Sure, but why bother? Think about what the asset was supposed to give us—intel on Sofia leaving her hideout, right?"

"Exactly. If Maximo is on her payroll, he could've arranged the hit to keep us from getting too close."

"But that's a lot of exposure, getting two Agency contractors killed. Maximo could have just warned Sofia to change her plans. She's already well aware we can't hit her hideout."

"Unless," Cancer pointed out, tapping his cigarette ash into the open mouth of the can, "she has to travel for something too important to cancel."

3

Relieved to hear the chime of an incoming email, Ian leaned forward and saw that it came from Duchess's operations center in response to the data they'd sent.

He eagerly clicked open the message, unable to temper his expectations.

The asset's body had no intel whatsoever—whatever he knew was in his head alone, and he'd been too worried to pass it over the phone—but the four men who'd come to kill them in the museum had a combined six cell phones among them. Two had identification cards, probably fake, but Ian took them nonetheless and had snapped a picture of each face before hastily departing with David and Maximo. Upon returning to the apartment, he'd sent all that information directly to his team's CIA handler, hoping for some kind of link.

His shoulders sagged as he read the email, then turned to David in the seat beside him.

"Agency's got no info on the shooters."

David snorted. "Are you surprised? It was probably a few small-time gangbangers."

"Not gangbangers," Maximo said behind them. Ian looked up to see him standing with his arms crossed—he never seemed to sit outside of a vehicle—and glaring at David. "They were sicarios, working on behalf of a cartel or, more likely, an independent trafficker."

"How can you be sure?"

Maximo chuckled.

"Designer clothes, fancy sneakers, the latest cell phones...of course they were sicarios. I promise they each left behind a Japanese motorcycle and a few beautiful girlfriends."

David objected, "Those shooters were in their twenties, at most."

"Murder for hire is a young man's game, my friend. Few sicarios live to see thirty. But if we find who they work for, we will know who tried to make us see the devil."

Cancer called out from the kitchen, where he and Worthy were preparing dinner.

"What does it matter?"

"Because," Ian said, sparing Maximo the trouble of explaining, "sicarios are loyal to one employer. Those employers are accountable for anyone their men kill. Whoever ordered this hit assumed some personal risk, which means they have considerable incentive for whacking a couple American contractors."

Maximo nodded. "Yes. This."

"And if we link the order to kill us to...well, to Sofia, then we've got bigger problems."

Ian left the obvious possibility unsaid—that Maximo had arranged the asset's murder himself, a not-unlikely possibility in the web of corruption, betrayal, and conspiracy that earmarked Colombia's history since its independence from Spanish rule, much of which was related to something as simple as the coca plant.

Instead he asked, "Max, is there any chance your asset set up the hit, not expecting to die in the crossfire?"

Maximo shook his head. "Elonzo was vetted. I have worked with him for almost three years, and if he said he had knowledge of Sofia leaving her village, it was because he did."

He couldn't tell if Maximo was truly confident in his source, or merely playing to the American team's steadfast resolution to kill or capture Sofia Lozano—a resolution the man could never know the full scope of.

Ian's team had followed a trail of clues spanning four countries that indicated the existence of a completely unknown terrorist syndicate of unprecedented scope, headed by a man under the pseudonym Erik Weisz. Their intel from Nigeria had revealed an unsettling connection between Weisz and Sofia.

Three years ago, Weisz paid the female drug trafficker a lump sum of twenty million; lo and behold, he orchestrated the July 4th attack a scant 13 months later. Weisz was clearly using cocaine to finance terrorism, putting Sofia in the team's crosshairs.

Far more troubling, even as the team made their final preparations to enter Colombia, Weisz attempted a second transfer to Sofia, this one for 25 million dollars. While the CIA was able to freeze that exchange before it reached its intended recipient, there were now two certainties for everyone at Project Longwing. One, Weisz would find a way to get that money to Sofia sooner or later. Two, he was planning a major terrorist attack, likely in a year or less.

With extremely few people in the world able to summon a single shipment of 25 million dollars' worth of cocaine—at Colombian wholesale pricing, somewhere around twenty tons—killing Sofia would disrupt Weisz's receipt of the product and ensuing funds, thus delaying his attack. This would buy global intelligence agencies some time and space to continue pulling at the threads of his network.

Maximo said, "As of the last contact with my source, and according to all the intelligence I have seen and word on the street, there is no possibility that Sofia could move the amount of product you claim. Twenty tons, you say?"

"At least," Ian replied.

Maximo grimaced. "A single ton, maybe two or three at a time...very few people can accomplish more than this. She is not one of them."

"Yes," David said, folding his arms, "she is. You'll just have to trust us on that."

Maximo opened his mouth to speak again, then halted at the sound of an incoming text message. Withdrawing his phone, he checked the display and said, without a trace of surprise, "My organization has no information on the sicarios."

Ian rubbed his temples.

Maximo's organization was the *Dirección Nacional de Inteligencia*, or DNI. It was, oddly enough, something of a fledgling startup—Colombia's previous intelligence agency was dismantled in the wake of a long series of scandals and confirmed links with drug trafficking, receiving funds from both left-wing and right-wing paramilitary groups, and spying on political opponents of the president. It was dismantled in 2011 and replaced by the DNI, which, for the most part, had maintained a relatively clean record.

That success was due in large part to professionals like Maximo, who had transitioned to national intelligence after a storied and elite military career. Though in the wake of the museum shootout, Ian wasn't quite sure what to make of their attached host nation representative.

David offered, "So if the CIA and DNI are both at a loss, our odds of figuring out who tried to have us killed are as dead as those four fuckers who pulled the triggers."

Maximo gave an odd little smile. "I would not say this. Where does your team fall on the...how should I say...ethical spectrum?"

"Far right," David quipped, leaning forward with a hungry expression. "Priorities one through three are getting the job done. Why, what do you have for us?"

Before Maximo could reply, there was a knock at the door.

Ian knew full well that Reilly stood on the other side, but as Worthy unlocked the door and their lone remaining team member barged in, it still came as something of a shock.

Reilly was a hulking giant of a man, bigger even than Maximo, and his bulk was accentuated at present by a massive duffel bag slung over his shoulders. He made it two steps into the apartment, just enough for Worthy to close the door behind him, then sniffed the air and said, "Cancer smoking in here again?"

"Quit your bitching," Cancer announced from the stove, not bothering to look up while he stirred the contents of his saucepan with a wooden spoon. "You get the stuff, or what?"

Reilly surveyed the group. "Not supposed to smoke in government facilities. But yeah, 7th Group hooked us up. Local garb, intel dump, a ton of contacts across the country. There's more in the van, can I get a hand?"

Cancer killed the stove and said, "Me and Worthy will get it. Just treat David."

Reilly dropped his duffel, eyes going wide as he looked to the team leader.

"You got hit?"

David shook his head. "It's just a fragment. Don't worry about it."

Too late. Reilly had gone into full medic mode, shaking his head adamantly. "No way. I'm getting my aid bag and checking you out right now. There's always a risk of infection with—"

He stopped talking abruptly at the sight of Worthy, who procured two brown paper bags from the counter and lifted them enticingly. Then he drawled, "Got you some more Scooby snacks."

Reilly looked from the bags to David then back to the bags before seizing them eagerly.

"Correction," he said, "I'm checking you out after I eat. It's just a fragment, no need to whine."

David frowned. "I wasn't."

Cancer and Worthy exited the apartment as Reilly, ever hungry, began to eat—strips of meat from one bag interspersed with handfuls of crunchy pea-sized morsels from the other.

Maximo wrinkled his nose, looking as if he was about to object, when David quickly rose, tapped him on the shoulder, and gave a grim shake of his head. The two men watched Reilly eat in silence. Ian felt sick.

Taking his seat, David resumed speaking as if Reilly had never entered.

"So now that we've covered our position on the ethical spectrum, how can we proceed?"

Maximo made no move to sit, instead giving a wistful sigh and speaking in a low, almost conspiratorial tone. "I must bring this information to Vega."

Ian felt his jaw drop. "Vega as in *Quinlan* Vega? The trafficker?"

He nodded. "A former colleague of mine, before DNI."

At this Reilly took another mouthful of meat and, without bothering to swallow, said, "I thought you were special forces before DNI."

"I was," Maximo confirmed. "And so was Vega. That is why he is so good at his second career."

It was common knowledge that some of the more successful Colombian traffickers were former cops or soldiers with firsthand experience in the industry, but Ian had never heard of a member of the country's premier counterterrorism unit crossing over. That would be quite a professional transition, he thought: spend years targeting the highest-level traffickers and narco organizations as a member of Colombia's equivalent to Delta Force, then use that knowledge to go into business for yourself with devastating effectiveness.

Maximo continued, "I will meet him tonight."

"I'm going with you," David said.

"Your country's rules dictate no affiliation with drug trafficking."

"And we both know how comical that concept is when we're operating in Colombia. Half of your politicians are paid off by traffickers, and half of mine are snorting their product while advocating a drug war. My team has been off the grid before, and I don't relay anything to the Agency that could get us in trouble."

"I understand that. But Vega will not speak with you."

"Then it's up to you to change his mind."

Maximo was silent for a moment, taking them in before speaking again. "You think I had something to do with the hit today."

"I didn't say that," David replied, a bit too quickly.

Maximo's temper flared. "That is why you do not want me going alone. I hate to tell you this, my friends, but if I had known the assassins were coming, I never would have let my asset place a foot in that museum. Much less you or Ian."

"Then it shouldn't be a problem for me to accompany you."

"Maximo," Ian began, trying to de-escalate the situation before the man could dwell on a potential slight to his honor, "it wouldn't be a bad idea to have David present as team leader. If Vega knows who you work for, then he'll know who we work for, and it's no secret that the Agency will gladly ignore or outright facilitate narcotics trafficking in the interests of countering people like Sofia. It could also assure Vega that we can provide some level of protection against extradition if he gets caught in a bind, or even financial compensation if he generates sufficient leads."

The Colombian scoffed, his eyes narrowing. "If you think he needs money or protection from your government, you know nothing. Let me explain why you cannot meet him. If anything happens to Vega afterward, if he is arrested or killed by another trafficker, they will naturally assume it was because you informed on him. Your entire team will die, and I will be just as accountable for introducing you to him."

David said firmly, "I'm going. That's final."

At this, Maximo relaxed, a smile playing at the corners of his mouth.

"I am telling you not to go. You want to ignore me? Fine. We will see how that works out."

4

I rode alone in the backseat of the BMW X5, watching my surroundings through a two-inch-thick pane of ballistic glass.

Medellín nightlife was in full swing, traffic moving at a crawl as pedestrians packed the sidewalks at 11 p.m., making their way between bars and clubs to the soundtrack of car horns and street vendors announcing their wares. By all accounts, the evening was peaceful. No shouting or street fights, and the only indications of criminal activity were the groups of young boys inconspicuously making their way through the crowd.

And yet I was glad our SUV was armored: while we had guns in the vehicle, they would remain there. Personal firearms were the norm at our destination, but not for representatives of intelligence agencies. The criminals could and would be armed, but their guests could not.

From the passenger seat, Maximo asked, "You see the *carteristas*?"

"Yeah," I said, "how many of these kids are pickpockets?"

"Too many." Maximo laughed. "And they are good, very good. Petty street crime is an art form. By the time you feel fingers in your pocket—if you do at all—and grab the kid's arm, your phone has already been handed off to someone else. Five minutes later it will be scrapped for parts."

The driver nodded and muttered, "*Impuesto turístico*."

"*Sí*," Maximo agreed, translating for me, "we call this the 'tourist tax.'"

the armored door and stepping onto the sidewalk in a charcoal suit I'd brought for the possibility of an embassy visit. Beneath it I wore a silk dress shirt without a tie, the closest I could manage to nightclub attire. Maximo, by contrast, wore a black suit with cowboy boots, a look that the tall Colombian pulled off with surprising panache.

The thumping bass notes of techno blared within the building as we approached the trio of bouncers standing guard at the door, the air smelling faintly of marijuana smoke. Despite the fact that no line of people waited to get in, the club held a distinct air of exclusivity. Combined with the music, it indicated that the VIPs had already arrived and the party was raging, and I braced myself for the drug-and-prostitute-fueled debauchery I was about to witness on the other side.

Maximo came to a stop before the bouncers and said, "*Soy* Maximo Ospina, *estoy aquí para ver a* Vega. *Me está esperando.*"

All three of the bouncers were men of uncommon size, unbuttoned suit jackets draped over the bulges of what must have been considerable handguns. They each wore radio earpieces, which made it all the more surprising when one lifted a walkie-talkie to his lips and relayed, "Maximo Ospina *pidiendo encuentro con* Vega."

I glanced down the street in either direction as we waited, feeling vulnerable without a weapon and growing increasingly suspicious that no one else was approaching the Hora Dorada club while a steady stream of traffickers and their entourages trickled from the parking lots into the surrounding buildings. The sound of a vehicle engine rapidly approaching caused me to spin toward the street, anticipating the sight of a rifle or submachine gun barrel out a car window, but instead I saw a low, wide Lamborghini, the throaty exhaust note of a V12 engine fading to the sounds of techno music after it slid past.

By the time I turned back to the door, the lead bouncer's radio squawked with a return transmission. He replied, "*Afirmativo*," then nodded to Maximo and said, "*Puede seguir, señor. Una escolta lo llevará a su anfitrión.*" And while the only words I understood were "affirmative" and "sir," two of the bodyguards stepped aside while a third pulled open the door for us to enter.

Thumping bass notes increased in volume as I glimpsed a long corridor of flashing lights, silhouetting the figure of a fourth security man approaching. I started to follow Maximo until he announced, in English, "Just me. The gringo will wait in the car."

At these words, two of the bouncers stepped between us to block my path.

I said, "Max, what the fuck?"

Looking over his shoulder, he replied, "He will only talk to me if I am alone. I told you not to come."

Then he slipped past the entrance, disappearing from view as the door slammed shut behind him.

5

"Rise and shine, buttercup."

Reilly recognized Worthy's voice, though after detecting no particular sense of urgency in his words or tone, he elected to keep his eyes shut.

"What time is it?" he murmured.

"Almost ten. We let you sleep in as long as we could. But I brought some street treats to help you wake up."

Reilly's eyes flew open to the sight of Worthy at his bedside with the two brown paper bags that, even at this early phase of his stay in Colombia, elicited a Pavlovian hunger response.

Eagerly accepting both bags, Reilly considered his choices and opted to open the one with a grease-stained bottom first. There he found glistening pieces of meat wrapped in newspaper, the perfect street food. Reilly pinched one and lifted it out, lowering it into his open mouth and chewing to savor the explosion of flavor.

Swallowing with approval, he murmured, "Why can't we get pork like this in the States?"

"You can," Worthy replied. "Just have to go to the right Colombian restaurant, I suppose. The vendor said it's all in how they cook it. Coconut milk, sweet chilies, that type of thing. We'll find a place that does it right when we get back."

Reilly opened the second bag and reached inside, shoveling out a handful of the chickpea-sized nuts and eating them. Crunchy, salty, roasted perfection.

"Thanks, man."

He noticed Worthy looking at him strangely then, taking unusual interest in the act of watching him eat.

"Why are you looking at me funny?"

Worthy frowned.

"Because I spiked your food with Devil's Breath. We know you leaked the details of the asset meet at the museum, and now you're going to tell us who you work for."

"What the hell are you talking about?"

"I'm messing with you, man. Eat up, because you'll need your energy. We're going out tonight."

"Sofia left her hideout?"

"Not yet. Come on, David will explain."

Reilly got out of bed, taking his bags of food with him as he followed Worthy into the living room, wearing only boxers. No sense getting dressed—the team members had all seen one another at their absolute worst, and if there had ever been any boundaries between them, they'd since evaporated in the Philippines, Syria, China, and/or Nigeria. So, he thought, fuck it.

The first indication that something was amiss came at the sight of the gear preparation currently underway in the living room. Cancer was laying out not fatigues but local garb, the name-brand knockoff clothes and soccer team attire he'd gotten from the Special Forces guys who kept a stockpile of that sort of thing for low-visibility work and asset meets. But next to the clothes were an addition that Reilly hadn't seen before: a set of black ski masks.

"Hey, man," David called from the desk, where he was seated beside Ian, "over here. I've got to talk to you."

Only then did Reilly fully understand that something was wrong. They'd let him sleep in, plied him with his favorite local foods, because they were trying to get on his good side. Whatever was going on here, they were afraid he was going to object.

But he brushed the thought aside, dropping into a seat beside David and holding the brown bags toward him.

"No thanks," David said, "already had some. You go ahead."

"Ian?"

No response from Ian, who was typing away with an intense focus on the screen, clearly in the zone. Reilly shrugged and set the bags down, procuring another strip of meat as he asked, "So how'd it go last night?"

David's face went slack, his dead-eyed stare indicating extreme anger.

"Maximo fucked us," he said. "Let me get all the way to the nightclub entrance and then told the bouncers I had to wait in the car."

Reilly felt his eyes narrow. "This guy is starting to skeeve me out—first the asset meet, now this."

"Yeah, I know. But Duchess did another round of vetting, and it was clean."

"Clean for Colombia, maybe, but that doesn't mean much. So what'd he get from his narco buddy?"

"The sicarios who tried to schwack us work for a guy called Andres Jiménez. He's a young trafficker who's been coming up through the ranks, killing civilians, doing mass shootings of entire families. The more senior traffickers like Vega are worried he's going to disturb the peace."

"Last I checked, we were in Colombia," Reilly replied, grabbing another handful of nuts and tossing them into his mouth. God, he thought, were these things good. "What peace is there to upset?"

David said, "Ian?"

The intelligence operative finally stopped typing and looked over from his keyboard, speaking quickly as if inconvenienced by the need to explain.

"Disarmament of the FARC and the degradation of Colombian cartels was supposed to put a dent in cocaine production. Obviously that hasn't happened, as this country is producing more than ever. What has changed is how the coke is moving: the new system is a lot of independent traffickers, for the most part, with no one in charge. That means an uneasy peace in Medellín, which could turn into an all-out narco war if someone tries to consolidate power. Right now the traffickers are policing each other, and Jiménez hasn't been playing ball."

Then he resumed typing, leaving David to continue, "Apparently he's been killing way too many innocent people, bringing too much attention to the traffickers. These guys aren't like the old-school drug lords, carrying gold-plated pistols and openly defying the government. They're low-key, moving product with more bribes than bullets. Jiménez has been moving up on their collective shit list, and Vega's volunteered to take him out."

Reilly reached back in a bag only to find he was down to his last strip of meat. He mournfully lifted it to his mouth, then asked, "How does that help us?"

"Because Jiménez has no reason to know who we are, much less want us dead. That means he ordered that hit on behalf of someone, and until we find out who it is, we can't adjust our risk matrix to operate much less run a hit on Sofia."

With his meat gone, Reilly turned his attention to the remaining nuts. "You think she's behind this?"

"I fear she is. But how would she know we're even in the country? There's only one answer to that, and it's a mole in the DNI if not the Colombian government. If we confirm Sofia ordered the hit, then we'll know there's a leak in the exceedingly small list of people who are aware of our presence and purpose. Which means we have to radically change our plans, and do it as soon as possible. First, though, we have to find out for sure. Because it would change everything."

Reilly abruptly stopped eating, pushing the bag of nuts away.

"So you're not talking about killing Jiménez, you're talking about torturing him for information. No fucking way."

"We're not torturing anyone."

"Oh," he said, reaching for the bag again. "Good."

"Because Vega's people will do that for us."

Reilly slammed a fist on the desk, his blood pressure rising. Now he knew the reason they'd tried to butter him up this morning—Reilly was as close as the team had to a conscience.

"Come on, man. I didn't sign up for this shit."

"None of us did," David countered, "but here we are. A few days ago Jiménez rolled up some of his competition, and he's been keeping them in his chophouse. Vega's going to hit him there tonight, and we've got permission to accompany the raid."

"Permission from who, Duchess?"

The team leader gave a short laugh. "Duchess doesn't know a thing about this, and she never will. Otherwise we're on a fast track to prison."

"Yeah, no shit. So what happens when one of us gets killed raiding a damn chophouse?"

"Vega's men are doing the hit. We're not setting foot inside until it's secure, at which point—"

"At which point," Ian interrupted, "I'm going to ask Jiménez some questions."

Reilly leaned forward in his seat. "If he's captured alive, which is a big 'if.' And Maximo's okay with all this?"

David nodded. "Maximo negotiated our presence on the hit. So yeah, he's okay with it."

"Unless he's trying to get us killed, in which case tonight is our last night on earth. You two clowns barely survived a hit from four sicarios, and now we're supposed to put ourselves in the middle of an army of them?"

"It's a calculated risk," David said flatly.

"No, it's a risk period. A big one. Am I the only one who has a problem with this? Going off the reservation to partner up with a bunch of narcos who may or may not want us dead?"

Ian pointed out, "Jiménez wanted us dead, not Vega."

"Sure," Reilly said, "if we believe Maximo in the first place. David wasn't even at the meeting last night. Are we really going to trust this guy?"

David parried the question.

"Vega's a legit trafficker, one of the top independents in the country. He's got the manpower to pull this off, and we've got an invite to go along and find out whatever we need from the man who ordered that hit against us. So no, I don't trust Maximo any more than a guy on the receiving end of that museum bloodbath could. But we've got a rare chance here, and we're going to take it. Still, I'm not going to force anyone to go. You want to hang back tonight, then hang back. But we could really use a medic in case shit hits the fan."

Reilly had never wanted to blast David in the face so badly as he did in that moment, as he watched the team leader calmly eye him. Dangling a carrot like that in front of the only fully qualified medic on the team was the lowest form of manipulation, a personal and professional insult of the highest order. Reilly felt his hands balling into fists, the onset of muscle tension that had preceded many a bar fight in his considerable experience brawling his way into and out of trouble.

He rose from his seat and strode out of the living room. He didn't yet know where he was going, but he couldn't stay here.

David had given him no choice at all.

6

Worthy sat cross-legged, surveying the back of the SUV through the green hues of his night vision as it drove uphill without headlights. The vehicle throttled over a rock in the trail, jostling him violently before veering around a bend.

This Renault was the best off-road rental option, paid for in cash by Maximo; after all, they couldn't exactly take a vehicle from the Agency fleet on this unauthorized excursion. As far as Duchess was concerned, the team was in their apartment safehouse right now, and they needed to keep it that way.

For all the Renault's 4x4 performance, what it lacked was a comfortable suspension—particularly, Worthy thought, since he didn't have a seat to speak of.

Instead he squatted awkwardly in the back, wedged between Reilly's medical equipment atop the folded down rear seating. As soon as Worthy and Cancer were dropped off, the Renault would relocate to serve as a casualty collection point for the raid that was to commence in roughly two hours. And just as awkward as his attempts to remain even semi-comfortable was the ongoing debate occurring up front, between two people who would be mortal enemies if they weren't on the same team.

"Relax, man," Cancer went on from the passenger seat, "this'll be over before you know it."

Reilly downshifted as the trail inclined, powering the vehicle up the muddy trail. "Easy for you to say. You're a sociopath."

"My moral proclivities don't matter. Getting the information we need does."

Worthy heard an audible scoff from Reilly, who countered, "So what if we find out Sofia ordered the hit? It wouldn't change anything."

"Sure it would, because if that's the case, then it means we can't trust anyone here except Maximo, and maybe not even him. That means taking this show off the grid—limited or intentionally deceptive reporting to the Colombians, maybe Duchess finding us a new partner force. Until we find out who tried to have us whacked, we won't know where to begin. And Jiménez is just the guy to tell us all about it."

"We're supposed to be representing our country. Torturing intel out of some poor bastard isn't what we stand for."

"Think of it more like an opportunity," Cancer said in an upbeat tone, one that he normally reserved for situations where he'd be shooting people in the near future. "Jiménez is going down whether we're around for it or not. So what if we take advantage of the situation? Sofia's probably the worst person in the entire country, and she's helping Weisz. There are civilian lives at stake here."

"So that's it? The end justifies the means?"

"This ain't America, Reilly. It's Colombia, and we're playing by local rules now. When everyone's corrupt, then working with the least corrupt people is a virtue. Besides, our country snorts more coke than the rest of the world combined. So if we're representing America, putting ourselves in the middle of a narco ring is a pretty good place to start."

Reilly shook his head, his night vision swinging from side to side. Then he commented, "You're awfully quiet back there, Worthy. Where do you stand on this bullshit?"

Worthy adjusted the grip on his rifle, a suppressed M4. Normally his team selected Heckler & Koch, but in the interests of blending in as well as resupply, they'd sided with the weapons used by Colombian defense forces and their US Special Forces advisors. As far as the narcos conducting tonight's raid were concerned, advisors were exactly what his team was. Vega himself may well know they were CIA and not Green Berets—hell, Worthy thought, for all he knew, Maximo had told him as much—but that was supposed to be a secret from everyone else. If word of their participation in what was essentially a blood feud between traffickers somehow reached Langley, his team was done for.

Finally Worthy responded, "Reilly, I understand your reluctance, I really do. This is an insanely risky operation on any number of grounds, highly illegal by every conceivable metric. I'm with you there."

"Exactly," Reilly said.

"But that's not the main thing. Bottom line for me is that if any member of our team is going into harm's way, then so am I. That's why I'm here right now. We succeed or fail together, and that's that."

No one spoke, leaving Worthy to check his heavily customized Android phone, seeing the satellite imagery of the mountain slope with his icon threading its way along the road. He cross-checked the coordinates against the GPS on his wrist, confirming that they were fast approaching their drop-off. Smooth progress so far, no major delays to speak of, a rarity in this business, though that could change at the drop of a hat, particularly once the dismounted portion of this little charade commenced.

"Almost there," Worthy said, setting down his M4 in order to don his assault pack. Slinging his rifle, he gave his GPS a final check. "This is close enough. Cancer, you ready?"

"Yep. On you."

"All right, Reilly, here we go. Three, two, one."

Reilly braked, and Worthy opened his door and stepped onto muddy ground, then pushed the door shut just hard enough for it to click into place without slamming. Cancer did the same and the Renault glided forward again, making its way uphill with precious little audible indication that it had just discharged two armed men in the jungled hills. The only visible evidence would be a few boot prints on the side of the road, and no one would find those unless a full-scale search was in progress—and if that occurred, they had bigger problems.

Worthy plunged into the wet foliage, using his rifle's infrared floodlight to blaze a path through the trees and undergrowth. The chatter of insects masked his movement completely, and he picked up the pace as much as he could—there'd be time to stop and get a precise heading later, but Worthy wouldn't pause until he was at least thirty meters away from the trail.

Wet leaves slapped across him as he fought his way deeper into the jungle, toward the cliff edges beyond.

7

"Jesus," Cancer said, clapping a hand on the back of his neck, "did we put on bug spray, or blood scent?"

Lying prone beside him, Worthy whispered just loud enough to be heard over the chanting insects, "Don't forget these mosquitoes bite narcos too. They probably get enough cocaine in their regular food supply to power right through our DEET."

Turning that over in his head, Cancer replied, "You know, for such a backwoods inbred redneck, you make some legitimate points."

"For a piece of degenerate white trash from Dirty Jersey, you're not so bad yourself."

Cancer grinned.

Other than the mosquitos, he couldn't have asked for better conditions. The night air was in the mid-sixties, more than bearable since his clothes were more or less soaked by the foot movement through the wet foliage to get here. An inflatable pad insulated his body from the rock surface below, keeping him comfortable as he aimed his sniper rifle off the cliff edge toward the target area.

The pair had been in position for just over two hours, waiting for this thing to kick off. Which wasn't so bad, Cancer thought, on two counts. First, he'd had much longer waits on previous ops, sometimes stretching into multiple days. And second, he had Worthy for company.

Cancer said, "I'm just glad it's you up here with me, and not Reilly. Think I've already had all the moral self-righteousness I can handle for one mission."

"He means well," Worthy noted, rising to one elbow to give a periodic scan of the trees behind them.

Cancer didn't disagree. Reilly was just young, idealistic, and, compared to himself at least, wildly inexperienced. Once you'd globe-trotted to various shitholes as much as Cancer had, you began to realize how equal everyone in the world truly was. Some cultures weren't on the receiving end of violence, but their appetite for commodities that only flowed through bloodshed—cocaine chief among them—made them a direct participant whether they wanted to be or not. Accordingly, Cancer had zero concerns about working in the gray area to accomplish the task at hand.

Worthy seemed to be considering the same thing. "Frankly I'm surprised Vega let us accompany the hit in the first place."

"Don't be," Cancer said. "Maximo sold him on the bargaining chips David offered."

"What bargaining chips?"

"The finest sniper and medical support that American taxpayer dollars can provide, offered in exchange for a few minutes with Jiménez after he's captured."

Worthy was quiet for a fairly long pause after that. "We better not let Reilly ever find out his services were sold to a drug trafficker."

"I don't intend to."

Clucking his tongue, Worthy muttered, "Accompanying narcos on our first operational night of the mission. Going to be a fucked-up deployment this time around."

"Yes." Cancer grinned. "Yes, it is."

But his smile faded as he wondered whether any of this would prove worth the effort.

Because in the end, their ultimate goal was to kill Sofia Lozano. Whether that would save as many lives as the Agency thought it would wasn't Cancer's role to say; his was to execute, leaving the justifications to the policymakers who debated such matters in climate-controlled offices and conference rooms far removed from the actual battlefield.

In his experience they were wrong just as often as they were right, and maybe more—one need look no further than the best-laid plans set aflame in Vietnam or Afghanistan, to say nothing of Iraq nearly falling to ISIS, to testify to that sad truth. Intentions took a distant backseat to outcome, he'd learned, and as a sniper who loved his job, the only truly objective determinant of effectiveness was his ratio of rounds fired to confirmed kills.

Then he transmitted, "Suicide, how's the wind down there?"

David replied over his radio earpiece, "*Still light and variable. We're getting a breeze every now and then, nothing consistent. Adjust for range and you should be good. How are you and Racegun holding up?*"

"We'll manage. Any updates on ETA?"

"*Jiménez left the club 52 minutes ago, so probably another ten to fifteen before he arrives. No change to plan.*"

"Got it," Cancer confirmed. "Standing by, let us know when you've got visual."

Then he resumed his grip on the rifle and conducted another scan of the target below.

While US Special Forces advisors possessed every conceivable high-grade sniper system, there was precious little overlap with the weapons carried by members of the Colombian military. Cancer wanted to straddle that divide to facilitate both their cover story as well as easy battlefield resupply if this op turned expeditionary, and as a result selected a time-honored classic: the M24 with suppressor.

Produced in various iterations ever since its inception in the '80s, the M24 was a staple of military snipers around the world for good reason. Bolt action, with a five-round magazine of match grade 7.62x51mm rounds, it was a supremely reliable and accurate weapon with an effective range of 800 meters, far exceeding anything he was likely to encounter in the cities and jungles of Colombia.

Though to be fair, this particular objective had given him ample reason to reconsider his choice. Worthy's laser rangefinder confirmed that a straight line distance of 582 meters separated them from the front door of the target building, much farther than he'd anticipated shooting over the entire duration of this deployment, much less on his first night of actual operation.

No matter, he thought; the adjustable night vision scope and its thermal attachment enabled him to see the objective almost as clearly as if it were day. The target building was an otherwise unremarkable warehouse located on the outskirts of an industrial park at the base of the jungled hills.

That much was no surprise, at least. One of the key considerations for what went on inside that building was solitude. Screams and anguished cries were better left unheard by outsiders, and anyone who became aware of the warehouse's true purpose would be putting their own life in jeopardy by notifying the police. It was clear from Vega's plan that no hasty withdrawal was necessary after the raid, indicating his people had enough local cops on the payroll to take their sweet time.

David transmitted, "*Lookouts have visual on the Audi, two minutes out. Cancer, how copy?*"

And while the team leader was looking for confirmation, he wasn't going to get it from Cancer, who'd already made the final adjustments to his shooting position and was now peering through his optic to reassess guard positions. Observation aside, his goal at this point was a regular breathing cycle, speaking as little as possible and preferably not at all.

Worthy transmitted for him, "Copy two mikes, we're all set here. Guards remain stationary in their fixed positions."

Cancer was scanning those positions now, taking in the three guards in the brilliant hues of his scope.

From his position at an oblique angle to the building's rear wall, he could only get a glimpse of the left side guard, who was partially concealed by the corner of the warehouse. Depending on how he shifted his weight, Cancer had seen traces of his leg and shoulder, the muzzle of a rifle, and nothing else—not enough for a good shot unless he repositioned himself, which wasn't going to happen.

The rightmost guard stood on the opposite side of the structure, leaning against the bricks with one foot on the wall and his rifle slung, barrel pointed down. For the past couple hours his main focus apart from staring at the adjacent unoccupied buildings was to fuck around with his phone.

Last but most prominent to Cancer's vantage point was the guard positioned at the warehouse's rear door, which served as the primary entrance for people to come and go unseen by the rest of the largely abandoned industrial park. This man was facing Cancer directly, an easy broadside shot, and had been passing the time by smoking, the lucky bastard.

But none of these were his primary targets.

More than enough of Vega's shooters lurked below to make those guards a matter of convenience, and the real necessity for a sniper with an elevated vantage point would soon be arriving in the Audi RS7—a pair of bodyguards that accompanied Jiménez everywhere, one as his driver. If Cancer couldn't eliminate both in the fleeting seconds between them exiting the vehicle and escorting their employer inside, there would be zero chance of capturing Jiménez alive. No one on the ground level could obtain a sufficient firing angle to accomplish the task without compromising the entire assault force or, worse, killing Jiménez in the crossfire.

Worthy said, "All right, I see the Audi. Twenty to thirty seconds out."

Cancer didn't break his gaze from the scope, nor did Worthy expect him to; the pointman provided all the verbal cues necessary as the approaching headlights gradually brightened the ambient illumination visible through the M24's optic.

"Fifteen seconds...driver's side is going to be three meters off the back door."

Adjusting his aim to account for that disparity, Cancer watched the sleek sedan crest into view at the bottom of his scope, then come to a stop and kill the lights.

The driver and passenger doors opened immediately after that, and two suited men exited. He held his fire—at this distance and at night, their features were nearly indistinguishable, and the last thing he needed right now was to smoke Jiménez by mistake.

The first confirmation that the man from the passenger seat was a bodyguard came when he took up a position facing the treeline at the base of the hill where, unbeknownst to him, a tremendous number of Vega's people had taken up positions. Cancer trained the crosshairs on his chest, then glanced upward in his scope to see the driver moving to open the Audi's rear door.

Good enough.

Cancer felt the buttstock jolt into his shoulder pocket as the M24 discharged a subsonic round, then worked the bolt with blinding speed before taking aim on the standing driver, now holding the door ajar with his torso visible above the car's roof from the elevated vantage point. By the time Worthy reported the outcome of his first shot—"Hit"—Cancer was squeezing the trigger a second time, and then he racked the bolt before seeing the driver drop in place.

"Hit," Worthy called again as Cancer swept his aim to the back door. The guard there was already advancing toward the woods with his rifle raised, and if Cancer didn't drop him now, then Vega's people would open fire and likely kill Jiménez in the process. The trafficker was darting toward the building entrance, having apparently decided that his odds of survival for getting inside were preferable to remaining in the open and fishing around his dead driver's pockets for the Audi keys. Cancer aligned his crosshairs on the door guard and fired a third shot.

He'd just finished working the bolt when three of Vega's largest sicarios completed their dead sprint toward the warehouse door and tackled Jiménez to the ground. Worthy announced "Hit" as Cancer transitioned to the guard stationed at the building's sidewall, only to see he was far too late. The man fell in a hail of gunfire, the source apparent only when Cancer scanned for another target.

But it appeared he was done shooting for the time being: with Jiménez safely pinned to the ground, a flood of shooters streamed toward the warehouse from three separate positions in the jungle, long rows of men with assault rifles and submachine guns who soon disappeared inside to begin the real slaughter.

~

Ian peered through the leaves with his night vision, watching the shooters converging on the target building as he heard Worthy's transmission with an odd sense of disbelief.

"Three hits, all probable EKIA, looks like they took Jiménez alive. Transitioning to overwatch."

"Copy," David replied, *"nice shooting. Doc, stand by for my word."*

Ian had only seen two of the enemies killed in action despite doing his best to get a sufficient view at the exact moment of Jiménez's arrival, and heard none of them—the effect of a hidden sniper firing subsonic bullets was essentially to watch bodies fall dead for seemingly no reason at all. After the long patrol across the lower slopes of the hill, with David on point leading an endless string of Vega's men before positioning the three assault teams with the benefit of night vision, Cancer's opening salvo was almost anticlimactic.

But that all changed in the next thirty seconds.

He heard volleys of unsuppressed gunfire inside the warehouse, a low popping sequence of snare drums that underscored distant shouts and battle cries, the entire cacophony punctuated by the dull explosions of grenades. He glanced left, where David and Maximo knelt behind the cover of tree trunks, and no sooner had he confirmed their location than the *crack* of an incoming round snapped overhead. Ian reflexively shifted behind the tree he'd chosen, second-guessing whether it was big enough to stop a high-caliber bullet, but no other incoming fire followed the seemingly random shot.

Had it been fired by Vega's sicarios, or men defending the warehouse? There was no way to tell. At this point a free-for-all raged inside the building, and Ian was thankful no one from his team had to conduct the assault themselves. Plenty could still go wrong tonight, of course, but securing the building was half the challenge.

The gunfire reduced to a smattering of pop shots, then silenced altogether. Ian saw Maximo answer his cell phone, then confer with David beside him, before the team leader transmitted.

"Objective is secure. Racegun, Cancer, how are we looking?"

Worthy answered, *"Coast is clear all the way up to the back door. Got you covered."*

"Moving. Angel, let's go."

David led the way through the brush, with Maximo and Ian following him downhill out of the jungle, through a strip of high grass, and finally over a retaining wall and onto the concrete surface beyond.

They spread out into a loose wedge formation, scanning for targets as they jogged toward the building. When their initial foray into the open ground resulted in no enemy fire, David sent his next transmission.

"*Doc, bring it in.*"

"*On my way,*" Reilly replied.

They continued jogging, and Ian swept his suppressed M4 in a search for movement among the unlit buildings surrounding the objective. Seeing none, he glanced at the Audi RS7, all four doors now ripped ajar as Vega's people searched the interior.

"*Fuerzas amigas,*" Maximo shouted, waving a flashlight in a preordained signal to prevent them from getting shot by the trigger-happy sicarios. And while those men were supposed to return the signal, their response was a collective series of victory whoops that made Ian's blood run cold.

He looked past them at his destination, dreading what they'd find inside. Despite the seismic shift in the organizational structure of cocaine trafficking, very little had changed in the grand scheme of things, and the warehouse was a perfect embodiment of that fact.

When the major cartels were dismantled at the cost of decades of effort, to say nothing of billions in US funding and military aid, the thousands of former members—foot soldiers, assassins, logisticians, middle management, and surviving senior leadership—didn't simply show up to the unemployment office to look for legitimate work. The grinding machinery that was the global cocaine trade continued to churn at ever-faster rates, with the facilitators melding and merging into a dizzying array of new organizations, partnerships, and paramilitary groups that were ever harder to target and kept the precious white powder circulating worldwide. So while independent traffickers had mostly filled the void, the cartel's *casas de pique*, or chophouses, had continued their uninterrupted operation, sometimes in the same physical locations.

When it became necessary to extract information, exact revenge, gain repayment of debt by non-financial means, or merely punish someone for an offense—real or imagined—the chophouses served an invaluable purpose to their owners. They were private prisons, morgues, secure locations where people could be systematically dismantled for days on end, their existence serving as a warning to keep the loyal in line and the final destination to any who betrayed the established order.

Ian was halfway to the building when his thoughts were interrupted by the sudden appearance of headlights to his right. The Renault sped into view and accelerated, then braked to a stop beside the Audi as Reilly leapt out and lifted the tailgate, then transmitted, "*CCP established.*"

"*Copy,*" Worthy replied, "*we've got you covered from the high ground.*"

With the truck now serving as a casualty collection point from which to treat injuries among Vega's men—if, Ian thought, any of them survived—Reilly spun to face the three-man element jogging toward him.

The effect was almost comical despite the sheer violence of the situation. Reilly was attired in the same uniform of sorts as Ian, David, and even Maximo: Colombian-style civilian clothes, tactical vest and weapon, and black ski mask. He looked nothing short of ridiculous, as they all did—CIA contractors and a local guide straddling the line between professional intelligence operatives and narcos.

Reilly said nothing to them, and rightfully so—what was there to say? —and the trio moved past the Renault on their way to the warehouse's back door.

They'd almost reached the open doorway when two sicarios exited, one assisting his wounded comrade outside to Reilly's truck. David stepped out of the way to let them pass, allowing Ian to take in the finer details of what would normally be considered an act of battlefield valor, only to find that it was anything but.

The uninjured sicario wore an AK-47 dangling from a sling, his eyes wide and jumpy as he passed. One arm was slung around his friend, who gripped an M4 while blood poured from a probable bullet hole just below his left pec, the wound probably indicating a lung collapse in progress. Yet the man's ragged, wheezing breaths were marked by laughter, his gaze as wild-eyed as the sicario assisting him out of the building. Both were high, Ian knew, though on what combination of substances or in what quantities, he couldn't begin to speculate. Prior to the raid he'd witnessed men snorting powder and eating pills, and a teenager with a silver flask who, by contrast, seemed to be the most restrained of the bunch.

Hell of a job, Ian thought—get the order for an assassination, a mass shooting, or a building assault, and then get high and try to make it out alive. Rinse and repeat. Cocaine asked much of its servants, and neither of these men appeared to mind the cost.

Maximo and David slipped in the doorway after they passed, and Ian entered the chophouse to an almost overpowering gut punch of revulsion that only worsened with each passing step.

His surroundings were the stuff of slasher films: blood sprayed and splattered in epic quantities across walls, floors, and furniture; human limbs protruding from burlap sacks; a limbless, headless torso propped against a corner. Tools of the slaughter were everywhere: axes, machetes, hatchets, a chainsaw coated from blade to handle in the dried, rust-colored residue of the people it had shredded at the hands of some drug-ridden lunatic who'd been paid handsomely to perform the act. Vega's men were moving about the facility now, searching the bodies of its slain defenders.

How many people had been chopped into oblivion here, Ian couldn't say; the only means by which he could begin to speculate how long this building had served its intended purpose was the smell, a combination of urine and feces, the musk of coppery blood, marijuana smoke, and rotten flesh that tinged the back of his nostrils like pork that had soured long ago.

But David, who seemed unperturbed by the grotesque monstrosity of this place, asked Maximo as they walked, "How much time do we have?"

"All we need," Maximo replied. "The sicario team leader will tell the police when they may respond."

Unconvinced, David glanced at Ian.

"Make it fast. I want us out of here asap."

Ian said nothing, his thoughts consumed by the human cost inside this building, itself little more than a microcosm for the violence that had ravaged Colombia for decade after decade. Many of these bodies would go unidentified, adding to the toll of over a hundred thousand Colombians who had disappeared in the endless battles between left-wing and right-wing groups, traffickers and the populace, with key members of the government playing both sides and getting rich in the process.

Their small procession sidestepped around a fallen sicario, apparently one of Jiménez's men. An assaulter knelt over him, stripping the wristwatch, wallet, and gold chains.

Someone called out to Maximo in Spanish, and he relayed the message. "This way—Jiménez is down the hall."

As far as sending a message to other traffickers, he had to appreciate Vega's sheer brazenness. Ian was witness to a cautionary tale that would spread throughout the underworld for generations: the man who got out of line, disrespected the rules, and was captured alive to be dragged into his own chophouse.

The thought made him almost as nauseous as the sights and smells around him, and yet he steeled himself for the encounter ahead. Interrogation was only as effective as the questioner's ability to seem totally in control. If he seemed hesitant, fearful, or overwhelmed, it would be all the easier for Jiménez to withhold some crucial piece of information.

Ian followed David to the final doorway, where a sicario standing guard handed Maximo a cell phone, surely the one they'd pulled off Jiménez. He felt vaguely uneasy over leaving Maximo unsupervised to toy with the device, but there was nothing he could accomplish that would escape the CIA's analysis once Ian transmitted the phone's contents, and if there was any tampering at this point, they'd have the Colombian intelligence operative dead to rights.

As he passed through the doorway, Ian ascertained in one fell swoop both why Jiménez had been taken to this room and why withholding information wouldn't be on his agenda this evening.

The space was a communal shower for warehouse employees, rivulets of dried blood leading across the concrete floor to converge at a central drain. Flies swarmed over an unidentifiable mass of meat in the corner, and Ian looked up to see that the showerheads had been replaced by metal bolts from which chains ran the length and width of the ceiling, allowing the building's occupants to do what they were currently doing to Jiménez himself.

His arms were drawn to either side, wrists handcuffed to the chain overhead. Gucci loafers barely made contact with the ground, his dress shirt ripped open to expose an intricate full-torso tattoo of the Virgin Mary benevolently exposing both palms. Andres Jiménez was 28 years old but looked far older now, his blood-marred face swelling with bruises that had already rendered one eye to a slit.

The remaining eye looked greedily at Ian's rifle, as if the prospect of death by firearm was the most merciful of all available options at present. He wasn't wrong, and Ian pushed the slung weapon to his back by way of directing the man's focus.

"You speak English?" Ian asked.

"*Sí*. Yes."

Ian nodded. "Then listen to me very carefully, and speak the truth. You tried to have me killed at *Museo Casa de la Memoria*. I want to know why."

No hesitation.

"She told me to."

"Who?"

"Sofia. Sofia Lozano."

His response was so immediate, spoken with such conviction, that Ian knew at once he was telling the truth. And while that should have been encouraging, it instead elicited the tug of sinking despair in Ian's belly that spoke to the obvious implications. Interrogations like this were not just commonplace in Colombia but so frequent that Jiménez knew the score: he offered no resistance, merely wishing to take the quickest possible route to a fatal bullet rather than any of the imaginative range of alternate fates that awaited at the hands of Vega's men.

Ian asked, "Why would she want you to kill us?"

"I have no idea. She knew of the gringos in Medellín, knew they were coming for her."

That was a particularly valuable piece of information: with an already very limited number of Colombians who knew of their purpose, Sofia's possession of the knowledge indicated a leak. This changed absolutely everything about the mission at hand. They could no longer trust anyone outside of their own chain of command stretching back to Langley, and even that provision would only be as good as the assumption that the leak didn't stem from Maximo himself.

"How did she know this?"

Jiménez gave a helpless shake of his head. "She did not say. But she had the details of the museum, what time the meeting would take place. There were to be no survivors."

Ian took a step back, as if to leave, and spoke to Maximo. "He's lying."

"No!" Jiménez cried. "Please, this is what happened."

Spinning to face the man, Ian asked, "If she knew so much, then why didn't she do the hit herself?"

"She is a *montañera*, one from the mountains. Her strength is in the jungle, not the city. She relies upon connections for places such as Medellín. She uses locals who know the area."

Another useful data point, if true. Sofia's reputation certainly preceded her, but Ian had no idea that the majority of her urban effectiveness came from outsourcing the work.

He said, "There's no shortage of hitters in Medellín. Why did she choose you?"

"Sofia did not say. I may only presume it was due to how many I have killed."

"And what was your reward, if you pulled off the hit? How much was she paying you?"

"Fourteen hundred kilos."

Ian cocked his head.

"Did you just say fourteen *hundred*? As in, a ton and a half?"

"Yes. All fully processed, all pure."

Ian did some mental math. Sofia had essentially placed a bounty of two million dollars on his team.

He asked, "How were you going to receive the cocaine?"

Jiménez probed the inside of his cheek with his tongue, then spat a stream of blood downward. A molar clattered against the concrete.

"Within a day," he said, "she was going to send me a location to meet her and pick up the coke."

"A location...at her hideout? She expects you to go all the way to Putumayo?"

"No. Another place, I do not know where. She wanted to meet me in person, discuss further business together."

Ian looked from David to Maximo. Both men were watching Jiménez intently.

"You expect me to believe she actually planned to leave her village?"

Jiménez winced, as if having trouble putting his thoughts together. "No, I am saying she already has. Her call was from the cellular network, not Iridium. She could not possibly be at her hideout with that kind of access. It is too remote."

Ian cut his eyes to Maximo, who looked up from his phone and gave a short nod.

Then Ian said, "Tell me where the exchange was going to be. Where she was calling from, and where she is now."

Jiménez began to cry, his chin trembling. "Please, *señor,* I do not have this information. She was going to tell me once the job was done. The last time I spoke with her was only to report that the first hit failed, and tell her I was working on a second attempt."

"Good," Ian said, nodding, "because in about an hour, you're going to call and tell her that you killed us all. Then you're going to demand your coke, and set up a time and place to meet her in person. You understand?"

David interrupted, not bothering to whisper. "How can we possibly ensure he's not going to tip her off?"

Maximo interrupted, speaking Ian's thoughts aloud. "Vega's men will gain his full cooperation."

Then, returning his gaze to the restrained trafficker, Ian nodded and continued, "And unless you do exactly what they say, the chophouse hospitality you receive will be considerably worse than you've provided."

8

CIA Headquarters
Special Activities Center, Operations Center F2

Duchess entered her operations center with a mug of tea in hand, surveying her domain with the peculiar sense that for once, things seemed to be unnervingly calm.

A majority of her staff were already present fifteen minutes prior to the official start to the duty day, seated at workstations spanning the length of descending tiers. The television screens at the front of the OPCEN presented muted displays of US and Colombian news networks, their standard configuration when there were no aerial surveillance feeds indicating an operation in progress. At first glance there was precious little to differentiate this space from any number of classified military or intelligence operations centers, save perhaps for its location in the remote reaches of the CIA's Special Activities Center.

In reality, its existence was known only to a handful of politicians and the president, plus, of course, the members of Project Longwing itself, every one of them an Agency employee or contractor. It was a tiny program with enormous implications for national security, kept sufficiently discreet due to its controversial purpose of conducting targeted killings of rising terrorist leaders across the globe.

She crossed the short distance to her workstation, centrally positioned at the highest tier of the OPCEN and flanked by a desk where a middle-aged woman with a Naval Academy class ring was already seated.

"Good morning, Jo Ann," Duchess said, setting down her tea and taking a seat.

Jo Ann replied in the Wisconsin accent that never ceased to strike Duchess as bordering on comical.

"Isn't it a refreshing change of pace to be in the same time zone as our ground team? Night shifts get exhausting. I think we need to select more targets in South America."

It was hard to imagine that outside Agency headquarters and dressed in a Navy uniform, this frumpy woman transformed into Lieutenant Commander Brown, an intelligence officer whose area of expertise was special operations. In that capacity she probably wasn't half bad, but as the military oversight for Project Longwing, she was by assignment a potential whistleblower waiting to happen.

Although as the Nigeria operation neared its end, Duchess thought, Jo Ann had shown a dark side that provided at least some assurance that she was fully committed to what needed to be done, rather than what was, strictly speaking, legally acceptable.

They hadn't discussed the event since.

"I agree," Duchess replied, unlocking her computer, "and there's no shortage of targets to be had on the continent. Though how many of them have ties to Erik Weisz remains to be seen."

"Or not," Jo Ann noted, "depending on whether we can keep the team operational."

She wasn't wrong. Everyone knew they were playing the long game in Colombia, pre-positioning David's team to be ready when Sofia left her jungle hideout and was thus vulnerable for a targeted killing operation. Until that occurred, the deployment should have been a milk run—living in an upscale apartment in Medellín, liaising with US advisors from the 7th Special Forces Group, and collecting intelligence with DNI support.

Instead, the first asset meet had resulted in the deaths of civilians and a source with presumably promising information, and very nearly killed David and Ian. And while the ground team were no strangers to the possibility of violent death at the hands of their enemies, the fact that their presence was compromised from the outset spelled the very real possibility of a total mission abort. DNI assistance was virtually a prerequisite for operating effectively in Colombia, and that "assistance" now clearly involved a rat in the mix. Duchess should have pulled her people out already, but hadn't yet only because David pleaded for more time to determine the exact source of the attack.

At this point they were desperate for answers. Given Sofia's connection to Weisz, there was simply too much on the line.

The quiet conversations across the OPCEN ended as David Rivers's voice broadcast over the speakers.

"*Raptor Nine One, this is Suicide Actual.*"

Duchess snatched the radio hand mic from her desk and responded, "This is Raptor Nine One, send it."

Today had just taken a turn for the worse, she decided—the team was in their Medellín apartment, and could have just as easily called over the encrypted phone. Using the radio indicated a matter of urgency; the last time she'd received a SATCOM call, the team's second in command was reporting the museum shootout.

David began, "*Be advised, our DNI attachment was able to run down the origin of the hit through his asset network. It was ordered by Andres Jiménez, an independent trafficker with a long list of murders under his belt.*"

Duchess recoiled, seeing no possible way to reconcile that particular bit of information.

"Why would Jiménez want you dead?"

"*He wouldn't, and that's why our DNI guy did some more digging. Maximo and his guys rolled up Jiménez, who provided information to avoid extradition to the States. Jiménez implicated Sofia as the mastermind behind the museum attack. She was going to pay him off with a ton and a half of pure cocaine—*"

"Hold on," Duchess said flatly. "My DNI counterpart has made zero mention of any of this."

"*That's what I was about to explain. We both know there's a leak in the DNI, and it's not from Maximo. As a result, he's restricted his reporting to a few key individuals, and ensured that nothing related to this reaches any potential source of compromise.*"

She swallowed, feeling her first inclinations of a lie-in-progress growing with each passing second.

Then she asked, "Could Jiménez pinpoint the leak?"

"*Unfortunately, no. He specified that Sofia knew a team of, and I quote, 'gringos' had arrived in Colombia to kill her. She had all the details on the asset meet at the museum, but didn't have the people in Medellín to pull off the hit. And whoever the DNI or government mole is, I doubt they have a direct line to Sofia; more likely, they're communicating through an intermediary.*"

"How could Maximo have possibly conducted a snatch operation against Jiménez without full DNI approval?"

"*To hear him tell it, they've got compartmentalized cells within the DNI. Trusted people who limit their reporting to combat trafficking without certain members of management alerting the bad guys. He didn't even tell us about capturing Jiménez until they had him in custody.*"

"Has your team personally questioned Jiménez?"

"*Negative,*" David said, "*they've got him at an off-site location, it's extremely low-vis, and they don't want to raise the profile by bringing in outsiders. He won't tell us where.*"

"Any video or audio confirmation that confirms Maximo's claims?"

A pause. "*No, but we assess the information is accurate.*"

Or, Duchess thought, they didn't want to admit having documentation because it implicated the DNI in torture.

"Can you obtain said documentation?"

"*Negative, we've been informed it's off-limits. Marked for Colombian eyes only.*"

Torture it was, Duchess thought. If America had dipped its toe into the murky area of unsavory methods—and it had, with Guantanamo Bay being the tip of the iceberg; far worse occurred at the black sites—then she could only fathom what select members of Colombian intelligence were capable of. She decided not to press the issue, switching instead to a more obvious contradiction.

"Yesterday you were concerned about Maximo's vetting on the grounds that he was late to the asset meet. What makes you think he's a hundred percent reliable?"

"*Because he just handed us Sofia.*"

"Wait one," she replied, setting down the radio mic.

Then she looked to the workstation of her legal advisor.

No words were needed; the man stationed there had already risen, opting to approach rather than broadcast his advice across the OPCEN. That act alone assured her that they were straying into dangerous waters; nothing new for Project Longwing, but troubling when the program's very existence placed her at risk of facing a closed trial with the slightest misstep of her authorities.

As he approached, Jo Ann leaned in and whispered, "Okay, so he's lying. Sofia might not be worth the risk of playing along, but Erik Weisz *is*. That 25 million we intercepted is even more than he paid her to bankroll the July 4th attack, and we have no idea what he's planning. If we don't stop this coke transfer, we won't have to guess what his next operation will be. We'll see it on the news."

Duchess nodded, considering the implications of everything David Rivers had just said, not against the facts she knew but rather against her gut instinct that she was being categorically lied to.

On its face, that would seem like a reason to shut down this line of operational reasoning at once and in full. David's team was well-versed in coloring outside the lines to achieve results; after his return from China, he'd come clean with her about exactly what had occurred in stark contrast to his official reports, and why. And with the benefit of hindsight, she'd concluded that his rationale was both well-intentioned and well-executed, having spared her the necessity of aborting the entire mission long after it had passed the point of impossibility.

That was, of course, to say nothing of the fact that her career had been spared in the process, albeit only through the ground team's ability to salvage victory from the ashes of defeat.

Now, her primary consideration wasn't whether or not David was lying to her, but whether she could brief his "update" with any meaningful semblance of a straight face to the authorities on the seventh floor, each of whom had their own political leadership to consider. And God forbid that

Senator Thomas Gossweiler, chair of the Senate Select Committee on Intelligence and her own oversight-slash-personal nightmare, fail to believe the official narrative being briefed to her now.

Gregory Pharr arrived at her desk, wearing his usual immaculate suit, an odd juxtaposition against his considerable beard and slicked-back silver hair. The Agency lawyer leaned down to address her quietly.

"The fine print of our legal authorities allows cooperation with the DNI as an organization. It doesn't limit us to specific individuals, so as long as Maximo is a card-carrying member, we're in the clear."

While comforting, nothing in his statement warranted a personal conversation versus calling out across the OPCEN, and she knew the other shoe was about to drop.

"But?" she asked.

"But," he went on, "I'd treat this as if the powers that be will scrutinize your decision for any errors in judgment. If you want to move forward with this, I advise you to frame the justification for proceeding as an OPSEC concern, and do so on the record. Just in case this thing goes sideways in the near future, which, frankly, our program has a lengthy historical precedent for."

She gave him a nod and he departed, leaving her to bite her bottom lip and consider how to articulate her response for the benefit of the official recordings being generated with each passing moment of the call.

Lifting the hand mic, she transmitted, "Understood, and I concur that a certain degree of compartmentalization is in the best interests of operational security. Maximo Ospina is an official representative of the DNI, granted to us with all relevant authorities for your team's effective and legal employment in Colombia, and if select elements of his organization see fit to regulate information sharing in the interests of continued mission success, then so be it. However, I will caution you to continue close supervision of Maximo's conduct and intelligence sources to ensure fidelity." With that out of the way, she continued, "Moving on to Sofia...how, exactly, has she been 'handed' to us?"

David was quiet for a time after that, but resumed an otherwise seamless delivery of, well, whatever half-truths he was telling her at present.

"Part of Jiménez's deal was to conduct a bait-and-switch. He'd already told

Sofia that the museum hit failed, but said his people were continuing to look for our team. After his interdiction, the DNI had him call her to report that he'd found and killed three of us, and that story was backstopped by a planted breaking news report that three unidentified Caucasians were killed in Medellín. Sofia has given him a location in southwestern Colombia, near the Pacific coast. He's supposed to arrive by boat at quarter to midnight, day after tomorrow, to take delivery of his cocaine and have a personal meeting with her."

"Send the grid."

A moment later, Duchess watched the central screen as her intelligence officer pulled up satellite imagery of the location.

The view told her precious little—the only markers in an otherwise solid blanket of treetops was a snaking river linked to jagged tributaries, one of which had a sharp turn marked by the icon indicating the specified grid.

Her J2, Andolin Lucios, turned to face her, narrating the implications in his Spanish accent.

"It's a mangrove swamp in Nariño Department, ma'am. Indirect access to the Pacific, and a labyrinth of tributaries for her to escape by boat. Likely too much overhead cover for us to determine what's there by satellite or even thermal measures. But with the geographic disparity from Sofia's usual hideout, I'd say it's unlikely she'd risk going there."

Duchess keyed her mic and said, "The linkup is in a mangrove swamp in an entirely different department than her hideout. What makes you think she'd take the risk of leaving her village just for Jiménez?"

"*That's the thing,*" David replied, sounding overeager, "*she's already left her hideout. Jiménez received calls from her on the cellular network, not satphone. Ian's preparing the data shot to send that info over to you now, but so far it checks out.*"

"If she's planning on a meet at that location, she's going to have considerable security and an airtight escape plan, *particularly* if there's that much cocaine present. That's not what we had in mind when we deployed your team, and as much as I like the idea of you going in while she's expecting Jiménez, it's not tactically feasible."

David's response was immediate. "*I agree one hundred percent. Given the amount of resources it'll take to isolate this objective to prevent her escape, we think the solution is a joint raid. Utilize the Colombian military and accompany their strike force, ensuring she's either killed or taken into custody. Either way, the Colombians take the credit and Sofia is off the battlefield for good. And Weisz doesn't get his cocaine."*

No way, Duchess thought, and said as much without bothering to censor herself. "If we can't trust everyone at the DNI, then it's guaranteed that someone in the military would tip her off."

"Exactly what we thought, at first. But there's one unit in Colombia that's tasked with counterterrorism, has the skills and operational security to pull this off, and full access to redirect any military assets they need with zero notice to prevent word getting out. And Maximo used to be a member."

"You want to go in with the AFEUR," she transmitted back, considering whether that would be possible, much less the best option. Because at first glance, it seemed to be both.

"Exactly. With your permission, of course, and provided your OPCEN can conduct some backside coordination– the unit is under the direct control of the General Commander of Military Forces, so it's going to require a political touch-point to pull this off. But Maximo still has plenty of contacts at AFEUR, and he assures us they'd be ready and willing to move on this if we provide the intel."

Duchess surveyed her OPCEN staff, letting her gaze drift across the staff primaries for intelligence, operations, logistics, and communication, searching for any indications of dissent that would counter her immediate thoughts on the matter. She was met with resolute expressions and subtle nods, finally ending her scan on the legal desk, where Gregory Pharr shot her a thumbs up.

Keying her mic, she transmitted, "I need to speak with the seventh floor, but I don't anticipate any resistance. Get your men ready."

9

Worthy stared out the window of the Colombian Army helicopter, watching the landscape below.

Aside from the occasional road or river, the view consisted of a wrinkled mass of jungled hills interspersed with agricultural fields. He idly wondered if any of them contained coca plants as the aircraft threaded its way southeast in the general direction of Bogotá. The capital city nestled in the Andes was known for its dining, women, and nightlife—none of which mattered at present, because regrettably they'd never set foot there. They had a different destination in mind, and were on their way in high fashion.

The helicopter was a Sikorsky Black Hawk, a staple of military aviation worldwide. It was just one of dozens sold as part of Plan Colombia, a US counternarcotics initiative that didn't seem to put much of a dent in cocaine production—now at record highs—but had succeeded in keeping the FARC from marching on the capital while equipping the nation's military and police with some of the finest equipment available. Worthy was enjoying the fruits of that relationship now; in stark contrast to some previous missions, there were no ratlines facilitated by local nationals with dubious motivations, no packing themselves into the back of a van and waiting to run into an armed checkpoint.

Instead, they were being whisked to their destination in an aircraft almost identical to those operated by the US military, and doing so without any considerable risk of getting shot in the process. Easy day.

But Worthy was in a foul mood regardless, harboring the sinking suspicion that this entire endeavor would amount to one wild goose chase.

He felt a tap on his arm and looked over to see Ian in the seat beside him. Reilly was on the other side, passed out; all three of them faced the cockpit, while David, Cancer, and Maximo were behind them and out of sight as they discussed the mission ahead.

Ian leaned in and spoke over the churning rotor blades.

"You've been awfully quiet. Regretting your decision to join the DEA?"

Worthy snickered, looking down to stroke the DEA Velcro patch now applied to the shoulder of his fatigues.

"What do you mean? I'm honored to be representing an agency with an efficiency rate under one percent. Besides," he added, affectionately patting the suppressed M4 carbine now pointed barrel-down between his legs, "I'm pretty sure they'll know who sent us once they look at our equipment."

Still, Worthy had to admit, there was a good reason for this particular cover. Posing as special agents made them non-threatening to the assault force—the DEA wasn't authorized to seize drugs or make arrests outside the US, so their inclusion on the raid was, ostensibly, in the capacity of advisors and observers. No tactical authority over the proceedings, and no real interference aside from perhaps being an annoying addition to the Colombian soldiers who'd actually conduct the raid, a very small price to pay in exchange for the intelligence that would put them on target. And besides, if a photograph emerged in the aftermath of tonight's raid showing one or more armed gringos had been present, the Agency needed some plausible deniability that they'd had a hand in the affair.

Ian said, "Don't be so sure our equipment will give us away as members of the Christians In Action." Worthy had to chuckle at that euphemism for the CIA as Ian continued, "Ever see pictures of the DEA burning hashish in Afghanistan? Those guys looked like regular storm troopers. Not that burning hash made much of a difference."

"Exactly," Worthy agreed. "They've got to be the biggest money suck in the US government."

Ian waved a dismissive hand. "You can't blame the DEA."

"Sure I can. Because I just did."

Ian glanced at the aircraft ceiling as if considering his words. "All right, look at it this way: the DEA is tasked with the same impossible problem set as the poor bastards who were supposed to stop alcohol in the early 1900s. Except it only took our country thirteen years to realize Prohibition was a disaster. The War on Drugs has been raging for a half century, and in that time it's accomplished two things. One is that America has incarcerated almost a quarter of the entire world's prison population, most of them minorities."

"And the second?"

Ian gave a lighthearted shrug. "We've started legalizing marijuana. So take it easy on the DEA—keep in mind the hero of the Prohibition was Eliot Ness, and he died an alcoholic."

Worthy nodded slowly, as if inspired by the insight. "And here I thought *I* was in a bad mood. You're just a regular ray of sunshine today."

"Hey, man, just stating the facts. I'm in great spirits."

"Yeah? Why's that?"

Ian's eyes widened, glinting with excitement. "We get to meet Sofia tonight. Or see her body growing cold. Either way, I'm good."

Worthy hesitated. "I don't know, Ian. Personally, I don't think she'd stick her neck out for a meeting with someone as inconsequential as Jiménez. My money is on her sending him into a trap so she doesn't have to pay her end of the deal."

"You mean to tell me you doubt the morality of drug running psychopaths? She'll be there, I guarantee it."

"How do you know?"

"More of a feeling, I guess. It's in her best interests to build a working relationship with the most violent trafficker in Medellín, and start expanding her urban reach. As for sticking her neck out, she's not doing it for Jiménez."

Worthy cocked his head to the side. "How so?"

"Sofia didn't leave her hideout to meet up with him," Ian explained. "She's meeting up with him *because* she left her hideout. And the fact that she traveled all the way to the mangrove swamps confirms that Weisz found a way to get that payment through, and his coke transfer is underway."

As if to confirm his point, David transmitted from the rear seats of the Black Hawk.

"*Update from Duchess*," the team leader began, "*they intercepted a communication on the network from Jiménez's phone exploitation. Someone linked to Sofia referenced his meeting in the mangrove swamps. They said, and I quote, 'We cannot afford any mistakes—over twenty million worth of product will be there.' Angel, you thinking what I'm thinking?*"

"Yep," Ian replied over the net, keeping his gaze fixed on Worthy. "Weisz's coke will be in the immediate vicinity. Meeting with Jiménez is just a convenience because she's already out there, supervising the main shipment. We take that down, we'll nab her and disrupt a terrorist attack. It's a win-win."

But Worthy was unconvinced, leaning in to tell Ian, "We *hope* the attack will be disrupted. What if Weisz just makes up that money somewhere else?"

"Law of supply and demand, my friend. The more governments try to restrict supply, the greater the demand and thus, the price. There's nothing in the world that compares to the margins on cocaine."

"I don't know," Worthy replied, adding humorously, "what if he's got stock in Amazon?"

Ian looked at him blankly, as if the pointman just didn't get it.

Then he said, "Sofia promised Jimenez 1,400 kilos. That's a little over 1.5 tons. Worth roughly two million dollars if sold in Colombia. Not bad, right?"

"Not bad," Worthy agreed.

"Now consider that value increases the farther the cocaine is transported. The same quantity would earn seven times that if Jiménez sold it to the Mexican cartels, which most Colombian traffickers do. But if he moves it to Miami? He's just turned two mil into 35. All the way to New York and he's looking at 56. And if he's got the resources to push it all the way to London, then those 1,400 kilos are worth *84 million*. Think about it."

Worthy did, and felt gobsmacked by the figures. Ian let the point settle before adding casually, "That's just wholesale pricing, by the way—cutting it up for retail would triple those amounts. Pair that information with the fact that Sofia is delivering over *twelve times* that quantity of coke to Weisz, and then imagine what kind of terrorist attack he could finance with the proceeds. Or don't imagine, just consider the sheer scope and magnitude of the July 4th attack if it had been carried out as planned. Stopping this coke transfer is going to save more lives than we'll hopefully ever know, brother."

Then, looking past Worthy and out the window, Ian said, "Hey look—we're here. That's Facatativá."

Worthy glanced outside to see the countryside had given way to a densely packed city, every inch of space brimming with structures between a tight grid of streets. As with Bogotá, there was probably a vast array of dining, drinking, and local culture to absorb, and as with Bogotá, the team wouldn't get to see any of it.

The helicopter thundered over the city, whose northeastern periphery ended in an enormous swath of massive buildings sprawling across open ground. This was the military base, home to a cavalry school, communications battalion, and one of Colombia's countless anti-narcotics units. But the base wasn't their destination either; at least, not the main portion of it.

He caught a glimpse of an isolated compound within the main grounds, its tall perimeter fence's chain link filled by slats that blocked the view to outsiders, the upper edges lined with concertina wire. From his elevated vantage point, however, Worthy got a good look inside as the Black Hawk banked right and made its way toward a helipad.

The compound's inception, Maximo had explained, stemmed from 1985.

That was the year a now-defunct terrorist group called M-19 seized the Palace of Justice in Bogotá, less than thirty miles from where Worthy's team now flew. The terrorists claimed 300 hostages, including all 24 justices in Colombia's Supreme Court, before demanding that the president appear to stand trial. He kindly refused the invitation before ordering an army raid to commence on the morning of the siege's second day.

The results were disastrous: 98 dead, including nearly half of the Supreme Court Justices. That much wasn't a surprise, at least to Worthy—utilizing conventional troops to conduct a hostage rescue was like getting pro basketball players to perform neurosurgery. Worthy's team could shoot, move, and communicate at a level equal to any number of special operations unit members, and even *they* were wildly unqualified for the particulars of that mission set.

The truth was, the split-second timing of hostage rescue required already seasoned people who were then selected, trained, and constantly practiced with minimal red tape or administrative requirements. His own nation had concluded the same in the wake of the massacre at the 1972 Summer Olympics in Munich, and as a result the US possessed Delta Force. And while those newly-christened professional shooters were fully prepared to execute the insanely audacious plan to rescue American hostages in Iran, 1979, the aviation and command capabilities weren't sufficient to support them, and Operation Eagle Claw failed. Enter the 160th Special Operations Aviation Regiment as well as the Joint Special Operations Command, both created as with many uber-specialized military organizations in the wake of a crisis.

Likewise, Colombia's response to the Palace of Justice siege was to create the *Agrupación de Fuerzas Especiales Antiterroristas Urbanas*.

How that mouthful of Spanish translated into the acronym AFEUR, Worthy didn't know and hadn't bothered to ask. But their English designation was Urban Counter-Terrorism Special Forces Group - Alpha, and his helicopter was currently descending into their compound.

No one on his team had worked with any members of the secretive unit, nor were there any glorious tales of past successes. Everything was classified, and even Maximo provided no insight beyond the assurance that not only was the AFEUR qualified to kill or capture Sofia tomorrow night, but that he was confident they would.

Worthy's initial glimpses inside the compound revealed sterile administrative buildings and outdoor shooting ranges, fast rope towers, and a conglomeration of multi-story shoot houses arranged into a mock town for practicing urban assault. These guys had the proper facilities and certainly the right equipment. All that remained to be seen was whether they possessed the skills of planning and executing a complex, multi-phase operation against a remote riverine target, and by the time the sun rose in a couple days, the answer would be clear one way or the other.

The pilots slowed the Black Hawk for landing, alighting gently atop the helipad as Worthy prepared to open the door.

10

The AFEUR commander addressed the assembly from a podium at the head of the small auditorium, speaking quickly in Spanish. Ian's grasp of the language was passable, but he was only vaguely aware that his team was being introduced, him in particular.

Instead his thoughts were consumed by the magnitude of the mission ahead, which was to be nothing short of a massive effort no matter how great the payoff. While he was relatively certain Sofia would be there, it was entirely possible she'd escape no matter how well his team or the Colombian main effort did their jobs. And if that occurred without the assault force seeing her in the first place, then all the blame would be on him alone. He considered that he was about to deliver the equivalent of former Secretary of State Colin Powell's speech to the UN in February 2003, more or less declaring that Iraq had weapons of mass destruction. No matter how much Ian personally believed in his own intelligence, he knew there was no such thing as a guarantee in this business.

As the commander continued to speak, Ian glanced at the men seated before them, considering that the gathering was oddly small considering the size of the ultimate raid. Then again, he thought, the vast majority of resources required would be requisitioned from other military elements shortly before the operation commenced. Only the AFEUR operators were trustworthy enough to notify this far ahead of time, and the audience reflected that: the organization's combat arm consisted of six squads containing fifteen men each, thirteen operators and two officers.

Many of those officers were present now, along with various staff types and mission planners. It wasn't hard to distinguish who was who: amongst what he would consider an average disposition of body types scattered among the attendees, the first seats were filled by Colombian men with an eerily similar look to any number of current or former US special operations forces members he'd met during his career. Incredibly fit, albeit ranging from the Herculean to relatively diminutive, with the poise and expressions of utter confidence in their abilities.

And, given the sudden presence of five Americans in their headquarters, extreme skepticism.

Ian looked beside him, where the other four members of his team along with Maximo sat nonchalantly in foldout chairs arrayed on the stage. In a way they had the easiest jobs of anyone, at least before the raid commenced—the particulars of tactical planning were no cakewalk, but the AFEUR operators would certainly be unified in the effort. It was up to Ian to convince them of the necessity of risking their lives to conduct the raid in the first place, and accomplishing that required him to divulge a series of closely guarded secrets within the US government and, in particular, the CIA.

He suddenly realized that the AFEUR commander had stopped speaking, and turned to the podium to see the man waiting, eyebrows raised, as an indication that it was Ian's turn to take the stage.

Flustered, Ian quickly proceeded toward the podium, intending to exchange a brief word of gratitude only to see the commander breeze past without a glance. Off to a bad start, he thought, more so since he'd been so preoccupied with his own internal monologue that he'd missed his entire introduction.

A long glass case beside him held a row of gleaming silver trophies inscribed with *Copa Fuerzas Comando*, awards from winning the annual US-sponsored Commando Forces competition between fifteen national teams. He was about to brief the nine-time champions of this event, some of the finest shooters not just in Colombia but anywhere in Latin America.

No pressure, he thought.

Stopping before the podium, Ian faced the room and began.

"Good morning, gentlemen. I'm Senior Special Agent Cohen of the US Drug Enforcement Agency."

He'd barely finished his sentence before one of the front-row attendees called out, "How do I know you won't get my people killed?"

Ian cut his eyes to the speaker, a thirty-something bulldog of a man with ostentatiously gelled hair. Not tall, maybe five-seven, his rank impossible to tell with a fatigue blouse draped across the back of his seat. But his upper body was covered in a virtually shrink-wrapped brown undershirt, and the visible skin of both arms was covered to the wrist in tattoos.

Ian paused for a moment to provide the AFEUR commander an opportunity to intervene, but when he merely folded his hands and smiled, Ian knew he was on his own.

He looked back to the interrupting party and asked, "And you are, sir?"

"*Capitán* Gomez, *Comandante* AFEUR *Numero Uno*. I will be leading the strike force."

Well, Ian thought, shit. No wonder the AFEUR commander hadn't shut down the line of inquiry; he'd be coordinating the overall raid from afar, not slinging lead on the objective's front lines. By now he'd undoubtedly learned that the best leadership style for this particular group of men was to give them a wide berth.

"Very well," Ian said. "*Capitán* Gomez, if you're concerned about my team being a liability, don't be. Every one of us served on the same DEA FAST squad—that's the Foreign-Deployed Advisory and Support Teams—with myself as the intelligence specialist and"—he swept a hand to David—"Supervising Special Agent Connelly as team leader. We've all got experience being forward-deployed with special operations forces in Honduras, Guatemala, and Afghanistan. When the FAST program was disbanded, all five of us were reassigned to a compartmentalized program where we continued to deploy to various classified locations. Training aside, I can assure you we've been in our share of gunfights. We're not here to get in your way."

With those false credentials established, Ian gestured to Maximo and said, "We've been working closely with the DNI to obtain actionable intelligence on tomorrow night's raid, where a minimum of 1,400 kilos will be changing hands."

But Gomez was undeterred, pointing out the obvious inconsistency in the team's cover.

"There is a significant difference between providing intelligence and going into the jungle."

That was Ian's first inkling that this entire brief, much less the mission, could turn disastrous in extremely quick fashion. It was entirely possible that the AFEUR shooters would suspect that the *cinco hombres blancos* hailed from an altogether different three-letter government agency than the one tasked to enforce controlled substance laws.

But the boldness with which this man had proclaimed himself leader of the first of six squads in the AFEUR, combined with the unit commander's reluctance to intervene in the unfolding engagement, indicated to Ian that he was dealing with an apex predator within the incredibly seasoned Colombian special operations community. They'd been mixing it up with bad guys in the jungles for close to sixty years, and prior to 9/11 comprised one of the most combat-experienced forces in the world.

If the DEA was dealing with an impossible problem set, as he'd assured Worthy they were, then the AFEUR were surely diehard believers in their cause.

So instead of trying to suppress the inquiry, Ian not only encouraged but congratulated the somewhat obvious implication.

"I agree," he said. "That's a very astute observation, *Capitán* Gomez. I've been in this line of work for quite some time, and this is the fastest anyone has called bullshit on my formal brief. My hat is off to you, sir."

Gomez gave an affirmative nod, and a majority of the room following suit in what should have been a reassuring gesture.

Ian continued, "The reason we're here is Sofia Lozano."

Gomez looked surprised at that, while the other men in the room perked up, leaning forward in their seats. The mention of her name was like flipping a light switch; a tangible, electric energy filled the room in a split second.

"And I'm here to tell you," Ian continued, "that much of what you think you know about Sofia is wrong. In fact, the only truth behind her legacy is the beginning—Daniela Milena Lozano was born in a tiny village in Caquetá and joined the Communist Youth at nine years old. She enlisted in the FARC at 14, where she was given the alias 'Sofia' that she uses to this day.

"While other female FARC members gained special privileges by sleeping with their commanders, Sofia became one herself. By 26 she was a field officer in the Southern Bloc, leading the 13th Front and both ordering and personally participating in what she referred to as 'parties'—mass executions of villagers, including children, after allowing the systematic rape of their women. When a farmer trying to defend his village nearly killed her with a sawed-off 12-gauge, Sofia took the weapon and put it to the womb of his pregnant wife. She's carried that shotgun ever since, which is where the nickname 'Sawed-off Sofia' comes from."

After pausing to let that comment sink in, he continued, "Then she became a FARC emissary, trusted by the high command with traveling to Libya to deepen their ties with the Gaddafi regime. This resulted in a prosperous relationship that lasted until Gaddafi's death in 2011. All the while, Colombian and US intelligence failed to locate her—understandable, given there are only two known photographs and a set of fingerprints from a petty arrest in her teens, along with a handful of intercepted radio transmissions. And in that time she not only developed a cocaine trafficking empire in FARC-controlled areas as a means of financing the movement, but also gained a reputation for political assassinations, including at least two left-wing presidential candidates."

His audience was sitting at rapt attention now, and it was easy to see why—this terror of a human being, a woman who had transformed so seamlessly and naturally from a childhood peasant to engaging in hideous acts of barbarism, would have been a dream come true in the crosshairs of any counterterrorist operative. The AFEUR missed their shot for years, and now they were about to get a golden opportunity.

Ian continued, "When the FARC demobilized, we know that she disappeared into the jungles of Putumayo Department along with her hardline followers. It now appears she leveraged her status to establish an extensive network that would outlast the organization's peace deal with the government, one that she must have seen coming. Sofia Lozano remains heavily involved in providing cocaine to known terrorist organizations. My government has tied her product to financing eleven bombings in Colombia, Ecuador, and Venezuela, with a combined death toll of 247. And tomorrow night, she'll be co-located with a shipment of somewhere in the neighborhood of twenty tons of pure cocaine, all of it destined to finance an as-yet-unknown terrorist attack."

He stopped short of mentioning that the load was destined for a mysterious international terror syndicate. For one thing, he wasn't allowed to disclose that, and for another, it wouldn't be necessary: if the room was attentive before, now they were on the edge of their seats.

Time to drive home his final points.

"Her normal bed-down location is a small village in Putumayo, where she resides in a riverside encampment with a number of rural communities in all directions. To Sofia, the civilians are human shields; to the civilians, she's their savior, a mix of Robin Hood and"—he hesitated—"Jesus Christ."

Then Ian continued, "And while the government has abandoned those civilians to the jungle, Sofia feeds their families, pays their children's teachers, provides for a far better life than they've ever known. They will fight to the death to defend her. As a result, any incursion by ground or air would be reported to her immediately. If that occurs, she'd vanish into the jungle, and it could be years before we get another lead. And by virtue of the innocent people she's surrounded herself with, even a precision airstrike is unfeasible for fear of collateral damage, as is the public relations fallout: she's taken up residence in a church."

He concluded, "This is what my government and a select few members of the DNI have known for the past year. Now, you know it too, and tomorrow night you have a chance to stop her once and for all."

Given all Ian's concern before his brief, he should've anticipated the immediate response, but, as with all too many things in the intelligence field, predictable outcomes were in startlingly short supply.

Gomez called out, "Your government also 'knew' that Saddam Hussein had WMD."

Ian flinched at that, his worst fears coming true, but the shouted statement was followed by uproarious laughter from the crowd and, he saw upon glancing to his side, his own teammates and Maximo as well.

Now that their skepticism pivoted to acceptance and, more importantly, keen interest, the real work could begin.

"Point taken, *Capitán* Gomez," Ian said, "and conceded."

Then, straightening behind the podium, he continued, "And since we've gotten that out of the way, let's discuss your objective."

11

I sat near the edge of the deck, cradling my suppressed M4 as our boat slipped across the nighttime tributary in Colombia's western mangrove swamps.

The jungle was eerily loud—the roaring chant of insects and amphibians was punctuated by shrieking monkeys announcing the presence of our vessel, which was just as well because we were traversing this particular stretch of water with the help of a spotlight mounted on the bow. Not very subtle, to be sure, but that was the point. And traveling by boat at night with a group of heavily armed men, I was having flashbacks to my team's last infiltration into Nigeria.

With a few notable exceptions.

The Niger River had a petrochemical scent, and was largely devoid of wildlife as a courtesy of international oil conglomerates operating in the delta. By contrast, this river offshoot was teeming with animals, giving me a degree of anxiety at present.

I pushed myself upright to glance at the periphery of the boat's spotlight beam, seeing clusters of glowing orange eyes reflecting the light from either side of the riverbank—these were caiman, large reptiles akin to the American alligator but purportedly faster and far more aggressive. We caught our first sight of one shortly after our boat traded the Pacific coastline for the mangrove swamps of western Colombia. The creature was thrilling to spot, until I noticed a second, then a third. The further downstream we went, the more of them we saw, both visible near the banks and swimming out of our path like a Red Sea of crocodilians parting to make way for our boat. If anyone happened to go overboard, I thought, they'd better bring a firearm along with them.

But the appearance of an eight-foot-long serpent draped across a branch overhead gave me some measure of comfort, and I eagerly keyed my mic.

"Hey Cancer," I said, "lots of anacondas in the trees. Big ones."

His tinny reply came over my earpiece a moment later, hardly audible over the background noise in his transmission.

"*Fuck. Off.*"

Ian's contribution to this exchange was far easier to hear—the intelligence operative was located in one of several boats trailing us at a distance under blackout conditions, prepared to speed to the objective and reinforce our highly vulnerable lead vessel.

"*Actually*," he said helpfully, "*we're a little far west for their native range, and they'd be in the water, not the trees. You're probably just seeing boa constrictors.*"

"I stand corrected—lots of boa constrictors in the trees. Now Cancer will know what's wrapped around his throat if he gets inserted tonight."

I'd barely finished my sentence when the boat rocked hard, either from the current or clipping a mangrove root. The motion sent me forward, and I reached out to brace myself against the gunwale, the upper edge of the hull that was particularly tall on this vessel. That gunwale provided both adequate concealment for a crouched man and the ability to install ballistic reinforcement—namely, armored panels that had been bolted to the interior side—and were one of two reasons this boat had been selected for tonight's operation.

The other was speed.

Both the boat and its driver had been selected from the Colombian Navy's AFEUR equivalent, a highly specialized maritime force attached to the Marine Corps. With the ability to seize vessels from drug runners and retrofit them with upgraded engines, the unit maintained a honed ability to covertly transport assaulters to and from various objectives along the country's thousands of miles of rivers and tributaries.

I surveyed the dark figures of men around me, taking in the relatively immense number of assaulters. Colombia had established dedicated SWAT-style military elements for its major cities, leaving AFEUR as a truly national assault force. That made it perhaps all the more surprising that the entire unit consisted of less than a hundred officers and operators, and close to a third of them were strung out across the boat, sitting as I was behind the protective cover of gunwale.

One of those AFEUR operators in full kit rose quickly and approached. I could tell from both his height and his actions—namely, moving to interact with one of the two gringos on board—that this was Gomez.

He knelt beside me and asked, "Enjoying your cruise on the *Caballo de Troya*?"

I nodded to the gleaming caiman eyes off the bow and said, "As long as I don't have to swim."

Gomez chuckled at my discomfort. "I wanted to inform you: our drones have spotted a light source ahead."

"At our linkup site?"

He shook his head. "Four hundred and fifty meters past that. East side of the river, on the water."

"You think she's there?"

Even in the distant glow of the spotlight, I could tell he was smiling. "I know she is."

"Thanks for the update."

Gomez departed without further word, rejoining his comrades behind the armored plates that would soon, I was sure, be desperately needed. And I had to hand it to these Colombian commandos: they were bold. Very bold.

The plan was simple but ambitious, hinging on the obvious fact that anyone as successful at eluding capture as Sofia would never provide her exact location. Everyone knew the linkup grid was for a preliminary security site, where guards would confirm that Jiménez was indeed on board and search the vessel before providing instructions to proceed to another location in the tributary. And since Jiménez was most certainly not up to the task—Vega's people kept the trafficker detained for the sole purpose of maintaining communications up until the bitter last second, now fast approaching—the AFEUR operators had designed an ingenious solution. Gomez had christened this vessel *Caballo de Troya*, Trojan Horse, for good reason.

Three of their men were in civilian clothes, one of whom was chosen for his physical likeness to Jiménez. Once we reached the security checkpoint, this element would serve as decoys to maintain our ruse as long as possible. And when Sofia's people tried to board for a search attempt, they'd encounter a hailstorm of suppressed gunfire from the AFEUR men on board. Once our shooters had seized all radios and intelligence materials, we'd simply proceed downstream to the actual meeting point—and with a light source confirmed less than half a kilometer past the ordained linkup site, it looked like we'd already found it. After all, Jiménez was supposed to accept delivery of 1,400 kilos, which ruled out the possibility of overland travel to some jungle location and allowed us to arrive in a relatively large vessel without drawing suspicion—until, of course, the assaulters went to work. All that meant Sofia was currently on the waterfront, and with a little luck that would be where she was killed or captured.

And in the event she was able to flee, well, the Colombians had a contingency for that too.

Keying my radio mic, I transmitted, "Net call, be advised Colombian drones have located a light source 450 meters downstream of our linkup. It's on the waterfront, east side, and looks good as Sofia's actual location."

I received sequential confirmations from my trio of teammates at three separate locations with various AFEUR elements, each prepared to converge on the objective when the time was right—everyone but Reilly, who I could see approaching on the deck. He'd chosen an IWI Galil ACE chambered for 7.62x51mm NATO for this mission, and he wore it well. While Cancer was my team's sniper, Reilly usually served as the long-range marksman and, when necessary, machine gunner; his size and strength were more than sufficient for carrying heavier weapons that packed a bigger punch.

The hulking medic knelt beside me, adjusting the rifle across his thigh. "You think this is actually going to work, boss?"

I shrugged. "It's as good of a shot as we're going to get, given the circumstances. But as for your part in this little charade?" I jerked a thumb toward the stern, where Reilly's aid bags and medical supplies were staged alongside those of two AFEUR medics, a grim reminder that the odds of coming out of this without casualties were inconceivably low. "It's going to be a hot minute before the cavalry arrives. I don't think you'll be bored."

"Yeah, me neither. Before this kicks off, I want you to know I think this entire plan is terrible. Bordering on lunacy."

"Of course it is," I agreed. "But can you come up with a better one?"

When Reilly didn't respond, I said, "Yeah, me neither."

My voice faded to the sound of whispers passing from Gomez down the row, and I strained to make out his Spanish order over the song of insects. Reilly's hearing must have been better than mine was, because he informed me, "Five minutes out. Better get back to my station."

"Send over my translator, would you?"

Reilly gave a nod and departed, and I lowered my night vision before taking a final glance over the side—a wall of jungle on both sides of the tributary, tree trunks giving way to a maze of vines and plants, all of it crawling with venomous snakes and jaguars.

Then I knelt, positioning myself behind one of the armored plates bolted to the side of the hull. We'd be taking fire sooner or later tonight, and I didn't want to end up as one of Reilly's patients if I could avoid it. The AFEUR operators on either side of me were doing the same, hunkering out of sight and adjusting their slings for the inevitable firefight. Only one man remained standing, strolling across the deck in a surprisingly casual manner for someone in body armor, night vision, and a suppressed assault rifle.

Maximo crouched wordlessly behind the armored panel to my left, the sole DNI representative at the pointy end of tonight's spearhead operation.

I asked, "Think we'll get the jump on her?"

"Not by much, if at all. But Sofia Lozano always has an escape plan."

"That's what the second wave is for," I pointed out. "We've got the waterways covered, and if she flees into the jungle—well, I put my money on Worthy and Cancer."

Maximo grunted thoughtfully.

"Perhaps."

"You don't like our odds?"

He drew a breath and replied, "I have come close too many times. So I will rejoice only when I see her dead."

"I'll drink to that. Mind translating for me once we get where we're going?"

He cut his eyes to me and asked accusingly, "How can you not speak Spanish yet?"

"I've been in Colombia for, like, seven minutes."

"Spanish is not so hard a language. You should try harder."

I sighed. "*Sí, señor.*"

He clapped my shoulder. "Was that so hard?"

Another call was passed down the row of shooters, this one a hand signal as each man flashed a single raised index finger.

"That means one minute," Maximo whispered.

"Yeah, I get that."

He shrugged. "You asked me to translate, *sí o no*?"

"*Sí.*"

The AFEUR stand-ins for Jiménez and his bodyguards clustered near the bow, armed but in civilian clothes as would befit a self-respecting gang of traffickers, and appearing for all the world like this was just another day at the office. While their tactical effectiveness remained to be seen, I had to admit their *cojones* were not up for debate—they had full military kit tucked out of sight in preparation for a hasty transition into assaulters at the final objective, but at the moment they were the most exposed individuals on an already exposed boat. How would I react in their shoes? I had no idea, and hoped to God I'd never have to find out.

I transmitted a final update to my team. "Stand by, approaching linkup."

My first indication that we'd reached our grid came by way of a glaring light sweeping the boat from our front, causing the AFEUR man at the helm to slow our vessel and angle left, subtly exposing the row of crouched shooters to whatever lay beyond.

"*Dónde está Sofia?*" the Jiménez stand-in shouted.

A shouted reply in Spanish ended in an interrogative note.

Maximo whispered, "They want to know his childhood address. Not good."

No, I thought, this was definitely not good. The AFEUR man had studied Jiménez on a short timeframe, to be sure, but there was only so much he could memorize.

He responded in an irritated, rapid-fire tone that indicated he was trying to bluff his way through. I watched him closely as he spoke, waiting for the inevitable. The plan at this stage was simple: the moment he and his "bodyguards" determined the risk to be too great, they'd hit the deck. That was our cue to pop up and take out whoever was beyond the hull, using overwhelming suppressed firepower to quickly and stealthily decimate the enemy.

But no such thing happened.

Whether Sofia's people detected something was amiss or simply had a short fuse when it came to getting answers, I had no idea. Whatever the case, our Jiménez lookalike was scarcely five words into his response before he and his compatriots flung themselves down amid bursts of unsuppressed gunfire; two of the men dropped behind the protective barrier of the gunwale in time, but the man playing Jiménez was too late, his body jolting amid a barrage of bullet impacts.

The row of shooters rose to kneeling firing positions before he hit the ground, and my first view over the gunwale revealed a much smaller vessel lit by our spotlight. It looked like a bass boat, and two standing men aboard it were still firing assault rifles.

By the time I took my first shot, so had everyone else. It was impossible to see where my rounds were landing, the enemy gunfire going silent amid a chattering racket of suppressed shots that bowled one man backward into a fountain spray of bullet impacts on the water. The other dropped to his knees, then fell forward with his arms over the side. He was dead three times over, and more than a few AFEUR operators seized on his stationary status as an opportunity to begin delivering headshots, brain matter spilling into the murky water below.

I lifted my barrel and swept the treeline, looking for any land-based elements and finding none. There would be no time to search the enemy bodies and no use searching for intelligence—Sofia probably hadn't heard her people's gunfire over the jungle sounds at this distance, but if they'd had time to shoot, they quite possibly had time to get a radio call out.

Either way, the race was on.

I fell to my side as our boat throttled forward, the bow angling downstream as the engine spooled to full power.

~

Reilly braced himself against the deck, recovering from the sudden acceleration as he started to rise and make his way to the bow, toward the casualty.

But the AFEUR medic beside him grabbed his sleeve and jerked him down, tapping his radio earpiece as he relayed a transmission in accented English.

"He is dead. Prepare to fight."

Jesus, Reilly thought, they'd just lost one of their operators in the blink of an eye and this medic's six-word response had all the emotional fervor of a takeout order. The man would mourn later, of course—who wouldn't?—but the immediate lack of anguish struck Reilly as borderline sociopathic.

The judgment faded when his own team leader transmitted with similar detachment, "*Boat compromised at the security checkpoint, one AFEUR KIA, two EKIA, we're moving toward the light source. They're bringing in all elements now.*"

Resuming his kneeling position, Reilly gripped the gunwale with his free hand while keeping his Galil barrel angled over the side, watching the jungle whip by in a flurry of green hues under his night vision. He could feel the boat churning around a bend in the tributary, barreling southeast as fast as the navy driver could pilot it.

Getting revenge was a distant second to helping the wounded, but given the circumstances, it would have to do. Fuck it, he decided, if they wanted him to be ready to fight, he was happy to oblige—Reilly readied his rifle, preparing to add his contribution to the upcoming engagement in the form of accurate 7.62. He could empathize with the ideological differences between himself and various hardline opponents around the world, but the people he was about to fight bore a degree of near-religious zealotry for money and money alone, and he simply couldn't abide that without a measure of disgust.

There was, of course, one small and exceedingly obvious problem.

The uncomfortable fact remained that they were tear-assing down the waterway with no other destination than a purported light source a few hundred meters ahead, beyond which they had absolutely no idea what they were looking for. What were they supposed to do if they arrived at the destination to find nothing at all—get off the boat and march endlessly into the jungle? Continue down the tributary in the hopes they'd spot something of note indicating Sofia's presence? The decision was up to the Colombians, and at this point even David was powerless to intervene.

That particular concern faded, however, the moment his vessel rounded the next bend in the waterway and Reilly caught his first glimpse of what was, unquestionably, their primary objective.

He had no idea what he was looking at, only that it was of great significance. Whatever light the drones detected had been extinguished, but his night vision conveyed a structure of sorts in the form of a long, narrow peaked roof held upright by vertical support beams. It rose twenty feet high on the shore, providing an excess of overhead cover to what seemed little more than a muddy section of riverbank descending into the water.

Why anyone would bother to conceal this meaningless slab of river was beyond him at present and, soon thereafter, completely irrelevant.

Figures were scattering to defensive positions along the shore, darting behind trees amid the first glinting muzzle flashes of incoming fire. The AFEUR shooters along the bow were already returning the favor, and Reilly swept his infrared laser across the trees, struggling to distinguish his beam from a dozen others in the vicinity as he searched for a target. If Sofia had advance warning of their arrival, it wasn't by much; these fighters were scrambling to react to the incoming boat, and no sooner had he realized this than he found his first opportunity to deal himself into the unfolding gunfight.

It wasn't that there weren't enough men on board to cover the objective, merely that any enemies amid the dense tree cover were almost impossible to spot. Reilly managed to locate a rifle-wielding figure making a break across open ground, moving for an advanced firing position in what, if all went well, would be the last mistake he ever made.

Orienting his laser beam toward the man, Reilly faced the near-impossible task of taking aim as the boat slowed to a stop broadside to the objective. The combination of a running target and a moving firing platform caused his odds of achieving a hit to dwindle perilously close to zero, and Reilly compensated with volume of fire.

His first two shots were interrupted by the clanging *thump* of incoming bullets hitting the armored gunwale, one aligned with his sternum and vibrating the metal surface he braced himself against; but Reilly recovered in a fraction of a second, driving a third and fourth shot in rapid succession.

Surely these guys had a moment of confusion as to whether they could eliminate this waterborne threat that arrived at their doorstep—after all, everyone on the boat was firing with suppressors that concealed any meaningful muzzle flash, so determining how many shooters were aboard was an impossible task. But there was a very tangible shift in the gunfight, a breaking point where the enemy seemed to realize their murderous numbers were no match for the accuracy aboard the newly arrived vessel.

It was too late to save them; Reilly himself was scoring probable hits on multiple fighters thanks to the now-stationary boat, although his confirmation came only in the form of muzzle flashes extinguished among the trees, never to return. In any case, the volume of incoming fire dropped to a few sporadic pop shots in a matter of seconds, while the AFEUR operators seemed to just be warming up. The audible cues were now a cacophony of chuffing suppressed fire, the clanging of magazines hitting the deck as shooters reloaded, and distant enemy shouts in the trees.

There must have been a radio call over the Colombian frequency, because the boat surged forward and sidelong, its forward hull thumping against a tangle of mangrove roots.

Gomez shouted, "*Avanzar!*"

This caused the landing team of AFEUR operators to advance along the bow, leaping over the side to establish an initial foothold as the men along the stern provided covering fire. Reilly did his part, driving rounds toward the few remaining muzzle flashes where clusters of infrared lasers converged. He remained optimistic that he'd be able to trail the assault, establishing a forward casualty collection point alongside the AFEUR medics, but those hopes were dashed when he heard the first call of

"*Médico*." That meant casualties were inbound and he'd be assisting with treatment aboard the boat.

He glanced right, seeing a pair of operators fireman-carrying wounded comrades toward him. With his role in the operation irrevocably shifting from shooter to medic, he placed his weapon on safe and started to move to his aid supplies.

But Reilly's last glimpse of the objective told him that the fight wasn't over.

Deciding that discretion was the better part of valor, a cluster of enemies took off into the jungle, the dense trees saving them from immediate annihilation as infrared lasers chased them without result.

Reilly was about to transmit this development to David when the team leader spoke over their team net.

"*AFEUR is making landfall, we've got six to eight squirters fleeing northeast. Worthy, Cancer, you're going in.*"

~

Cancer momentarily thought he'd misheard David's transmission, attributing the confusion to two possible factors.

First was the noise. He was seated aboard the floor of a Black Hawk helicopter screaming over the treetops at near maximum power with both doors open, the wind whipping through a cabin packed with AFEUR operators. Second, if he was being honest with himself, was the fact that he really, really didn't want to be employed in the capacity of squirter control.

At least not in the way the Colombians intended on doing it.

Hesitation wasn't a normal part of his repertoire, however, and he duly transmitted back, "Cancer copies. Shit."

Worthy's response was slightly more professional. "*Racegun copies. We're on it, boss.*"

Cancer looked out the starboard side to see the adjacent helicopter flying blackout, visible only as a sleek profile against the sky in his night vision. Aboard was Worthy along with a half-squad of AFEUR operators, and the bird banked a hard right turn out of its formation slot, reorienting to a separate insertion point.

Then Cancer's helicopter tilted left, a subtle course correction but one made with such speed that he felt his stomach lurch. With six to eight enemies attempting to flee, the race was on for the men aboard his and Worthy's Black Hawks in addition to the three others currently spreading out to insert unilateral AFEUR teams. Given the sheer number of men the Colombians were dedicating to the squirter contingency and the speed with which they were responding, Cancer felt good about their odds of a successful interdiction.

He tightened the sling of his Galil ACE, chosen because his usual sniper rifle would be of little use in the maze of vegetation below, and shifted the weapon to his back while trying to stay out of the way amid the AFEUR operators clustered around him. Cancer was used to functioning as second-in-command, ensuring David's orders were translated into appropriate actions at the tactical level so the comparatively young team leader could focus on managing the big picture and liaising with their higher headquarters.

Accompanying a partner force as a straphanger was new territory for him, and not a particularly comfortable one at that.

It didn't help that he'd been relegated to squirter control, which the Colombians were pursuing with reckless abandon—the AFEUR squad leader was untethered, leaning halfway out the open door as he communicated with the pilots to determine an appropriate insertion point. Matter of fact, the only person aboard who'd bothered clipping into a tie-down point was Cancer himself, which was troubling on two fronts. First, a hard landing would turn the seating area into a pinball machine, and second, if he was the most safety-conscious person in any given setting, then things were straying into truly sketchy ground.

He donned a clear set of shooting glasses before rotating his night vision back into position, seeing that his counterparts aboard the bird were also taking at least that minor precaution. Cancer had been expecting to ride with a bunch of hot-blooded Colombian warriors fist bumping each other on their way to the objective, but these AFEUR shooters were stone-cold, all business as they unclipped thick leather work gloves from their kits.

Cancer retrieved his safety lanyard from the metal clip on the floor, hooked the newly freed end back onto his kit, and then pulled on his own leather gloves as the helicopter suddenly angled to the left. Confirmation that the pilots and squad leader must have found what they were looking for came when the latter man leaned back in the aircraft and yelled, "*Veinte segundos*."

He shifted his position to make way for the AFEUR shooters moving away from the massive rope coiled on the cabin floor, its fixed end attached to a metal pylon extending a short distance beyond the left door.

"*Diez segundos*," the squad leader called, each man onboard rising to a knee by the time he updated, "*Cinco*."

Then the bird transitioned to a hover over a clearing that was little more than a slightly less dense section of jungle canopy, and before Cancer could contemplate how ludicrously inappropriate it appeared for what they planned to do, the squad leader shouted, "*Cuerda, cuerda, cuerda!*"

The AFEUR men shoved the rope out the left door, where the fat coil cleared the final threshold of metal and fell out of sight as the squad leader watched its descent to determine, if he even could at this height, whether the bottom end made it through the trees, much less all the way to the ground.

And apparently he liked what he saw, because seconds later he spun into the cabin and jabbed a finger toward the closest operator.

"*Vamos*."

The first man dangled his legs over the side, gripping the rope with gloves and boots before vanishing in a downward flash of motion. Without taking his eyes off the man's descent, the squad leader repeated, "*Vamos*."

A second operator was gone then, disappearing down the rope as the helicopter wobbled slightly with the redistribution of weight. The AFEUR shooters shuffled forward, their departure intervals controlled by the squad leader and elapsing in remarkably quick succession given the conditions. For once, Cancer was glad to be one of the last men out the door; whether these Colombians were used to doing this on a regular basis or not, he was in no hurry to catapult down a rope that may or may not be entangled twenty feet in the canopy, a situation that was an eight-man pileup waiting to happen.

Although, he reasoned pragmatically, falling to his death may be preferable to safe landfall amid a snake-infested jungle.

He moved on his knees, edging forward as the man to his front mounted the rope and dropped out of the doorway. By then only two other men were left in the cabin: the Black Hawk's crew chief, who would remain aboard and detach the rope after the last man was on the ground, and the squad leader who surveyed the descent of his operators.

Cancer sat at the edge of the doorway, gripping the rope with one hand over the other and pinching it between his boots. A quick glance downward revealed the previous shooter dropping between the treetops, or through them—it was difficult to tell amid the churning mass of jungle canopy being whipped by rotorwash. Upon hearing one last *vamos*, he committed his weight to the rope and spun sideways for his assault pack to clear the aircraft's bottom edge.

Then he spiraled downward, past the Black Hawk's blazing heat and gas fumes and into a tropical night sky, the horizon a spinning green disc that rose up to meet him. He caught glimpses of two other helicopters conducting similar fast rope insertions, both appearing in a blur of motion until the view was gone altogether, replaced by the whipping treetops that he plunged into like a dive into the ocean. Once the battering assault of leaves and branches clawing for purchase against his body had passed, Cancer slid into an entirely new world beneath the canopy's surface. It was infinitely blacker than the sky, glimpses of vine-laden tree trunks dancing around the periphery of his vision as he looked downward, seeing the man below touch down at the center of a perimeter of kneeling men before darting off to join them.

Cancer applied maximum pressure with his hands and feet, the friction heating his palms through the gloves as he prepared for landing. He managed to slow his descent, albeit barely, before spreading his boots and thumping down into a soggy blanket of leaf litter.

Releasing the rope before the squad leader could crash down on top of him, Cancer ran toward a gap between two kneeling AFEUR shooters. He used his teeth to rip off the leather gloves one at a time, spitting them out to their final resting places in the jungle and reaching back for his slung rifle as he heard the *whomp* of the squad leader making landfall behind him.

By the time Cancer took a knee, his weapon's pistol grip was in his right hand, his left putting slack into the sling so he could bring it to a firing position as he heard branches cracking overhead. The rope was falling free from its anchor point, and he hoped the perimeter was of sufficient diameter to prevent one or more members from getting clobbered by the thick mass of woven fiber racing down toward them.

No sooner had Cancer put his weapon into action amid the fading dizziness of the spiraling descent than his night vision turned to a uniform shade of pale green that erased all details of the jungle beyond. He was in the process of yanking the shooting glasses from his face—they'd saved his eyes from branches on the way down but were fogged by the muggy air in seconds flat—when the rope thundered to the ground, emitting a deep concussion that faded to the sound of the Black Hawk departing to the north.

As the AFEUR men swiftly rose and assembled into a file, Cancer heard a third sound: his team leader's voice, transmitting in an urgent tone.

"Objective is clear—Sofia's not among the dead. Cancer and Worthy, don't screw this up—she's got to be moving with the squirters."

"Copy," Cancer whispered. "I just got inserted, we're moving now."

He'd just assumed his place in the center of the formation, shadowing the squad leader and scanning the surrounding trees for snakes, when Worthy finally checked in over the net.

"*My element is boots on the ground,*" he said, "*starting movement to the target.*"

Worthy crouched to slip beneath the fallen tree suspended five feet above the ground, edging his way past it before rising and scanning the jungle ahead. Only a single-file formation was possible in this terrain, and even then it was a challenge to locate the AFEUR operator to his front, now little more than a shadow slipping between the trees as Worthy hustled to follow.

The air was thick with humidity and the smell of rotting vegetation as swarming clouds of mosquitoes surrounded his head, seemingly unbothered by the generous quantities of insect repellant he'd applied before boarding the helicopter. A laundry list of tropical diseases ran through his mind with each bite to his face or neck—yellow fever, dengue fever, malaria—and he could only hope that Reilly's mandatory regimen of vaccinations and daily antibiotics was sufficient to keep his immune system boosted.

He trailed the leader of this seven-man AFEUR element, moving in the center of the formation as they continued toward the tributary. The jungle only grew more dense the further they moved, plant growth already well-supplied by substantial rainfall increasingly bolstered by the rising water table. About the only thing working in their favor was the fact that they were moving downhill, and even that presented its own challenges. Worthy's footfalls were met with exposed roots, sliding patches of leaves, and spongy mud; with his night vision impinged by a lack of ambient light beneath the canopy, he took a step onto the most stable surface he could identify only to realize too late that he'd just committed his weight to a rock. His left boot sole displaced the moss there, which shifted along the slick rock face with heart-stopping speed as his foot got stuck and he went off balance, managing at the last second to arrest his fall with his free hand and very nearly punching his suppressor into the mud in the process.

Pushing himself upright, Worthy pulled his left foot from between two stones, a narrow wedge that could just as easily have broken his ankle. He turned to face the obstacle and traced a circle around it with his infrared laser, highlighting the area for the man behind him before continuing to move.

David's estimation of six to eight squirters meant his element was almost equally paired man-to-man; the US military strove for a 3:1 friendly-to-enemy ratio before committing to an engagement, but these AFEUR operators were plunging ahead regardless. Of course they were, he thought —waging war far from your own shores was one thing, but these men were combating a threat in their families' backyard just as they'd done their entire career. And by all appearances, the maneuver was routine to them: they negotiated the jungle with relative ease, making steady progress through the byzantine corridors between trees and thorns, brush and vines.

Of course, "steady" didn't mean fast, and there were patches of jungle where the Colombian pointman had to stop the formation and test several patches of foliage before committing to one and proceeding. Twice they'd had to back out and try an alternate route, all the while proceeding in a generally southwest direction toward the main objective. Worthy questioned the efficacy of doing so at all; the jungle was endless, and if they reached the objective without finding the squirters, then this whole effort would have been for nothing.

A pair of considerations gave him hope, however.

One was that the AFEUR had inserted so many men along the squirters' last known path that the sheer numbers worked in their favor. Better still was the jungle's inhospitality, which worked both ways; if the Colombian elements were limited to certain routes among the microterrain, then so were the enemy who'd fled. The odds of a head-on collision were very real and getting better with every meter of ground covered.

He followed the procession down a steep slope and into a muddy stream, then up the far side before giving a rearward glance to confirm the presence of an AFEUR man continuing to follow. The formation threaded into the plant cover beyond, their rate of movement increasing as he realized the pointman had stumbled upon a game trail of sorts in the undergrowth. It was narrow and winding, providing little in the way of horizontal clearance from the surrounding brush, but given the terrain Worthy had seen so far, even that was a tremendous blessing. He was in the process of checking his GPS when he received Cancer's transmission.

"Hey Racegun, be advised: aside from a pack of pissed-off monkeys, my group hasn't found shit. If anyone on our team has a chance of taking her out, it's you."

Worthy keyed his mic twice in a nonverbal response.

His blood was really pumping now—the prospect of witnessing Sofia's death, if not personally administering it, was far too tantalizing to ignore. Of Project Longwing's four previous targets, two terrorists had survived. The other two had been killed only after an absurdly long list of attempts and changes to the original plan, coloring the targeted killing program's early history with a very checkered success rate, to say the least. Gunning down Sofia this early in their deployment would be an unprecedented victory, so long as the Agency never found out they'd collaborated with a known trafficker to do so. And if Worthy pulled the trigger, so much the better.

The moment this thought occurred to him, the formation stopped dead in its tracks. He heard the squad leader transmit a response to some radio traffic over his frequency, causing the front half of the formation to fan out to the left, and the rear half to the right, with alarming speed. Someone must have heard movement ahead, he thought, because this was the AFEUR contingency to form a hasty lateral ambush. When his Colombian counterpart assumed a kneeling position to the left of the narrow game trail, Worthy reflexively sought the cover of a tree trunk on the opposite side and whispered a transmission to his teammates.

"*Got movement. Stand by.*"

He'd barely taken a knee when he detected the reason for the sudden dispersal—crashing brush perhaps twenty meters to his front, the sound highlighted by the sudden silence of jungle insect calls to an even greater extent than his own element had induced. On top of that, he could see a pale glow increasing in brightness to his front; the incoming runners were moving under white light, a fatal mistake in nighttime warfare. Best of all, Worthy was alongside the AFEUR leader, positioned almost dead-center in the squirters' direction of movement, meaning he'd without a doubt be able to put his suppressed M4 to good use.

Judging by the tremendous racket they were making, these people were booking it as fast as they could move. The helicopters had made a point of approaching from far inland and, after inserting the shooters, departed the way they'd come. Breaking brush through the already-loud jungle made a lot of noise, firefights more so; and Worthy realized it was entirely possible that the squirters were unaware that they'd encounter any resistance whatsoever in this direction. Unless they'd managed to hear choppers in the distance, why would they?

And that single factor, he thought, was probably the key to decisive victory in the engagement ahead.

Then again, the benefit of night vision and uncompromising accuracy wouldn't hurt either. Sure, this would be a one-on-one matchup or very close to it, but the holy trinity of training, tactics, and equipment tended to win the day. He brought his M4 to a high ready firing position, holding his place in the line for a now-imminent clash as the sound of footsteps and crackling vines being pushed aside increased in volume.

Their lights grew brighter, and he could tell by the sounds of movement they were around ten meters out now. He angled for a shot, deciding to hold his fire until the AFEUR operators initiated contact—the last thing he needed was to be viewed as the "DEA agent" who spooked the enemy element too soon, causing them to disperse for a messy chase amid the undergrowth. If he were alone with his team under these circumstances, they wouldn't trigger their ambush until they could figuratively if not literally smell their opponents.

To their credit, the small AFEUR force did largely the same.

Worthy couldn't see the first squirter from his covered position, but could tell from whatever flashlight or headlamp heralded their progress that he—or she—was less than three meters distant before three or more suppressed weapons opened fire upon the enemy force.

And then, all hell broke loose.

What he hadn't considered was the fleeing enemy's sheer desperation. They knew turning back meant encountering the main assault force they'd just fled, and thus the only hope of survival lay in moving forward. And they acted accordingly, with nothing short of savage ferocity.

Glaring white light was cast in every direction to his front as the fighters scattered in a mad dash, their headlamp beams sweeping above visible muzzle flashes as they began blasting rounds. Worthy took single and double shots with his M4 at likely and suspected enemy positions; at this point determining both was more of a best-guess situation, with forward fire permissible only because he knew without a doubt that every friendly fighter was spread evenly to his left and right.

The ensuing engagement was chaos. With his own element operating under night vision and the squirters barreling through the jungle with headlamps, Worthy's view went from crisp green to blinding flashes of white amid a backdrop of impossibly dense vegetation.

He heard a crash behind him and whirled sideways to see that one squirter had penetrated a gap in the AFEUR ranks and was plunging through the trees without a visible source of light, apparently having extinguished a headlamp in the interests of stealth. Worthy stood and raised his weapon, trying to draw a bead from his current position—if he broke from the formation to pursue, his odds of getting shot by either the squirter or an overeager Colombian commando went up by a factor of ten.

But his infrared laser only shimmered off leaves and vines, crossing tree trunks in pursuit of a shadow. Finally the squirter made a move that exposed their body for two fleeting seconds, running away at an oblique angle. As a former competitive shooter, it was far from his easiest target but not the hardest, either. Worthy fired a controlled pair of subsonic rounds, then chased them with six more shots as the darting figure tumbled and fell.

There was a shout in Spanish, and while Worthy couldn't understand it, he imagined the import was something along the lines of "engagement complete." The AFEUR operators activated the taclights on their rifles to transition to a thorough search of the enemy bodies.

Worthy did the same, flipping his night vision up and using his taclight both to advance on the squirter he'd just shot and to signal his location to the AFEUR men. No one followed him, at least not yet; they had their hands full with the squirter bodies spread out among their hasty ambush line.

So Worthy proceeded through the foliage alone, keeping his weapon at the ready and aimed on the patch of brush where the body had fallen. He moved to a chorus of refrains from the main objective, men calling out "*Negativo*" as they checked the corpses and found none were Sofia.

Clearing a tree, Worthy found his target.

The final body was lying face down with a bullpup assault rifle at its side and wearing mud-covered rain boots rising to mid-shin, khaki cargo pants, and a plaid shirt with the sleeves rolled. There was a hat, too, that had remained in place despite the fall. It was a floppy bush cap of sorts, with long black hair pulled into a loose ponytail beneath it.

Worthy moved slowly now, watching for movement and finding none. Which wasn't to say that the person wasn't necessarily alive, but he'd seen the fall, pulled the trigger himself, and knew that whoever it was didn't have time to lay atop a grenade with the pin pulled as a de facto boobytrap. Given the necessity of facial recognition, he considered drilling a pair of subsonic rounds between the shoulder blades just to be sure, but the intelligence value of a surviving captive couldn't be overstated, particularly if it was Sofia herself.

He could hear AFEUR operators crashing through the brush toward him, and decided that the arriving backup was more than sufficient for him to make the identification himself without assuming undue risk. Reaching down with his free hand, Worthy grabbed a fistful of shirt at the shoulder and rolled the body onto its back, stepping back and shining his taclight at the head now rolling to face him.

Ian stood alongside a row of Colombians at the bow of his boat, the last to arrive at the main target.

Vessels were now clustered alongside the objective, with David's *Caballo de Troya* hard to distinguish amid the follow-on vessels that had ferried additional waves of shooters and, once a sizeable security perimeter had been established, forensic and intelligence personnel.

That latter group was visible moving along the shore and in the jungle beyond, spreading across the now-secured objective to conduct site exploitation. They'd already fired up a portable generator to give life to a long row of tripod-mounted work lights, illuminating the ground to daylight conditions as they searched bodies and used biometric devices to compare fingerprints to a database of former inmates. All in a day's work, he thought, when your job consisted of trying to decipher connections between an ever-growing list of trafficking organizations.

Ian wasn't interested in any of that. First, the Colombians were more than equal to the task, and second, his attention was drawn to the single structure growing in his field of view as the boat approached.

It was a hangar-like tin roof, braced by wooden planks and held aloft by vertical support beams. There were no walls and, aside from the muddy bank, ostensibly nothing underneath. Behind it were stacks of construction materials, long slats whose composition he couldn't visually determine at this range. But the combination of all these elements and, more importantly, their location in this obscure tributary along the Pacific coast, told him everything he needed to know about Sofia's intention here tonight.

Keying his mic, Ian transmitted, "Suicide, I'm coming up on the objective now."

"*I see your boat,*" David replied. "*I'll meet you at your stopping point. You're not going to believe this.*"

Oh, Ian thought, I bet I will.

His boat cut power as it neared the shore, gliding the final few meters before the hull brushed up against the muddy bank and they came to a complete stop. Ian was surprised when the Colombians aboard made way for him to depart first—none had so much as spoken to him since the assault had begun, instead conferring among one another in hushed tones as they monitored their internal frequencies.

"*Gracias, señores,*" Ian said as he passed. He mounted the hull ladder and climbed down, then leaped off to plunge into knee-deep water and muck before striding up to solid land. There he could make out his team leader threading a path through the intelligence people and soldiers pulling security.

When David finally arrived, he shook his head and said, "I've never seen anything like this." He turned to point to the piles of construction materials. "So the stack of planks over here is—"

"Fiberglass," Ian cut him off, turning to see the Colombians disembarking from his boat and assembling on shore to receive a hasty briefing from Gomez. "Show me the sub."

David looked stunned. "How do you know there is one?"

"Because this is a clandestine shipyard, probably one of three dozen operating at any given moment. Point is, that's why Sofia was here—she wasn't just transferring the coke to Jiménez, she was going to surprise him with a ready-made vehicle for him to transport it. Pure profit for him, and a guaranteed jumpstart to a viable working relationship for her."

David frowned. "That's what Maximo said."

"Cool. Let's go."

As they began moving toward the tin-roofed scaffold, Ian asked, "So where's the twenty tons?"

"They haven't found it yet."

That comment settled like a brick in Ian's gut. The load should have been in the immediate vicinity, and the fact that no one had found it yet was troubling, to say the least. He consoled himself with the knowledge that the jungle was thick, and Sofia would have kept it out of Jiménez's view. Surely it would be uncovered in short order.

"They will," he said with confidence, then asked, "Any updates from squirter control yet?"

"Not since they confirmed insertion, but those guys have their hands full trying to cross Jurassic Park to reach the objective. It's going to take them all night, but with the number of squads they dropped into the jungle, I feel good about their odds of finding the squirters."

"Anyone captured alive here?"

David laughed, not breaking stride as he gestured to the surrounding area—blood-splattered bodies lying in every possible orientation, being administered to by the forensic and intelligence teams.

"So far, no one's talking."

They arrived underneath the roof, where David shined his taclight over the surface of the water and then held it over a pentagon-shaped slab of metal and a curved section of pipe.

Ian gave a knowing nod. Of the two or three tons of cocaine leaving Colombia every day, close to 80 percent went via the Pacific—most of it on go-fast boats, customized high-power vessels that relied on speed to run the gauntlet of US Coast Guard efforts to detect and stop them.

But the barely visible cockpit emerging a foot or so above the waterline belonged to a vessel built solely for stealth.

He activated his own taclight, then swept it left and right. Barely visible beneath the murky depths was an exceedingly long and impossibly narrow hull spanning perhaps forty feet.

After they both killed their lights, David asked, "Everyone keeps calling this a sub. So why is it out of the water?"

Ian half-grinned at the inquiry, which indicated his team leader had been too embarrassed to ask Maximo. He replied, "Full submersibles are extremely rare. Most narco subs are actually low-profile vessels. Technically this one is a semi-submersible. They're virtually impossible to spot from the air, or on maritime radar. Anyone searched it yet?"

"They were waiting for EOD to arrive on your boat. Gomez wants them to check it for boobytraps."

The explosive ordnance disposal team arrived a moment later, escorted to the site by Gomez, who'd apparently just concluded his lengthy brief.

David and Ian got out of their way, advancing up the bank so they could survey the proceedings without interfering. Then they watched the Colombians perform their clearance with casual proficiency. First they recovered a ladder placed by narcos for the purpose of moving to and from the vessel, sliding it over the surface of the water to the exposed cockpit before sending three men across the rungs. They tested the narco sub's hull, probing with boots in the water to either side of the cockpit before committing their weight and clustering around the hatch.

Ian's focus was shattered by a transmission over his team frequency that caused his lungs to constrict in hopeful anticipation that Sofia was confirmed dead.

But instead, Cancer spoke in a bored tone. "*Hey Racegun, be advised: aside from a pack of pissed-off monkeys, my group hasn't found shit. If anyone on our team has a chance of taking her out, it's you.*"

With sagging shoulders, Ian heard a double spike of static as Worthy confirmed receipt.

Looking back to the sub, he saw that an EOD man was already cracking the hatch a few inches, allowing a teammate on all fours atop the hull to scan inside with a flashlight before inserting a tactical cable camera. It was attached to a display screen held by a third man, who issued quiet instructions on where he needed to see before confirming it was clear.

Then Worthy transmitted, "*Got movement. Stand by.*"

Ian involuntarily held his breath, locking eyes with David to exchange a hopeful glance. They faced a potential multi-hour wait for the squirter interdiction teams to achieve results, if they did at all—it was a big jungle, after all—and with this early progress it was impossible not to get his hopes up.

He forced his eyes back to the water, but found his thoughts in gridlock as he awaited an update from Worthy. As such, he was only peripherally aware that the EOD team had fully opened the hatch, and he was completely unconcerned when their first man entered the narco sub. After all, he knew what they'd find—Jiménez's load of cocaine and nothing else, a hollow victory that would amount to nothing if Sofia and Weisz's twenty tons weren't stopped in the process.

And when Worthy spoke again, Ian lapsed into a state of complete denial.

"*Engagement complete. Eight EKIA, no friendly casualties. Sofia's not here.*"

Keying his mic impulsively, Ian asked, "Are you sure? We've only got a couple pictures to go off of."

"*Pretty sure, Angel,*" came the unapologetic response. "*Because unless we just killed the eight ugliest women in Colombia, these are all dudes.*"

A voice behind Ian said, "Didn't you guarantee she'd be here?"

He turned to see Reilly, his first view of the medic since arriving. His fatigue sleeves were rolled halfway up the forearms, revealing dried blood on the exposed skin above the cuff of his tactical gloves.

"Are you okay?" Ian asked numbly.

Reilly looked confused, then glanced down and said, "Oh, this. AFEUR blood, not mine. They took three KIA and five wounded, none critically. And a narco who I tried to keep alive for intel but...yeah, that didn't work out. Too far gone. So," he continued, repeating the question, "didn't you guarantee she'd be here?"

Ian glanced to David, whose jaw was set, then to the Colombians below. News must have spread via the AFEUR frequencies, because Gomez was glaring at him. The intelligence operative had sold them on an extensive mission that had claimed the lives of three men while the squirter interdiction teams would remain in harm's way until they arrived safely at the objective.

That realization snapped Ian back to reality, somewhat at least, and he muttered, "I was sure of it. I don't...I don't know what happened."

By now the EOD man aboard the sub had emerged from the hatch, clutching an armful of kilos that he began tossing to the men on shore.

One of these was caught by Gomez, who turned to face Ian and made a sickeningly ill-timed announcement.

"Congratulations, America. We have just won the drug war."

He hurled the brick of cocaine with startling accuracy. In Ian's shocked state, it would have hit him in the face if David didn't step in to intercept it.

A knot of nauseating, nervous tension was forming in his stomach now.

Ian didn't know what was worse, the fact that Sofia hadn't been here and the twenty tons of cocaine were nowhere to be found, or the fact that despite the meaningless loss of life tonight, Colombian politicians would parade this load of cocaine before the television cameras as a sign of "progress" in the endless fight against it. Yet for every kilo captured, he knew, nine more made it to the street.

Then Gomez shouted, "Twenty tons? There are only two aboard the sub."

Not even, Ian thought, his lips silently parted as the Colombian officer shouted, "And no Sofia!"

He stormed off then, moving away from the sub with a long string of rapid-fire profanity.

Maximo arrived a moment later, looking oddly natural in his tactical attire. Which was to be expected, Ian supposed, since he was a former member of AFEUR.

He grabbed Ian's arm and squeezed it powerfully, giving him a shake as if enraged, but his eyes bore a twinkle of mischief and he spoke without malice. "I told you, Sofia cannot get her hands on twenty tons. But did you not say she would be here?"

Ian pulled his arm away and rubbed it. "Funny."

Maximo clapped his shoulder in apology, then leaned in and said, "It is not the first time she has slipped a noose. I merely hope it will be the last."

David, who suddenly appeared angry, lowered his voice and said, "I trust Ian's assessment that she was here. But she must have had advance notice, and we're looking at the reason why. Look how many people it took to isolate and raid this objective—we're dealing with professionals, sure, but it only takes one leak for Sofia to have known we were coming. The next time we go after her, we're not doing a huge joint operation. We'll do it like we usually do, slipping in and out with a small, agile team."

"How do you propose we do that?"

David glanced from Reilly to Maximo to Ian before he said, "Maybe there's an opportunity in this. There's twenty tons of coke missing, and only hitting her hideout will tell us where they're at. She's going to flee back to her village, right?"

"Undoubtedly," Ian said. "It's the safest place for her."

David shrugged. "So we hit her there."

Reilly looked at the team leader as if he'd just gone mad.

"No one's been able to hit her there for a reason, otherwise the Colombians could have finished the job without us."

"No one," David agreed, "because there wasn't a way to slip in undetected."

Ian countered, "The Colombians have almost everything we do, or at least a watered-down version of it. The War on Drugs has seen to that. What's changed?"

David nodded toward the narco sub, its cockpit barely visible above the waterline.

"That," he replied, adding helpfully, "at least, if we can find someone to drive it."

All eyes turned to Maximo, whose gaze was fixed on the vessel in silent rumination.

A smile crept across his face as he nodded to himself with a look of grim satisfaction, then said, "I believe I know just the man for that."

12

The interior of La Paz Penitentiary Center was about as warm and inviting as the maximum security exterior—which was to say, not at all.

But as Maximo and I crossed the visitor check-in lobby, I was taken aback by how decrepit the facility was. Overhead lights flickered or were out completely, the concrete floors were water-stained from leaks in the ceiling. No family members or children made their way to or from the reception desk; instead, we saw only uniformed police and men in business casual with badges clipped to their belts, most of whom looked like they were trying to get in and out as quickly as possible.

We dutifully waited in line until reaching the receptionist, if you could call him that. The grumpy-looking old man was hunched in front of a paper ledger that looked like it hadn't been used in some time. But he did have a radio, which I supposed counted for something. Maximo took the scene in stride, greeting the man warmly and reciting his name, organization, and the prisoner we'd arranged to speak to.

And while none of this seemed to impress the man, I watched Maximo procure a thick wad of local currency, stuff it in the crease of his DNI credentials, and hand that particular master key across the desk.

This had the effect of animating the receptionist from his stupor, and he discreetly counted the money before giving a half-glance at the ID and handing it back, sans cash.

Then he lifted his radio and spoke commandingly in Spanish, procuring two authorized visitor badges from beneath the desk and shoving them toward us. I picked one up and examined it—the visitor number had been scratched off from overuse sometime in the past eighty years, I estimated—and dutifully clipped it to my shirt pocket as Maximo did the same.

A side door opened to reveal a morbidly obese guard in a uniform stretched to maximum tensile strength around his midsection. He summoned us by way of a sharp whistle, causing Maximo to stroll toward him as if this was standard prison protocol, which here, I supposed, it was.

I, however, felt like I was entering a pseudo-reality version of hell as I hurried to catch up. It would be the last time I had to rush, however, as we entered a hallway only to assume a glacially slow pace behind the colossal guard. And while the electric and plumbing capacity was even more downtrodden in this corridor, the real distinction was the smell. It was an almost chokingly thick scent of human excrement and urine, mingled with sweat and mildew that must have seeped into the walls at this point. I shuddered to think of what we'd encounter once we entered the actual cellblock.

The guard unlocked a side door and held it open for us to enter, then closed and locked it behind us. The room was sterile and split in two by a wall of bars, with a reinforced door on the far wall.

"What's this?" I asked.

"Our interview room. They put Felix in a holding area this morning. It should not take long for them to retrieve him."

"I thought we were going to his cell."

Maximo unleashed a guffaw, a startling display of humor for the ordinarily serious Colombian.

"His *cell*? You are in Colombia, friend. La Paz is filled to 200 percent capacity, which is not bad—Riohacha Prison is almost 500 percent. And La Modelo in Bogotá is a battlefield. They put the right-wing inmates on one side, left-wing on the other, and let them slaughter each other in the middle. Inmates have grenades and guns, and the guards do not dare set foot inside the housing area. Here, I could at least bribe the guards to find our man and pull him out for an interview. Otherwise, I do not know what we would do."

Stuffing my hands in my pockets, I asked skeptically, "And you're sure this is the guy we need to talk to?"

"Absolutely. As the navy became more successful at finding shipyards near the coast, the builders had to move deeper into the swamps. You see the problem?"

"Yeah," I said, "trying to drive a sub through that labyrinth of a river network."

Maximo nodded. "Run ashore, or damage the sub, and they will kill you. Deliver the sub to its crew on the coast, and you make a fortune. To do this job one must be crazy or very, very good."

"So which one is Felix?"

"Felix is both."

At that moment we heard a deadbolt open in the far door, and it was pulled open on rusty hinges. A single man was shoved inside from behind —no prison uniform, just a filthy T-shirt, shorts, and sandals that, from the looks of it, may well have been the same outfit he'd worn upon being incarcerated. Then the door slammed shut again, leaving the three of us to watch each other through the bars.

Getting my first in-person glimpse of Felix Pinzon was entertaining on several counts.

First, he was a hideous man in every regard. He had a hawk-like nose and a narrow face, with deep-set eyes glowering at us over sunken cheeks. Tall and rangy, he looked like a man stranded in the desert in the throes of death. Locks of greasy hair partially covered his eyes, and even the stubble on his chin and face grew in strange patches.

Then there was the fact that his gangly arms were handcuffed to his front, exposing forearms with absurdly minimalistic tattoos. I made out a ship anchor and whale, though much of the rest was hard to discern; he must have either gotten these in prison or done them himself, or both. At least I hoped he had, because if I'd paid for someone to administer that kind of ink, I'd want my money back.

But best of all was when he lunged for the bars and shoved his arms through a gap in them in an attempt to grab Maximo's throat.

The DNI agent didn't move or flinch; hell, he didn't even blink at the attempted assault, merely standing still as Felix's long fingers clawed at the air a few inches in front of him.

Finally Felix abandoned the effort, jerking his arms back through the bars and spouting a tremendously animated stream of Spanish at the silent Maximo.

"Slow down," I said. "Let's stick to English. What's the problem?"

Maximo gave a slight shrug and calmly explained, "He is upset because I apprehended him."

"Apprehended?" Felix cried, outraged. His eyes were wild, darting, the eyes of an addict in desperate need of a fix. "Is that what you call your *justicia callejera*?"

I looked at Maximo, who explained, "Street justice."

"He beat me," Felix continued, "like I gave his wife gonorrhea."

"You ran," Maximo retorted.

"Of course I ran! You monsters kicked in my door."

"With good reason, it seems. Many narco subs began crashing in the swamps after I put you in here."

Felix rolled his eyes before throwing up his arms in frustration.

"Are you mad? Has the War on Drugs somehow been won during my stay at the shit palace? Only a *caremonda* believes he could stop the White Goddess."

I asked, "*Caremonda?*"

Without taking his eyes off Felix, Maximo responded, "The face of a penis."

"Dickhead," I muttered, giving a nod of understanding. "Okay, proceed."

The imprisoned sub captain did so without hesitation, glaring at the man who put him in this cell. "And now you come here with this *mono* to show off? Let me tell you about life here. I sleep shoulder to shoulder in a room with twenty men. The water is on for three hours a day and I am fortunate to receive two cups to wash down the fly-covered meat they feed us. Outdoor showers broke down a few years before I arrived and they have mysteriously not been fixed since."

I remarked without thinking, "Your English is excellent."

"Fuck off," he spat back, looking like he could kill Maximo with eye contact. "And best of all, our bathroom is two buckets that we all have to wait in line for. Sometimes they even allow us to empty them once per day."

Maximo grinned. "Not unlike life aboard your subs, no?"

Felix yelled his response. "For 250 million pesos per trip, I will shit in a bucket with pride." Then, calming himself, he continued in a mockingly conversational tone, "So now you may explain what brings you to the Ritz and why this ghost is beside you."

Leaning toward me, Maximo whispered, "He is racist."

"Thanks for the clarification," I replied, then addressed the prisoner.

"To hear my friend tell it, you're the best sub driver in Colombia."

Felix winced. "Only because de Zurara is dead, which again..."

He paused, almost as if mentioning the name had caused him to lose his train of thought, and then lunged at Maximo once more.

This time, he didn't try to strangle the man; instead he grabbed the bars with white-knuckled intensity, shouting at the top of his lungs, "Because of this *hijueputa* and his posse of thugs."

Maximo replied calmly, "AFEUR did not kill your teacher."

As Felix opened his mouth to shout again, he continued, "We simply called in the airstrike."

This seemed to deflate Felix's resolve at once. He staggered backward, placing his back against the wall and leaning forward to cup his face in his hands.

"What do you want."

I held up a hand to Maximo, indicating I'd take the lead lest any more taunting commentary cause us to lose the best chance we had of getting Sofia.

"You made a name for yourself driving narco subs. We want you to do it again, for us."

This piqued his curiosity, and Felix looked up before brushing a strand of greasy black hair away from his eyes. "And you are...who, exactly?"

"It doesn't matter who I am. What matters is what I can offer you, which is—"

Maximo interrupted, "A full pardon and release back to Buenaventura.

Under the conditions that you swear never to engage in narcotrafficking again."

Felix appeared uninterested in this, fixing his eyes on me as he asked, "What is the job?"

I said, "Me and my friends are looking for someone, and I want you to help us until the job is done. Starting, and probably finishing, with driving a sub down a river. At night. Once we reach the destination, we'll need a few hours to do our work. Then you take us back."

"What river?"

"You take the job, I'll fill you in on the rest. You don't, I've got other sub drivers to talk to."

"Unless *Capitán* de Zurara has returned from the dead, you will find no one as good as me."

"I have no doubt. But just the same, if you refuse once I'm not going to offer again."

Felix took a step forward, assuming an odd little smile as he said, "No, if you are serious about this thing you need the best. Any dirt farmer could drive a can through the east Pacific to Mexico. But a river..." He clucked his tongue thoughtfully. "This is another beast, *mi amigo*. You must start with the depth charts, working backward to determine how steep the banks are and in what areas, analyzing the satellite photos to anticipate tree roots and mudslides that could leave your can broken or beached. Then there is the act of piloting across dozens of turns with precision accuracy, sometimes in places with only a meter or two of draft. And you say at night? Well, you have come to the right place. But I do have my terms."

I sighed. "Let's hear it."

He raised his handcuffed wrists, lifting individual fingers as he counted off the conditions.

"You will bring my girlfriend Isabella to me. I cannot risk setting off while fully loaded, if you understand. A man must be able to focus. Next, I will require prime accommodations—a hotel suite will do nicely—and seven days and nights with a fat wallet for all the drinking and fucking I can manage. Then we will begin preparations."

I looked at Maximo, who returned my gaze in a manner that indicated we were thinking largely the same thing. After all, if I was feeling bad for

Felix having to endure the conditions here, then surely the DNI agent who put him here had at least a shred of sympathy.

Turning back to Felix, I said, "Yes to Isabella. Accommodations are whatever the hell we say they are. And you get one day—"

"And one night," Maximo concluded.

I added, "Then you sober up and we start planning and rehearsals. Those are the terms. Take it or leave it."

Felix's eyes lit up, and he clapped his hands together with a crooked-toothed smile that served as the first indication of positivity I'd seen him display since we arrived.

"Wonderful," he said cheerily, then gestured to his attire. "And since I have nothing to pack, we are wasting time that I could be using to revive my *pene*."

Before Maximo or I could speak, Felix effortlessly stepped backward, using the heel of his foot to bang on the door three times as he watched us and shouted, "Guard! I am ready to leave this shithole forever."

13

Reilly had seen a lot of shit in his time with the US Army, having served in the 75th Ranger Regiment—as had David, incidentally, though they'd never crossed paths until running into one another in the mercenary realm. That second career was a whole other plane of existence, exposing both men to horrors and triumphs inconceivable even in the existence of an elite military unit.

Now Reilly was in the third and, God willing, final phase of a professional life where both success and survival required a high degree of proficiency with firearms. This time David had recruited him directly into the startup Agency team he'd been appointed to assemble, and Reilly had been honored to receive the call to serve his country once more.

But right now, he wanted to find David Rivers and wring his fucking neck.

He'd spent the better part of an hour sitting on this uncomfortable fold-out chair, waiting in an otherwise abandoned hallway spanning a row of empty one-bedroom apartments. The DNI and other Colombian government agencies maintained the building for asset debriefs, safekeeping, and the like. Considering the task here today, Maximo had in the interests of privacy selected an unoccupied floor.

Or more correctly, Reilly thought as the door beside him opened, almost unoccupied.

Felix stumbled through the doorway, casting his glance in both directions.

"Where is my Isabella?"

No, Reilly thought, there was no amount of military, mercenary, or CIA training that could prepare any self-respecting man for this kind of indignity.

"She's not here yet," Reilly responded without rising. "And how are you drunk already? We threw you in there an hour ago."

"What makes you think I am drunk?"

"Because it smells like you took a bath in rum."

"If you gave me enough to fill the bathtub, I would have," he said with a laugh. Then he grew more solemn. "But in all seriousness, I am almost out of rum."

"You know it's nine in the morning, right?"

Felix belted a volley of laughter, emitting a smell that Reilly found revolting. Before he could react, Felix slapped a claw-like hand on his shoulder and said, "You are too serious, *mi amigo*. When life seems dark, when all hope is lost, I look to the one who has always been there for me, sustained me, indeed, carried me through difficult times. And never, ever failed me."

"Jesus?"

"My liver."

Another whoop of laughter, exposing misaligned, stained teeth as a blast of booze and nicotine fumes roared across the space to Reilly's nostrils.

Then Felix was gone, slamming the door shut and leaving Reilly to massage his temples and wonder what the hell David had gotten his team into.

After being released to DNI custody, Felix had spent the better part of the previous day consuming takeout, food, beer, and water in quantities that made even Reilly nauseous. In that time they'd made contact with his girlfriend, who Worthy was presently picking up in Medellín. They were due to arrive any minute now, which meant Reilly was one unenviable step closer to seeing the woman who'd voluntarily subjected herself to the sight of Felix on a regular basis prior to his incarceration.

Felix's requested shopping list for this authorized recreation was, as with everything else about this bizarre fisherman-turned-narco sub runner, extreme.

First was a 1.75-liter bottle of Antioqueño aguardiente, a sugarcane-derived liqueur which was, according to him, a national staple. To this he added a fifth of Ron Viejo de Caldas rum, two cases of Club Colombia beer, one case of champagne cola, a carton of Marlboro Menthol Smooth cigarettes, three pounds of cocktail shrimp, and...that was it.

David had adjusted the order significantly, downgrading the quantities of liquor to 750-milliliter bottles and trimming off a case of beer. It still seemed excessive to Reilly—after all, this guy was no good to them if he died of alcohol poisoning. That was to say nothing of the fact that Reilly had sampled a few cans of Club Colombia, and he wouldn't even use it to boil bratwurst.

But the team leader loved alcohol with a fervor matched only by Cancer's affinity for cigarettes, and seemed to recognize a kindred spirit in the sub driver. As such, David approached the matter more like an anesthesiologist assessing whether Felix's tolerance was up to the task. The cigarettes had survived David's culling process, and they'd added three cases of bottled water, which would, he suspected, remain untouched until the hangover set in, together with Tylenol and a fridge and pantry stocked with food.

The sound of an elevator chime caused him to look up with a mixture of relief and resignation, wanting to start the clock on this appalling charade only so they could end it sooner rather than later.

A moment later, however, all these thoughts vanished from his mind.

He was barely aware of Worthy exiting the elevator, riveted instead by the sight of Isabella.

Reilly had seen women like her before, of course, though only in magazines and on television. To say she was stunning would be insufficient to capture the magnitude of this woman before him—she was a vision, a force of nature, her proportions the stuff of schoolboy fantasies and never, ever real life.

Isabella strutted down the corridor on high heels, her tanned and sculpted legs rising to an absurdly high skirt shrink-wrapped around wide hips. Her narrow waist was exposed beneath a low-cut blouse struggling to contain ample cleavage, while dark cascading hair shimmered with blonde highlights, parted to reveal pouty and surely velvety red lips and exotic eyes...it was all more than Reilly could comprehend.

Leaping to his feet, he compulsively blurted the first words that came to mind.

"Name's Reilly."

He almost cringed upon hearing his own outburst, spoken an octave higher than usual.

But this siren before him didn't seem bothered; in fact, she didn't react to his overture at all, merely continuing her hip-shifting stride as she extended a manicured fingertip to the doorway beside him and asked, in a deliciously accented and pointlessly sultry voice, "This door?"

"Uh-huh," Reilly stammered, knocking three times with such force that the plank of wood rattled on its hinges. He heard the sound of shattering glass and a curse from inside, followed by Felix ripping the door open with an angry expression that faded to relief at the sight of Isabella.

"*Hola, chimbita.*"

"*Hola, guapo.*"

She pressed her body into Felix, taking his hideous face in her perfect hands and greedily pressing her lips to his. Reilly no longer felt like he was on Planet Earth—this had to be some kind of a horrid nightmare from which he'd soon awake to find that order still prevailed in the universe along with some meaningful degree of justice.

He looked to Worthy for explanation, only to find the pointman standing patiently with his hands folded, a vision of consummate professionalism. Worthy had once been a bodyguard, Reilly recalled, and had probably seen worse if there was such a thing.

When Isabella finally advanced into the apartment, Worthy started a timer on his watch and said, "Twenty-four hours starts now."

Felix lingered in the doorway with a dreamy expression as he replied, "At least wait until I have closed the door, *mi amigo*."

Reilly gasped, "God, she smells good." Then he looked to Felix and struggled to formulate the obvious question. "What the—I mean, how, or why, or what the fuck." He concluded with a tone of sheer awe. "Nice, dude."

Felix smirked.

"Now you know my secret. Some women are shallow enough to focus on looks, *sí*. And I am not the most handsome. But other women, like my sweet, sweet Isabella, are wise enough to focus on *chimbo* size alone." With a suggestive eyebrow wriggle, Felix added, "Enjoy your guard shift."

Then he slammed the door shut, and Reilly could hear the deadbolt locking into place followed by uproarious laughter from within.

Turning to face Worthy, he shook his head and muttered, "I'm starting to question everything I thought I knew about life."

"Don't. She's a prostitute."

Reilly's jaw fell open. "No, that can't be..."

"Yep. Gave me her rates on the way over, so this is one more charge Ian's going to have to fudge when he accounts for our operating expenses."

"But...but in America, she'd be a supermodel."

Worthy sighed.

"Yeah, well, this is Colombia and women like her more or less grow on trees. You can always retire down here, you know."

"I might have to do that." He sighed with frustration. "I just wish we didn't have to delay this whole thing so Felix can party until tomorrow morning."

Nodding respectfully, Worthy replied, "You know, I mentioned the same thing to Ian. Know what he told me?"

Reilly shook his head.

"First, we need confirmation that Sofia is back at her hideout before we can move. Second, we've still got a full week of rehearsals to make sure the sub is seaworthy and to iron out our boarding and debarking procedures."

"And to make sure Felix is sober."

"Or relatively sober, at least," Worthy agreed, "and third, Felix would be useless if we threw him straight in a sub. He hasn't tasted freedom in eight months, and that's to say nothing of where he's been living all that time. Because there's prison, and then there's *Colombian* prison. The man deserves some time to unwind."

Then the laughter inside faded to decidedly more graphic sounds, and Worthy quickly excused himself.

"All right, I'm out of here. See you in three hours for guard rotation."

He retreated quickly down the hall, leaving Reilly to dig in his pocket for his one and only respite from the most demeaning assignment of his professional career. Inserting a headphone bud in the ear not occupied by a radio earpiece, he swiped through the musical options on his phone with an increasing sense of urgency, and selected a Journey playlist.

Then he resumed his place in the folding chair, closed his eyes, and with a wistful exhale, let the opening notes of "Wheel in the Sky" take him away.

14

As Worthy escorted Felix from the helipad to the closed off-warehouse ahead of him, he considered that Army Aviation Base Bogotá was an extremely unlikely location to plan and launch a covert operation.

It wasn't for lack of facilities. The base was home to two aviation battalions—one for fixed-wing aircraft, one for logistics and service—along with a training unit to qualify the army's flight students. There were plenty of aircraft going in and out, and more than enough building space for the DNI to temporarily commandeer a relatively conservative storage area.

What made it unique as far as special operations support went was its location on the north side of a very busy El Dorado International Airport, as evidenced by a huge passenger jet that roared overhead on its way to touchdown.

Worthy plugged his ears until the rumbling wave of deafening sound had passed over, and when he unplugged them it was to the sound of Felix shouting over the echo.

"This *guayabo* is killing me. Can we wait until tomorrow?"

"No," Worthy called back, closing with the warehouse. "And what's a *guayabo*?"

"How do you say in English..." He pointed to the side of his head.

"Headache?"

"No. Far worse."

"Hangover."

Felix snapped his fingers. "This one. Hangover."

He'd been fully expecting Felix, who was an eyesore under the best of circumstances, to far more closely resemble death on this fine morning.

But to the contrary, the sub driver actually appeared rejuvenated after his 24-hour bender, his formerly ghastly pallor now a healthy if slightly pale version of a normal human being. The only reason he could tell Felix's undernourished body was still processing psychotic quantities of alcohol was from his words, although Worthy had a pretty good theory as to why that might be.

Raising his hand in greeting, he called out to the Colombian Army guard stationed at the warehouse door. The pleasantry wasn't returned and Worthy presented his access badge to the guard, who inspected it, then warily eyed Felix.

"He's with me," Worthy said.

The guard sent a radio call in Spanish, receiving a quick reply before he opened the door and allowed them to enter. Worthy understood his suspicion; the poor guy had no idea what he was protecting or why, only that he'd been tasked with guarding the entrance with his life and seen nothing but strange-looking gringos coming and going with a DNI representative.

Once they'd begun moving down the corridor, Worthy looked over his shoulder to confirm the door had been sealed, then spoke to Felix.

"All right, here's the score: we're going after Sofia Lozano."

With a mock shudder, Felix replied, "If this is true, I hope you do not expect me to join you."

"You'll stay in the sub."

"Wonderful."

"Under supervision," Worthy added, eliciting an angry sidelong glance from the Colombian.

But the expression faded to one of astonishment when Worthy stopped before a door labeled *ENTRADA PROHIBIDA - Sólo Personal Autorizado* and pulled it open for Felix to see the storage bay beyond.

He practically staggered past the threshold, eyes wide at the sight before him: the forty-foot narco sub was propped upright on a mobile trailer, all streamlined hull with the exception of a low cockpit and inverted-U-shaped air intake rising a few feet over a nonexistent waterline that Felix must have been able to envision all too clearly. The body was a dull mid-blue color, with darker hand-painted splotches of camouflage, looking more like an elite naval commando vessel than a semi-submersible hand-built in the swamps for the sole purpose of transporting cocaine.

Ian was seated at a fold-out table covered by maps, laptops, and planning materials, though Felix didn't seem to notice him.

Instead his eyes were fixed on the sub, which he approached unsteadily before stopping, running both hands through his hair, and whispering, "*Jesucristo.*"

Ian rose and walked over to him, ever to the point as he began, "We captured this from Sofia. The military categorizes this as a Panther-class LPV-IM-12.2, for Low Profile Vessel, Inboard Motor, second iteration of the Type 12. They're extremely rare, with only one captured at sea—"

"Stop talking," Felix snapped. "Yes, it has an inboard motor. About everything else, you are wrong."

"How so?"

Felix looked supremely irritated by the question, fixing Ian with the kind of glare normally reserved for parents whose toddler's every response was the word, *why*?

"No one on your side of the drug war may comment on the rarity of such vessels. You only know what you have captured. What you call rare, we call successful. If Sofia had this built, it was because it was the best tool for the job."

"It's still a low profile vessel, though—"

"No. What this is, is an utterly magnificent can."

Worthy interjected, "I thought we were looking at a sub."

Felix was pacing the length of the vessel now, stopping at the rear section before kneeling down to examine the propeller screw. "No, *mi amigo*. To almost everyone in the world, this is a *narcosubmarino*. But to the crew it is *el bidón*, the can. And I can see why Sofia had it built—it is a masterpiece. Quick, give me a flashlight."

Worthy removed a Surefire from his pocket and handed it to Felix, who made no effort to use it.

Instead he took a step back and scanned the sub from stern to bow, then said, "Cargo area is fore of the cockpit, and the inboard motor is aft—a good design. In the old days, we had to rely on the cocaine placement and quantity to ride low. This is far, far better. The bow remains underwater, but look at the hydroplanes on the stern, to control running depth even more. The inboard motor reduces noise, and just look at the hull—almost no wake at low speeds. And the skeg"—he pointed to a protective extension built around the sub's rudder—"allows the crew to push off in the swamp without damaging the screw. The *maestro* has gotten even better."

Worthy asked, "*Maestro*?"

"Master shipbuilder," Felix replied. "He drafts the plans and sells them. These are not so difficult to build, you see." He rapped a knuckle on the hull. "Wooden frame, a few sheets of plywood. Fiberglass for the hull, plexiglass cockpit, and engine. Assemble the parts in a factory, then transport them to the shipyard for welding. The key is in the design, and we have come a long way since the Tigers."

That comment seemed to catch Ian off guard, and he asked, "So it's true about the Sri Lankans?"

"*Sí*, of course it is true. This was before my time, but *Capitán* de Zurara worked with them in testing the early designs. Before they came, it was mostly the Cali Cartel building scrap heaps that could barely make it to Puerto Rico."

"Hold on," Worthy interrupted, "what do Colombian narcos have to do with Sri Lanka?"

Felix didn't respond; he was occupied climbing aboard the trailer, then pulling himself atop the sub as Ian addressed the question.

"In the early 2000s, we started seeing captured narco subs with a nearly identical design to those built by the Tamil Tigers during the Sri Lankan civil war. The Tigers ran drugs overwater from India to finance their operations, and it was speculated that the traffickers here hired the Sri Lankan engineers to build a Colombian fleet. It was all circumstantial, until the Coast Guard captured a vessel with a Tamil machinist."

"His name was Shriyan," Felix said, pulling open the hatch. "*Capitán* de Zurara said he hit on a narco's mistress, so rather than kill him they put him aboard the bait."

Worthy shook his head. "What do you mean by 'bait?'"

Felix knelt before the cockpit opening, responding impatiently as he shone Worthy's flashlight inside.

"When there is a major load going across the water, they will load a can with a smaller amount. Drop a tip to the known informants, and let your Coast Guard send their boats and helicopters to catch it. And the major load slips past on a different route. It is a big ocean, *mi amigos*. Sometimes your people get lucky, but mostly they are catching the scraps, the bait, that the traffickers sacrifice."

Then, without warning, he dangled his legs into the open hatch and dropped inside.

Worthy looked at Ian and said quietly, "Where did Maximo find this guy?"

Ian simply watched the sub, now emitting the dull metallic thunking of Felix making his way through the interior, and said, "As long as he can get us where we need to go, who cares?"

"Fair point."

"And look at it this way: if you're Sofia, and you had a near-miss at the clandestine shipyard, how long would it be before you ventured out again? We could spend another six months waiting for her to leave her hideout, and by then, Weisz's plan will already be funded and in progress. We'll only find out about it after the fact."

Worthy's eyes narrowed as he watched Ian, wondering whether the intelligence operative was being delusionally optimistic about his own analysis or merely suffering from an extremely short and selective memory.

He said, "Ian, she wasn't at the shipyard. Or in the jungle."

"Maybe not when we hit it. But she was there, all right. She *had* to be."

Before Worthy could respond there was a high shriek from inside the sub. It served as their only warning before Felix burst back through the hatch, flashlight in hand, and shouted two words.

"Ballast tanks!"

Catching his breath amid their dumbfounded expressions, he clarified, "We have ballast tanks."

"So?" Worthy asked.

By then Felix was clambering out of the sub, then down onto the trailer before leaping to the ground and tossing Worthy's flashlight back.

As he caught it, Felix strode toward him and excitedly explained, "So together with the hydroplanes, we can submerge all the way to the tip of our air intake and exhaust pipe. Not dive, of course, but move like a swimmer with a...what do you call the pipe, the tube—"

"Snorkel," Ian volunteered. "You're saying we have a snorkel sub."

"Yes, this."

Unimpressed, Worthy asked, "What kind of crew do you need to drive this?"

"Crew?" Felix laughed. "For two weeks in the Pacific, I would need a machinist, no question. The engine appears to be in good shape, so this will not be necessary for a short trip in a river. But I will require a navigator."

Worthy pointed to the air intake. "We'll put a GPS receiver there. Plus or minus three-meter accuracy, and I'll navigate."

Felix shook his head resolutely. "On the open sea, perhaps. But the jungle will block this GPS nonsense in the river, and a delayed update will get us killed. Listen closely: map, pencil, and stopwatch to time each leg and calculate distance traveled using our speed."

"So, like, math?"

"*Sí*, my friend. Math."

Worthy jerked a thumb sideways and said, "Ian will navigate. What else do you need?"

"It is not what I need that matters. You *bebecos* need a captain, and you have chosen the right man." He turned to appraise the vessel once more. "It is twelve meters in length. Not the best, for a river. The compact models they build inland and transport to the coast by truck would be easier to maneuver. Though unless our route is like a coiled string, it should be no problem."

With his hands on his hips, he concluded, "Now we may begin charting the course."

"Yeah," Worthy grimaced, "so about that coiled string..."

"Yes?"

Worthy waved him over to the table. He cleared a swath of notepaper and protractors from the map, then grabbed a pen to use as a pointer as he indicated a spot.

"*Río Caquetá*," Felix said knowingly. "That is a highway compared to what I have driven. It flows east, into the Amazon. This is no problem."

"I sure hope so, because the Caquetá River isn't our destination. This spot is a navy training area, and we're going there to run rehearsals and get our procedures down."

Squinting in confusion, Felix pointed to the sub and asked, "How will we move the can there?"

"The same way we got it here—sling load it to a Black Hawk just like an artillery piece or Humvee, except they'll fly under cover of darkness. Once we get to our site, the DNI will resupply diesel by boat, but other than that it's going to be a camping expedition."

Felix wrinkled his nose. "I hate the jungle."

"Everyone hates the jungle. Once we get final clearance to launch our raid, we're going to move down the Caquetá to right about here"—he used his pen to trace the river—"this tributary that breaks west."

Felix nodded. "Easy. This will be easy."

"Hang in there," Worthy cautioned him, continuing to outline the winding route, "because we've got to follow the tributary and proceed to right about...here."

Tapping his pen on a location within walking distance of Sofia's village, Worthy glanced up to see Felix looking aghast. His reluctance was understandable—the spot was along a narrow channel of water with more turns than anyone on the team had cared to count.

Except, apparently, Ian.

"Forty-seven turns between the river," Ian supplied, "and our team drop-off. Our guys will cover the remaining distance on foot, then return to the same spot for pickup."

Felix appeared completely sober now. "You cannot be serious, *mi amigo*."

Worthy crossed his arms and said, "Serious as dick cancer, *mi amigo*."

"Is it too late for me to return to prison?"

"After we pulled guard on you for 24 hours," Worthy began, "while you and Isabella repeatedly tried to sneak out and score coke—*more* coke, I should say, since as much as Reilly would've liked to search her, he didn't, and you're a little more bright-eyed and bushy-tailed this morning than cigarettes can account for—far, far too late."

Felix grabbed the map and scanned it closely, shaking his head in disbelief.

Then he lowered it, looked from Worthy to Ian with a haunted expression, and spoke matter-of-factly.

"Listen to me closely: if you want me to attempt this thing, I am going to need more rum."

15

Ian kept the red glow of his headlamp oriented on his clipboard, where a laminated sheet was filled by rows of painstakingly calculated data that would make or break their mission tonight.

In addition to the plotted turns, there were columns of time estimates based on varying speeds of travel. Using a dry erase marker to check off the current row—without such basic measures, it'd be far too easy to lose track of their progress in this insanely complex route—Ian glanced at his stopwatch to determine his next time hack.

After a full week of rehearsals, he didn't feel any more comfortable than he had the very first time he'd boarded this death trap.

He said, "Thirty to moderate left, Turn 46."

"Thirty seconds," Felix repeated.

The sub driver's seat was positioned before a control panel that was so primitive as to be ludicrous for daytime operation, much less tonight's task. There was a steering wheel, twin sticks to control the throttle and ballast, a panel of boat gauges with the label and logo of *CUMMINS MARINE*—not a sub manufacturer, to be sure—and an honest-to-God tiny key to start the engine, like something you'd see on a lawnmower. A cluster of exposed wires led to bilge pump controls for the fore and aft sections, an unsettling reminder that they could take on water at any moment. The sub's plexiglass windows were a series of narrow, angled slits wrapping Felix's position, the view beyond nothing but the dark tributary waters they slipped through, thus far unnoticed.

Ian was positioned behind him, seated on one of two crudely fashioned bunks presumably installed to accommodate sleeping rotations for the normal crew of four. The other bunk was occupied by David in full combat equipment plus a black life jacket and dive fins strapped over his boots, the team leader appearing only slightly more composed than Ian as he tracked their progress on a map.

David asked, "Wouldn't it be funny if we were struck head-on by an outgoing narco sub?"

"Not going to happen," Felix assured him. "No one can drive a can through here but me and *Capitán* de Zurara, may he rest in peace."

Felix removed a hand from the wheel to cross himself, then kissed his knuckles before resuming a two-handed grip.

Ian said, "Stop talking, David. We need his hands on the wheel. Felix, ten seconds to your left at Turn 46."

"Ten seconds."

"Five seconds...three, two, one—"

Ian braced himself against the seat as Felix executed a gut-churning turn resulting in a series of thumps and curses followed by strained grunts from the storage space below the bow. It was the now-familiar noise of Cancer, Reilly, Worthy, and Maximo occupying an unforgiving gap intended for up to two tons of cocaine. Theirs was, quite frankly, the least enviable role aboard—the cargo area was a four-foot-high channel stretching the front half of the sub, requiring them to lie in the prone like sardines and be mercilessly flung into wooden support ribs with each of Felix's aggressive maneuvers.

And as much as Ian liked the idea of using the narcos' own tools against them, and even with his relatively cushy seat, this couldn't have been any more uncomfortable if they'd ridden into battle in the back of a cement mixer. To be fair, there weren't many concessions the sub captain could make for his passengers' comfort. Throttle around a bend too fast and they'd strike the far bank; too slow, and the sub wouldn't have sufficient momentum to make the turn at all.

It was a fine balance that Felix negotiated not with ease but rather a hyper-focused derivative of sheer joy. It was less a job for him than a performance: like a concert pianist, he was in some kind of spiritual zone that was almost enthralling to watch.

Ian's heart seized up when the sub shuddered with a soft thump at the stern, but Felix quickly leveled the craft after turning the corner, not only unbothered but elated as he proclaimed, "The skeg bumped a mangrove root, and yet we made the turn. This is beautiful, *mi amigos*, simply beautiful."

A maniacal burst of laughter followed, that of a mad scientist bringing his creation to life, and Ian didn't know whether to be comforted or terrified as he reset his stopwatch and called out the next hack.

"Twenty seconds to hard right, hard right, Turn 47."

Felix echoed, "Twenty seconds."

"Speed?"

"Six knots."

Ian made a check on his clipboard, consulting the stopwatch and then the tablet display beside him.

The sub was running with only the tip of its exhaust above the surface, the metal pipe disguised by branches to make it blend in with the various debris floating down the tributary in their direction of movement. Though what that exhaust accomplished mechanically, Ian wasn't sure—the cabin was filled with hot diesel fumes as it had been on every training run.

The exposed snorkel of sorts did, however, allow their single advantage in terms of forward visibility at present: thermal and night vision cameras they'd retrofitted to the assembly, both live feeds now piping into a trio of split-screen tablet displays situated so Felix, David, and Ian could monitor their proximity to shore. There was also a radio transmitter and various scanners that had, fortunately, detected nothing in the way of enemy communications thus far. With the certainty of numerous observation posts as part of Sofia's early warning network, *especially* along the water, Ian's confidence in this vessel's stealth continued to increase with each passing minute.

He'd also fitted a GPS receiver to the exhaust tip, though as Felix predicted, it had been a wasted effort ever since they departed the main river. Its readout next to Ian's seat was so slow to update as to be completely useless, and he'd long since stopped consulting it out of anything beyond morbid curiosity.

Ian caught a flash of motion in the red glow of his headlamp—a cockroach skittering across his thigh. He reflexively swiped the bug back into the shadows. The sub was infested with them, a disconcerting reality that Ian took to be the norm for such vessels. Felix barely seemed to notice the insects, casually brushing one off if it managed to reach his neck.

"Ten seconds to hard right at 47."

"I see it."

"Five seconds...three, two—"

Felix initiated the maneuver before Ian got to one, basing his timing off the display, and this time he was certain they'd strike the shore.

Ian struggled to remain in his seat as the sub groaned in protest, its wood and fiberglass frame creaking against a low metallic howl that signaled the final and hardest angle on their route. The hairpin turn required Felix to push the limits of his craft's mechanical capability, inducing a wave of nausea in Ian's gut as the sub driver chanted, "*Dios te salve, María, llena eres de gracia...*"

He abruptly reversed the control input, swinging the sub upright and applying throttle in equal proportion in an effort to keep the stern from smashing into the far bank as they regained momentum and, quite miraculously, proceeded without incident.

And with that realization, Felix's prayer gave way to jubilation.

"I am the greatest—the greatest!"

"Shut up," David ordered, eyes fixated on his periscope display. "Port side, twenty meters, looks like a five-foot cliff embankment. You see it?"

"*Sí*," Felix replied sullenly.

"That'll be our drop-off, and unless I tell you otherwise, the pickup." Felix pulled back on the throttle as David called out to the cargo area, "Thirty seconds to surface. Cancer, let's go."

Cancer crawled through a low opening into the sub cockpit where Felix, Ian, and David were tightly packed in what was essentially a Bel Air mansion compared to the cargo area.

Forward progress was complicated by the black life jacket with a pair of dive fins clipped to it, a bulky and inconvenient addition that he wouldn't don over his boots until the last possible second. They didn't have far to swim, but when weighed down by fighting equipment—ammunition, medical supplies, and an assault pack serving as a blowout bag in the event they had to scatter into the jungle rather than re-board the sub as planned —it wasn't worth the risk of drowning in near-zero visibility. That was to say nothing of the necessity in reaching the shore as quickly and quietly as possible, if they even made it that far without being compromised in the first place.

"You ready?" David asked.

Cancer replied in the affirmative.

"Fuck it."

He scanned the nearest tablet to see grainy night vision and thermal feeds of the riverbank and with it, the short rock face that his team leader pointed to now.

"I'm going to have Worthy take us there, then get to the high side and cover our transition to shore."

Cancer squinted at the screen, trying to discern whether there were any people in the cameras' expansive field of view. The task proved impossible, the jungle too dense and remote to make out something so slight as a human figure, particularly with rain obscuring the view. Though that may well change, he thought, the instant he was able to survey their surroundings in person.

"All right," he concluded. "Let's jam."

"Stand by," David called to the cargo area. Then he rose in a crouch, positioning himself with a handle on the overhead hatch before he addressed Ian and Felix, giving a penultimate command before the insertion proceeded in full.

"Kill the lights."

The cabin was cast into near-total darkness, the only light sources a faint ambient glow from the displays of their homemade periscope assembly, before David said, "Felix, take us up."

Cancer kept his night vision raised on its head mount, feeling the sub shakily floating upward as a result of Felix manipulating the ballast tanks with the pull of a handle at his side. The sensation wasn't unlike an elevator ascending, and Cancer heard the scrape of equipment as his teammates in the cargo area edged forward to the cockpit.

No stranger to combat, he nonetheless felt the rising tension at the task ahead, which was equal parts long-range marksman, split-second assessor of enemy presence, and, least enviably of all, exposed target to draw fire if anyone happened to be watching the sub's cockpit break water. And if that occurred, he'd have little choice but to drop back into the vessel for a hasty evacuation as incoming fire laced into the sub, risking a mechanical failure that could leave them stranded in this desolate wilderness with a swarm of enemy fighters closing in.

He adjusted his grip on the suppressed Galil, keeping his gaze focused on the narrow slit windows in front of Felix. It wasn't much help—without night vision it was impossible to determine where the tributary depths ended and the black jungle sky began. His only indication came from Felix, who made his announcement as the sub transitioned to a gentle sideways rocking.

"Cockpit is just above the waterline. Get off my can."

There was a metallic shriek as David cranked the handle and pushed open the hatch, quickly stepping aside in the cabin's tight confines.

Cancer filled the void immediately, angling his weapon through the gap in the ceiling as he rose to full height and put his "eye to the glass," looking through the adjustable scope of his Galil and, more importantly, the thermal attachment mounted in front of it. After all, if the enemy had night vision of their own, then using an infrared laser to take aim would be as good as heralding his exact location to everyone in sight. Sweeping his rifle clockwise, Cancer began his first scan of the jungle outside Sofia's camp.

The diesel fumes gave way to dank jungle air and the feel of chilly rain drizzling over him, his hearing overpowered by the sudden exposure to the calls of night creatures, amid which it would be almost impossible to hear a person speaking a few feet away, much less from the shore. He appraised the trees through his scope, quickly zeroing in on a dissonance in the marbled black and white hues of his thermal device.

Not twenty meters away, on the elevated shore to his left and practically on top of the rock ledge David had designated for their insertion, was a barely distinguishable signature of white heat that suddenly shifted.

Then the amorphous shape grew, clearly a man rising beyond the trees and stepping forward as if he'd heard something. There was no urgency in the motion, merely a curious readjustment of his position to get a better view, and Cancer was taking aim when he caught a glimpse of a second heat signature, this one seated beside the first.

Cancer fired two subsonic rounds into his standing target and then angled his barrel toward the seated man, loosing another two rounds before transitioning back.

The first man he'd seen was now toppling forward into the undergrowth as Cancer chased him with another controlled pair, then repeated the process with the seated man as he heard the brass casings from his expended rounds clinking off the raised hatch behind him. A single piece of brass bounced back and landed in the collar of his fatigue shirt, painfully singeing the back of his neck as Cancer fought the urge to respond. Instead, he pumped another flurry of rounds into the brush at his best approximation of where the fallen fighters had landed.

Then he swept his aim clockwise, scanning across the tributary to the opposite shore, searching for any signs of movement and finding none. His arc ended at the raised hull, and Cancer hoisted himself upward to sit on the edge, a potentially fatal decision that left him even further exposed to enemy fire as he completed a full 360 before settling his aim on the site of his first engagement. There he watched for swaying vegetation that would indicate one or both of the men had survived his fire.

He transmitted, "Scanner traffic?"

"*It's clear*," Ian replied.

"Go."

Cancer lifted his legs above the hull opening, attempting to rise to a crouch until one boot slid off the slick fiberglass hull and he barely arrested his fall—if he was wearing his fins, he'd have gone in the drink already. So he sat cross-legged instead, shifting forward on the bow before settling into a seated shooting position to pull security for Reilly, who was now emerging atop the sub to cover their backside in the same fashion.

Using his free hand to grasp the hot brass pinned at the base of his neck, Cancer flung it into the water and transmitted.

"Two-man LP/OP," he began, using the military parlance for listening post/observation post, "ten feet right of our insertion point. Racegun, you're gonna have to clear the bodies."

Worthy's response came as an audible whisper behind him as the pointman said, "Got it—"

The second word of that statement was rushed, spoken with a strained emphasis amid the squeal of dive fins on the hull, and Cancer grinned.

~

Worthy's uncontrolled descent down the side of the sub was considerably less graceful than he'd planned, but no sooner had he replied to Cancer than the bottom of his left dive fin lost traction as he shifted his weight over the hatch. Now he was riding the lightning toward the water.

His final act before striking the surface was a crude attempt to roll onto his left side, holding his suppressed M4 skyward as he plunged into the tepid tributary waters with a splash that momentarily drowned out the night creatures and rain. If any enemy observers were present to witness the act, he thought, they were surely laughing their asses off.

Worthy bobbed to the surface, a testament to the buoyancy of his life jacket more than any display of aquatic ability. He kicked from the hips, gaining an initial surge of momentum from his fins that increased as he side-stroked toward the shore, using his right arm to prop his rifle above the surface. By his second stroke he heard the soft splash of David entering the water behind him, followed in short order by Maximo before the chanting chorus of insects drowned out any further ability to discern his team's progress.

But he knew well enough from their rehearsals what would occur: Cancer would be the last in the water while Ian would seal the hatch and remain aboard to supervise Felix, whose mission in life would transition to an immediate submersion of the vessel as far as it could go, followed by turning around to stage for pickup. A routine one if everything went well, but an emergency exfil if everything went to shit, which, Worthy thought, had an inordinately high risk of occurring.

The success or failure of their insertion hinged upon him alone at this point—until he reached dry land and established a foothold to cover the continued transition of his team from sub to jungle, they remained vulnerable to whatever curveballs the enemy could throw at them. Worthy side-stroked with all the efficiency he could manage given the tactical kit, assault pack, and flotation device, periodically bumping into floating branches and sickeningly thick patches of floating algae that congealed in the stagnant water near the shore. He glanced ahead, confirming he was only a few meters out, when Reilly transmitted, "*Doc going feet wet.*" He felt a momentary surge of panic that he hadn't made landfall before only Cancer remained pulling security atop the partially-surfaced sub.

His fins caught the first edge of mud when the next transmission came over his earpiece.

"*Cancer going feet wet.*"

It was immediately followed by Ian's sendoff message. "*We're submerging and moving to turnaround point. Happy hunting, guys.*"

Worthy gave one more powerful stroke, feeling his left ribs beach against the bank before rolling into a prone firing position and sweeping the area for any threats that Cancer had been unable to see from the sub.

Three seconds of angling his suppressor left and right revealed this to be a futile endeavor; the space ahead was an unoccupied tangle of sand and mangrove roots, with the rock face rising up a slope of muddy ground.

Worthy rose, feeling ridiculous to be marching onto the soggy mud, lifting his knees high and keeping his legs bowed to maintain clearance for the dive fins, which had all the glamor of clown shoes as soon as he cleared the water. Hollywood loved to play up the elite stealth of maritime infiltration; the reality, as Worthy had discovered, was far less flattering.

When his secondary scan of the jungle revealed no movement, Worthy knelt and stripped off the straps of his dive fins, kicking them off his waterlogged boots before writhing out of the life jacket. He left the swimming aids abandoned on the shore—his teammates would gather them and add them to the collective cache, but for the moment Worthy desperately needed to provide security for them.

After making a beeline for David's preordained destination, he found that the five-foot-tall ledge was closer to six and a half when viewed up close and personal. After determining that the wooded slopes to either side presented a black thicket of vines and potential thorns, Worthy resorted to scaling the miniature cliff, rotating his M4 to his back and using both hands to ascend as quickly as he could.

Once he cleared the top edge, Worthy thrust himself forward and brought his weapon into a kneeling firing position, prepared to gun down any immediate threat to his follow-on teammates. But there were none, and he transmitted, "*Racegun feet dry*," before moving out to his right in an effort to find the LP/OP that Cancer had reported obliterating moments before Worthy hit the water.

Slipping through the brush, he saw the seat first—a canvas camp chair sitting erect, with an identical one bowled over and greased with blood splatter beside it. The occupant of the former was motionless on his stomach, night vision device knocked sideways on his head and a trio of gaping exit wounds stitched across his backside. The second man must have been seated when he received Cancer's personal delivery of subsonic 7.62mm rounds; he was in a contorted fetal position beside the fallen chair, still wearing his night vision, and while it was impossible for Worthy to determine the bullets' points of impact from his position, the man was dead beyond all doubt.

Worthy leaned in to deliver a follow-up headshot to each man, placing his suppressor close enough to remove any need to activate his infrared laser, then scanned the ground to analyze the weapons: two AK-47s, an unsurprising choice given they could withstand the constant jungle humidity and continue to function with minimal maintenance, along with an M79. The single-shot grenade launcher was more commonly known to US troops as "Thumper," and Worthy didn't need to check the ammo satchel beside it to know that it held illumination rounds for signaling intrusion high over the jungle canopy.

There was also an open backpack on the ground, and he pulled back a flap to find it was filled with a considerable amount of food—a telling detail—the provisions resting beside a radio that appeared to be a modern, long-range unit.

But Worthy's real concern at present was locating the narrow trail leading from the observation post between the trees, deeper into the jungle.

He paralleled it then, slipping a few meters past the downed fighters before taking a knee behind a fallen tree trunk and scanning the jungle. He heard no man-made sounds, just frog and insect calls above the rain.

Keying his transmit switch, he whispered, "LP/OP clear, two EKIA. Night vision, flares, and radio. I'm posted up twenty feet down the trail leading away from their location."

David replied, "*Suicide inbound from your six.*"

"Come on in," Worthy said.

The linkup didn't take long; David appeared at his side moments later, kneeling beside him and picking up a sector of fire. They'd be alone for a few minutes at least, left to defend the trail as Reilly, Cancer, and Maximo stashed the dive fins and life jackets that they'd hopefully have time to don before swimming back to the sub. Then there was the small matter of searching the observation post for intelligence and disabling the radio that was too big to carry.

David whispered, "What do you think?"

"I think this game trail leads to a small camp," Worthy began, "where there's probably two more guys to rotate with the ones Cancer popped. If I'm right, that means a main trail running alongside the water, linking the camps behind each LP/OP. We must've passed a dozen of them on our way in and heard zero radio traffic, so they're disciplined. Their night vision is going to make our lives a lot harder, but we were expecting that."

"So the question is whether it's worth following this trail to the camp so we can schwack their buddies before they find the dead."

Worthy agreed, "That is the question. And my call is that we don't."

"Why do you say that?"

"Backpack at the LP/OP had a pretty significant picnic basket for two that looked like it'd gone untouched. That's indicative of a long shift, so I'd say we're looking at day and night rotations. Their replacements probably won't arrive until sunrise, by which time we'll be long gone. And if the camps are linked like I believe they are, we run the risk of a resupply effort finding bodies a whole lot earlier."

Worthy was proud of his assessment, particularly given that he'd made it in the ten seconds or so that it took him to clear the observation post. The fact that David tended to accept his intuitive judgments about such matters served as further validation, and he waited for the team leader to voice his agreement.

But David merely looked over and whispered, "Jesus. It's on your cheek."

Worthy reached up as David said, "Your other cheek."

Then he felt it—a long, rubbery mass suspended from his face. Worthy peeled the leech off and tossed it to the dirt, shuddering with the thought that he hadn't felt a thing and would have unknowingly worn the parasite until someone pointed it out or he made it to a mirror.

Cancer transmitted, "*Swim gear is stashed, on our way to the LP/OP.*"

"Copy," David replied, then whispered to Worthy, "How confident are you in your assessment?"

Worthy swallowed, speaking just loud enough to be heard over the rain. "I don't see any other way it could play out. The observers have freedom of movement from camp to camp, and each camp has a game trail to the observation post. It's the only way Sofia could run such an extensive early warning network for so long."

"I get that. I mean, how confident are you that no one's going to notice they lost two spotters until daybreak?"

"Ian hasn't intercepted any radio checks yet, so it's unlikely they're transmitting on a regular basis. Which is a smart play on their part because the Colombians could have a SIGINT bird overhead at any given time. And since Sofia has been living like this for quite some time, they've got no reason to doubt their system."

Before David could respond, Cancer's voice came over the frequency.

"*We've searched the bodies, no intel. Angel, their radio was operating on FM frequency 92.7. Racegun and Suicide, we're heading to you now.*"

"Got it," Worthy answered, "let's get this show on the road."

When the remaining three men arrived, no words were spoken. Worthy remained in place as David relocated to expand the modest security perimeter, each man facing out in what was to be their final consolidation before transitioning to a relatively short but exceedingly dangerous foot movement. It was one last chance to spot approaching enemies, adjust equipment, voice concerns, and gather thoughts before the real work began.

After a few seconds, David transmitted, "*All right, let's get off this game trail and proceed along our original route. If Racegun is correct, we'll have a linear danger area crossing at a main trail ahead. These people have night vision, so we'll keep it slow and steady, lots of thermal scans. Everyone good?*"

No response, least of all from Worthy, who agreed that, tactically speaking, this wasn't just the most sound plan but the only feasible one.

David concluded, "*Racegun, take us out.*"

16

As he trudged through the cold raindrops splattering down from the treetops, Reilly realized exactly how much moving through the jungle sucked—heavy vegetation, thorns, banana spiders, poison dart frogs, and a couple species of snake that could kill you with a sideways glance. Fucking super.

His left boot plunged into a random sinkhole of mud, a reminder that combining all those elements at night left them vulnerable to mishaps like this. Breaking the suction to pull his foot free required a herculean effort, even for him, and he rushed ahead to keep Maximo in sight through the enormous palm fronds ahead.

Reilly was used to sweating like a whore in church under even slightly warm conditions, but after the swim from sub to shore, there was no telling where the perspiration ended and the bacteria-laden swamp water began. Or the rain, for that matter. At least, he thought with great relish, his teammates were finally getting a glimpse of what it was like to be him. Not in terms of rakish good looks, sex appeal, or physical stature, to be sure, but most certainly with regard to being soaked to the bone during these little jaunts toward the objective.

He glanced back to see the final man in the formation, Cancer, walking as if this were a literal stroll in the park. Just like always. As much as Reilly was wary of the sniper's moral leniency and overall shitty attitude toward life in general, he had to hand it to him—the man could don as much weight as any of them and seemingly walk forever without showing the slightest degree of discomfort. Hell, his biggest concern at present was probably not being able to smoke.

Looking forward, he located Maximo once more and resumed his patrol through the pouring rain.

Infiltrating during a storm had its advantages: precipitation would mask the sound of their movement, lessen the effective range of the enemy's night vision, and allow the team to rely on superior optics and thermal devices to spot natural, man-made, or human obstacles in their path while hopefully remaining unseen.

But the downsides were many, comfort least among them. Night vision lenses fogged constantly and had to be rubbed off with a fingertip, while maintaining any semblance of a formation required slow and methodical movement given the reduced visibility. Worse still, communication with other team members was problematic with the ambient noise.

Reilly heard an unintelligible transmission through his earpiece and thought, case in point.

Keying his mic, he said, "Say again."

Worthy's drawl came through then, louder, "*Coming up on the village.*"

Peering through the trees to his right revealed nothing of the sort, and Reilly saw little but the same jungle underbelly he'd been trudging through for over an hour. Worthy must have made the determination based on his navigation rather than any visual indicators to speak of—or at least, that's what Reilly assumed until he proceeded to roughly where his pointman had made the call. But as soon as that happened, he knew beyond a doubt that the question wasn't whether or not they'd be compromised, but when.

The reports of Sofia surrounding herself with clusters of human shields were true, he realized in a split second, and given the sights and sounds to his right, she was financing them quite well.

Even through the trees and rain, Reilly could sense a virtual jungle nightlife amid the populated area, the buzz of generators powering visible white lights through the undergrowth, a chorus of reggaeton blasting from unseen speakers. He glimpsed a covered plaza where a crowd of dozens was dancing, not just men but women and children as well. That made Reilly's stomach churn—once the shooting started, they'd be severely hindered out of concern for civilian life. Sofia and her fighters, by contrast, shared no such reservations. If these innocent people were to come out of this unscathed, his team would have to strike fast and hard, and fade into the jungle before the narcos could mobilize a full response.

No sooner had this occurred to him when he froze in place, squinting at the distant lights. Using night vision to peer into a backlit area was difficult under the best of circumstances, more so when your lenses were fogging. Reilly wiped them clean with a gloved fingertip and re-assessed to confirm that a human figure was slipping through the jungle toward them.

"Halt movement," he transmitted.

David replied, "*Say again.*"

"Halt, halt, halt. My three o'clock, one mover at fifty meters and closing." No visible light, he noted with dismay—a surefire indicator of night vision. "Anyone else have visual?"

No response, and why should there have been? With the dense vegetation, each line of sight was fleeting, arriving with one footstep and gone the next. It was a miracle Reilly had been looking in the right place at the right time to identify the person, and he fixated on the location to realize there was not one but two.

"Fuck, there's two of them. Could the villagers have seen us?"

Worthy answered, "*Not at this range. Maybe we got spotted by an LP/OP.*"

"*If we did,*" David replied, "*they'd be sending out a lot more people. Hold fast, let the situation develop. Doc, you keep eyes-on no matter what—we can't risk losing visual.*"

Reilly disobeyed that order almost immediately, casting a quick glance to identify Maximo to his left and Cancer to his right, both behind cover but facing opposite directions to maintain overall security. He burned their positions into his mind in one final verification of where he could and could not establish sectors of fire, knowing intuitively that this encounter was going to unfold faster than he could consciously react.

Then he glanced out from behind the tree, attempting to locate his quarry and failing. Every subtle movement revealed itself to be nothing more than leaves tumbling beneath the incoming rain.

But the sudden blaze of a flashlight fired twenty meters to his front, and Reilly ducked behind a tree before the glare could reflect off his night vision lenses. These people were moving fast, though he couldn't fathom why or to what end—Sofia's fighters should be traveling without white light, and there was zero reason for civilians to venture into the jungle amid a nighttime downpour. Either way he couldn't put this down to coincidence, particularly when the flashlight continued to bear down on him.

Cancer transmitted, "*I've got eyes-on the light, can't make out the source. Max?*"

Maximo replied, "*Same.*"

Suddenly the tree Reilly was using for cover seemed woefully small, though it was far too late to move. He keyed his mic and whispered, "*They're heading right for me, twenty meters and closing.*"

"*Say again?*" David asked.

Reilly hissed, "Twenty meters out."

He could hear a male voice now, only vaguely over the rain, but he noted an unmistakable tone of excitement, the inflection of a man closing in for the kill.

Well if it was excitement he wanted, Reilly was happy to deliver—in the form of subsonic 7.62mm rounds through the backs of him and his partner, delivered seconds after they passed his position.

There was just one problem; at this bearing, they wouldn't pass him at all. Instead they were on a collision course, and there was no way their flashlight would fail to illuminate a white amateur bodybuilder trying to remain hidden behind a sapling.

"Ten meters," Reilly transmitted as the men neared.

David replied, "*Say again.*"

This damn rain, Reilly thought, repeating his whispered transmission at the loudest volume he could without being heard by the closing fighters.

Now his team leader sounded angry, as if this entire thing were somehow Reilly's fault.

"*We can't hear you, and you're the only one with visual. Deal with them, you have control. Everyone else, stand by.*"

This was it, he thought. If he didn't get the jump on these two fighters, he was dead meat. There was only one way out of this—to expose himself at the last possible second and dispatch the men before they could return the favor.

The flashlight beam continued to spread beside his meager tree. Any second now they'd see him, and Reilly flicked his weapon's selector lever to semiautomatic the moment he leaned out and took aim.

His suppressor practically chest-thumped a man in a red poncho—a decidedly un-tactical piece of attire—and the only item in his hand was a flashlight. He froze in horror, the fear-stricken eyes beneath the hood belonging to perhaps a sixteen-year-old; not a man at all, but a boy.

"Oh," Reilly said, releasing his right hand from the Galil's grip and closing the distance with the stunned kid.

Then he swung a brutal haymaker at the boy's head, his knuckles cracking off skull before the kid vanished from sight, revealing the second half of this unlikely duo to be a girl of roughly the same age and equally unarmed.

She let loose a terrified scream in the two seconds it took Reilly to transition his rifle to his now-throbbing right hand, advance two steps, and deliver a hard left cross that turned her shriek into an almost comical yelp that ended when she hit the ground, motionless.

Reilly quickly recovered the flashlight and extinguished it, taking in the sight of his two unconscious opponents sprawled on the sopping leaf litter.

He transmitted, "Uh, it's two kids. I'm going to need support."

Reilly had flex-cuffed both of the young civilians by the time his team consolidated into a perimeter around him. He stepped back as Cancer hastily searched the bodies, then felt David's hand on his shoulder.

"You okay?"

Lowering his head, Reilly replied, "I've never hit a girl before."

"Well we came here to kill one, so get over it."

Cancer rolled the girl onto her back and said, "Her cheek is huge. Couldn't you have pulled your punch?"

"I *did* pull my punch."

"You're a fucking monster. Here's your intel, hero."

He tossed a plastic baggie at Reilly, who felt a crumbly substance within that he couldn't identify under his night vision. Opening the bag, he took a light sniff, and then, after determining the contents, a deep inhale. It wasn't just weed; it was very, *very* good weed, the kind of quality he'd rarely encountered even during his avid use of it during his high school and pre-dropout college days.

In a way, this was ironic in the extreme: everyone out here thrived due to the cocaine trade, and their kids still had to sneak out to enjoy a little ganja.

As soon as the search was complete, Maximo descended on the boy, slapping him awake and delivering a low interrogation in Spanish. The boy sounded terrified but he responded in short order, and Maximo translated.

"They were coming out here to get high and screw."

Reilly nodded. "That relationship is going to stand the test of time."

"I agree." Then, to the boy, he said, "*Dónde está Sofia?*"

Reilly could see the kid's face harden even through night vision—these people really did worship her, he thought. Maximo simply shrugged and unsheathed a knife from his kit.

At the sound of the blade scraping free, the boy sputtered, "*La iglesia.*"

Maximo abandoned him and moved to the girl, repeating the process. When she refused to respond with Sofia's location, he simply pinched her swollen cheek, squeezing and twisting until she shrieked, "*La iglesia!*"

"That's enough," David ordered. "We've got to move before anyone notices they're gone."

Maximo gestured to the two restrained teenagers. "What about them?"

"Doc, I blame you for this mess. Take care of them, and make it fast."

Reilly unslung his aid bag, hastily locating the only suitable tool to deal with such a contingency.

He recovered a pair of syringes referred to in medic slang as "pocket rockets," each containing 300 milligrams of ketamine and five milligrams of midazolam. The combination of a dissociative anesthesia and a benzodiazepine medication would not only render these unwitting patients unconscious for an hour or so but also cause short-term retrograde amnesia. Not quite so much as Devil's Breath, of course, but the teenagers would likely remember moving into the jungle and not much else.

Reilly told Maximo, "Tell them they're going to sleep. No lasting effects. And I'm confiscating their weed for safekeeping."

"Leave the weed," David ordered.

"You haven't smelled it. Believe me, you're going to want some."

"If you're trying to get fired, you're doing a hell of a job."

Reluctantly, Reilly stuffed the bag into the boy's pocket and then raised the needle.

The boy struggled mightily, requiring Maximo to hold him down just so Reilly could make the injection between his forearm and bicep. Which was fair enough, he considered, because he probably thought he was being poisoned. He quickly relaxed, then went completely limp, and Reilly turned his attention to the girl.

And whatever she thought about his ad hoc medical treatment, her reaction was far more dignified.

She spat in Reilly's face, a tendril of saliva penetrating his partially open lips with the taste of chicken and salsa. Wiping it away in disgust, Reilly muttered, "Kids these days. They have no respect."

Then he stuck her too, administering the remainder of the syringe and watching her slip into unconsciousness.

The team gagged the teenagers and bound them at the ankles, then used flex cuffs to tie their restraints together so they wouldn't be able to reach the village before sunrise. Then they fell back into their order of movement—Worthy on point, followed by David, Maximo, and Reilly, with Cancer on rear security—and continued the patrol through the jungle.

After a few meters, Cancer abruptly transmitted.

"*Hey, Doc.*"

"What?"

There was a pause before the sniper continued, removing any doubt that he'd seen the girl spit into his mouth.

"*How's it feel to have AIDs?*"

Reilly clenched his jaw. "Eat shit."

They continued their march, closing the final distance to Sofia's church.

17

I proceeded carefully through the waning jungle, my team strung out in a row to my left and right as we approached the village outskirts through rain that had slowed to a light drizzle.

We'd already performed a dogleg maneuver and lined up for a head-on approach, which we conducted with painstaking slowness in the knowledge that a direct line of sight would lay ahead any minute now, and that it would work two ways. As successful as we'd been thus far in bypassing Sofia's early warning network, there was simply no way that an outer ring of sentries didn't await us at the edge of this rural civilization. Her real security lay ahead, and the only way we could defeat it was to locate the bastards before they saw us.

Sidestepping a vine-covered tree trunk, I scanned ahead to see light permeating the wall of vegetation. The sounds of nighttime jungle were giving way to human influence, the drone of generators underscored by the distant reggaeton music blasting to our right flank. I glanced to my side, gradually identifying the figures of Worthy to one side and Maximo to the other, and slowed my pace to remain on-line with them. At this point we were all searching for a visual, and it wasn't until I'd managed to find a route through a thorn-laden patch of bramble and peered around a tree on the far side that I was the first to establish it.

"Hold up, I've got eyes-on," I transmitted, raising my rifle to peer through the brush at the view unfolding before me.

The jungle gave way to a series of surprisingly well-kept buildings spread between trees that had been left in place to provide concealment from overhead view. I scanned the rooftops in search of a deviation that revealed itself a moment later: a rudimentary church steeple supporting a cross that stood above every other structure.

Panning my view downward, I caught sight of a cluster of people sheltering from the rain beneath a pavilion beside the church—not sentries, but a crowd of perhaps ten facing away from me, all apparently focused on the same thing before they suddenly dispersed and revealed the focus of their interest.

Four figures were on the far side of the pavilion, now moving toward the church. They were virtually indistinguishable from one another, each carrying a rifle at the ready save one. But that final figure was the one that mattered—long hair pulled into a ponytail, a sawed-off shotgun slung over one shoulder.

By the time I brought my rifle to a firing position, it wasn't worth risking the exposure of activating my laser—Sofia and her entourage had vanished inside the building. It was the closest anyone had come to killing her in years, and I'd missed it. On second thought, I was probably the only person to actually see her in that amount of time who both wanted her dead and lived to bear witness to the sighting.

"Goddammit," I transmitted, "Sofia just ended a meeting under that pavilion and went inside the church. Three bodyguards with her, all toting rifles."

Cancer responded in my earpiece, "*All right, I can see the pavilion now—who are those people leaving*?"

"Probably her lieutenants. It looked like she was holding court."

"*You sure it was her?*"

"Long-ass hair and a sawed-off shotgun at the right spot. I'm sure. Shit, if we hadn't stopped to detain those kids we could've had time to set up and take the shot from here."

It was an unenviable admission that I hesitated to state aloud. Maximo transmitted a response.

"Gentlemen, we are missing the bigger question. It is raining, so why did Sofia not simply have that meeting inside the church in the first place?"

"I have no fucking idea," I replied angrily.

He answered his own question. "*She does not want anyone other than her bodyguards seeing what is inside, whether defensive measures or materials related to intelligence or future operations. This means we have truly reached her inner sanctum and established positive identification that she is inside. We are close now, my friends, very close.*"

Reilly asked, "*Think we can stage and wait for her to come out?*"

"No," I replied. "She probably turned in for the night, and it's a miracle we haven't been compromised already. Besides, someone's going to look for those kids we tied up. That rules out us exfilling now and re-cocking for another night."

I didn't mention the other obvious issue, one that would have held true even if we didn't have to detain a couple rebellious teenagers on our way in: Felix's narco sub. It was constructed for straight-shot ocean voyages, not the extended duration of hard maneuvering that we'd been subjecting it to during rehearsals to say nothing of our actual infil. And after hearing the groans and creaks of tonight's journey, I severely doubted the vessel's ability to survive a repeated attempt.

And before I could second-guess that conclusion, Cancer spared me the trouble.

"*I agree. We hit her now, hard and fast, and leave before the smoke clears.*"

Reilly quipped, "*Sounds like most of my one-night stands.*"

"All right," I said, taking a final scan of the village, "looks like a straight shot through the village and into the church, and we'll have to enter through the door Sofia used because every other entrance is likely booby-trapped. I can't see any sentries from my location but they've got to be spread out, facing the jungle. Let's creep forward until we can locate them. Hold fire unless you're compromised."

We resumed our forward movement in unison, now advancing with the full knowledge that not far ahead, Sofia's fighters were peering into the undergrowth with night vision. The element of surprise was still on our side—as difficult as it was for us to see into the clearing, determining any movement in the jungle's depths would be doubly tough, particularly in the rain. But something as slight as a swaying bush could nonetheless give us away, and we moved with all the stealth we could maintain while edging gradually forward, closer to Sofia.

Reilly was the first to locate a member of the guard force, speaking quickly as he transmitted.

"*Halt movement, I've got eyes-on a sentry position. Sitting in a chair with an AK, and I can make out an M79 so they're probably all packing flares. He's in a three-sided shack not much larger than a telephone booth—there must be more spaced out along the edge of the village.*"

I needed to proceed only another two steps before finding that he was right.

The small shack through the bushes to my front was so identical to his description that we could've been looking at the same structure, with the exception that the guard I now faced was on his feet and holding not an AK but a bullpup assault rifle of some kind.

Keying my transmit switch, I whispered, "Guard post ten meters to my front, same deal."

"*I've got one too,*" Worthy replied, "*on the far left flank. It's an oblique shot, but I can take him from here.*"

"Cancer, how are you looking on the right?"

"*Can't see a guard shack, but I've got a bunker or something directly to my front—looks like a wall of sandbags stacked ten, maybe fifteen high.*"

Maximo asked, "*Square perimeter, right against the trees?*"

"*Yeah, looks like it.*"

The DNI agent confirmed, "*Not a bunker, then. I have seen this before, in many places where a village is carved out of the jungle. This is how they store fuel cans for the generators, so if the depot is struck by an airstrike it does not destroy additional homes.*"

I offered, "Sounds like an ideal diversion."

Clearly, this was what Maximo had hoped I would say.

"*It does, does it not?*"

"Well since we can't get any closer, I say we do a simultaneous passive aim takedown of our three identified guards. Then plant the diversion and set up for final assault. Any objections?"

Worthy replied, "*Ready when you are, boss.*"

Then Reilly weighed in.

"I've got a clear line of sight, just give the word."

The optic mounted atop my M4 was an EOTECH holographic sight, and I'd already dimmed the reticle to a brightness level sufficiently low enough for use with my night vision device. Actually aligning the optic with the binocular device over my eyes required a bit of coordination—this was called passive aiming, certainly more time-consuming than simply using an infrared laser, but a necessity when you were vastly outnumbered by opponents with night vision.

Taking aim at the guard shack to my front, I sent a final transmission before we kicked off our festivities. "Cancer, give us a short count."

He didn't hesitate, announcing at once, "*Stand by, stand by. Five. Four.*"

My assigned guard suddenly took a seat, forcing me to drop my point of aim.

"*Three. Two. One.*"

The EOTECH reticle appeared as a faint green circle with a centered dot hovering over the guard's chest as Cancer said, "*Execute, execute—*"

My suppressed M4 jolted with the slight recoil of two precisely aimed rounds, followed by three more for good measure. I watched the sentry go limp and lean forward slowly as if he'd simply fallen asleep. Then he tumbled forward, dead, as I scanned the background, watching and listening for any indication that someone in the village had heard our sudden gunplay.

Instead I heard Worthy, then Reilly, check in.

"*My guy's dead.*"

"*So is mine.*"

Aside from the cycling of my own weapon, I heard no audible signs that three guards had been gunned down in the span of as many seconds, bringing our kill count for the mission to five with no more effort than applying a few pounds of pressure to our triggers.

"Same here," I added, conducting an extremely deliberate tactical reload to avoid broadcasting the sound. "I'm going forward to determine our scheme of maneuver. Doc, link up with Cancer and set the diversion."

"*Moving.*"

The immense size of our resident medic had won him the honor of hauling the diversion in question, and I continued my slow creep to get a better view of our objective as I waited for him to complete the drop.

Our reasoning behind bringing it was sound, at least in my biased opinion: we'd be taking out Sofia amid a village of people who would fight to the death to defend her. Once the job was done, there was a very finite amount of time to flee into the jungle before narco militants descended upon us, and absent any knowledge of the tactical situation, those fighters would be responding in a mob mentality to whatever stimulus presented itself.

So why not provide them one?

Reilly wouldn't be emplacing a massive amount of explosives, merely enough for a startling boom that should be sufficient for alarming anyone within visual and audio range, which, in this case, was almost every occupant of the village.

But paired with a large number of fuel cans packed as tightly as possible within the protective barrier of the sandbags, we were looking at an explosion that could practically be seen from space. Bad if you relied on the fuel source in question to power your electricity, but wonderful if you were trying to leave the area while everyone looked the other way.

Cancer transmitted, "*Explosives are in place, and I got a decent view of the clearing. Entire village is surrounded by guard posts, and we'd need all night to take them out in advance. We're gonna have to slip in and out between the three we already schwacked.*"

"Copy," I replied, feeling increasingly uneasy about my view of the village. "I can make out a couple observation towers among the rooftops. We're going to need sniper support."

It wasn't an idle observation—absent any imagery of our objective, we were reduced to planning our assault on the fly. And broadly speaking, the only two options were to bring all five of us into the building, or leave Cancer and Reilly as an impromptu sniper/spotter team covering the movement of three assaulters.

Cancer agreed, with a twist.

"*If she's got at least three bodyguards inside the church, you're gonna need Doc as an extra barrel on the assault. I'll post up alone.*"

18

Cancer felt relatively content with the shooting position he'd selected, which was about the only positive thing he could say about the situation at hand.

Amid the dense undergrowth and trees at the jungle's edge, he'd found a beautiful fork in the branches of a low hardwood with comparatively superlative views of the church and more than a few of the surrounding buildings. After nestling a Cordura-encased bean bag shooting rest in the fork, he'd settled the upper receiver of his accurized Galil atop it and confirmed that it wouldn't get much better than this. He only needed to squat down slightly to maintain a standing firing posture and, thanks to the vegetation around him, remain completely unseen as he dropped his two targets inside the village.

Cancer swept his scope and thermal device across them now, finding the two elevated observation platforms that each held a single target above the rooftops. Both remained stationary, at least for the time being. One hundred and fifty and 200 meters, respectively. Nothing he couldn't handle with relative ease. But what concerned him wasn't the targets he could see, it was the ones he couldn't—neither observer had a long-range optic, indicating their purpose was to watch for flares fired by the guard positions and then sound the alarm.

Which was all well and good until he asked himself, sound the alarm to *whom*? Certainly not Sofia's expendable, single-serving guard posts that formed a perimeter around the village, nor to her presumed lieutenants who'd vanished into the surrounding buildings upon conclusion of the meeting witnessed by David.

That disparity spelled the regrettable presence of a preordained and yet-unseen response force who would remain a mystery until their services were required. And if that occurred, he could quickly find himself pushing the limits of his otherwise ample ammunition supply.

The only way to avoid that fate was to have the four-man assault element slip into the church unnoticed, do their job in relative silence, and make it back to the treeline before the response force was any the wiser—an unlikely proposition growing more so every minute they took to stage the raid. Everyone on his team had trained extensively for just this type of dirty work, though, and from what he'd seen out of Maximo so far, the Colombian was no slouch when it came to tactical proficiency.

David approached him and whispered, "All right, brother, we're off to stage. If you have to displace, haul ass into the jungle and we'll worry about the linkup later."

"Thanks, Mom. Don't you have an assault to lead?"

"Good luck to you too." David's parting words faded to the sound of him moving through the undergrowth with the remaining three teammates in tow.

Although to be fair, Cancer thought, his team leader's concern wasn't unjustified: rule number one of all things tactical was to never, *ever* operate alone, and Cancer was breaking it now. But they were running and gunning with only five men, having no choice but to leave Ian aboard the sub to ensure Felix recalled his obligation to the mission at hand, potentially if not probably at gunpoint.

David transmitted, "*Cancer, we're set to move. On your mark.*"

"Copy," he replied. "Wait one."

Dialing in his crosshairs on the sternum of the further target atop an observation platform, Cancer exhaled and let his sights settle. Then he fired a subsonic 7.62 round that caused the man to drop in place—a clean kill, he could tell at once—and upon transitioning his view to the closer observer, Cancer was irritated to find the man had turned sideways in the interim.

So he drew a bead on the observer's bicep and fired, hoping the round would penetrate into the chest cavity. Cancer chased the bullet with a near-immediate follow-up shot, watching with muted pleasure as his target crumpled in place.

He scanned for additional targets and, seeing none, transmitted, "Go."

After sweeping his aim across the village, he took a momentary diversion to scan left and confirm that four shadowy figures were indeed sprinting out of the jungle and into the bushes at the edge of the clearing, making a straight line for the church.

Cancer scanned for targets again, anticipating the sudden appearance of rooftop observers or barrels emerging from doors or windows of the rural sprawl. Devoid of a spotter, his team's unhindered passage to their target building rested almost entirely in his hands, and he wasn't going to let them down.

But a moment later he saw that this entire mission was fucked no matter what he did.

A succession of sharp hissing noises to his front heralded a blinding array of flares shooting skyward—one of his teammates had run into a tripwire, probably strung at waist height in the brush to prevent wildlife from triggering it.

A human-sized intruder, however, didn't stand a chance, and even though the flares soon crashed into the treetops and extinguished amidst the dwindling rain, there was no going back.

Suddenly the bass rhythm of distant reggaeton music went silent, replaced by the howl of what sounded like a World War II air raid siren. Its blare preceded a series of floodlights blazing to life all around the village, casting the scene into a nightmarish juxtaposition of harsh glare and black shadow as Cancer struggled to locate his team.

If David had half a brain, he'd order the assaulters to retrace their steps with maximum urgency. Pursuing Sofia and surviving this already-botched raid had become mutually exclusive possibilities the millisecond those flares went up.

No such luck—he saw the four men accelerating their approach, now racing toward the church steps toward the threshold Sofia had crossed only minutes ago.

Cancer steeled himself for the inevitable fallout of that decision.

Worthy flinched as Reilly detonated his explosive charge, blasting the church door clean off its hinges.

That was his cue to move as the first man through the breach, an advance that was cut short by the thundering rattle of a belt-fed machinegun firing from inside the building. Worthy flung himself to the stairs as a streak of green tracers whizzed by overhead, a problem whose only solution lay in the round pouches on his tactical vest.

Withdrawing a fragmentation grenade and thumbing the safety clip free, he yanked the pin and let the spoon pop before beginning his mental count.

One thousand, two thousand—

Then he hurled the grenade inside and drew another, this time keeping the heavy metal sphere in hand: throw too soon, and the blast from the first could eject it right back toward his team.

Worthy felt the shuddering blast inside the building as a shockwave of scorching debris flew by overhead, the machinegun going instantly silent from within. He flung the other grenade inside anyway; if the gunner was merely stunned or momentarily concussed, it would be Worthy who ate the next burst. Transitioning his grip to the suppressed M4, Worthy felt the steps beneath him tremble with the blast of his second grenade. He waited a beat to allow the metal fragments to embed themselves within the church interior before pushing himself upright and charging through the door.

Cutting right through a smoky cloud of dust and explosive residue, Worthy activated his taclight and visually cleared his corner, then swiftly approached it while sweeping his barrel left. The beam illuminated a five-foot-high figure standing motionless, and he very nearly engaged it before registering it as a statue of the Virgin Mary—or at least it had been. The head and one shoulder had been sheared off by a grenade blast while the hands remained benevolently outstretched.

By the time he reached his corner and proceeded down the far wall, the entire space was lit by an additional three taclights gliding toward one another as each shooter collapsed their initial sector of fire. He saw a sandbagged machinegun position, its gunner sprawled over the fortification with all the ghastly wounds expected from a pair of close-range grenade blasts, one of which had probably been postmortem. He looked like he'd been shoved halfway into a woodchipper, the eeriness of the sight doubled by a large crucifix suspended overhead that cast a shifting shadow across the wall behind him.

Worthy reached his point of domination at the second corner and stopped, dropping his aim to a fallen figure that revealed itself to be a second Virgin Mary statue, this one holding a scorched and fragmented baby Jesus. It was the final indication that they'd just cleared a church at all—there was no pulpit, no pews, and Worthy angled his barrel upward to illuminate nothing but rafters overhead as the raid siren continued to wail outside.

Sofia and her remaining bodyguards were gone, and Ian chose that exact moment to transmit, "*Guys, I'm picking up a lot of radio chatter—they know you're there.*"

Reilly took up a position to cover the doorway while every other taclight dropped to the floor, searching for an entrance to what was surely a bunker beneath the building, somewhere Sofia could take cover in the event of an airstrike or assault on the village.

Cancer sullenly responded to Ian's transmission, "*Thanks, asshole, we got it. Suicide, you better call it quits and bail. Like, now.*"

Aside from scorched blast marks within sooty discs fanning outward, Worthy saw no visual aberrations among the wooden planks lining the largely bare floor. That minor setback didn't seem to trouble Maximo, who leapt out into the center of the room and began stomping around like a madman, seeking to find the concealed hatch and succeeding in remarkably short order. Worthy and David had scarcely joined in the process when the burly DNI agent knelt and pried back a section of planks, revealing a plywood square with metal handles embedded beneath the false floor. He yanked on the handles without result—it was locked from within.

"Demo," David called, moving to the door to relieve Reilly.

The medic advanced on the hatch entrance and quickly applied a breaching charge as Maximo and Worthy retreated to the walls, then assumed prone firing positions facing the main door that still remained clear of intruders.

The building shook as Reilly detonated his explosives, sending a wave of choking black smoke into the air. Worthy rose and advanced on the hole, determined to continue his streak of being first in and prepared to order one or more hand grenades into the void before doing so.

He saw that the medic's demo had succeeded in blasting the hatch down into a subterranean bunker, though what was inside, he had no idea. Gray smoke continued to belch upward from the void, far more than the explosives alone could have accomplished. Worthy realized in a split second that rather than allow planning materials of immeasurable value to fall into the hands of her pursers, Sofia had set them aflame.

Every second that slipped past was one less to save the intel, which was so critical to her that she'd quite possibly just immolated herself in the process of safeguarding it.

But there was only one way to know for sure.

Worthy crouched before the hole, clutching his M4 as he took the largest breath he could manage and held it.

Then, without waiting for confirmation from the men around him, he leapt inside.

~

Cancer exhaled, momentarily held his breath, and squeezed the trigger.

The man in his sights had been running toward the church, and his momentum carried him another two steps after the 7.62 round ripped through his chest. Only then did he collapse, the rifle tumbling from his grasp.

Cancer was scanning for a new target before the body settled. It didn't take him long to find one—the thermal signature of the next responding fighter indicated a young female, probably no older than the one they'd detained in the jungle, racing toward the echo of an explosion from Sofia's church with what looked like a Lee-Enfield rifle. Exhaling, Cancer took his next shot and put her down like a sick animal.

She was the fifth runner he'd capped in less than a minute since his team had fought their way into the church, and when a sixth didn't immediately present themselves, he took the opportunity to key his radio.

"Get out of there, you bastards."

Then he was back on his Galil, scanning for the response force he knew was coming. Every possible indicator pointed to their presence: the elevated observation posts, the flares at every guard position, the goddamned tripwire. They were coming, he knew—so where were they?

Only when he finally saw them did he realize that any delay in their arrival wasn't due to a lack of either courage or willingness to die. Instead it was a simple matter of time required to retrieve their weapons—villagers were emerging from the buildings on either side of the church, forming collective mobs to overrun their attackers.

He saw mothers handing weapons to their children, fathers corralling their entire family toward the battle, an eight-year-old boy struggling to hold an assault rifle nearly as tall as he was. And in those fleeting seconds, Cancer realized that the villagers *were* the response force, and there were far too many of them to kill.

He wasn't one to shy from a fight; among his teammates, he was almost uniquely qualified to engage potential threats without a wayward thought to age or gender.

But he also knew an unwinnable battle when he saw one.

Cancer transmitted in the quickest possible terms to convey this unfortunate reality. "She's trained the villagers. We're not making it out."

David replied without a moment's hesitation, "*All right, so we're not. But* you *are. Move to the sub, now. That's an order. Angel, stand by to receive intel as we locate it—she's set her bunker on fire.*"

Reilly followed that up with a lighter counterpoint over the team net.

"*Avenge me, Cancer. Avenge me!*"

The sniper faced two choices: flee and save his life, or commit to certain death alongside his teammates. There was no real thought process to speak of, merely a single-minded focus on the physical actions required to execute his decision.

Lifting his Galil from the fork in the tree, Cancer abandoned his Cordura shooting rest to the jungle. After palming the radio detonator in his left hand, he rounded the tree and huffed an irritated breath at the necessity for his second most hated thing in the world, narrowly edging out snakes for the number one spot.

He ran.

Though the term "ran" was, perhaps, too flattering for what transpired then.

It wasn't that a love of smoking since his teenage years had considerably impacted his ability to sprint, much less run sustained distances almost as fast as his teammates. Whether by sheer grit or merely genetics, he was one of those rare breeds who could undergo cardiovascular exertion at a relatively high rate while continuing to routinely suck down cigarettes like his life depended on it.

Instead, the reason for his clumsiness was the stress of doing so under the circumstances: an enraged mob closing in from either flank, and an indeterminate amount of time remaining before they'd see him in the glow of floodlights, much less discern the significance of a shadow racing out of the jungle with a rifle.

He was halfway across the open area when gunfire broke out from both sides—these crazy bastards didn't care about killing each other, only protecting Sofia. Which, to be fair, was probably where he'd be if raised in a country whose government gave them nothing while a purported villain provided ample resources to feed, clothe, and educate their families.

Cancer threw himself to the ground in a sprinting lunge, extending his left hand as he mashed the transmit switch on his radio detonator.

The delay was substantial enough for him to consider the possibility that the diversion would fail altogether, whether by a transmission or connection issue.

But his chest had barely impacted the spongy ground when the concussion sucked all the air out of his lungs in a microsecond, a shockwave of heat and light catapulting overhead as he curled into a fetal position as if in the wake of a nuclear blast. The noise was beyond deafening—the decibel cutoff in his earpieces was activated immediately, transmuting any ambient sound into a dull roar of white noise as the explosion soared overhead. Cancer rose and stumbled forward on the remainder of his sprint.

The diversion had, for all intents and purposes, worked surprisingly well; he sensed no further bullets cracking past him, although there was a great chorus of screams on either side. Fuck 'em, he thought; if they were fine benefiting from Sofia's reign of destruction, they could stand to bear a few seconds on the receiving end.

It wasn't until he reached the church steps that he realized the detonator remained clenched in his left hand. Tossing it over his shoulder, he secured his Galil at the high ready and raced up the stairs and inside to conduct a one-man clear.

But security wouldn't be required right now, at least not at the moment and not inside the building. Beneath a cloud of acrid smoke accumulating on the ceiling, the only enemy in his taclight beam was a machine gunner who looked like he'd been killed several times over. To an outside observer, it was a sight of horrific proportions; to someone who was about to join his team in a suicidal last stand, however, it was a breathtaking vista of survival, however fleeting, in circumstances where every breath was a blessing.

Except his team wasn't there.

Cancer looked down to find the source of the smoke: a hole in the floor, and below it an open fire that, from the looks of it, must've been consuming the bodies of his former teammates.

"I'm in the church," he transmitted. "Anyone still alive down there?"

Sofia's bunker was a smoldering wasteland. Maps and notebooks were aflame on every table and desk, gas cans staged for the purpose now strewn about the floor with their liquid contents burning everywhere. Only a set of sleeping cots lined up beneath a flag on the wall had remained untouched as we desperately tried to smother flames and snatch up documents that turned to ash in our hands, the entire chaotic scene underscored by the troubling realization that our target wasn't here.

That detail was of particular concern because absent the possibility of finding any useful information and transmitting it to Ian before we were overrun, ensuring Sofia died alongside us was about the only good thing we could still accomplish.

But her absence presented at least a temporary ray of hope. There had to be another hidden panel somewhere that led to a second bunker or, God willing, a tunnel, and we feverishly searched for it while looking for salvageable intelligence materials.

And while myself and the others had been stuffing singed scraps of documents in cargo pockets and dump pouches, it wasn't until I kicked a stack of hopelessly flaming pages that I spotted my first viable piece of intelligence: a single business card, the thick cardstock more impervious to flame than the thin papers that had been scorched atop it.

I snatched it up, pocketing the card as I watched Maximo drop to all fours and dart his arm into a mini-bonfire of flame to retrieve a partially exposed prize from the bottom: a laminated map that he hastily rolled into a tube, then stuffed in his cargo pocket before racing to the untouched cots, which he kicked aside. Not his first rodeo raiding these types of bunkers, I could tell at once. He knew exactly where to go.

Above the upended cots was a FARC flag. It was a standard Colombian tricolor with the addition of a silhouette of the country bearing an open book, crossed AK-47s, and the acronym FARC-EP. It was also hung upside down in a not-so-subtle indicator that Sofia had been less than pleased when her former organization signed a peace deal with the government. Maximo ripped the flag off the wall, casting it into the flames to reveal the explanation for every contradiction we'd uncovered since entering the church—the gaping black void of a tunnel entrance.

A death trap, to be sure, but nonetheless our greatest hope of overtaking Sofia.

"Tunnel," I shouted to Reilly and Worthy, my view of them reduced to hazy apparitions through the heat and flames. Maximo was already hoisting himself into the gap, and he'd disappeared inside by the time I reached it, yelling, "Max, hold up."

It was no use; he was gone, and as I rushed to follow, my earpiece transmitted the voice of someone who should have been running through the jungle by now in a desperate solo exfil.

"*I'm in the church,*" Cancer said. "*Anyone still alive down there?*"

That fucking idiot, I thought—gangster in combat, loyal to a fault, but a fucking idiot nonetheless. I keyed my radio to reply, "Tunnel on the sublevel, we're taking it."

"*On my way.*"

I pulled myself through the tunnel entrance, casting a final rearward glance to confirm that Reilly and Worthy were following suit.

Then I lowered my night vision and rushed to follow Maximo.

Only then did I fully process the grave risk inherent in proceeding along this narrow corridor—forward progress was possible only by moving in a half-crouch, the tunnel's confines delineated by wood panels in the periphery of my night vision. I could barely make out Maximo, who was moving ahead of me like a man possessed, significantly taller than I was and yet somehow running so fast I could barely keep up. No stranger to finding the entrance to such tunnels, he'd clearly gained a lot of experience traversing them as well.

"Max," I transmitted, "let me take point."

He replied over my earpiece, "*No sir—she came from my country, and she will die by my country.*"

Sure, I thought in my rush to pursue him, right up until Sofia's remaining bodyguards turned around and emptied a magazine in our direction. Because that's all it would take to kill or wound all of us, and I realized in that moment that Maximo's seemingly refined professionalism as a DNI agent was a facade. In actuality, he was a lunatic whose drive to see Sofia dead eclipsed even that of my own team.

Even then, I had to admit that our options were somewhat limited. Sometimes you just had to roll the dice and see where they landed, and this was undoubtedly one of those times. After all, we'd just narrowly escaped certain death by the grace of Sofia's escape plan, and however this was about to unfold, it was very likely preferable to being torn limb from limb by a mob of furious villagers.

The next transmission was from Cancer.

"*Just made it into the tunnel.*"

"For Christ's sake," I replied, "try to seal it behind you with a grenade before the villagers catch up. We're committed at this point."

Cancer, for his part, didn't disappoint; his one-word response so closely followed the dull reverberation of a shuddering blast that the two events were almost simultaneous.

"*Copy*," the sniper said, coughing as he appraised his work. "*Tunnel is sealed.*"

I felt immeasurably grateful for the update—given Sofia hadn't even allowed her senior lieutenants to enter the church, it was unlikely anyone outside her inner circle of bodyguards knew where the tunnel led to.

The answer to that question wouldn't reveal itself for long minutes of racing through the tunnel. Its direction continued to shift at irregular intervals, every step we covered crackling with the anticipation of unsuppressed gunfire from our front. Impossibly, this didn't occur, though it wasn't until I rounded a final corner that I saw the tunnel's single endpoint.

Maximo slowed before a water-soaked shaft through which rain poured down. He stepped into the stream of water, aiming upward without firing before mounting the single ladder positioned there and scrambling upward.

By then I was moving as quickly as I could, legs burning with the exertion of this entire night as I raced to back him up. I considered yelling at him to wait, thought better of it given the possibility of enemies overhead, and transmitted, "Hang on, Max, I'm almost there."

But his legs vanished up the shaft, and I scrambled to a stop at the base of the ladder and began climbing, looking up through the rain at a square hatch that Maximo cleared a second later.

I was halfway up the ladder when I heard a shotgun blast overhead.

Maximo was gone from view, though not necessarily out of the fight—his weapon was suppressed like the rest of ours, and I held out hope that he'd given better than he'd gotten in his engagement with Sofia.

My continued ascent was tactical lunacy at this point, but I had no choice. Maximo was up there alone; there were certainly worse fates than death, and abandoning a teammate was chief among them. The closest I came to hedging my bets was to angle my M4 upward as I watched for Sofia to appear in the gap, feverishly climbing with a free hand while intermittently bracing my back against the wall behind me.

I cleared the hatch to swing my rifle in a wild scan of the ground level, seeing no standing opponents but clearly registering a startling, angry buzz to my right—I was looking at one of the hundreds of tributaries snaking throughout this region, and the stern of a small powerboat racing away.

Scrambling above ground, I raised my suppressed M4 and opened fire at the quickly receding vessel, hoping to hit an outboard engine if not kill Sofia outright. But it was already too far away and moving too fast, slipping out of sight through the trees long before my bolt locked to the rear, a full magazine expended in my futile effort.

No conscious thought was involved in my emergency reload; the act was seamless, conditioned by thousands of repetitions on the range. Then I spun to clear my backside only to find Maximo on the ground.

The shotgun blast had opened up his chest at the sternum, exposing a ghastly crater of internal organs pulsating among shattered ribs. Incredibly he was still alive, mouth gaping, staring up at the rain as he tried to talk.

I fell to the ground beside him, leaning in to hear what were surely the last words he'd ever speak.

"I almost had her—I almost had...almost—"

Reilly appeared then, shoving me aside and yanking up one of Maximo's sleeves to deliver a lethal dose of morphine. Maximo's mouth continued to move, but no sound came out.

I placed a hand on his shoulder and said, "We'll get her, Maximo. I swear to you, we'll get her."

It was too late—his lips had gone still for the last time, and I was talking to a corpse.

My first instinct wasn't to run or even set an ambush for any responding fighters. Instead I wanted to take my team back to the village and gun down every single member of the cult that was willing to trade their life for that of the woman who'd just slaughtered Maximo.

But a hard shake snapped me back to reality—it was Cancer, although I only heard the last fragment of his sentence.

"—out of it, you bastard."

I impulsively reached for Maximo's pocket, wrenching out the rolled map he'd recovered from the bunker and securing it in my drop pouch.

Rising quickly, I said, "Worthy, get us out of here. Reilly, you carry Max and set the pace. We'll figure out a linkup with the sub once we get some distance."

Reilly hoisted Maximo's body over his shoulders in a fireman's carry. It was a sickening sight—blood and gore poured down the medic's back, but we had no alternative, or even time to consider whether the rain would wash away the trail of blood we'd leave in our wake.

They'd either track us or they wouldn't; we'd either kill more of their number or escape from this abomination of a mission without further casualties. At this point I didn't give a shit either way.

Worthy determined our azimuth and we began moving, melting into the jungle on our way back to the sub.

19

Ian stood alone at the apartment window, holding a mug of coffee that had been poured with the best of intentions.

Now it was growing cold without him taking so much as a sip, his mind churning through a torrent of thoughts that had plagued him since his team's return to their homebase in Colombia. He stared out at the surroundings of the El Poblado neighborhood and beyond it, Medellín as a whole.

He'd previously been awed by the city's sheer beauty. Now, in the wake of Maximo's death, it seemed a horrendous reminder of everything that was wrong with this country—all he could focus on were the impoverished barrios spreading endlessly up the surrounding mountain slopes, contrasted by the affluent professionals in the city who he couldn't help but suspect had built their wealth from cocaine. He'd spot a garishly attired thirtysomething and wonder if he was a narco; a gym-toned female made him wonder whether he was watching some trafficker's mistress.

Even the city's name was synonymous with the violent excesses of Pablo Escobar, whose Medellín Cartel had amassed 60 million dollars per day at the height of its stranglehold over Colombia—and that was in 1980s money. Adjusted for inflation, it was a solid indicator for the kind of drug cash that continued to change hands freely in ever-increasing amounts. Because while the Medellín Cartel was eventually dismantled, the demand for its product remained. The only difference now was the structure of the operation. While current mega-cartels were devastating Mexico and leaving hundreds of thousands dead in their wake, Colombia's contribution to the cocaine trade had fragmented a hundred times over into its current status quo, a complex network of smaller organizations and independent traffickers who'd taken production to levels that Escobar could have only dreamed of.

While Ian had no illusions that he would ever serve the drug war, his place to make a difference in this world was to stop terrorists. His team had racked up some not-insignificant successes in that fight, and he'd done everything in his power to shape their operations against Sofia.

And had, without a doubt, failed them.

Now he stood alone in the apartment, feeling like he was bearing the full weight of their crushing defeat in the jungles of Sofia's village.

Maximo's corpse, at least, had been transferred to DNI custody for return to his family. It was bitter consolation at present, but at least they'd be able to bury their husband and father, he thought, which was no small accomplishment for his team; if they'd been forced to abandon him, it would have been as devastating as if they'd left behind one of their own.

Felix's now-useless narco sub faced a different fate: the Colombians were going to transport it to their main naval base at Malaga Bay to be displayed alongside its captured counterparts, all of them intended to serve as symbols of victory in the war against cocaine.

His rumination was shattered by Reilly, who groggily shuffled into the living room-turned-operations center. The medic walked stiffly, looking like he'd just crossed the finish line for a marathon, before he reached the desk and wordlessly lowered himself into a seat.

Ian sighed, taking his place in the seat beside him and setting down his coffee. Reilly reached for the mug, sniffed it, and took a sip of the lukewarm liquid.

Then he downed the rest in chugging gulps, slamming the mug down as if he were a frat boy with a beer bottle before wiping his lips with the back of his hand.

"What's new?" he asked then, and Ian hesitated to answer out of concern for Reilly's current condition. He looked like shit—unshaven, dark circles under his eyes, his normally robust cheeks appearing sunken and drained of color. It was for good reason, Ian supposed. After the failed raid, the medic had single-handedly carried Maximo's body for a majority of the jungle flight that had nearly lasted until sunrise.

Now the team was rotating through rest cycles, trying to recover for the next phase of their hunt for Sofia—if there was going to be one at all.

"What's new?" Ian replied. "Nothing, really. Still waiting on Duchess for the official word, but I'm convinced everything we found in the bunker is critical."

"You figure out the significance of Michelena?"

"No."

Reilly sniffed and squinted at Ian. "You think that 25 million Weisz paid Sofia might not have been for cocaine?"

"What else could it be for?" Ian scoffed.

The medic shrugged, and then they both looked at the material laid out on the desk, all rescued from the flames of Sofia's lair—which was, unenviably, not much.

Of the little that had not been rendered illegible or destroyed in rain-soaked pockets and drop pouches, only two items bore promise.

The first was the partially intact, laminated map that Maximo had recovered. With a scale of 1:50,000, the majority that hadn't been burned covered over 500 square kilometers of inland countryside.

Sofia had wisely kept this map sterilized of all markings in the event of its capture, but that hadn't stopped Ian from exploiting it. His first analysis, occurring while still aboard the outbound narco sub shortly after his navigational services were no longer required, had been to smell the sheet. The act garnered no shortage of concerned glances from his teammates, but he'd at once discerned that cutting through even the still-fresh scent of smoke and soot was a faint trace of rubbing alcohol, just as he'd hoped.

Not until they'd returned to Medellín was he able to fully exploit it, however.

The laminated map had been creased when Maximo rolled the sheet and stuffed it into his pocket. Ian's first examination with a flashlight held at a shallow angle illuminated shadows from the creases, along with something else: hairline traces of markings that had been erased.

Normally, fine-point alcohol markers were used to mark laminated maps like these; they tended to leave behind a surface impression, however fine, on the acetate covering. That was in large part why Ian always procured a double set of maps for each team member; one was for planning, to be marked up freely until the route had been memorized. Those maps would be left in the planning bay while a fresh map would be brought on mission. Because while their digital devices and radios could be "zeroed out" of all data in the event of capture or imminent death, something as simple as a marker impression on an accidentally carried planning map could compromise their destination, exfil route, and plan as a whole.

Aligning a blank sheet of paper over the map, Ian had shaded the entire surface with a pencil in the hopes of identifying the impressions but found none. Undaunted, he'd ordered tracing paper and charcoal from a local art store, then systematically worked over the map in gridded segments to assemble a coherent image of the impressions he was looking for: three possible routes traced over the roads on the map, all leading into a town called Michelena.

There was also text delineating a time and date: noon on the 24th, transpiring in just over two days. And while there wasn't an exact destination at this scale beyond the town itself, that final detail told Ian that not only was this location critical to Sofia's arrangement with Weisz, but that she was headed there herself.

Ian had pored over both the open source and classified intelligence databases for information on Michelena and the surrounding area, searching for its strategic value to a dedicated trafficker and finding none. It was an unremarkable town with seemingly zero significance beyond the fact that the nearest airport was two and a half hours away. That made it no different from hundreds of others across the countryside, most of which were far closer to Sofia's usual area of operations. Ultimately he concluded that whatever Michelena's significance, it was known to Sofia alone.

Regardless, the map in and of itself should have sent the team into motion at once. As far as Sofia knew, it had been destroyed, and even if it hadn't, he knew enough about the woman to be assured she'd proceed there regardless. She'd been operating with sociopathic impunity for many years, and she wasn't about to stop now.

No matter the case, Michelena was the team's obvious destination. Once there, they could set a trap and wait for her arrival with a little help from the Agency in tracking her movement.

And yet they sat in this apartment, impotently awaiting Duchess's go-ahead, due to one indisputable and exceedingly inconvenient detail.

Michelena was located in Venezuela.

Reilly leaned forward and tapped the other piece of intelligence: the singed remnants of a business card.

"Think Duchess is going to find any dirt on him?"

The name on the card was Vicente Benavidez, who was listed as an import export broker based in Medellín. That job description could mean everything or nothing; it would be difficult to find anyone in that line of work who wasn't at least peripherally involved in the cocaine trade, even if only paid to ignore certain goings-on. But given the facts, Ian was certain that Benavidez had been commissioned to transport twenty tons of cocaine to Weisz.

"God," Ian almost gasped, "I certainly hope there's some connection between him and Sofia. Because if he's clean on paper, Duchess will forbid us from taking any action against him."

"That's never stopped us before."

Ian turned to face the medic with a mixture of empathy and pity. Reilly wasn't an intelligence operative, but you didn't have to be in order to see the obvious.

So he patiently explained, "Now that we've asked for a background check on Benavidez, if anything happens to him—police report of a mugging, a break-in, or dare I say a disappearance—Duchess will know it was us. She'll have us recalled to the States and disbanded, if not prosecuted and *then* disbanded, especially after all the shit she either knows or suspects we've done in the past year."

"No, I get that," Reilly replied. "But you've spent half your time here warning us about the dangers of scopolamine."

"Devil's Breath? What has that got to do with anything?"

"It puts you in a fugue state, like one of my 'pocket rockets' of ketamine and midazolam, but a hundred times worse. So we could drug this guy with it, and he'd tell us everything we need to know and never remember a thing."

Surprisingly good theory, Ian thought, especially coming from Reilly.

But he shook his head and countered, "Sure, he'd forget everything except the twenty minutes between ingesting it and actually losing his ability to remember. Scopolamine has a limited effect of retrograde amnesia. So he'd still have a physical description of at least one of us, and that's definitely making it into the police report."

Reilly shrugged. "So we don't do it. We use Isabella."

"Who?"

"Felix's girlfriend. The smokeshow. She's hot enough to get close to Benavidez, but there's so many beautiful women here that they'd never find her. And that's how it works, right? Some chick in a bar spikes the dude's drink, gets back to his apartment and robs him. So what if he reports it to the police? It happens thousands of times a year in Colombia. Duchess couldn't tie that to us, not officially. No one could."

Ian didn't reply, though not for an unwillingness to consider the prospect as novel. Instead, David entered the room.

"Reilly, you big bastard, I'm going to need that chair. It's time for my call with Duchess."

20

Duchess stirred a double measure of honey into her tea, tapped the spoon twice on the rim of her mug, and replaced it in the porcelain holder.

Then she turned to face her spartan personal office within the corridors of the Special Activity Center, the only workplace refuge where she could be alone with her thoughts.

She took a seat at her desk, deliberately avoiding the eyes of her son and grandchildren watching from photo frames, and glanced at the wall clock. Then she lifted her phone from its receiver.

An Agency switchboard operator said, "Go ahead."

"Project Longwing, scheduled call with Suicide Actual at Medellín location 0-4-8."

"Stand by."

She heard a few clicks as the call was routed, followed by the operator concluding, "It's ringing now."

"Thank you."

The switchboard operator transferred the call then, not that it mattered—all this was being recorded in an archive somewhere—and as she waited for the final connection, Duchess considered how much she'd grown to dread these calls.

Whether over SATCOM or encrypted telephone, the conversations were never good. But they were far worse on the heels of a failed mission attempt that, under slightly different circumstances, could have accomplished the team's stated aim. A clean victory would give her the bargaining chip she so desperately needed to justify Project Longwing's continued existence to those who saw it as little more than a costly and inefficient political and public relations disaster waiting to happen.

Instead, her reward for explaining the near miss with Sofia to everyone from the director to Senator Gossweiler was this, a phone call with one extremely pissed-off David Rivers. Despite all his tactical audacity, he knew nothing about the political tightrope she negotiated on his behalf and even less about how close Project Longwing was to being shut down, despite her best efforts to convey the realities of both.

As the call connected, David's opening line didn't disappoint.

"Are we cleared to hit Benavidez?"

He may have been unpredictable to his enemies, but Duchess never failed to anticipate his reaction to the situation at hand.

She injected a forced measure of professionalism into her voice as she replied, "Vicente Benavidez has no known ties to narco terrorism, or even organized crime. We've run his finances and cross-referenced accounts with the intel from Nigeria. There are zero connections, which places him outside our purview."

Duchess left off the fact that her appointed legal advisor, Gregory Pharr, had made exactly that point in no uncertain terms.

David said, "Give me a break. Sofia had his business card in her bunker, and the fact that you found a 'clean' import export guy in Medellín should be probable cause in and of itself."

"And if that were damning enough evidence for our legal department, it might mean something. But unless you want to try your hand at selling used cars upon completion of a thirty-year prison sentence for violating orders, Benavidez is off-limits."

"Fine," David sulked. "I can find out his role in all this when we interdict Sofia at Michelena. Have you gotten us cross-border approval?"

That ungrateful little shit, she thought.

"The odds of getting you into Venezuela are better," she admitted, "which is to say there are odds in the first place. But SECDEF is withholding approval until we can present a valid plan."

"Plan? Is that code for him providing us zero additional resources, heaping on a bunch of constraints, and expecting us to figure it out as we go? If so, that's more or less what I was banking on in the first place."

"Nothing so simple, I'm afraid. Baseline requirement is Colombian accompaniment through every phase of the operation."

David snorted a laugh. "As soon as the DNI assigns a replacement for Maximo, we can check that box. But I haven't heard from them since we returned his body."

"And you won't," she said, "because I've already spoken to my counterpart. DNI has revoked all support."

A long pause before he replied, "If Colombia's intel agency is turning us down, how are we supposed to get anyone else to commit their people to this?"

"I explained as much to the director," Duchess explained. "Now everyone agrees it's critical we get Sofia, particularly considering the implications of a major attack by Weisz."

"Fuckin' A."

"Which is why the parameters for your support have been expanded to current *and former* members of the Colombian military and intelligence establishments."

"You're telling me all I have to do is find an ex-private and we're good to go?"

"You have to find a suitable commander, David, who can bring sufficient manpower and local area expertise to escort your team through the narco country along the border. And that commander must be vetted."

"Vetted?" he asked incredulously. "Duchess, half the war criminals on the continent were trained by us at the SOA. The other half don't have records to vet."

Her jaw clenched. "I've got my own powers to answer to, David, so listen carefully: we're looking for a current or former member of the Colombian military or intelligence community with a clean background. It'll be all the better if you can find someone who meets those parameters and is also a graduate of SOA or WHINSEC."

She considered the sheer absurdity of this requirement, momentarily wondering whether it would be a blessing or a curse for their odds of finding Sofia.

SOA was the School of the Americas, a US institute run out of Fort Benning, Georgia. It was impossible to serve at that base without being keenly aware of the school's presence, which incited an annual protest whereby human rights advocates and Hollywood celebrities alike climbed fences at the base perimeter to be arrested by military police. Their resentment wasn't unfounded, owing to oversight documentation of a laundry list of Latin American graduates who had gone on to commit widespread torture, massacres, assassinations, and either facilitated coups against their government or benefited from them by establishing themselves as dictators. By 1993 that list comprised over 60,000 people, and it had only gotten longer.

And even Duchess felt a bit silly using the term WHINSEC.

After decades of uproar by human rights groups, Congress had enough and the School of the Americas was no more. Which was to say, it changed its name to the Western Hemisphere Institute for Security Cooperation and continued running the same program of instruction ever since. And while less-than-amicable political relations caused Venezuela to boycott the school several years later, they weren't alone. Human rights concerns had likewise caused Uruguay, Argentina, and Ecuador to stop sending students.

That still left ten or so Latin American countries in the running, however, Colombia among them. And with tens of thousands of WHINSEC grads drifting around the continent, finding one was the program's best chance of gaining validation for any significant adjustment to the failing mission at hand.

"All right," David said finally, "let me see what I can do."

Duchess reminded him, "You've got 24 hours, David. That's the only window we've got for me to make a case amid already waning political support."

She anticipated some profane outburst; instead, he replied with relative optimism.

"I'll call you as soon as I have more info, but we're not throwing in the towel yet."

She warned him, "We are all throwing in the towel, David, the instant the seventh floor or administration says so."

David didn't say anything, but his silence spoke volumes—the team leader was never at a loss for a pithy comeback or disrespectful retort. Duchess knew at once that he was at that very second considering if and how to go rogue to finish the job.

The pause chilled her; but a moment later he spoke calmly, assuredly. "We've come this far, just let us work our magic and see what we can come up with. I'll get back to you asap."

Duchess ended the call and replaced the receiver. She considered what he meant by the word "magic," and whether his personal definition would put him at odds with her role here at the Agency. Because if David forced her to choose between throwing his team to the wolves or risking the entire future of Project Longwing in its fight against terrorism, then her decision was already made.

21

Reilly sat behind the wheel of his Hyundai sedan, parked curbside on the busy Carrera 35 street of Medellín.

The lanes were packed with cars despite it being after seven p.m., well past any excuse for rush hour, and as unappealing as the stop-and-go traffic would be to drive in, he was getting tired of just sitting here. Not that the situation didn't have its advantages, he thought; the benefit to operating in a city with a thriving tourist industry was easy availability of rental vehicles and, perhaps more importantly at present, relative ease in staking out Vicente Benavidez's place of business without attracting undue attention.

The only unsettling thing about his role in tonight's foray, in fact, was the presence of his passenger.

Isabella was breathtaking even when he'd seen her in streetwalker clothes, but with the finest makeup money could buy, Bvlgari glasses, a form-fitting business suit and skirt, Prada handbag, and 900-dollar heels—all expenses Ian would have to fudge in his post-mission accounting—she looked like the kind of woman you'd propose to on the first date, if you could even manage a first date.

Reilly asked her, "You remember all your social engineering talking points?"

She sighed, her thickly accented voice as sultry as ever. "Yes, but I do not need them. Benavidez is a man; this is all I need to know."

"This is important," he insisted. "Don't get overconfident. I mean, I see why you would be—you're you, after all—but this is our only shot."

She was quiet for a moment, then looked over at him with the city lights reflecting off her glasses.

"If I may give you some small advice?"

"Sure," Reilly said.

"You try too hard."

He frowned. "I don't follow."

"You men who idolize women...how should I say...if your jaw drops, we are not interested. We see this every day, and it is too...too uncomfortable."

Reilly felt a deep pang of shame at the statement for several reasons—first, Isabella detected his obvious attraction and apparently didn't have to try very hard to do so, and second, she'd just lumped him in with every creep on the street.

His face flushed, embarrassment setting in as he considered how to apologize.

But he composed himself in seconds, and rather than try to pardon himself, he asked, "So what should I do?"

She looked out the passenger window, watching people pass on the sidewalk.

"Before you are a man, before I am a woman, we are both...human. Same doubts, same insecurities, same...dreams. You see?"

"I think so."

"Stop acting like you are talking to a pageant queen—"

Reilly cut her off.

"And start acting like I'm just talking to a fellow human being."

"Yes." She nodded. "This. Then you will relax, and be who you are. And the women, they will see this. Many men cannot do it, they just stand and drool."

He considered her admission, a rare insight into the female psyche that made a lot of sense.

Then he said, "So by relating on a universally human level instead of acting like I'm on the opposite side of some massive gender divide, I'll stand out. I can be a human, too, just like she is."

"Yes." She nodded with encouragement. "You can be human, if you stop trying to be a man."

"Huh."

Reilly's brow furrowed. He looked over and replied with boyish enthusiasm, "Thanks, Isabella. You rock." He lifted a palm and she high-fived it, and then Reilly stared out the windshield, turning her advice over in his mind.

But Isabella's eyes remained locked on him, a smile playing at her lips. "See? Was this so hard?"

"Oh, shit," he whispered. "I just did it, didn't I?"

"Yes, you did."

"Does this mean that—"

"No," she swiftly responded, looking away. "You cannot just do it once. All of the time, Reilly. All of the time."

"Okay. Got it."

She reached into her purse and procured a tube of lipstick, waving it at him mockingly.

"Do not make me use this on you."

His gaze dropped to the lipstick, whose vial had been cleared to accommodate a measured portion of tasteless white powder. It was the dreaded scopolamine, Devil's Breath, and as much as Ian warned of the dangers of getting randomly dosed by a thief, only Reilly had any experience with the substance.

And while that experience was limited to assisting postoperative care during a hospital rotation as part of the Army's Special Operations Combat Medic Course, he knew what even a low dose of the anticholinergic drug could accomplish. It quite literally disrupted the brain's connection to the body, blocking short-term memory neurotransmitters in the central nervous system. A neat little trick, if you were treating a patient who'd just undergone a surgery that would otherwise leave them vomiting for hours.

But Isabella would be administering a large amount of scopolamine in a decidedly non-clinical setting—not her first time to do so, he'd learned, as it was apparently a staple of the Colombian working girl. And after consulting with her on what that dose should consist of, he was alarmed to find her recommendation consisted of roughly three times the amount he would've dared use on his own.

The ensuing dilemma made Reilly wish he hadn't suggested this course of action to Ian in the first place: here he was, a medic, not only trained but hardwired to save people, and Project Longwing was continually forcing him to use his knowledge to condemn them instead. Knocking out a couple teenagers in the jungle, ensuring Maximo's last moments would be as painless as possible, drugging a Colombian businessman who may or may not have any knowledge of Sofia's cocaine transfer to Weisz.

David had left it up to him to determine how much scopolamine to use on Vicente Benavidez while ensuring he didn't overdose, and in lieu of any medical data on the subject, Reilly had no choice but to side with Isabella's recommendation. Too little, she said, and the target wouldn't "become a zombie." Too much, and he'd black out too soon. According to Reilly, of course, too much meant anaphylactic shock, respiratory failure, or death, and he had significant medical supplies on hand to intervene if Benavidez's condition trended in that direction.

Still watching the lipstick vial, he asked politely, "Can you put that away?"

Seeing his fearful gaze, Isabella began laughing, so Reilly laughed too, albeit nervously. When she went silent, so did he.

Then his phone rang—it was Ian—and he hastily answered and put the call on speaker.

"Benavidez is on the move," Ian said. "Exiting the lobby, blue dress shirt and gray slacks. Get her on the sidewalk, I'll be three or four paces behind him."

Reilly gave his passenger a final glance as she slipped the lipstick tube back into her purse. "Showtime, Isabella. Just get him into a bar or restaurant, and I'll be a few minutes behind you."

She replied flippantly, "Do not be nervous. I do this for a living, you know."

Then she stepped out of the car, closing the door and adjusting her purse strap.

But she didn't depart in Benavidez's direction, instead letting foot traffic pass her by as she pretended to text on her phone.

"Twenty feet out," Ian announced over the phone. "Is she moving?"

"No, she's just—standing here, right outside the car."

"Is she going to play ball?"

"I don't know. I think so."

Ian's voice grew tense. "Ten feet. Does she see him?"

"Can't tell, she's pretending to text."

"Five feet."

Reilly watched as Isabella continued staring at her phone, taking a distracted step forward onto the sidewalk—and colliding with a businessman in a blue shirt, her purse thumping to the sidewalk.

Isabella chirped, "*Dios mio, lo siento,*" and knelt to retrieve her purse, exposing a generous portion of cleavage to a stunned Vicente Benavidez.

The man was way out of his element, stammering a response as she swiftly rose and put her hands on his chest, smoothing his shirtfront and continuing to apologize profusely. Reilly shook his head. No way was this going to work—Isabella was being far too obvious, the entire event nothing more than an obviously contrived boy-meets-girl moment that Benavidez would be far too savvy to fall for.

He registered Ian slipping past on the sidewalk with a phone pressed to his ear, then heard his next update.

"I lost visual."

Reilly replied, "Well I've got it, and it's not looking good. We should've hired an actress, not a sex worker."

But shockingly, Benavidez continued to engage with Isabella. Reilly kept his eyes forward for fear of giving himself away, but he could hear the delighted tones of Spanish conversation beside the car.

Those tones faded a moment later—she'd lost him, he knew, and would be getting back in the car any second now—but when he looked up, both were gone. He checked his side-view mirror, seeing that Benavidez had reversed course and was now strolling back the way he'd come.

Isabella was keeping stride next to him, a hand on his arm as she threw back her head and laughed.

"What the hell," Reilly gasped. "I think she's got him. They're headed back the way he came."

Ian sounded angry. "I thought you said it wasn't looking good."

"It wasn't, I mean, there was no way any guy could fall for that."

"Doc," Ian began, "I love you, brother. But you can't tell me you'd react any differently. Keep me posted on where they go."

That didn't take long—Reilly's phone flashed an incoming message from Isabella, and he read the contents aloud.

"Vortex Rooftop Bar." Then he added, "Man, she works fast."

"Got it. Now get in there, and don't let them out of your sight."

"Yeah, yeah, I'm going. David's going to be sorry he missed this."

"What are you talking about?" Ian asked incredulously. "As far as tonight's festivities go, he's got the best role out of any of us."

22

I exited the cab into the cool night air, breathing in the scent of car exhaust and lingering marijuana smoke. Medellín, I thought, was quickly becoming a second home.

Striding across the sidewalk, I glanced up at the neon red sign proclaiming *HORA DORADA* and felt the bass notes reverberating in my chest long before I reached the door. As with the time I'd come here with Maximo, no lines of people waited to get inside the nightclub. That placed it in stark opposition to the other clubs in the district, and spoke volumes about Hora Dorada's place in the hierarchy of afterhours establishments: you were either a known trafficker or the guest of one, or you didn't get inside.

All I had to do was achieve guest status, and by now I knew exactly how to do it.

Two bouncers were stationed outside the door, and while I didn't recognize one of them, the other was the same man who had admitted Maximo into the club. Off to a good start, I thought.

"English?" I asked him.

The bouncer simply tilted his head at me, twirling the antenna of his walkie-talkie in my direction as if to say, *Of course, you idiot. Hurry up and spit it out.*

"Good," I said, "because my Spanish sucks. I need to see Vega."

He cracked a grin that faded as quickly as it appeared. "Get lost."

I held up a hand and said, "I was here three weeks ago, with Maximo Ospina. I'm Maximo's friend, and Vega will know that. It's very urgent that I see him now, tonight. He's not expecting me, but he needs to hear what I have to say. Five minutes, that's all I ask."

That seemed to get his attention more than my initial request, and he asked, "Name?"

Entering a face-to-face meeting with a hardcore trafficker, the last thing I needed was to be caught in a lie.

"David Rivers."

He relayed that information in Spanish, and there was a long and exceedingly awkward pause before a return voice spoke over his walkie-talkie.

"*Sí entiendo*," he replied, then looked at me with a warm expression, as if we'd just become best friends. "One moment, please."

I gave him a grateful nod and tried to appear patient, though I felt anything but under the circumstances. Already down to five men—plus Felix, not that he counted for much outside the controls of a narco sub—we were in such an insane time crunch to deliver a viable plan that I'd had no choice but to split up from my team. With the added difficulties from losing our one link to the Colombian intelligence with Maximo's death, we had less than a day to come up with something before the Agency pulled the plug and Sofia continued to evade the usual efforts to locate her.

Someone opened the nightclub door from within, and I saw three men standing inside, one cordially waving for me to join them.

I couldn't tell exactly what the trio was supposed to be—they had earpieces, though not the unbuttoned suit jackets of the door bouncers. Attired in metallic dress shirts, gold jewelry, and designer belt buckles, they appeared more club rats than armed security.

All three were large, though the one who politely addressed me was nothing short of gargantuan.

"Good evening, *señor*. We are here to escort you to Mr. Vega."

"Thank you," I said, stepping through the entrance and following them into an interior hallway of flashing lights that led toward the club proper.

Turning to see the bouncers closing the door behind me, I mentally reviewed my sales pitch for Vega as I followed the men and the wake of their industrial-grade cologne. The club music grew louder with each passing step. I was curious to catch a glimpse into this side of the cocaine trade, the lavish wealth and extravagant consumption that poured out of the depths of jungles like the one I'd just departed.

But they diverted me out of the main hall into a side corridor, explaining, "We will need to search you, *señor*."

"No problem," I said, following them down a short hallway and into a concrete-floored storage room stacked high with cases of liquor bottles.

I'd come here prepared for anything from a basic metal detector sweep to a literal strip search, and seeing the room made me think it was going to be the latter. These men could search all they wanted—I hadn't brought a weapon or, for fear of compromising my team, even a cell phone. Unless they were looking to steal either the pen and blank notepad or the taxi fare in my pocket, this should be a relatively short process.

The upside, as I soon found out, was that they weren't looking to shake me down for money.

But the downside was that they weren't particularly interested in searching me, either.

The largest of the three men spun and threw a fist into my gut so fast and so hard that I dropped in place. Only the intervention by his partners on either side kept me from hitting the ground, though the alternative proved to be debatably worse.

They wrenched me upright and pinned my shoulders against the wall, after which my assaulter advanced a step and placed a choking meathook of a hand against my throat.

"You DEA?" he hissed.

I didn't answer him, though not to deliver some steely-eyed, defiant stare. I simply couldn't breathe, much less speak—if the punch hadn't knocked all the air out of my lungs, then the palm against my larynx would have done the trick regardless.

Whether he realized this or expected it in the first place, the man released his choke and grabbed a fistful of my hair, flinging me to the concrete floor as he repeated, "DEA?"

I rolled onto my back, gasping for air.

"Come on, man. Do I have a"—I took a rasping breath—"shitty government haircut?" Exhaling, I went on, "Do I look like I care about drugs?" A final gulp of air before I concluded, "You'd better call Vega now, before you really"—gasp—"piss him off."

"I have called Vega," he replied. "He has no idea who you are."

The last word still hung in the air when he drove a kick into my ribs, causing me to convulse into a fetal position as I yelled my response.

"I'm Maximo's friend. Maximo Ospina. Your boss helped him deal with Jiménez, you understand?"

Another kick, this one impacting my kidney as I writhed away. "If this was true, you would not come alone."

Before I could respond, his pair of goons descended upon me, wrenching me partially upright and dragging my back against a shelf of liquor crates for their boss to drive a swift right cross down on my face.

The fist impacted below my cheekbone and sailed across my mouth, splitting my lip open as I felt a hot gush of blood against my tongue.

"Where is Maximo?" he roared.

"Maximo is dead," I shouted, hopefully in time to preempt another assault.

I heard the *snick* of metal and instinctively looked to the source, gongs clanging in my head as he knelt before me. Before I could so much as flinch in response, he pressed the tip of a switchblade against my testicles.

Nothing in my life had ever been so immediately sobering—the gongs vanished, all thoughts of air intake forgotten as I focused on the knife with laserlike attentiveness, unable to pull my gaze away or, thanks to the shelves behind me, even move.

"If you lie," he said, "I take your manhood."

"Maximo is dead," I repeated, spitting a stream of coppery-tasting blood onto the floor beside me. "Sofia killed him."

Then I met his eyes and concluded, "And if Vega wants payback for that, if he wants her gone from his competition, then I'm the guy who can make it happen."

There was a glimmer of recognition in the giant's eyes, though how much of this made sense to him remained to be seen. I had no idea if he was a knuckle-dragging hired gun or one of Vega's trusted lieutenants, but if my admission failed to sway him, then I was soon going to regret coming here far more than I already was.

The metallic *clack* that followed sounded louder than any gunshot or explosion I could recall, despite the source: the blade retracted into the knife's handle, while the huge man wielding it rose and transmitted.

What followed was a low murmur of Spanish. I could only make out the words "Maximo" and "Sofia."

The response only took a few seconds to arrive, though that span of time seemed considerably longer given the fact that I was off the grid for both my team and the Agency, completely on my own and subject to whatever imaginative torture and/or execution would follow if Vega didn't like what he heard.

But my tormenter visibly relaxed upon hearing it, then addressed the remaining two men curtly and in English, presumably so I could understand.

"Clean him up, bring him upstairs."

He turned to leave then, and his men hoisted me to my feet.

23

Ian sat on the bench in the back of a parked panel van, his legs propped up on a medical aid bag as he impatiently checked his watch.

Worthy called back from the driver's seat, "How much longer do you think this is going to take?"

Ian rolled his eyes. "How should I know?"

"You're an intel guy," Worthy explained. "You should know everything."

"You do realize that my training and experience has at no time involved date rape drugs, right?"

"Me neither. But it's been over an hour now. Give him a call and see what's up."

Sighing, Ian produced his phone and redialed a number for the third time since Benavidez had taken Isabella's bait. He placed the call on speaker so Worthy could hear the conversation that Ian was certain would be short and uneventful.

Reilly answered, "What's up?"

"You tell me," Ian replied. "We still haven't heard from Isabella. What do you got?"

"I mean, they're still drinking. Looks like it's going well, but I can't tell if she's dosed him yet or not. He looks completely normal; they're both talking up a storm. And I've discovered that club soda without alcohol tastes like shit."

"All right, thanks."

Reilly ended the call.

Great, Ian thought. He and Worthy were stuck in a van, Reilly was sitting at the bar ogling Colombian women, and David was at the nightclub with zero ability to communicate his progress or lack thereof. The clock was ticking down to getting pulled out of the country for lack of results, and his ability to divine any intelligence value from Benavidez's connection to Sofia hinged on a ludicrous plan.

Getting Benavidez to sit down for a drink was a critical first step, but there was no telling how long it would take Isabella to slip the scopolamine into his cocktail, if she would at all. There was a very real risk that he'd never look away from his glass, particularly given the prevalence of Devil's Breath in Colombia, along with a not-unlikely possibility that their femme fatale would cut her losses and bail with her initial payment and new outfit, never to be seen again. And while Reilly was in the bar to keep eyes-on and prevent that latter outcome from occurring, Ian's read on Isabella was that she was not to be underestimated. If she delivered Benavidez on a silver platter it would be because she'd chosen to, not due to an inability to lose Reilly in the crowded streets.

But as Ian considered which outcome was more likely, Isabella called and removed all doubt.

"Hey," Ian answered.

He could tell from her voice that she was smiling. For her, this must've been something akin to a recreational sport.

"My friend is ready to meet you now."

Thank God, he thought, hastily responding, "We're at the planned pickup next to the taqueria, but we can move wherever you need us."

"No, I will come to you. He is quite...cooperative right now."

"Are you sure he's under?"

"I am one hundred percent certain. The time to speak is now. We will see you in a few minutes."

"Showtime," Ian announced to Worthy, who keyed the van engine to life.

Ian dialed Cancer next, speaking quickly as the call connected. "We're a 'go,' he's inbound to primary pickup. Get ready."

The background noise of traffic was loud over the phone—the sniper was parked with the windows down, he surmised, smoking in the rental.

"Sweet," Cancer replied with an audible exhale, "I'm ready for the demolition derby."

He ended the call before Ian could, and in the final moments before Isabella arrived with Benavidez, Ian desperately hoped that the demolition derby wouldn't occur at all.

Cancer was currently behind the wheel of a chase car, and would trail them until Ian had finished his interview with Benavidez. If a cop tried to pull over the van, it was up to Cancer to stage a traffic accident by getting in a fender bender with the offending patrol car. That wasn't without its own set of risks, but easily explainable as a dumb tourist texting while driving, and certainly preferable to the officers of Medellín's *Región de Policía Numero Seis* discovering a van full of gringos with a drugged Colombian businessman.

Ultimately the decision to conduct the interrogation from a moving van was a no-brainer—the only viable alternative was to enter Benavidez's apartment. While they'd take him there if the need arose, doing so presented far more opportunities to leave forensic evidence that pointed straight to them.

Watching his side-view mirror, Worthy called back from the driver's seat, "All right, here they come. Get that door open."

Without the benefit of any windows to confirm who was outside the van, Ian took the pointman at his word and pulled the sliding door ajar.

Sure enough, Isabella was standing at the curb, flanked by Reilly.

And between them stood Vicente Benavidez.

Aside from poring through his social media to create talking points for Isabella, Ian had no real idea what the man was like when he was sober. But the first sight of him caused the intelligence operative's fears of being remembered the next day to evaporate.

He looked younger than his 42 years, with curly dark hair and a gaunt frame. And while he stood with remarkable coherence, the scopolamine had clearly taken effect. His pupils were constricted to pinpoints, eyes fixed in a blank stare as he looked at the van interior as if this were the most normal situation in the world.

Isabella assured him, "These are my friends, baby. They are going to take good care of you."

"Friends," Benavidez said with a dreamy half-smile. "I like friends."

"I am going to get dressed. I will see you at the party."

"Yes," he replied as Reilly helped him into the van, "the party."

As soon as Benavidez was inside the cargo area, Ian handed a cash-filled envelope to Isabella and thanked her with more genuine gratitude than he'd felt since entering Colombia.

She took the remainder of her payment and slipped it into her purse, giving the type of goodbye that only women of Isabella's caliber of beauty could pull off. With a wink, she blew him a kiss, and Ian slid the door shut in her face.

"Go," he announced, and Worthy pulled the van into traffic as Ian seated himself across from his interview prospect for the evening.

Reilly was next to Benavidez, applying a blood pressure cuff over his bicep as he explained, "Mr. Benavidez, I'm just going to check your blood pressure, make sure everything looks fine."

The man stammered groggily, "But the...the woman."

"She'll meet us at the party, but first I've got to check you out. You don't want to get a woman like that sick, do you?"

"What woman?"

Reilly looked at Ian and said with grave concern, "You may want to speed this up."

Ian tested the waters with a simple request. "I'd like to see your phone."

Benavidez produced his iPhone, and when he handed it over, Ian noticed a yellow gold Rolex on his wrist.

Taking the phone, Ian asked, "Passcode?"

"One-four-nine-two."

Ian entered the numbers and the phone unlocked. So far, so good.

He continued, "Mr. Benavidez, I need to know about some logistical support you offered to Sofia Lozano."

The man squinted in confusion.

"Who?"

"Sawed-off Sofia."

He slowly shook his head, and Ian offered, "Real name Daniela Milena Lozano."

Benavidez thought for a moment. "The woman from the bar?"

"No. She may have used a representative, though. But you were asked to help transport a large quantity of cocaine out of Colombia. You were paid a lot of money, and told to keep it a secret. No customs, no police."

"I do this...all the time." Then he emphasized in a singsong voice, "Aaaall of the time."

"Good. Because this shipment was for around twenty tons."

Another dreamy smile as Benavidez replied, "That is an entire year's work, my man. Not a single shipment."

Ian winced. It was entirely possible, of course, that Benavidez's only connection to Sofia was facilitating the routine transport of her coke, not Weisz's order. If that was the case, then this entire foray was little more than a tremendous risk of arrest by Colombian authorities and, worse, Duchess closing the noose around his team for good.

But Ian suspected, no, *knew*, that Benavidez's role went far beyond everyday drug smuggling. Sofia had been running coke for ages, so why would she have a fresh business card for a routine associate?

The only conceivable answer was that she wouldn't, which meant that Sofia had her people commission Benavidez for some component of her transfer to Weisz, whether the broker realized it or not.

Ian continued, "Okay, fine. Then the order I'm concerned with is one that stands out in your memory because whatever it was, it paid extremely well. Think, Mr. Benavidez. It was an unusual request, and you found it strange. It may have been your biggest payday all year."

Benavidez blinked slowly. "Do you have any water? My throat is...too dry."

Ian nodded to Reilly, who handed a bottle to the drugged man.

Benavidez took it in a loose grip, then seemed to forget it was there. His eyes fluttered shut, and the bottle fell to the floor.

Leaning toward him, Ian spoke loudly. "Mr. Benavidez, focus on my voice. You were paid a lot more than usual for one smuggling job. What was it?"

Benavidez's eyes flew open and he blurted, "The New Panamax."

"What's that?"

"A container ship. From Tumaco."

"A ship," Ian repeated, "good, excellent. You're doing great. When did you get the New Panamax job?"

"Two...no, maybe three weeks ago. Rush order."

"What did this rush order consist of? What was being moved?"

The man giggled. "Nothing."

"What I'm asking is, what was on the ship?"

"Nothing. Lots of things."

"What were the 'lots of things?'"

Ian could barely stand to hear himself talk right now. This was like trying to reason with David after he'd blacked out on alcohol but somehow continued to function.

"Ah," Benavidez mumbled, "the usual. Cargo. Containers."

"No coke?"

"No coke."

Ian gave a frustrated sigh. "Then what were you being paid extra to transport?"

"Nothing."

Suddenly furious, Ian said, "Mr. Benavidez, if you don't answer me I will start cutting off your fingers one at a time—"

Benavidez laughed, then looked at Reilly. "Your friend, he has a problem."

Then he faced Ian again. "I was paid. To move. Nothing. Space. Air. Nothing."

Ian nodded eagerly. "So you had to clear space on a cargo ship."

"That is what I said. The dropped shipments, the companies...the companies were given double the value not to load."

"Did you deliver payment to anyone else as part of this?"

"Ah, yes. The captain and his crew were paid quite well. You should talk to them."

Swallowing hard, Ian asked, "How much space was cleared on the New Panamax?"

"A lot."

"What's a lot? Two containers? Ten?"

"Two hundred. Maybe two-fifty."

Ian's heart sank. Sofia would need eight or nine containers, tops, to pack in twenty tons of coke. It didn't make sense to raise her signature by disrupting a routine shipment any more than that—so if she was paying for that many containers, then what else was she supplying to Weisz?

And only one answer came to mind. People. An assault force of some kind, trained and provided to Weisz to execute some massive raid, something like the Palace of Justice siege.

"Where was the ship going?" he asked.

"I do not recall...the usual stops, I suppose. No deviation from the normal route, I can tell you this."

Well that was a wrinkle, Ian thought.

"And when does the ship depart Colombia?"

Benavidez giggled. "It already has."

"Listen carefully," Ian began. "I need the ship identifier, point of departure, every single destination. And I need it now."

Benavidez threw his head back and groaned.

"I am so tired—"

Ian grabbed his shirtfront and shook him hard. "Then wake the fuck up. You're not sleeping until you tell me what I want to know."

"My phone. Give me my phone."

Ian did, though only under close supervision. He rose to hover over the man, prepared to smack the device from his hand if he tried to place a call.

But as it turned out, he had no such intentions. Instead, Benavidez groggily thumbed through work emails, eventually finding a digital bill of lading for a container ship, listed as departing the port of Tumaco at 2:45 that morning with ports of call in the European Union.

Ian pointed to the screen. "You're sure this is the right one?"

Benavidez was fading fast. "Yes."

"You're positive?"

"I made millions."

His eyes were closed now, and Ian slapped him hard across the face.

But the only result was Benavidez snorting and murmuring a final word.

"Millions..."

Reilly shook his head. "That's all she wrote, bud. He's going to sleep for six, eight hours, and then wake up with a splitting headache."

Ian took the phone from Benavidez's limp hands, then sat on the bench and stared at the data, trying to anticipate Sofia's intentions.

"All right," he said with an air of grave finality, "let's dump him."

Worthy drove to *Conmemorativo Inflexión* Park, where Ian and Reilly dragged Benavidez to a bench before depositing him for the night. The park was in a safe area of Medellín, not that it mattered much—no one was going to mug Vicente Benavidez, because the team already had.

To make the interdiction plausible as a robbery, the broker's wallet, watch, and, most importantly, cell phone remained securely in Ian's possession. With their interrogation complete, they made their way back to the team apartment in the El Poblado neighborhood to await David's return.

24

I followed the two men back into the nightclub's main hallway, the music getting louder as my heartbeat quickened. A trio passed us on their way out; two of them looked like sicarios, and they were half-carrying an older man—probably their *patrón*—who was drugged to the eyeballs and struggling to place one foot in front of the other.

But his sicarios were sober enough, both appraising me for a split second before looking away without a hint of interest. A half-beaten gringo with a blood-splattered suit wasn't sufficient enough to warrant interest here—my attacker's order to clean me up, apparently, meant being escorted to a bathroom to splash some stinging tap water on my cut and swollen face. As they passed us and we proceeded down the hallway, I now knew the trial I'd just endured hadn't been the first one administered in the club's backroom.

In light of my recent beating, I questioned the efficacy of the meeting ahead. Vega would very likely be high on coke, presumably paranoid, and in that state the promise of vengeance and facilitating his business interest only held so much weight. Maybe he didn't care that Maximo was dead; perhaps he'd agreed to see me out of little more than morbid curiosity. Either way, these thoughts slipped from my mind as I got my first glimpse of the club's main dance floor.

The music was deafening, the entire massive space quaking with the low, sharp blasts of a techno beat. I couldn't even see the main dance floor, packed to the brim with churning bodies—two or three stunning women to every trafficker or sicario grinding against them. Hands clutched at the women, held open bottles of liquor pumping to the beat, raised small vials for a bump of powder to keep the party going.

Like any American bar or club, sobriety appeared to be in short supply, but unlike the many places where I'd downed overpriced alcohol in my day, the eyes of every dancing man and woman had transcended reality to a state of unadulterated bliss. This wasn't a scene where a few people in the crowd were tweaked out on whatever drugs they could buy on the streets; this was a place where every patron in sight was dosed with the purest of the pure, a substance that had made them rich and immediately demanded the gains back in the form of consumption and, ultimately, their lives.

That risk of death was tangible now, a malevolent force that hung over the partiers like a storm cloud. Every combat instinct I'd honed across a hundred battlefields on multiple continents was firing at once, telling me to get the hell out of here while I still could, if I still could at all. There was the distinct aura that gunfire could break out at any moment, that life in this place was a fleeting luxury to be celebrated while it lasted.

Fortunately, this wasn't our destination. The men led me to a staircase and I felt grateful to ascend above the fray, to seek whatever distance I could from the sight of traffickers and their assassins that had triggered my fight-or-flight response as surely as audible gunshots.

We emerged on the second floor, and I could tell at a glance that I'd just entered the rarefied air of a VIP section.

If the dance floor was where the partying occurred, then this level was for business—clusters of men engaged in animated discussion at tables whose surfaces were littered with drinking glasses and cell phones, the proceedings monitored by groups of bodyguards looking bored as they sat or stood nearby, watching me enter.

The two escorts led me through this somber fray toward a railed barrier at the balcony's edge. Below, the dance floor continued to pulsate with human bodies, its occupants completely oblivious or otherwise uncaring as to the extent of violence and misery they inflicted to fuel this level of debauchery.

But I'd jump into bed with the devil himself to get my team across the border into Venezuela, if it led to us stopping Sofia. However many people had met their fate at the hands of the man I was about to sit down with, Weisz could snuff out a far greater number with a single attack. Which, if I believed the intel reports, was exactly what he was trying to do.

I saw my chosen devil a moment later, seated alone at a table near the rail, sipping from a cocktail glass and by all appearances completely unmoved by my approach.

Quinlan Vega looked more like a movie star than an AFEUR commando-turned-trafficker.

He was handsome, beyond handsome even, in a collared shirt unbuttoned to the sternum. He had dark skin and gelled hair, eyes concealed by lightly tinted sunglasses, and cuffs rolled to expose a gold bracelet on one wrist and what appeared to be an inordinately expensive watch on the other.

"*Patrón*," one of my escorts announced, "*Señor* Rivers."

Vega made an odd little gesture with two fingers, presumably indicating I could seat myself across from him. It was a power gesture, the kind of subtle cue that only a man who'd had his every desire catered to would be capable of making.

Undeterred, I said, "Thank you for meeting with me. Maximo spoke very highly—"

I went silent as Vega lifted a finger, his attention shifting to the sudden illumination of one among several iPhones laid out on the table. He lifted the device and flashed a smile of distractingly white teeth as he stared at the screen.

Fuck it, I thought, pulling out my chair and lowering myself into it with a sidelong glance at the dance floor below.

Vega made an announcement in Spanish to his bodyguards. A smattering of applause from his entourage followed and he set the phone down, making his first eye contact with me.

"I had a very large delivery to make tonight. It just arrived safely."

"Congratulations," I replied, without enthusiasm.

He shrugged ambivalently; this was all in a day's work.

"I pay one million for each ton," he said, unprovoked, "and my friends in Mexico send back ten times that in cash."

I wasn't sure how to respond. My natural inclination after a few weeks in Colombia was to inquire how many people had to die for each kilo that reached its destination intact, but the odds were extremely high that wouldn't go over well among the present company.

So I settled with, "To get those kind of profit margins where I'm from, you'd have to make a sex tape and star in your own reality show."

He smiled again, snorting dismissively. "Parasites."

Then he leaned forward and noted, somewhat insultingly, "You look a little banged up."

"Apparently I bear a striking resemblance to an undercover DEA agent."

Vega leaned back, laughing.

"Octavio did not think you were DEA. I had to have him shake you up a bit, to make sure you were not a *coño*. I have no patience for these. Are you a *coño*, Mr. Rivers?"

"No, Mr. Vega," I said, having no idea what that meant but taking from context that I was better off denying the charge. "No, I am not a *coño*."

"Then we may talk like men. So Maximo is dead."

"Yes."

"Sofia killed him."

"That's right. And I've got a plan that would require your help—"

"Slow down," Vega interrupted. "We have just met. Maximo spoke of the Americans, so I know who you work for."

Well at least that particular cat was out of the bag, I thought. Though the CIA had been involved in anti-communist efforts in Colombia for so long that my involvement with them may have been a bygone conclusion, whether Maximo had explicitly stated it or not.

He continued, "But I do not know *you*."

"Not for lack of trying," I replied. "But our mutual friend made sure I didn't get in the club on our last visit."

"Then let me explain something to you: you do not simply come in a place like this and start barking orders. I want to know who I am working with."

I conceded, "Fair enough. I'm new at this."

"At what?"

"Let's just say my job doesn't normally require me to go in nightclubs, or try to gain the cooperation of—"

"A trafficker?"

"Right."

He tilted his head, watching me closely. "I am first and foremost a businessman, and you may speak to me like any other businessman. What were you expecting, a mountain of coke like Tony Montana?"

"Something like that," I admitted.

Vega waved a hand as if the very notion was ridiculous, the stuff of Hollywood tripe. "I never touch it. At my level, I never see it—at least not packaged for transit. There are people for that."

The thought of a murderous drug kingpin who exercised his craft while completely sober was somehow infinitely more terrifying than one who did so while high, and as I considered how to frame any meaningful response, Vega saved me the trouble.

He removed a small tin from the inside of his suit jacket. The lid was emblazoned with a golden skull, and he opened it to reveal the contents: small, round white pills with star imprints pressed into the flat sides.

"2C-B," he explained, sliding the open tin across the table toward me. "The world becomes a watercolor painting. It is a psychedelic with all the rush of cocaine, but sells for far, far more. If we can smuggle thousands of kilos, you can imagine what we will make with these."

I plucked one of the pills from the case and examined it. "You make this in a lab?"

He nodded slowly. "We have no choice. Because your government"—he slammed a fist on the table with such speed and force that it startled me—"your *fucking* government, is going to legalize cocaine."

I deposited the pill back in its case, unable to suppress a rueful smile. "My government is still conflicted about how to handle marijuana, and you could buy a dime bag of that off any given teenager for the past couple decades. Given the price point of cocaine, I don't think we're in any danger of seeing it legalized in our lifetimes, at least not in America."

His eyes were imploring, trying to read me as if I held some secret information. I recalled Maximo mentioning that the greatest fear of all traffickers was legalization, and given Vega's current expression, he seemed to think my Agency placement granted me some unique insight into the matter. Which was entirely false, but the more I could put his mind at ease, the better.

I continued, "Look at it this way: way more people die from Big Pharma products than any illegal drugs. More from tobacco than all illegal drugs combined, and my country doesn't do anything to stop either of those products from generating hundreds of billions in tax revenue."

"But in a few years," Vega countered, "marijuana will be legal across the entire US. We have already stopped producing it because any money that is not gone now will be soon. Cocaine must be next. And with this decriminalization madness in Portugal and Switzerland, I fear America will follow."

I couldn't tell if he was serious, and tried to frame the stubborn reality in a way that left no room for misunderstanding.

"America's the absolute last country you have to worry about. Look, the War on Drugs was started by Nixon, my country's most corrupt and racist president, and I'm including slaveholders in that assessment. And today, you can't find a single politician who will publicly say that the drug war has been anything other than a monumental failure for the past fifty years, yet every administration keeps it going as strong or stronger than the one before it. Know why that is?"

A flurry of gunshots rang out from the dance floor.

I felt bizarrely vulnerable, every natural response denied to me at present. Taking cover would have indicated weakness to Vega and his men, none of whom had so much as flinched, and I had no weapon to draw. Instead, I mirrored the actions of those in the VIP section, which mainly consisted of looking toward the dance floor with a detached spectator's interest.

What I saw there confirmed that this kind of thing was a more or less routine occurrence.

The crowd spread away from the center of the dance floor as if a fistfight broke out in a mosh pit, only one man was lying dead while another stood over him with a drink in one hand and a pistol in the other, maintaining his weapon with a wavering aim amid the stupor of drugs or alcohol, or more likely both.

Contrary to the movies, no record scratched to a stop—the techno continued to blare, though as club staff rushed to drag the body away, the DJ conducted a fadeout to a new track by way of encouraging the party to continue.

"*¿Quién?*" Vega asked.

A bodyguard standing by the rail called back, "Blanco Hugo."

"Faggot had it coming," Vega grunted to no one in particular.

I looked back to the dance floor with disbelief as a member of the janitorial staff quickly wiped down the bloodstains before scuttling off, and the crowd closed back in to continue dancing as if nothing had happened. The shooter remained, shakily holstering his pistol as a few men slapped him on the back. Christ, I thought, based on that reaction it might not have been the last shooting of the evening.

It may not even have been the first.

"Mr. Rivers," Vega said angrily.

"Hm?"

"I asked you, why is that?"

"Why is what?"

He heaved a sigh of frustration.

"Try to keep up, Mr. Rivers. You said everyone knows the drug war is a failure. Yet it continues. You asked if I know why, then some *maricón* spilled a real man's drink and went to hell where he belongs, and then I *did* ask why. You did not answer, so I asked again."

"Right," I said, trying to recall my train of thought. "The drug war."

At this point it took the sum total of my concentration to recover from witnessing what appeared to be a recreational homicide, and I tried to deliver Ian's data points with clarity. "At this point it's a self-licking lollipop of campaign promises and budget justification that's never going to end. In my country, politicians get elected for vowing to be tough on crime. As long as your product remains illegal, then everyone wins. The politicians, the private prison industry, Big Pharma, everyone who keeps the entire machine running. They all get a boogeyman to point to—that's you, by the way—and the solution to every setback is more funding for an endless drug war. Besides, the last study I read on the subject estimated that somewhere around 200 billion dollars in drug money is laundered through US institutions every year."

"Your government knows this?"

"*Knows* it?" I scoffed. "They count on it. Our banking lobby works day and night to ensure that any meaningful investigation gets suppressed long before the money train is interrupted. So rest easy. America is legalizing weed now, sure. But my government still has a long time remaining to claim cocaine is the worst thing to happen to the human race, and by the time my great-grandkids can legally buy that, America will have moved on to fighting synthetics, lab products"—I waved a hand at the case on the table —"2C-B, or whatever. I don't know what to tell you, Mr. Vega. The only people who want drugs to keep selling at record prices more than you guys do is the US government, whether they realize it or not."

He visibly relaxed, the fire in his eyes calming slightly.

Then, without warning, he muttered, "Thank God," and popped one of the pills into his mouth before amicably pushing the case over to me.

I closed the tin without accepting the offer. "Thanks, but no thanks. I've got my own drug of choice, and it doesn't come in pill form."

Vega lifted a hand to summon one of his bodyguards, who leaned in to receive my order.

"Double of Woodford Reserve, on the rocks."

"*Dos*," Vega said, causing the bodyguard to quickly retreat. Then he asked, "So tell me what happened to Maximo."

I tried to conceal my disgust at the sudden pivot in conversation. His first concern was for his money, and only once his irrational fear of legalization had been quelled did he bother to ask about his friend.

Added to that was the unsettling fact that the man had just taken a psychedelic pill, and God only knew how many before I arrived. He could be watching me turn into a giant panda or a talking tree right now, which made the prospect of discussing business more than a little uncomfortable.

Whatever, I decided. If he was granting me an audience, I'd shoot him straight and hope that the drugs didn't stop him from comprehending my words as they were intended.

I began, "We hit Sofia at her jungle camp."

"Maximo said no one could reach her there. How did you accomplish this?"

"She was close to a tributary. We used a narco sub."

Vega's eyes widened, as if I'd just given him a glorious revelation.

"Bravo," he said. "And then?"

"We raided her building—a church, as it were. She fled down a system of tunnels, and we pursued. Maximo was in the lead, and he was the first one up the ladder."

"Who was second?"

I paused. "I was."

"You were," he paraphrased, eyes growing darker.

"I was on the ladder when I heard the shotgun blast. By the time I made it up, he was mortally wounded and Sofia was fleeing by boat. We recovered his body and returned—"

"Any last words?" he cut me off. "A message to his wife, his sons?"

Swallowing hard, I told him the truth.

"He said, 'I almost had her.'"

"And you, motherfucker"—he leaned forward—"mister second on the ladder. Why could you not defend him? Taking your sweet time to save your own skin?"

I locked eyes with him, anger welling up from my gut. This wasn't going to end well for me—controlling my temper was an even greater weakness than drinking in moderation, and in both cases there were times it wasn't even worth trying.

This was one of them, and I folded my hands on the table in a white-knuckle grip.

"You used to be AFEUR like Maximo, so I'll put it to you like this: I've slung more bullets in more shitholes than I care to count. I've watched friends lose their lives and limbs for my government's agenda in the military, and for money on the mercenary side. War is all the same. I tell you this to say, as one fighting man to another, that if we didn't share that experience I'd have broken your goddamn jaw by now. If I could have been first up the ladder, I would have. If I could have given my life for his, I would have. But my entire team endangered themselves to bring his body back. And I watched him bleed out in the rain while you were sitting here eating your *fucking* pills—"

I flung his tin of 2C-B off the table and leapt to my feet, standing over him as he watched me in a drug-laced expression of awe as I thundered, "—and *you* call *me* a coward? I don't get to sit around in the VIP and have other people do my killing for me—"

And that was as far as I made it before his bodyguards reached me.

My first indication was the thrust of hands flinging me back to my seat and holding me there, followed by the less subtle escalation of a pistol muzzle in the base of my neck, angled toward my heart. I did nothing to object, just tried to breathe normally as my view of Vega shuddered with unadulterated rage. All the while I felt my pulse hammering, a vein in my neck struggling to maintain blood flow against the tremendous pressure of the barrel.

"*Patrón?*" the bodyguard asked.

Vega shook his head and waved at someone behind me, gesturing to the table. Great, I thought, this psycho had just determined a bullet to be too merciful and decided to side with something more blunt. Knife? Rope? Chainsaw? None would have surprised me—and the next man to arrive leaned down to set a pair of objects on the table before me.

Two glasses of Woodford Reserve, on the rocks.

"Drink," Vega said.

The pressure of the hands against my shoulders released, followed a moment later by the pistol leaving my skin.

Heaving an angry sigh, I snatched the glass from the table and lifted it, giving the ice a swirl and inhaling the fumes that had restored balance to my life since I was a teenager.

Then I took a long sip, never taking my eyes off Vega as he spoke.

"You are an emotional man, Mr. Rivers." He frowned and took the remaining glass, tasting the drink once, then again.

"This is quite good," he noted.

I said nothing, just glared at him and took another drink. If this was going to be my last night on earth, I may as well lace as much of my bloodstream as possible with the king of all bourbon.

Vega went on, "I must caution you, do not disrespect me again. Once is a mistake. Twice, and you go to the chophouse. I can have them put you right next to Jiménez."

Unable to suppress my curiosity, I asked, "He's still alive?"

"I did not say he was alive, I said he was in the chophouse. And he is. In pieces."

Setting my glass down, I replied, "If you don't want me to join him, I suggest we move on from any topic of conversation that implies I let Maximo die to save myself."

"You say you did not." He shrugged. "I must take you at your word. So tell me, what else shall we discuss?"

Onto business, at-fucking-last.

"I can't bring Maximo back, but I can avenge him. And I can remove Sofia from your competition, with any intel on her routes going to you and you alone. I know where she's headed, but I need your help to get there."

"My help?" he scoffed. "What is the problem, the DNI cannot take you there?"

"They bailed on this mission as soon as we returned Maximo's body, and if I can't find a way to get Sofia in the next"—I checked my watch—"16 hours, then so will my government."

"Cowards," he muttered. "Governments want the easy wins, the victories. When things go wrong, when they get difficult, the institution will turn on the very men it sent."

"That has been my experience," I agreed. "And what about you, Mr. Vega? Will you help me and my men get Sofia?"

"This depends on what you need."

"She's headed to Venezuela. A town called Michelena, a couple hours over the border from Cúcuta. She'll be arriving at four p.m. on the 24th, and I can't make it there with a handful of gringos—I need mercenaries who can take us across, men who know how to fight. And in order to ensure I receive permission from my own people," I continued, thinking at this point I may as well confirm that meant the CIA but refraining from it nonetheless, "I'll need the name of a partner force commander who used to be in the Colombian military or intelligence."

"That part is no problem. I employ many."

"Preferably a WHINSEC graduate."

"What in the fuck is WHINSEC?"

"School of the Americas."

"Ah." His face lit up. "Of course. Yes, yes, I have these as well. They are the gold standard. I give them a bonus."

"With a clean record," I concluded. "No human rights offenses, no documented activity on behalf of traffickers, death squads, and the like."

Vega cringed, his gaze fluttering to the ceiling in silent consideration before he replied, "I may be able to find one."

"I hope so, because I need to submit a name for vetting as soon as humanly possible. But that should get me permission to cross the border, at least. After that, you're my only hope of safe passage through Venezuela."

His expression grew solemn then, a moment of complete and total sobriety.

"There is nothing safe about going to Venezuela, not right now."

"I agree. So why would Sofia be headed to Michelena?"

"If you ask me why a trafficker would go there, I would tell you there is no reason. If there is business to be done, you send someone to conduct it. You see, Sofia runs coke but she is not a trafficker. Me and Maximo hunted that cunt all across the country. She is *agente del caos*, an agent of chaos. What she really deals in is death, and cocaine is merely a means of financing that."

His words were, in a way, incredible. The man was clearly intelligent, which was nothing exceptional. But the fact that his delivery was well-timed, clearly articulated, and spoken with confidence told me this man must have eaten so much 2C-B on a routine basis that his overall tolerance rivaled that of my own liver.

I asked, "But logistically speaking...why go there?"

He sighed, then took a drink.

"There are two main groups of buyers for our product. One is the Mexican cartels, who send it to North America. The other is the European mafias—Camorra, Cosa Nostra, Ndrangheta—and to sell to them, we must ship through Venezuela. If you meet a Venezuelan who is not starving right now, he is either a politician, military man, or someone handling these shipments. So perhaps Sofia has routes to move her product to Europe." He shook his head. "As to why she would incur the tremendous risk of traveling there, particularly with the current situation in Venezuela? I can tell you now, there is no reason. Whatever her purpose, it is not drugs. It is death."

It was a surreal moment. I sat across the table from an extremely high yet articulate drug lord. He offered no apology for my injuries, and I asked for none. Likewise with the small matter of me insulting him in front of his men. We were, after some minor negotiations, here to take on the problem of Sofia, period, and in that regard I actually liked Vega better than a majority of the commanders I'd ever worked under, whether military or mercenary. And he was a hell of a lot easier to deal with than Duchess; if I could simply take an ass-whipping and a pistol to the neck in lieu of every lecture on authorities and political considerations that she liked to deliver at every possible opportunity, I'd gladly volunteer for the privilege.

He continued, "But let us say I use my people to get you to this town—what did you say?"

"Michelena."

"What is in it for me?"

"I'll kill Sofia."

"Not good enough." He chuckled. "If I do this for you, Mr. Rivers, you must do something more."

"Let's hear it."

Vega smiled, his teeth glowing under the club lighting. "You must bring me her head."

I laughed uproariously, partially out of his tacit agreement and partially because my odds of not ending up in a chophouse had just gone up by a factor of ten.

But my laughter trailed off when Vega continued to stare at me with a deadpan expression.

Clearing my throat, I asked, "Her...head?"

"*Sí*, her head. Her shotgun too, if possible. But mainly I want her head. Pack it in a cooler," he said thoughtfully, "with dry ice, or regular ice. But I want it, as you say, 'on the rocks.' Because I want to look into her eyes, you understand?"

I nodded dumbly, entranced by his hypnotic gaze, as he continued, "You will do this for me?"

Composing myself somewhat, I took another drink and considered the inquiry. He was proposing that I, in my capacity as an Agency contractor and team leader, mutilate a human corpse and deliver part of it back to him.

"Done," I said. "You have some people take me to Michelena, and I'll come back with Sofia's head. Hell, I'll put a bow in her hair for you."

"This is not a casual request, Mr. Rivers. If you accept my support, you take on this responsibility and will personally deliver her head to me. You will be killed if you do not comply."

I set my drink down and extended my hand toward him.

He gave a leering smile and shook it, sealing my pact with the devil.

Then he leaned back and said mournfully, "I have a load headed that way, and I can send your men with it. But it does not leave immediately."

I nodded eagerly. Considering that I'd just put my life on the line to commit a war crime that would require Duchess to obtain cross-border authorities for my team in record time, the more delay the better.

But Vega continued, "Tomorrow afternoon, at three o'clock. I will text you the location to meet my people."

I swallowed. "Tomorrow afternoon?"

"I want my head, Mr. Rivers."

"Right." Suddenly conscious of the late hour, I checked my watch again and said, "I'll have to make preparations immediately."

Retrieving my notepad and pen, I scrawled my phone number on a sheet and tore it out, sliding it to Vega with the words, "I should go."

"Yes," Vega agreed, folding the paper and pocketing it. "You should. Because you are not a bad-looking man."

My eyes narrowed at that, and he explained, "But it is getting late, and I still have actresses to fuck. Life is short, is it not?"

25

Worthy filled a mug to the brim with steaming hot coffee, checking the microwave clock to see that it was half past one in the morning.

He turned to face the living room—Reilly and Cancer were passed out on separate couches with their rifles within arm's reach, leaving Worthy to tend to the only other team member in the apartment. He approached the desk that Ian had been hunched over for the better part of an hour, guzzling caffeine as he worked at the computer connected to Benavidez's phone.

Worthy set the coffee beside him and lifted an empty mug from the desk.

Ian didn't notice the unprompted replacement coffee for a full ten seconds, and once he did, he didn't even bother shifting his eyes from the screen.

Instead he removed his left hand from the keyboard and probed along the desk until his fingertips found the mug and rotated it so the handle faced him. Then he drank, set it down, and muttered, "Thanks, David."

"David's not back yet," Worthy said.

Only then did Ian break his focus on the computer, looking up at Worthy and blinking like a mole that had just seen sunlight after a year underground.

"Oh. Right."

"You okay, man?"

"Yeah," Ian muttered, waving a finger at the screen. "I've got access to all of Benavidez's email accounts. Now it's a matter of copying all his data before he regains consciousness and locks everything down. So far, though, there's not many links to the New Panamax ship aside from the email he showed me. Thank God for Devil's Breath, right?"

Worthy grunted. "I'd thank God if we could just punt all this to the CIA."

Ian's shoulders sagged. "What I wouldn't give for that right now. As it is, we'll be lucky to inform them about the ship without Duchess tearing us apart. A fine balance—if I spend too long scrubbing this data, we might not stop whatever's aboard that ship. But if I don't examine every angle, we could miss a detail that the Agency can act on."

A knock on the door caused Worthy to spin around, and he actually gasped with relief when the sound was followed by David's muffled voice on the other side.

"Don't open the door, it's a trap."

Not the most elaborate technique to assure everyone inside that he wasn't being forced home at gunpoint, Worthy thought as he moved to answer, but sufficient for keeping his pistol in its holster for the time being.

He set the empty mug down on the counter and unlocked the deadbolt before flinging the door open to allow his team leader to enter.

"How'd it go with Benavidez?" David asked.

"Forget about Benavidez," Worthy responded, locking the door behind him, "what happened to you?"

David stopped in his tracks, seemingly confused by the question. Then he glanced down at the blood splatters on his suit that had dried a muddy brown color, and raised a hand to his split lip.

"Oh. It's nothing. Some narco dick-measuring is all. We're good for Venezuela, so long as Duchess gets approval."

Ian looked ecstatic, arm draped over the back of his chair as he surveyed the proceedings.

"Really?"

"Yeah, Vega's putting together some people under a grad of SOA, or

WHINSEC, or whatever the hell they're calling it this week. He wants us to meet them tomorrow." David checked his watch and corrected himself, "Make that today, at three."

Worthy grimaced. "That's going to be tight."

"I know it, but still better than getting no support at all."

Reilly sat up on the couch, apparently awakened by the proceedings.

"Well this is perfect," he yawned. "I mean, if Duchess can come through for us in the first place. Vega's just going to have his people take us there?"

David hesitated. "Yeah. But there's a small concession I had to make in order to seal the deal."

"What's that?"

"He wants her head."

Now Cancer spoke, although he remained curled on his couch, eyes closed as if the conversation didn't warrant his full conscious attention.

"Shit, man, of course. We're here to kill her anyway."

"You're not getting me," David cautioned, adding tentatively, "I don't mean he wants Sofia's head as a metaphor for whacking her. What I mean is, he wants Sofia's head as in, he wants Sofia's head."

Worthy frowned. "Like, her...her head?"

"Yep, pretty much. No, exactly that. In a cooler, on ice. I have to deliver it personally. Her shotgun too, if we can swing it. But mainly her head."

Ian's eyes widened, voice squeaky with surprise as he asked, "You *agreed* to that?"

"What was I supposed to do, give up?"

"I don't know, maybe talk him out of making us commit an atrocity."

"You're being a baby," David said dismissively. "Look, there's already a billion things we're not going to tell Duchess about this mission. The decapitation will make a billion and one."

Rubbing his jaw, Worthy inquired, "Who's going to cut it off?"

"Well, obviously Ian."

Ian looked startled. "Why *me*?"

"Because you're the most bothered by this," David said, "and it'll be funny."

"But Reilly's got all the medical training."

Chuckling, Worthy offered his own consolation to the stunned intelligence operative.

"Relax, Ian, ISIS does this on a regular basis. How much medical training could it possibly require?"

Reilly shook his head. "Man, this whole mission just got really dark."

David's phone chimed with an incoming text, and he checked the screen with a triumphant smile.

"Vega just sent me our WHINSEC graduate: Eberardo Herrera, former Colombian Army."

Looking up, he continued, "All right, so that closes the loop on my end. I've got to relay this to Duchess asap, so she can run vetting and keep working our cross-border authorities."

Ian shook his head. "You may want to hold off for a minute, because that's not all we have to tell her."

"Right," David said, as if he'd suddenly remembered the second part of his team's efforts that evening. He swept across the room to Ian and dropped into the chair beside him. "What did you find out?"

Well this was going to take a while, Worthy thought. He walked to the couch and took a seat next to Reilly as Ian began his brief.

"Scopolamine worked as advertised, but the bottom line is that the only non-cocaine transaction that Benavidez admitted to, or that I've been able to find in his emails so far, was clearing deck space on a container ship. This was done at great expense to the requestor, who I believe was a middleman working for Sofia. Benavidez specified that he made 'millions,' but that's all I could get out of him before he passed out."

"And the container ship—"

"It's a New Panamax, 366 meters long, with a carrying capacity of 12,500 TEU, or twenty-foot container equivalent, that left Tumaco yesterday morning en route to Europe."

David gave a curt nod and asked, "How much deck space did he clear?"

"Two hundred and forty containers were dropped from a designated section on the far aft deck, which equates to over three hundred thousand square feet of space."

"And Sofia put her containers there instead?"

"No," Ian said quickly. "She—actually, whoever was working for her, if I'm right about this—just cleared the space. But the captain was paid so the crew could've loaded anything and Benavidez would have no idea. Bottom line is that's about 230 containers more than she needs to ship twenty tons of cocaine."

"What do you think she's moving?"

"Best guess? An assault force."

"Jesus."

"But even that doesn't make total sense. If she was moving people—"

"Why not just transport her fighters in ventilated containers?"

Ian nodded slowly. "Exactly. Human traffickers do that all the time, and there's no reason Sofia shouldn't do the same with a whole lot less effort than clearing that amount of space. If I had the time, I could probably generate a half dozen theoretical explanations. But with a cross-border trip to Venezuela in the cards, none of them would do us any good, and even if I landed on the magic right answer, we don't have the manpower to act on it. Particularly at sea. We've got to send this information up the chain. Let Duchess and her staff sink their teeth into this while we continue hunting Sofia. Which raises an obvious problem."

"Right," David said in a resigned tone. "Attribution. We can't admit we got it from Benavidez, and once Duchess looks into the ship she's going to realize he was the facilitator. Which puts our team in an extremely tenuous position. That being said, if the ship is linked to hauling even more than Weisz's load of coke, we can't afford *not* to tell Duchess, no matter the risk to us."

Ian nodded again. "And the catch-22 there is that she can run down the ship and still recall our team for violating orders by going after Benavidez."

"Which tanks our prospects of following Sofia into Venezuela."

"Exactly. But Cancer came up with a pretty ingenious solution, and if you approve, we can get this intel to Duchess in the next hour and potentially keep our cross-border option intact."

David turned to face Cancer, who was now sitting up on the couch but not returning the eye contact. Instead he slipped a cigarette between his lips, raised his lighter, and sparked it.

Throwing up his hands, David asked, "You going to tell me what that 'ingenious solution' is?"

Cancer extinguished his lighter and took a drag, exhaling as he spoke.

"I just did."

26

Reilly clustered alongside his teammates, watching Felix hunched over the desk as he transcribed Ian's neatly written script into Spanish longhand on a fresh sheet of paper. His writing was punctuated by inconvenienced huffs, a sound he made every ten seconds or so with impressive consistency.

The sub driver's frustration was, to an extent, completely understandable.

After all, his nighttime hours had been restricted to the apartment's asset debrief room—the only windowless portion designed to be locked from the outside—and sleeping on an air mattress that was, by Felix's account, roughly as comfortable as a pile of gravel. To add insult to injury, the team had just woken him up at three a.m. with the current writing assignment. It was a task that Felix was uniquely qualified to complete and, if he did a good enough job, one that would not be without its rewards.

Ian cautioned, "Take your time. This has to be exact."

Felix looked up with irritation and said, "It is exact, *mamón*. I am a criminal, not illiterate."

With a final scrawl, he handed the paper to Ian, who lifted the original sheet and compared the contents line by line.

Reilly cut his eyes to the page, unable to decipher anything more than elementary Spanish, but he saw the English version well enough on

Ian's original paper: all the info contained in Benavidez's email, from the designated containers to be left behind to the ship identifier and destinations.

Felix thrust an impatient hand toward Reilly, who only shook his head in stern rebuttal.

"Not until Ian says we're good."

"Ah!" Felix cried dramatically, crossing his tattooed arms. "You Americans are such *hijueputas*. Taking my phone, keeping me locked away in this room, making your constant demands. I am beginning to feel like I am back in prison."

David said, "We'd be happy to send you back there if you'd find it preferable."

"Your mother is a dirty, dirty whore."

"That's what I thought."

By then Ian finished his review, holding up Felix's Spanish translation for the team leader to see while confirming, "It's good."

"All right," David replied, scanning the page, "let's get it over to our documents guy."

Cancer snatched the sheet from Ian and crumpled it into a ball, then unfolded it and smoothed it out against the table.

Then he raised it in one hand and, using the other to operate his lighter, let the flame dance at the paper's edges. They singed immediately, and he blew out the fire racing toward the center of the page, repeating the process until it looked like a half-charred relic.

Ian said, "All right, that's good."

"Not yet," Cancer insisted, preparing the final coup de grace.

He held the lighter beneath the blank lower half of the page, letting the flame spear upward to create a hole in the paper, the effect of a single burning ember that had fallen atop it before being extinguished.

Only after he'd blown it out did he appraise his work and pass the paper back to Ian, narrating his altered version of the truth.

"I just found this stuck at the bottom of a drop pouch on my kit. Must've picked it up in Sofia's bunker, and missed it when I was clearing out the intel. Fog of war and all that, right?"

Reilly shook his head. "How'd you think of this shit?"

Cancer shrugged. "You ever play pirate as a kid? That's how we used to make treasure maps."

"My parents didn't let me play with fire."

"Well it's a good thing my dad left lighters scattered around the house, along with his cartons of cigarettes. Let's go."

He departed then, along with Worthy and Ian, to send the ostensibly new intelligence to Duchess along with the name of Vega's resident WHINSEC alumnus. That left Reilly and David alone with Felix, who held out his hand once more to the medic.

David nodded his consent.

Reilly reached into his backpack, removed a bottle of rum, and handed it to Felix. He was in the process of retrieving the glass he'd pulled from the kitchen cabinet only to see that it was no use. Felix had already stripped the plastic seal and discarded it before uncorking the bottle and taking his first pull.

The sight left the medic slack-jawed—the Colombian was chugging straight rum like a newborn at his mother's breast.

"Wow," Reilly said. "This is like watching a live-action reenactment of *Animal House*."

But David didn't look disturbed in the least. He just let Felix drink, and drink, knowing full well that short of alcohol poisoning, the more inebriated he was before receiving the upcoming news, the better.

Finally Felix came up for air, wiping his mouth before looking at them with sheer, glassy-eyed bliss.

"Now get the fuck out of my room," he commanded, looking at the bottle in rapture. "I have a date."

David replied, "Not so fast. There's something we need to discuss first."

"You brought me some *porro* too?"

"We have to follow Sofia. I need you to come with us."

Felix took another swig and shook his head sadly. "I do not know that our can will last much longer. We pushed her too hard in the river."

"That's okay," David said, "because this won't involve a sub."

Confused, Felix asked, "Then why would you want me?"

"Oh, let's see...you're a native Spanish speaker with an intimate understanding of the drug trade, you're already aware of what we're doing here, and we can trust you."

Felix cackled. "You cannot trust me."

"Okay, so I made up that last part. But we do need you, and you owe us."

"*Owe* you?" Felix slammed the bottle down on the table and began gesturing wildly with both hands. "No no no, I have completed my end of the arrangement. I stayed in the disgusting jungle for a week of practice, somehow drove the can through that nightmare of a tributary, and delivered you precisely where you wanted to go."

"But—"

"And if this was not enough," he cut David off, "I sat around until you made it back, and got you safely home."

Reilly pointed out, "We had to leave Ian with you, though. So that last part was at gunpoint."

"It still counts," Felix hissed.

David took a more measured approach, speaking calmly.

"The arrangement was to help us hunt Sofia until the job was done. Starting, and not necessarily finishing, with driving a sub."

Felix had calmed somewhat, whether due to wearing himself out in his counterarguments, the calming effect of saturating his bloodstream with rum, or both.

With a resigned breath, he asked, "Where are you following Sofia to?"

"Venezuela."

Any level of acceptance that Felix had reached prior to that point evaporated with the mention of that country, and he spun himself up into full battle mode once more.

"Shit on that, *mí amigo*. I am proud to have never gone to this scab on the face of my great continent."

Reilly intervened, injecting his own personal area of subject matter expertise into the ongoing debate.

"You're looking at this all wrong, Felix. Think of the women."

Felix threw his head back and declared, "I am from Colombia. We have the most beautiful women in the world."

"Do you?" Reilly asked. "Or do you simply suffer from nationalistic bias?"

"I do not know what this means."

Reilly leaned against the wall behind him and spoke assuredly. "Venezuela is the only country to ever win all four international beauty pageants in the same year, and repeat it multiple times."

Swallowing another gulp of rum, Felix declared, "Those contests are political."

"Oh really?" Reilly laughed. "You're telling me Venezuela's sterling record of wholesome administrations upholding human rights and the democratic process accounts for them having 60 percent more wins than the second most victorious nation, which, by the way, still isn't Colombia?"

David interjected, "There's a cash bonus involved. Ten thousand US."

Felix shook his head sadly. "This money is toilet paper compared to what I make driving cans."

"Maybe it is," the team leader replied firmly, "and if you go back to that line of work once we're done, you can be rich all over again. But now that the Colombian government has your number, if you get caught they're going to throw away the key. That's up to you, though, but either way I'd say ten grand is good enough walking-around money until you decide what you want to do. And there's something else—Reilly?"

Lifting his backpack from the floor, Reilly found the other item he'd carried into the asset debrief room for the purpose of convincing Felix to continue along on this little misadventure against Sofia.

He dangled it in front of the sub driver, who was suddenly rendered silent for long seconds before summoning the will to speak.

"That is fake."

Reilly set the object on the table before him—Benavidez's recently liberated, solid gold Rolex. "Feel the weight, Felix. Look at that second hand sweep."

The sub driver lifted the timepiece, weighing its heft and checking the dial and caseback with a scrutinizing eye.

"This is not fake," he murmured, then placed it on his left wrist and closed the clasp before admiring it with renewed enthusiasm. "It fits."

"Like it was meant to be," Reilly said. "But since money, women, and a Rolex isn't good enough, you can give it back right now."

Felix hesitated, appraising the watch as Reilly held out his hand and added, "Come on, man. If you're not taking it, I am."

Pulling the Rolex close to his heart, Felix used his right hand to paw for the rum and threw back another shot.

"After some consideration," he muttered, "perhaps I will see the women of Venezuela for myself."

27

Duchess checked the OPCEN clock, noting that three minutes remained until her staff's next update brief.

She surveyed their ranks, seeing the bustle of activity as the meeting approached. Then she took a discreet glance sideways, confirming that Jo Ann was gainfully occupied with a phone call. All clear, she thought, and pulled up an image on her computer screen before analyzing it once more with a scrutinizing eye.

It was the high-definition scan of a document allegedly found in Sofia's bunker.

And "allegedly" was the operative word, she thought.

It wasn't because the note had been handwritten. Non-digital forms of communication had become almost de rigueur among terrorist and criminal operatives seeking to evade the ever-growing surveillance efforts to stop them, as her Project Longwing team had discovered firsthand in Nigeria. If she'd received this image along with Vicente Benavidez's business card and a map depicting a swath of Venezuela that included the town of Michelena, she wouldn't have given it a second thought.

But she hadn't, of course, and that almost 48-hour disparity led her to wonder if the ship's logistical intervention had been facilitated by Benavidez himself. If so, she'd know without a doubt that David's team had taken extrajudicial measures to procure the information. That turned her attention to whether that possibility could be proven instead of merely suspected; and if Benavidez had mysteriously vanished, she'd have no choice but to take action because it would be forced upon her. At some level she didn't know or want to know exactly how the sausage was made, and neither did her superiors. This late-breaking intelligence, however, would force her to follow up on the status of Benavidez, if for no other reason than because her oversight would be doing the same.

She focused on the burn pattern on the paper itself, feeling a heightened sense of suspicion that if a documents analyst scrutinized it, they'd determine the marks to be consistent with a lighter rather than an uncontrolled bunker fire.

Hopefully it wouldn't come to that. If David was going to break the rules—and he'd shown a remarkable proclivity to do so when given the slightest opportunity—then the least he could do was not leave a trail of evidence.

She had, however, taken the liberty of comparing the handwriting on the note to her extensive samples of each team member. Along with bizarrely specific personal details, the handwriting samples were kept on file to confirm or deny proof-of-life should one or all of them be captured in the line of duty. To her great relief, if this was a forged document, they'd at least taken the precaution of using an intermediary to transcribe it.

"Hey," Jo Ann said beside her. "Wake up."

Duchess looked over, momentarily perplexed—and only then did she become aware of the complete and total silence in the OPCEN, the product of a sense of expectation before each update brief, particularly one that preceded the seventh floor issuing their final verdict on whether a mission would launch into uncharted territory or be aborted altogether.

She checked her computer clock and swiftly rose. Normally known for her split-second punctuality, Duchess was already a minute late.

"Let's begin," she announced. "Diane?"

Her personnel officer rose from the bottom tier of the room as the central screen flicked to a slide with the lone acronym *J1*.

Diane Goldhammer replied, "Our team submitted Eberardo Herrera as their partner force commander. He served in the National Army of Colombia for twenty years, retiring as a lieutenant colonel. Final assignment was as a battalion commander in the 31st Jungle Infantry Brigade in 4th Division, whose area of operations is eastern Colombia. Military training includes the Counter-Guerilla Course, Lancero School, and the Urban Commando Course. He also attended WHINSEC, formerly School of the Americas, graduating with honors at the rank of captain."

The next slide was split down the middle, with the left side consisting of bullet points highlighting Herrera's career from officer cadet to retirement. On the right was his official military photograph, and Duchess felt herself releasing a self-congratulatory sigh. This couldn't have possibly turned out any better. Herrera looked like a Colombian version of George S. Patton—stately, distinguished, with a square jaw and a chest full of ribbons.

Goldhammer continued, "For the past five years, he's been employed as a security consultant by various commercial firms—nothing unusual there, as Colombian veteran benefits are almost nonexistent and the 10,000 retirees per year usually seek contracting or mercenary work worldwide. His disciplinary record is clean, no charges of corruption or abuse of power, with zero human rights violations. Legal has confirmed his suitability, and J3 review of his military record indicates extensive counter guerrilla and counternarcotics experience in the border region with Venezuela. No red flags."

"Thank you," Duchess said, almost wanting to cut the woman off before anything could contradict this glowing prospect. With a clean human rights record, which was in itself a rarity among WHINSEC-trained personnel, her pitch to get the team over the border was looking more and more like a slam dunk. "J2?"

Andolin Lucios stood and began his presentation in the monotone Spanish accent that was either mildly charming or completely off-putting, depending on what news he delivered.

"Ma'am, we've focused our efforts on all information pertaining to the New Panamax vessel from the latest bunker intelligence. We can now confirm that Vicente Benavidez was in fact responsible for securing a section of deck space on the aft section of the ship, arranging the absence of two rows of containers from the far rear deck while maintaining the official loading manifest."

Duchess tried to suppress any visible reaction to this news, though it was the veritable nail in the coffin of her suspicion. She now knew beyond any possible doubt that David's team had violated her orders to leave Benavidez the hell alone. The only question now was whether that gross insubordination had been conducted in exchange for any meaningful information.

The slide flipped to an overhead view of the ship in question and Duchess scanned the screen for anything that looked out of place. By her initial estimate, at least, the picture was completely unremarkable.

Lucios narrated, "This is the most recent satellite image with the ship visible transiting the Panama Canal, taken less than three hours ago. Only 216 containers are present out of a possible 240: two stacks are missing on the port side, where a deck-mounted marine crane has been installed."

"Is that cause for concern?" she asked.

"In this case, yes. The New Panamax vessels don't come equipped with them—they're loaded and unloaded by harbor cranes that are far more powerful and don't take up deck space that could otherwise be used for cargo."

He swapped the slide for a zoomed-in view of the aft section of the cargo area, with a rectangular swath of containers outlined in red.

"These are the rear two rows of containers indicated in the latest intelligence. Per the arrangement with Vicente Benavidez, that should all be empty deck space. But as we see, it's almost fully loaded with containers now. Compare that to an image of the ship shortly after it departed Tumaco"—another slide flip, this one revealing an open strip of deck—"and we can confirm that while the crane was installed prior to the ship setting off, none of those containers were present."

Duchess felt her mouth go dry at the sight. "You think they were loaded at sea?"

"It's possible that another ship was involved, ma'am, but I think it's more likely our vessel made an undocumented stop prior to entering the Panama Canal. Given the existing satellite photos on the ship's known route, it could have been loaded at the port in Buenaventura or any number of coastal towns."

"As for the containers' contents, do you agree with the team's assessment of an assault force onboard?"

"It's possible," Lucios admitted, turning to analyze the screen, "but I doubt it. They could have simply loaded those containers in Tumaco using a front company, so why pay for the complicity of the entire crew and risk the plan getting leaked by scheduling a new stop?"

"Why indeed," Duchess remarked. "So what I'm hearing is that whatever the cargo, loading it at a separate port was a logistical consideration. Which means it consists of something that couldn't be transported to Tumaco, so it had to be picked up elsewhere along the coast."

Lucios gave a satisfied nod. "Exactly. Furthermore, a deviation of that magnitude couldn't be kept secret forever. Sofia must know that word would get out eventually, particularly considering both the captain and his 24-man crew are well aware. She may be planning to kill them all upon their return, but to me this indicates a high degree of confidence on her part that the plan will be completed before any national intelligence services catch on. That makes this extremely time-sensitive, and even if I'm wrong, nothing in this pattern of events is consistent with drug trafficking. I'd say this document is the most valuable piece of intelligence the team has uncovered."

Uncovered, Duchess thought, or fabricated in order to spare themselves the minor inconvenience of prosecution and jail time.

She asked, "What's the timeline on the ship making landfall again?"

"Scheduled stop in Gibraltar, Spain, fifteen days from now. But there's always the risk of another unscheduled harbor visit, or, given the crane, those containers being cross-loaded to another vessel at sea."

Duchess turned her gaze to a man seated on the opposite side of the OPCEN.

"Brian?"

Brian Sutherland didn't rise, or even consult his notes. He'd surely been expecting the inquiry, and replied with his customary level of expertise.

"It'll take about 18 hours from official tasking to begin a steady rotation of Global Hawks and Tritons for continuous coverage, but we can fill that gap using P-8s out of Naval Air Station Jacksonville. They've got two airborne south of Cuba right now, both on counternarcotics sweeps to identify unknown surface tracks. Closest one could be over that ship in two hours, tops. All I need is the official 'go' to set it in motion."

"Get it up and running as soon as possible, and start working on a second set of ISR to stand by in case some or all of the cargo is transferred to another ship and our air requirements suddenly double. J2, anything else?"

Lucios shook his head and the slide flipped to *J3*.

Duchess cut her gaze to a thickly muscled man with a ginger beard, her operations officer whom she'd learned by now to trust almost unequivocally despite his often abrasive level of candor.

Before he could speak, she said, "Wes, I want you to rope in DoD and have them start planning for a ship seizure. DEVGRU or MARSOC, I imagine."

He replied without hesitation, "1st Raider Battalion is running a company training exercise in Honduras right now. Those boys can take down a container ship without breaking a sweat, and it'd be an easy redirect to stage a couple of their teams at our base in Curaçao. Besides, ma'am, if you want the job done right, it's got to be the Devil Dogs."

No surprise with his affinity for the Marines, she thought—Wes used to be one.

Then he rose stiffly to his feet, the result of a leg prosthetic he'd earned during his later service with the CIA's Ground Branch. It was an injury that landed him here on staff, and Duchess filled the time delay it took him to stand with her next guidance.

"Whoever can reach the staging area first, Wes. And I emphasize that they are to prepare—no local surveillance that could spook the crew. We will cross-level all ISR feed with whoever supplies the shooters."

He nodded his understanding—without that clarification, they risked some overeager unit sending in a boat or local drones to get a closer look. And when you had an informational edge over your opponent, the only thing better than acting immediately was to play your cards close to the chest, surveilling and gathering intelligence before the enemy realized they were being watched. To do otherwise could scare them into a contingency plan that the Agency wasn't prepared for, with the trail potentially going cold as a result.

Nowhere was this more apparent than with Sofia Lozano, who, in addition to having received at least one large payment from Erik Weisz, had proven extraordinarily successful at eluding capture.

Wes replied, "Will do, ma'am, but I think there's an additional possibility we're not considering."

She raised her eyebrows.

"Well don't leave us all in suspense, Wes."

"We know the containers are on board, but not necessarily the cargo."

"Meaning?"

Wes drew a long breath and offered, "If the cargo is critical to Sofia's plan, and I'm sure it is, then why is she heading into Venezuela? Why not board along with the containers? Maybe they're specially rigged to support an assault force, but if those people were in Colombia in the first place she'd have no reason to go to Michelena."

Duchess considered that for a moment. "You think she's picking up the cargo in Venezuela, and loading it in the Atlantic."

"Could be," he said tentatively. "We follow the containers and we'll get our answer soon, but my money and my instincts say those fuckers are empty right now."

It was a bold proclamation, doubly so since he'd just voiced it to the entire OPCEN rather than shared it at her deskside. She glanced at Lucios and found the intelligence officer looking as perplexed as she felt, and yet, when she considered the outlandishness of this suggestion, Duchess found her mind unable to materialize any particular objection.

"Duly noted." She cued him to sit before she checked the clock and said, "Anyone else?"

At this point the slide flipped to the title *J6*. Duchess allowed herself a small groan that no one else, save perhaps Jo Ann, was remotely close enough to hear.

"Yes, Christopher?"

Christopher Soren looked like a nearly ideal briefer; with a hypervigilant gaze and almost reptilian level of alertness, he came across as a master of his domain. And as Project Longwing's designated communications officer, he most certainly was.

But then he opened his mouth and, as with every one of his overtures, made Duchess want to smother him with a pillow.

"Ma'am," he began, "a key piece of the team's latest intelligence submission was the point of contact information for the person who commissioned the cargo space aboard the New Panamax, presumed to be a middleman for Sofia herself."

"Yes," she said, and was about to follow up with a preemptive comment for him to get to the point. But even her single-word response went unheard—Soren was already launching into his second wave.

"We ran a full network analysis of the cell phone number in question and found outgoing calls, via international access number, to a heretofore unknown satellite phone number. Being as this was the only non-cellular number in the call history, we zeroed in on it and went through the historical data from our SIGINT birds collecting on the Gulf Clan along with monitoring FARC dissident activity to ensure short-term stability for the peace deal. Now only a few of those birds have the phased arrays to decipher a precise location from a satphone signal. There weren't many hits as the aircraft had to be relatively close to pick up on a signal in the first place, but we took what we had and conducted decryption and analysis to distinguish individual users—"

"Soren," she cut him off, using his last name for emphasis, "pretend you had thirty seconds and *only* thirty seconds to tell us *the most key* takeaways from all the data piling up in your brain right now.

He blinked. "Yes, ma'am."

"Now pretend that thirty-second clock started ticking down five seconds ago, and tell us what would be pertinent for the collective OPCEN. Go."

He whittled another three full seconds off his imaginary countdown with a blank stare, then composed himself and finally, *finally*, said something that truly mattered.

"There's a new satellite phone number, last four digits 2758, that pinged from a couple significant locations. Four hits from Sofia's jungle camp, spread over a 90-day period of time."

"And the other location?"

"The clandestine shipyard that our ground team raided with AFEUR.

An incoming call was received less than twenty minutes before the assault commenced."

"You're sure it wasn't one of the phones recovered in the post-assault collection?"

"Positive, ma'am."

Sofia had been at that shipyard, Duchess knew at once. So how did she get away?

Rather than voice that conclusion, she asked, "Who made the incoming call?"

"Another unknown satellite phone number ending in 7191. I've cross-referenced it with all available SIGINT data and found zero hits, so wherever that phone resides, it's outside any of our intercept capabilities at present."

Duchess smiled.

"Well I've just done my own cross-referencing between the current operation and global locations where we don't have intercept capability and deduced that the incoming call came from somewhere in Venezuela."

"Possible, ma'am, but we can't definitively say—"

"Thank you, Christopher. Is there anything else?"

"No, ma'am."

Turning her attention back to her operations officer, Duchess continued, "Wes, at the risk of disrupting our nation's unprecedented progress in the War on Drugs, I want you to see what SIGINT and ISR assets you can shift to the Colombian border with Venezuela. The intent is to pick up on any further satphone signals from the 2758 suffix and, if possible, get a correlating description of the dismounted or vehicle element in that location. We find that, we find Sofia and can extrapolate her route among the available options to Michelena, which will give us a rate of movement, and allow us to vector in our ground team to interdict."

"On it, ma'am."

The brevity of the former Marine's response served to restore her sanity at least somewhat, and after checking the clock and taking a deep, centering breath, she issued her conclusion.

"Solid work, everyone. I've got half an hour before my update brief with the seventh floor, at which time I'll make the case for approval on the border crossing as well as an on-order DoD raid while the ship is underway. Given the intelligence, I suspect both will be granted. In the meantime, we're going to keep laying the groundwork to interdict Sofia. Questions?"

There were none, and Duchess sat back down to the sound of keyboards clattering and phone calls being made, both of which were music to her ears. She detested being a chokepoint to mission progress: her staff was capable enough, and all they needed was for her to tell them which way to run. Few things in her job were more satisfying than seeing the OPCEN come to life in the wake of a key decision point.

Her reverie, however, was interrupted by Jo Ann in the seat beside her.

"Looks like everything's working out great, as long as we don't get caught."

Duchess felt the breath hitch in her lungs.

"I'm sure I don't know what you mean."

"Oh, come on," Jo Ann quipped. "That paper is an obvious forgery and you know it. I saw you reviewing the team's handwriting."

Without looking over, Duchess replied, "I'm going to make some tea before my meeting. Would you like anything?"

"Don't worry. Benavidez is alive, our guys aren't that stupid. They've got the tradecraft to break into his home or office. The only question is, will he notice and report it?"

"Coffee, Jo Ann? Maybe a sandwich?"

"Good God, Duchess. I'm no snitch."

"Nothing, then? Very well. I'll be back in a few."

She rose and departed, feeling Jo Ann's gaze burning a hole in her back. No matter, she thought—the woman was surely succumbing to the same heady emotion that was welling up within Duchess herself: the knowledge that barring some unforeseen complication, their team would be heading into Venezuela.

28

Cancer's body jostled on the wooden bench as the shoddy suspension relayed every rock, bump, and divot just as it had for the past six and a half hours since leaving the hardball streets of Medellín. Every breath brought with it the overwhelming stench of diesel fumes, which were, he could only hope, a result of the fuel cans scattered around the back of the flatbed truck rather than a leak.

Under the red glow of a headlamp in the canvas-enclosed cargo area, Felix was explaining, "The can Sofia built was quite nice, but nothing compared to the ones that go beneath the waves. No one can catch those."

Ian countered, "I mean, they get caught, just a lot less. It's like 25 low-profile vessels captured for every one true submarine, because Colombian authorities can only locate them during the construction process. *Sí o no*, Felix?"

Felix grinned widely. "Yes, this is true. Once they make it to sea...they are ghosts."

"And narco technology is growing by leaps and bounds," Ian continued, now gesturing as he explained to David on his opposite side. "They captured the first transatlantic sub off the coast of Spain. Three tons of coke onboard, and it came from Brazil."

Felix giggled.

"Something funny?" Cancer glared at the Colombian. Something about him irritated Cancer to no end—or maybe it was everything about him.

"*Sí*," Felix answered flippantly, "something is very funny. You Americans are so confident in your war on drugs." He looked to Ian and asked mockingly, "The first sub to make it to Europe, you say? We have been running *perico* across the Atlantic for over a decade."

"'We?'" Cancer said skeptically, wincing as the truck hit a hard bump. "You've done that yourself?"

Felix quickly corrected himself. "No. But my teacher, *Capitán* de Zurara, did so many times—they would pay to fly him back to Colombia first class. He had more fake passports than the cartel leaders. But that sub captured off the coast of Spain? It was only caught because of a first-time *capitán* who missed two linkups with the cartel boat, spent twice as long at sea as he intended, and was running out of fuel. For these reasons, he went for the shore. But the plan was to send that can to *el cementerio*, the graveyard, just like everyone else."

Ian asked, "You mean the Azores? Off the coast of Portugal?"

"*Sí*. There they cross-load the cocaine to ships, and scuttle the subs. There are hundreds of cans on the bottom of the Atlantic off those islands. Maybe a thousand or more. And you people celebrate the capture of one. It is like I told Maximo—"

"Easy," David warned him.

"—only a *caremonda* believes he could stop the White Goddess."

"*Caremonda*?" Ian asked.

David began to rise from his seat; Felix, dumbass that he was, remained completely oblivious. And as much as Cancer would love to see his team leader slap the degenerate off the wooden bench, he intervened before things got out of hand.

"Boss," he announced, "we're gonna need him."

This served to halt David in his tracks, though he jabbed an index finger at the sub driver and intoned in a low voice, "Keep his name out of your mouth."

Taking his seat again, David explained to Ian, "*Caremonda* means 'dickhead.'"

With the situation defused—or as defused as it was going to get for the time being, given that David had been taking Maximo's death quite personally—Cancer glanced toward the back of the truck.

Worthy and Reilly were seated there, prepared to react in the event of a checkpoint manned by unruly FARC dissidents who were, at this point, about the only element they were in any danger of running into. The truck was making its way across a remote jungle path, deep into cocaine country, and the final Colombian military checkpoint had slipped by hours before.

Reilly looked back at him and offered a bemused comment. "You've got to appreciate the irony."

"What irony?"

"I mean, we started out this mission as narco assassins. Assassins trying to kill narcos."

"So?"

"So now we're *narco assassins*, get it? Assassins working with narcos."

Unamused by the observation, Cancer glared at him, and Reilly's gaze dropped to the truck bed loaded with their team gear.

Cancer propped his feet up on that gear now, selecting the last rucksack in a row spanning the center of the flatbed. The team was down to what they could carry now, each man's pack filled to the breaking point in preparation for an expeditionary mission. Which was, in lieu of any meaningful information from Vega, about all they could plan for—the trafficker certainly wasn't going to reveal the details of his inroads into Venezuela to them in advance, which left them with the quite practical assumption that if they brought something, they'd have to carry it.

As for the rest of their upcoming cross border effort, all was a mystery.

It was possible they'd be so lucky as to complete a marathon road trip over some mountainous backroad, though far more likely that they'd be dropped off to cross the border on foot before linking up with a convoy on the far side. Or ride some ramshackle boat down one of the rivers stretching into Venezuela. Either way, any team gear that wasn't absolutely necessary had been packed up in their Medellín apartment, ready to be recovered by Agency support personnel and shipped back to Langley in the event the team was wiped out to a man.

Cancer suddenly felt the vehicle accelerate and wheel around in a half-circle, a maneuver that wouldn't be possible on the winding jungle roads they'd been traversing. As the truck groaned to a stop and cut its engine, he slipped past Worthy and Reilly to kneel at the tailgate. Then he pulled back a seam of the buttoned canvas flap a few inches to see outside.

On one hand, he was relieved at the sight. It would mean one hell of a lot less walking.

But that convenience would come at a cost, he could tell, and the cost was the risk of imminent death.

He appraised a linear field carved out of the jungle. It certainly wasn't the most sophisticated airstrip he'd ever seen, but sufficient to accommodate the aircraft parked before him: a silver, twin-engine DC-3 cargo plane, renowned for its ability to use dirt runways, which, he supposed, was appropriate given the current setting. The aircraft itself was a cutting-edge mode of aerial travel—in the 1930s. As for whether it would get them to their destination alive, the most promising detail at present was the fact that theirs wasn't the only truck in the clearing: a trio of similar vehicles lit the area with their headlights, and were in the process of being offloaded by daisy chains of men passing kilos from the flatbeds to the aircraft's rear doors.

Then the canvas flap was ripped from his hand, the button fasteners torn apart from the outside by a hideous Colombian man he recognized as the driver.

"*Fuera de aquí*," the man said gruffly, lowering the creaky tailgate and waving an arm toward the plane.

Worthy and Reilly donned their rucks and were first off the truck, taking up discreet security positions a few paces away.

Felix stopped at the tailgate, took one look at the plane, and asked, "We are going to die, aren't we?"

Cancer nodded. "Eventually, yes. But I'd rather be traveling with coke—Vega values that cargo more than our lives."

"But this is probably an insignificant load for him."

"Well," Cancer hastily added, "you've already tapped out my supply of optimism for the year. Beat it."

Felix clambered down off the tailgate, looking awkward with the massive hiking pack that he was clearly unused to carrying—inside was a hodgepodge of excess team fatigues, field rations, and water filtration equipment. Cancer would've loved to use Felix as a mule for much heavier gear, but alas, the odds of the greasy sub driver getting shot or simply running off into the jungle at the first opportunity were simply too high.

David appeared then, shaking his head at the seemingly endless supply of cocaine being loaded.

"Duchess is going to crucify us if she ever finds out."

"Then we better make sure she never finds out."

The team leader sighed and climbed out, leaving Ian as the last man aboard, surveying the crude airfield with a shrewd look as he said, "Just another day in Colombia."

Once he was gone, Cancer donned his own ruck, then conducted a headlight sweep across the interior to search for any accidentally dropped evidence that the dumbass driver could get caught with on his way back to Medellín. But aside from a few candy bar wrappers carelessly discarded by Felix, the truck was clean, and, draping his legs over the hanging tailgate, Cancer lowered himself to the ground.

Then he strode after his team leader, marveling at the efficiency of the loading operation. These guys were operating under white light, sure, which wasn't the most effective way of remaining unseen from overhead surveillance, but even this detail meant that Vega had cleared the way for this flight, along with however many others he ran on a monthly if not weekly basis. Whether by money or murder, he'd ensured the safety of his cargo.

Provided, of course, this rust bucket of a plane didn't fall from the sky.

Both the Colombians pulling security and those loading the aircraft looked at the team skeptically, and Cancer couldn't blame them—David had clearly had his ass kicked in the not-so-distant past, his split lip only just beginning to heal in addition to an oblong bruise running down his cheekbone. Worthy had a leech bite on his face that looked like a hickey, and he could only imagine the narcos' perception of the remaining three team members who, while uninjured, were probably the furthest thing they expected to see from an elite CIA paramilitary force: an old man, a dumb jock, and a nerd. Cancer, Reilly, and Ian in a nutshell.

David strode toward the operation's obvious figurehead, a tall, solemn-looking man who appeared to be the only one not gainfully occupied with either security or manual labor.

Cancer could tell at once that this was Eberardo Herrera, but he was fortunate to have seen a picture of the former lieutenant colonel in advance. There was no handoff from their driver to the loading detail, no introduction offered—narco hospitality at its finest, Cancer thought. Vega had cleared them to be there, which was the only reason they weren't dead already; as for the rest, it was up to them to earn the trust, however begrudging, of the grizzled old Colombian they now approached.

And once he was within a few feet of the former senior military officer with a 1911 pistol on his hip, Cancer saw that Herrera made Felix look like a wholesome Christian.

Whatever had transpired in the past five years since he'd left the military, it aged this man by a decade or more. He had ruddy cheeks crisscrossed with the spider veins of a full-blown alcoholic, which Cancer didn't need to see to arrive at that particular conclusion; booze was practically emanating from his pores, and while he didn't have a bottle in hand at the moment, one would surely appear soon.

David greeted him in Spanish and then asked, "Where are we headed?"

"To Venezuela."

"Where in Venezuela?"

"An airstrip."

David produced his map and asked, "Can you show me where?"

"We will have time on the plane. Until then, I can take you over the border, or I can answer all your questions and then go home. I have the patience for one, so choose."

Putting his map away, David said, "My men are ready when you are."

"Then get your shit on the plane."

David took the hint and departed, leaving Cancer to wonder what it was about the team leader that caused him to so consistently alienate almost every valuable host nation counterpart they met around the world.

Probably the fact that he was a stubborn, blockheaded asshole, he concluded, which of course Cancer was as well.

But age brought with it the benefit of experience, and while he would ordinarily be supervising the loading of his team and their equipment right now, he remained in place instead, watching Herrera procure a cigarette and, with shaky hands, make three attempts to light it.

Cancer chose that moment to step in with his own lighter, sparking Herrera's cigarette before finding one for himself.

"*Gracias*," the colonel said.

"*De nada, Coronel*," Cancer replied affably, using the Spanish term for the man's former rank. There was no rapport in the world quite like that between fellow smokers, he'd learned long ago, who were a dying breed both literally and figuratively.

Grunting with disdain, Herrera gestured to David. "That kid. I do not like him."

Cancer blew a cloud of smoke into the muggy night air.

"Don't complain to me, sir. I've been putting up with that *hijueputa* for years now."

Herrera bellowed a laugh in response, the chortle transitioning to a phlegmy cough that he attempted to clear by banging a fist against his sternum.

Jesus, Cancer thought, was that what he'd be like at this man's age? It wasn't terribly far away—but before he could dwell on the prospect, the colonel recovered with alarming speed.

"What is your name, soldier?"

"Cancer, sir."

"Ha!" He waved his cigarette. "How appropriate. You should be the one running your team, not that little *pirobo*."

With a lopsided grin, Cancer replied, "I hear that all the time, sir."

"All right," Herrera growled, seeing that the trickle of kilos onto the bird was nearing its end. "We should get moving. The Land of Lightning awaits."

And while Cancer had no earthly idea what Herrera meant by that comment, he nodded as if he was thinking the same thing, and moved out to board the plane behind his team.

29

The rain hammered in sheets outside, wind buffeting the aircraft as great flashes of lightning lit the windows like anti-aircraft fire.

At first, Ian thought that was exactly what they were; the great blasts of white started out as quickly as machinegun tracers and had since transitioned into one near-continuous pulsating glow of varying intensity.

But for once, Ian wasn't the one most uncomfortable with this arrangement. Felix maintained a white-knuckle grip on his seat, his body rigid with terror. Reilly, Worthy, and even Cancer appeared only slightly less mortified with the prospect of their plane being struck by a bolt of lightning.

That left David, who looked trapped in a nebulous standoff between trying to feign courage and suppressing the urge to puke.

A stomach-lurching descent followed, maybe twenty feet of altitude lost in a split second, before the aircraft resumed some semblance of steady flight.

David groaned.

"Why aren't they flying around the storm?"

"They probably *are* flying around the storm," Ian replied. "The Catatumbo region is the lightning capital of the world. Thought I said that in my intel brief."

"You didn't. I'd remember."

"Oh," Ian said innocently. "Could've sworn I did. Basically, you've got cold air from the Andes hitting the warm air from the Caribbean—"

"I don't give a shit," David cut him off, "about the goddamned weather patterns. Do they know how to fly in this or not?"

"Definitely. Locals call this 'the Never-Ending Storm of Catatumbo.' Lightning 300 days out of the year. And this crew probably runs this route, say, two or three times a month, so statistically we'll be fine."

"You sure about that?"

"I am," Ian said. Then, unable to resist the urge to indulge himself in the wake of Duchess's latest intelligence update, he added, "Keep in mind I was also sure that Sofia would be at the clandestine shipyard, and as the new satphone number indicates, she was."

"Yeah?" David asked. "Then how did we miss her?"

A thunderbolt crashed outside, and Ian let the sound dissipate before replying.

"Between the squirter control and all the troops that combed the jungle from the tributary in both directions? I honestly don't know."

"If I had a dollar for every time you said 'I don't know' every single mission we went on, I could go on a three-day bender with change to spare."

"If fishing were easy," Ian countered, "it'd be called 'catching.' My specialty is intelligence, and regrettably that doesn't come with a crystal ball. Why don't you go ask the colonel, and see if his assessment is more to your liking?"

They both glanced over at Eberardo Herrera, slumped in a seat near the cockpit.

He was staring into the middle distance with a haunted expression, sipping at regular intervals not from a flask but a liter-sized bottle. Its contents were impossible to distinguish at this distance, but it didn't take a master detective to know the man's blood alcohol content was steadily rising. To Ian, that was something of a comfort; a far greater evil at present would be the symptoms of withdrawal for a full-blown alcoholic whose cooperation they desperately needed.

Far more concerning, however, was the fact that he had yet to engage with

Ian's team, despite his proclamation on the airfield that they'd have time to plan during the flight. Instead he'd told the Americans to sit down and shut up, in so many words, and that he'd call them over when he was good and ready. Which, apparently, would not occur until his bottle had been sufficiently depleted.

David said, "When he calls us over, you'll need to do most of the talking. That guy hates me already."

Ian quipped, "So business as usual, then?"

"I hold my own with the locals."

No sooner had he said this than Herrera capped his bottle, slid it into a pocket of his field jacket, and waved them over.

Ian hastily rose, a gust of turbulence nearly sending him ass over teakettle before he steadied himself with an outstretched arm against the side of the cabin. Then he proceeded along with David, feeling more like he was surfing the plane's floor than walking across it until he took a seat next to Herrera.

"Good evening, *Coronel*," Ian began, speaking over the storm. "Thank you for escorting us across the border."

"What choice do I have?" Herrera grumbled. "Now tell me about the target."

"Sofia Lozano, sir, more commonly known as Sawed-Off—"

"I know about Sofia. What I mean is, who is with her? How many fighters? Are they on foot, or in a convoy?"

Valid questions all, Ian thought. He provided the unenviable answer in three words.

"We don't know."

"You do not know? How is it possible you intend to attack a force of unknown size?"

Clearing his throat, Ian clarified, "We know she'll be reaching Michelena tomorrow, and that she's considering three possible routes to get there. We should have an update on which one she's taking soon."

"And you will determine this how, exactly?"

David intervened, "Our people will tell us."

"Your people," Herrera grunted. "Fantastic. Wonderful. They had better be correct, because every mile we travel brings ELN, EPL, ex-FARC, and

Venezuelan military fighting for control of the coca fields and smuggling routes."

Ian nodded. "We're aware of the power vacuum after the FARC peace process, sir, and intend to move only when we have fidelity on Sofia's location."

He quickly pulled out his map and spread it open to expose the topographical depiction of the border region to their headlamps amid the flickering glow of lightning through the windows.

Using the tip of a pen to point to Michelena, he continued, "She'll be arriving here at or before noon tomorrow. And these"—he traced a trio of road combinations—"are the most likely paths she'll use to get there. Can you show me where we're landing?"

"Here," Herrera said, mashing a sausage-like finger on the map. His fingertip covered a square-kilometer swath of terrain west of Lake Maracaibo.

David asked, "And we'll have transportation on arrival?"

"Trucks, yes."

"How many men will come with us?"

"We will gain seven when we land. Plus a machinegun, and my top fighters."

Herrera gestured to the rear of the plane, where five narcos sat in a row beside ratchet straps securing enormous wooden crates, all of them filled with cocaine.

One of these narcos was tall and lanky, with a pencil mustache as his second most noticeable feature. Far more distinguishing at present was the fact that he was awake, a state which was, incredibly, not shared by the four men beside him. The sight of that was nothing short of impossible absent a serious narcotic intervention, which, given their location, was entirely possible.

After exchanging a worried glance with David, Ian continued, "Very good, sir. Now once we determine Sofia's route, we'd like to set up an ambush to intercept her."

"I should hope so," Herrera said gruffly. "You have no idea how many people she has. The only thing you possess is the element of surprise, so you had better keep it. Did you bring money?"

"Yes, *Coronel.*"

This was a delicate topic. As a matter of standard practice, it would be ludicrous to disclose the full extent of their Agency finances. To do so would be to provide a dollar sign over their heads, tilting Herrera's odds of betraying them from an inconceivable prospect given Vega's wrath, to a potentially feasible option with a very tangible risk-to-reward ratio.

"Ten thousand US," David said before Ian could reply, "for bribes and expenses."

The true figure, of course, was much higher, and Ian fully expected Herrera to continue probing to determine what it was.

But this seemed to satisfy the colonel, who nodded with approval. "This will take us far. The people of Venezuela are starving. The president has put the military in charge of all food shipments so they stay fed and do not rebel against him. But they do not receive much pay, if they get paid at all. The military can be bought, for a price."

His last sentence was rendered inaudible amid another crash of thunder, which preceded the entire plane shaking as if it were going to disintegrate midair. Ian kept his gaze locked on Herrera, whose reaction was considerably more casual.

He slipped the bottle out of his jacket, screwed off the top, and took another swig before presenting the bottle to Ian, who shook his head. Herrera put the liquor away, notably not offering any to David, who would have been all too likely to accept.

"*Coronel,*" Ian asked, "what about the other groups? FARC dissidents, EPL, ELN—can we pay them as well?"

"They can be paid, and they must," Herrera said with a jagged grin. "In bullets. If we encounter them, it is kill or be killed."

30

I proceeded down the stairs of the DC-3, exiting the cabin into the pouring rain.

My first view of Venezuela was little different from the airfield we'd departed: a primitive landing strip lit by vehicle headlights; three cargo trucks, presumably for the cocaine; and four Kia Sportage SUVs that appeared to be dedicated to my team and our accompanying narco mercenaries.

I set foot on the muddy ground, clearing the stairway for the unloading detail that was already lined up to begin shuttling kilos to the trucks. As with the men who'd loaded the plane in Colombia, this work detail looked dirt poor—their clothes were tattered rags, footwear nothing more than rainboots caked in innumerable layers of muck. Trying to reconcile this with the sheer excess I'd witnessed in the Medellín nightclub was mind-boggling, and yet the two scenes were merely opposite ends of the spectrum within a single industry.

Seeking some overhead cover amid the remote surroundings, I found that the closest I'd get was a decrepit shack at the edge of the field. More of a partial roof covered in a sheet of black plastic, really, with the walls having long since succumbed to decay, but sufficient for keeping me out of the rain. Only when I'd advanced halfway toward it did I realize the questionable judgment of departing the main element with zero security, and, glancing back, I saw Worthy following me through the rain without being told or even warned as to my intentions.

The very sight of him was reassuring. A former bodyguard, he was so switched on when it came to not letting me get killed that I'd probably have to try extremely hard to do so. Then again, I shouldn't have put him in the position of having to improvise to cover me, but I'd worry about that later.

I unslung my rucksack and deposited it in the center of the shack, the driest ground I'd find for the time being, then unfolded my laminated map atop it before checking my GPS. Herrera's crude finger point had been at least somewhat accurate; we were fifteen miles from the nearest highway and with it the town of Encontrados, my first official confirmation that we'd entered Venezuela.

Preparing my waterproof notepad and pen, I transmitted to Duchess.

"Raptor Nine One, this is Suicide Actual, radio check."

"*Good copy*," Duchess replied, far too quickly for comfort. "*I've been trying to reach you.*"

Retrieving my notepad, I replied, "We've been having some comms issues."

The actual reason was far less acceptable for our Agency handler: since we couldn't simply admit boarding a narco plane and being whisked into Venezuela atop a mountain of cocaine, I'd simply told her we were making our way to the border by vehicle at the behest of our mercenary partner force, who, as far as she knew, was being paid for the privilege.

With the CIA's assets tied up in the search for Sofia and our blue force trackers disabled due to suspicion of enemy SIGINT capabilities—a clever "assessment" that was standard practice for us—I felt confident that she wouldn't be able to trace the locations of my transmission.

Or at least, I hoped not.

I hastily scrawled on my notepad as Duchess began, "*We've had two pings—Sofia is on the move toward Venezuela. Last hit was correlated with visual on a convoy with description as follows: one white Suzuki Grand Vitara SUV, one black Toyota Prado SUV, and one silver Ford F-350 with a covered bed. All have scratch marks on the roof consistent with machinegun bipods, so we assess this is solid.*"

"Stand by," I replied, then told Worthy, "Get the guys over here with Herrera. We've got a lead on Sofia."

He relayed the instruction over the team frequency and I replied to Duchess, "What's her last known location?"

"Just north of Bogota, moving on Route 55. So she'll be approaching Michelena from the south, arriving as early as 10 a.m. tomorrow."

Holy shit, I thought, even with the benefit of Vega's plane we were scarcely thirteen hours ahead of Sofia, a lead that could easily evaporate given the slightest obstacle. I felt my neck burning when Duchess ordered, "*Send your current location.*"

"Give me a minute," I said, flipping to the back pages of my notepad. "Let me find a GPS signal."

Instead I consumed the rows of handwritten data calculated in advance: select GPS coordinates on both sides of the border, each correlated with a road and written beside a four-digit number that represented the no-earlier-than time we could have feasibly arrived there by vehicle.

They were marked on my map as numbered points across all three potential routes, and after checking my watch I selected the most appropriate location.

Then I transmitted the phantom grid as the remaining members of my team and Herrera arrived under the meager roof.

"We had to divert to Route 70 due to a mercenary tip about ELN presence on our primary road, but since then we've been making good progress."

"*Copy,*" Duchess acknowledged, "*how are Herrera and his merc force working out?*"

I glanced up at the husk of a man standing beside me, watching him polish off the final remains of the bottle before chucking it into the rain.

"He's all business," I replied. "We definitely found the right people."

"*I'm glad to hear that. Keep us posted on your plan of attack. I'll reach out as soon as we have another satphone ping.*"

"Wilco. Suicide Actual, out."

I summoned the men beside me with a wave, and they knelt in a semicircle as I used the map to narrate our findings.

"She's moving along Route 55, so she'll be approaching Michelena from the south and arriving as early as ten in the morning. Two SUVs and a pickup."

I scanned where that trajectory would take her relative to our current location. We'd already scrutinized potential ambush positions along her possible routes, the most feasible located at an appetizing turn on a paved road called *Troncal 1* a half hour south of Michelena.

Shifting the tip of my pen to the 90-degree bend, I said, "I think we should stage here. Set up an L-shaped ambush and wait for her approach. We push an observer element to the south, and once they identify her convoy approaching we can block the road with a vehicle. Then we hit her."

Herrera considered my assessment, looking from the map to his watch. Then, for the first time since I'd met him, he addressed me with something other than contempt in his voice.

"I know this area. We can be there by daybreak."

31

Reilly focused on the view out his window, trying to drown out the incessant monologue that had been going on for nearly as long as the drive had.

With the bulk of Herrera's fighters packed into the lead truck with Worthy and the trail vehicle with Cancer, the rest of the team had been relegated to the middle two trucks in the convoy. And since David insisted he and Ian accompany Herrera in the second vehicle, that left Reilly sitting in the back of the third Kia Sportage with mercenaries in the driver and passenger seats. Beside him was the only remaining member of the team, if you could call him a member at all—Felix, who started talking thirty seconds into the drive and hadn't stopped since.

"It was the time of my life," Felix was saying, responding with vigor to the driver's chuckles. "I would return to Buenaventura and party for three days straight. Sleep for two days, then drive to Cali for the real fun—"

Reilly sighed, resuming his focus on the view outside. In the jungles of Colombia, it had been hard to appreciate the scenery while slogging through it under a rucksack.

But driving south across the Venezuelan countryside, Reilly found himself struck by the staggering, awe-inspiring beauty of his surroundings. To his left, the rising sun lit an endless blanket of clouds hovering over vibrant green fields, rolling forest, and farmland, all backstopped by the unmistakable profile of the Venezuelan Andes. There was nothing to suggest the jaw-dropping poverty that this entire nation had sunk into long ago; instead, the panoramic vista was the stuff of tourist brochures and travel magazines.

"...and then," Felix continued, "when we said we had enough, that we had spent all our money, the girls would bring their friends. That was all it took—"

"Felix," Reilly snapped, "can you go ten seconds without running your mouth? Just ten seconds, that's all I ask."

"Relax, *mi amigo*. We are just talking."

"No, *you* are just talking. I don't think anyone else has gotten a word in edgewise since we left the airfield."

Felix snorted. "Can you blame me? Remember, I have been rotting away in prison—"

"I know," Reilly interrupted, "hard to miss the sweet jailhouse ink."

The sub driver looked confused, then glanced down to his arms, partially covered by the rolled sleeves of his fatigue top. What wasn't covered by the shirt, or the gold Rolex that he wore like a dumbass absolutely begging to be robbed, was filled by crude tattoos.

"These?" he asked, pushing his sleeves up further to expose the art. "These are not from prison. They are from my first trip in the Pacific..."

Reilly groaned to himself, looking back out the window. Only Felix could take a mild insult as an excuse to launch into another long-winded story, and the medic was relieved when he heard a transmission from Worthy—a reprieve, however brief, from the incessant ramblings of the Colombian beside him.

"*Suicide, we'll come up on the ridgeline shortly. Ten minutes or less before my drop-off.*"

"*Got it,*" David replied, "*just let me know when you need to stop.*"

Felix hadn't broken stride, continuing to talk without any apparent need to collect his thoughts, or even breathe.

"...I was just a boy. *Capitán* de Zurara knew my father and gave me a job, but he warned me that this was the season of the sea monsters, and we could well die on the journey. I thought he was joking, of course. But in

Buenaventura, I was lucky to make two hundred a year in fishing. Every year the catch was less and less, and I was saving to get married..."

Reilly saw the beginnings of the ridgeline to his left, his vista views ending with the rise of a sharply sloping hillside that closed in on the highway. All he could see now were crumbling rocks overgrown with vines, stretching upward to the jungle.

And all he could hear, as per usual, was Felix.

"We set off in the can, the only light through the captain's windows. At night, nothing. And then we could hear noises outside—squealing, groaning, like a rusty door being pulled open. Only much, much louder. *Capitán* de Zurara said this was a sea monster, and being young and stupid, I now believed him. It was terrifying. I began praying and *Capitán* de Zurara laughed at me, but no one laughed when the creature bumped us."

Reilly looked over and asked, "Bumped you?"

"It felt like thunder," Felix continued. "The entire can shook—it was not a hard strike, just a tap for something that large. But when your survival rests on a few pieces of fiberglass held together by wood, *mi amigo*, it feels like the hand of God."

He took a rare pause, blinking quickly before he resumed.

"The next morning, we opened the hatch. As the youngest man aboard, it was my job to empty our waste buckets into the ocean. I climbed up to see the sunrise, the most beautiful sunrise I have ever seen, and there, not one *cuadra* off our starboard side, I saw the creature."

"Kraken," Reilly said knowingly.

"What? No."

Felix held out his left forearm for the medic to examine, exposing the tattoo of a whale.

"One of these, a whale longer than two of the largest fishing boats I had ever seen. I was frozen, and before I could think, she shot a spray of water that made a rainbow in the sky."

The merc in the passenger seat half-turned and asked, "She?"

"*Sí*, because her baby was beside her. A calf the size of a city bus. But not just this; looking around I saw a dozen more, surrounding the can. I cried out to my crew, and of course *Capitán* de Zurara laughed as I had never heard him. Then he explained these were humpback whales, migrating north to the winter breeding grounds. I crossed myself, said a prayer, and vowed never to be afraid at sea again."

"And then?" the passenger asked, enraptured by the story.

"After two weeks, we reached the shores of Mexico. I returned home with twenty thousand and got these tattoos. As a reminder not to be afraid, because after seeing what I saw that day, if the sea wanted me, she could take me. Then I got married, bought a house for my new wife. One month later I was back at sea with *Capitán* de Zurara, and only then did he begin to teach me."

Reilly frowned at Felix's mention of a wife. Because whatever celestial realm Isabella had descended from to grace the earth with her presence, she was most certainly not a resident of whatever fishing town had given rise to Felix, the amoral junkie with an endless supply of self-serving tales to dish out when provided the slightest chance.

But his heart sank when Worthy transmitted from the lead truck, "*We've got refugees coming up on the right.*"

"I've got my aid bag ready," Reilly replied.

David came over the net then.

"*I already asked—Herrera won't let us stop.*"

Fucking savages, Reilly thought as he ripped open the rucksack between his legs and reached inside. He was momentarily distracted when the two narcos up front began shouting and making sharp whistles, though it took Reilly long moments of watching the file of refugees shuffling along the side of the road to realize why.

Nothing about the lead members of the procession was worth jeering about—men carrying sacks loaded with all their worldly possessions, moving hands to their mouths in rapid gestures to pantomime the motion of eating. They were begging for food.

The children behind them waved and smiled as if the vehicles were a town parade, gleeful despite the utter despair of their circumstances.

Behind them were the final members, who, he saw at a glance, explained the reaction of the two mercenaries in the vehicle—teenage and adult women making lewd gestures at the vehicles as they passed, soliciting male attention with a vigor that would make an Amsterdam prostitute blush.

Reilly rolled down his window after retrieving two field rations from his ruck, hurled them out, and turned to see the refugees descending on the tumbling packages before they slipped out of sight. That pair of meals totaled 2,500 calories, probably more than this group of families had collectively eaten in the past week.

"Wow," Felix said, laughing, "you were not kidding about the women here."

Reilly turned and slugged him in the arm, delivering as powerful a blow as the tight confines of the vehicle would allow.

"They're trying to sell sex for money to feed their kids, asshole."

Felix recoiled in pain, clutching at his bicep as he gasped, "*Maricón*! You were the one who told me—"

"About the Venezuelan women?" Reilly cut him off.

"*Sí.*"

"I told you whatever I had to," Reilly replied, huffing a breath of the muggy air pouring inside the cab before rolling up his window, "to get you to come with us."

Worthy's voice came over his earpiece.

"*Suicide, we're stopping here—got a clean route.*"

David replied, "*Happy hunting. I'll let you know when we reach the side road.*"

The vehicles came to a stop, though only for a few seconds. And as the convoy lurched forward once more, Reilly scanned out his window to see that Worthy's description of a "clean route" was relative in the extreme.

All he saw was a series of perilous rock ledges rising upward into a jungled slope, nothing he'd want to even consider climbing. Sure enough, however, he caught sight of Worthy and the gangly merc with the pencil mustache, both encumbered by rucksacks as they darted to the base of the hill and began their climb.

32

Cancer exited the trail vehicle with his Galil in hand, stepping onto the muddy side road amid the oppressive humidity.

Herrera's men left the trucks with equal urgency, though not with the same motivations—they quickly lit cigarettes and gathered in a group to bullshit until they received further guidance. No attempt to pull security, no noise discipline. A bad sign of things to come, if he couldn't get them under control.

He turned and began walking back the way they'd come, approaching the outlet onto the strip of pavement where their mission against Sofia would reach its conclusion, whether in victory or defeat.

The main road was largely free of traffic on their drive; despite Venezuela's vast oil reserves and gas that frequently sold for under twenty cents a gallon, the staggering ineptitude and corruption of its government had ensured whoever hadn't already fled to a neighboring country had little reason to drive. The country's loss was the team's gain, however. With four to six hours before Sofia's convoy passed, the fewer people who drove by their location, the better.

That being said, they'd still have to remain hidden, and the muddy side road appeared to serve that end well. The vehicles were already tucked out of sight behind the bend that he rounded now, walking uphill toward the main road.

He appraised the high ground to his left, steep and thickly jungled, bad for a protracted foot movement but ideal for setting an ambush and lying in wait. There'd be line-of-sight issues, to be sure, but they had plenty of time to selectively hack branches and vegetation to remedy that.

David caught up to him and asked, "What do you think about right-side security?"

It was a valid question. With Worthy and his counterpart posted to the south, they had left-side security covered. Ideally they'd mirror that position to the north, providing any advance notice of possible hostiles, but that would have left them short two men they'd desperately need for the main ambush.

This was the story of his team's existence, Cancer thought—never enough men, resources, or authorities to do the job properly. In the CIA's current foray into formal targeted killing outside of drones and elite military units, the strategy seemed to be dumping five guys with questionable mercenary backgrounds into a foreign country with limited intel, a local contact or two, and telling them to figure it the fuck out.

And given the results thus far, the Agency probably thought the strategy to be at least moderately effective; what they could never know, of course, was that the moderate string of successes was due in large part to what he could optimistically frame as his team's moral flexibility in getting the job done. Operating in such a gray area required a penchant for bending, breaking, or simply ignoring the rules, and in that, his team's unofficial motto of "fast and loose" was often exactly what the job called for. Good luck trying to achieve that with a team of card-carrying Boy Scouts. It'd be a disaster, though none of them could ever say as much on the official record.

Coming to a stop a few meters from the paved road, Cancer responded, "Boss, I don't think we've got the manpower to commit two more shooters, and even if we did, we'd have to put an American on it just to know these clowns don't fall asleep on us. But it's your call."

"I was thinking the same thing," David said. "And Herrera is going to feel better with you running the ambush. Set it up however you need."

Cancer turned to see the former lieutenant colonel approaching, trailed in short order by Reilly and Ian.

Facing David, he said, "I'll take care of it, boss. We stick with Racegun on left-side security, and don't worry about Herrera—you'll probably knock it out of the park with our next foreign contact."

"If there is a next one," David said sullenly. "To hear Duchess tell it, there's a lot of pressure to shut down Project Longwing. This could be our last mission."

"Then we better make it count."

Herrera came to a stop and immediately asked, "Cancer, what do you think?"

David was right—Herrera hadn't even bothered consulting the actual team leader, instead going straight for the American shooter whose age and general level of cynicism most closely reflected his own.

And truth be told, what Cancer thought was that he had a slam dunk on his hands. Even if the terrain were fifty percent less cooperative, they could still pull this off.

Then again, he'd been planning objectives and actioning them for his entire adult life, so experience was probably more important than their surroundings. By now Cancer could look at the lay of the land and determine at a glance the ideal fighting positions, how the enemy would react, and what could go wrong. Ambushes, assaults, urban combat, reconnaissance, long-range sniping—at this point in his career, all were as natural to him as breathing.

Returning home, trying to blend in with a population of sheep glued to their phones and possessing a need for instant gratification at all times, was another story altogether. *That* was the hard part of his existence, and he was grateful to be free of the burden now.

"*Coronel*," he began, eyeing their surroundings, "I think this location is perfect. Main road has a steep uphill throughout the turn, so by the time they see our roadblock vehicle it'll be too late for them to build up enough speed to ram it." He raised an index finger toward the high ground to their left. "Ambush line is too elevated for them to dismount and assault through. If they're smart, they'll go bumper-to-bumper and try to push through the roadblock, but that's going to cost them time in the kill zone.

Or they try to reverse out, but by then our machinegun will have taken out their trail vehicle. No matter what, they're about to have a really bad day."

He pivoted on his heels and pointed toward the trucks.

"I recommend we empty the roadblock vehicle of all fuel and supplies, then put your most reliable man behind the wheel. Once I give the call for him to move, he drives into the highway, pulls the emergency brake, and takes the keys with him, then hauls ass back onto the side road. He's dead if he doesn't."

Herrera cracked a grin. "Fabian is crazy. He will be happy to do this."

"Ambush kicks off on my mark. I'll remove my suppressor and initiate with audible gunfire."

"What about the machinegun?"

"Because it's an open bolt weapon, sir, the odds of a malfunction on the first round are higher. But once I kick off the ambush, Doc is the belle of the ball."

Cancer swung his gaze to Reilly. "I want you to find a machinegun position that gives you visibility down the long axis of the kill zone. Priority of fire is engine blocks from rear to front, and once you've booked all three trucks as mobility kills, I want you to dump all remaining ammo into the cabs."

Reilly gave a curt nod. "Easy day."

"I'll position the ambush line off of the machinegun and assign their sectors. Following initiation, their priorities of fire are runners, dismounting personnel, and vehicle cabs in that order."

Eyeing the high ground before letting his gaze drift toward the road, Cancer went on, "We blaze for the full 'mad minute' or until I call a cease-fire. Any movement or noise on the objective, and we repeat the process as many times as necessary. Then I'll order the assault. Ambush line hauls ass downhill, clears across the objective, slays any survivors, and confirms Sofia's dead. I'll establish 360 security and recall our OP, then post at the south to ensure there's no friendly fire once Racegun and Mr. Mustachio make their way back. The rest of our team transitions to site exploitation with Angel leading the charge. Once he says we're good on intel collection, everyone loads up on the trucks and we return to the airfield. *Coronel*, am I missing anything?"

"The head," Herrera replied, crossing his arms. "We need to bring back her head."

"Right. Angel will take care of that." He turned to the intelligence operative. "Got your knife ready?"

Ian's eyes narrowed in contempt.

"Thought I was supposed to be 'leading the charge' on intel collection."

"How long could a simple decapitation take? It's not like you're performing major surgery."

"This is bullshit, and you know it—"

"Fuck," Herrera snarled, "you are all children. I will cut off her head. It would not be the first time."

A sobering silence fell over the group as Cancer considered whether the man was joking—and after a second he concluded that no, he wasn't.

"Great," Cancer said. "Thank you, *Coronel*. Now aside from our roadblock driver, we'll need a small element to stay with the vehicles and provide ground-level fire once the convoy is stopped."

Herrera nodded. "I will remain here."

"So will I," David added.

As ground force commander, it was David's prerogative to position himself wherever he damn well pleased, and in partner force operations that would doctrinally mean staying alongside his direct counterpart. But David didn't have the best rapport with the colonel, and Cancer doubted the efficacy of combining the two in an unsupervised setting.

But they'd need at least one American to make sure the trucks didn't disappear, and if David thought he was up to the task, then so be it. Who knows, Cancer thought, maybe he and the hard-drinking Colombian would bond before the ambush kicked off.

Turning to Herrera, he said, "*Coronel*, with your permission I'll start emplacing the men."

33

Worthy knew the storm was coming.

It wasn't just a matter of the barometric pressure dropping. More notably, the amount of visible sunlight filtering through the treetops had been reducing as steadily as if Mother Nature had her finger on a dimmer switch, the effect of dark, rain-swollen clouds choking out the sun. Any minute now, he thought, it was going to start pouring.

And while Worthy didn't enjoy being soaked and miserable any more than the next guy, his real concern was visibility. He'd scouted this ridgeline extensively before committing to his current position atop a moss-covered slab of boulder, from which the ground dropped precipitously to reveal an eight-meter stretch of *Troncal 1* through the trees.

All he had to do now was watch and report any northbound traffic, though his ability to do so might soon be impeded by a veil of rain.

Beside him, Nikolai gave a remorseful sigh and said, "We are going to get pissed on."

Yes, Worthy thought, we most certainly are.

But he voiced no such pessimism to the Colombian fighter, commenting instead, "As long as we can see the road, it won't matter much. Sofia's convoy should be passing in the next hour or so, and we'll be back at the airfield before you know it."

"I hope so," Nikolai replied. "I hate coming to Venezuela. The countryside looks the same, yes. But there is evil in the air. You can feel it, *sí o no*?"

"*Sí*," Worthy admitted, glancing at the gunslinging narco and wondering how, shitty mustache or no shitty mustache, anyone so intelligent could end up in this particular line of work. Not that he was in any position to judge at present, but still—from being the only one of Herrera's men to remain fully alert on the DC-3 flight to his keen observations over the past few hours, Nikolai had proven to be a suitable counterpart to provide the only advance notice of Sofia's approach.

The high-pitched whine of an engine cut through the birdcalls, and Worthy quickly transmitted, "Incoming, stand by."

He heard two squawks of static in response, then caught sight of the intruder—a red motorbike zipping across the road.

Worthy relaxed and keyed his radio again. "Motorbike, single male, no visible weapons."

"*Copy*," David replied, the disappointment palpable in his voice. "*Hopefully we can make it out of here before the rain.*"

Good luck with that, Worthy thought. They had better odds of getting struck by lightning in the coming storm than they did of killing Sofia before the torrential downpour.

Finally he asked Nikolai, "So how'd you end up in this job?"

The man laughed. "How did *you* end up in this job, *señor*?"

Worthy wasn't about to provide anyone on this mercenary force with any traceable biographical details. But Nikolai throwing the question back at him was certainly fair play, so Worthy simply glossed over the details of his background as a competitive shooter but otherwise answered honestly.

"I've always loved guns, loved shooting. Eventually I got pretty damned good at it and once that happened, people noticed. Job offers started coming in, and that was a big deal because I grew up poor."

He regretted that last admission the moment he'd said it—what was considered poor in Moultrie, Georgia, was a scandalously good existence for much of Colombia, and the pinnacle of wealth in Venezuela given the current crisis. He hastily added, "I took the biggest paycheck I could get. The rest is history. May not have been the right thing to do, but that's what I did."

Nikolai considered this and remarked, "What else *could* you do? A man must feed his family, no?"

Worthy didn't reply, instead letting the words hang in the air between them as he kept his gaze on the road. The truth was, providing for a family hadn't entered into the equation; he didn't have a wife, or kids, and his parents didn't need any help from him. Instead he wanted to get the hell out of Moultrie and know what it was like to have real money. His decision had been driven by greed, pure and simple, as had his lengthy participation in the mercenary realm. Only later did he grow up, develop a conscience instead of blindly following orders. About the only good thing to come from the experience was meeting the men he served with now, and if he was truthful with himself, his service as a CIA contractor was more penance than profession.

Seeming to sense his uneasiness, Nikolai said without prompting, "I, too, grew up poor. My family is from a small village in Guaviare. When I was a boy, the American planes started flying over and spraying poison."

"Over your coca fields?"

"Coca, yes. Also our rice, cassava, beans, corn...there are no roads, no bridges unless the people build them, so we have no way to sell those crops. They were to feed ourselves, to survive, and once those plants died, our village was as good as dead. Many of the old people got cancer, and also the babies—the babies were born fucked up in ways I cannot begin to tell you."

"Jesus," Worthy muttered. "What the hell did they spray?"

"I told you: poison. The village could not survive. Our people fled, mostly east, to find work at other coca farms. But this was not good enough for *mi papa*, no. He moved us into Bogotá, with our uncle. We had nothing. I could have found work as a janitor and watched my family go hungry. But the traffickers offered much more. So just like you, I followed the money. And here we are."

"Here we are," Worthy agreed.

"But we should not feel ashamed. In this life, you do what you must to survive, no?"

Worthy barely heard the question. The sound of an approaching vehicle caused him to transmit, "Incoming, stand by."

He felt his heart thudding with anticipation as he awaited the first visual contact, silently willing it to be Sofia's convoy.

But the vehicle that slipped northward on the paved road was clearly not transporting Sofia, nor were the ones that followed it.

Keying his radio, Worthy said, "Suicide, we've got a problem."

My pulse was skyrocketing by the time Worthy finished his transmission.

"*Venezuelan Army convoy, three unarmored Tiunas with turrets—two medium machineguns, one heavy.*"

Shit, I thought, this was a bad development. Tiunas were a beefed-up Latin American knockoff of the US Humvee, and while I was glad they weren't armored, it didn't change the fact that three of them could mean twenty or more troops.

Our own vehicles were hidden around a bend from the main road, all positioned to exfil east along the dirt path save the last one, its front bumper facing me in anticipation of Fabian speeding it into position as a roadblock. But our concealment wouldn't do us much good if the Venezuelan convoy turned down this side road and found us.

I glanced at our meager defenses. Herrera stood beside me, along with an unarmed Felix and a scant two-man protective detail. One of those latter two mercenaries was Fabian, a sketchy-looking teenager with a ponytail who would serve as our dedicated roadblock driver.

But when I relayed Worthy's report, as well as my take on it, Herrera simply responded, "If they come this way, we must bribe. As I told you in the plane, the military is fed but has no money. We pay them, they go. It is as simple as that."

My apprehension grew when Cancer transmitted, "*I've got eyes-on. They're driving slow, gunners scanning the high ground. I don't like it.*"

As absurd as it seemed in that moment, Cancer's distress was the most concerning thing out of the entire situation. The man had an ability to foretell gunplay with an accuracy that bordered on the telepathic—I'd seen him go from calm to red-alert status without provocation in Nigeria, and minutes later we found ourselves racing to stop a massacre-in-progress.

Herrera remained ambivalent in the wake of this revelation, stating curtly, "Of course they are looking for an ambush. They are fighting the EPL, ex-FARC—be grateful we only have to deal with the army."

I immediately felt a wave of suspicion that Herrera had sold us out to the Venezuelans, but before I could consider the prospect, Cancer spoke again.

"*They've passed the side road, and I can hear vehicles stopping. Stand by.*" A moment later, "*Looks like two, wait, three dismounts heading your way with small arms. I've lost visual on the convoy.*"

"Three men coming toward us," I told Herrera.

"*Mierda*. They must have seen our ambush line. I will talk to them...do not worry."

He whispered an order to his men, who spread out on both sides of the path with their weapons ready.

I transmitted, "Cancer, any chance they spotted you?"

"*No way*," he replied without a trace of self-doubt. "*I camouflaged all the fighting positions myself, and we hunkered down as soon as Racegun gave the word.*"

I could hear the Venezuelans approaching now, footsteps squishing in mud and quiet murmurs of conversation. Any second now they'd smell the lingering cigarette smoke if they hadn't already, which didn't much matter; there was no place to hide ourselves, much less the four trucks behind us, and all we could do now was wait and see how the situation played out.

The three uniformed Venezuelan Army troops who rounded the corner carried their weapons with barrels down—two Kalashnikov AK-103s and an FN FAL. They clearly weren't looking for a fight, not yet at least, and came to a stop once they were within sight of our element. All were mildly overweight by American standards, but that made them morbidly obese compared to the refugees we'd spotted on our way in.

The central man was the heaviest of the trio, clearly in charge as he made a proclamation in Spanish until, his gaze falling upon me as the lone Caucasian, he promptly switched languages.

"Did you think we would not see your men in the hills?"

Herrera replied, "I do not have any men in the hills."

"Do *not*," the man shouted, then lowered his voice as he continued slowly, "lie to me. You want to stay here, stay. But you will pay for the privilege."

"I work with *Teniente Coronel* Mendoza. Is he with you?"

"He is not. Two thousand for us to go. Or," he continued suggestively, "I will call upon my men to convince you, and we take everything—"

Herrera barked a laugh, an eerie sound, before holding up a hand as if this was all one hilarious misunderstanding.

"*Relájate, relájate, Sargento. No hay problema. Un minuto, por favor.*"

He ordered his men to remain where they stood, casually waving at me to follow him as we moved down the row of parked trucks together. That was a subtle escalation that only Herrera and I would've spotted—I had five separate thousand-dollar stacks tucked away in various pockets for exactly this purpose, and he knew as much. By calling me away from the standoff, he was merely seeking privacy.

As soon as we'd cleared the bend and passed out of earshot, he stopped and whispered, "We are fucked."

"Meaning?"

"Commanders always collect bribes, because they cannot trust their men. That *bastardo gordo* is a technical sergeant. He is probing our defenses, trying to determine our positions. Believe me, he will return to his convoy and send them straight to us. Then they will kill us all."

While I didn't require much convincing on the heels of Cancer's gut feeling, my suspicion of Herrera's complicity evaporated. At least he knew he'd been wrong, and said as much.

I transmitted, "It's an attack. Cancer, reposition the ambush line to cover the outlet to the side road. Doc, you turn the first Venezuelan vehicle you see into a mobility kill, then hold off the rest until our shooters can establish a defensive perimeter around our trucks. Racegun, get your ass back here five minutes ago. Sprint, motherfucker."

Then, as they confirmed receipt of my message, I recovered two of the thousand-dollar bribe rations from my pockets and combined them into a single wad with a rubber band. To Herrera, I said, "I'm going to take out those three Venezuelans quietly, and buy us as much time as I can. Your men need to hold their fire, you understand?"

I was making reference to the obvious fact that I was the lone shooter on the side road with a suppressed weapon, but Herrera dismissed the notion entirely.

"You cannot kill all three before they get a shot off."

"Yeah?" I asked, fed up with the man's ceaseless doubt in my abilities first as a leader and now as a shooter. "Watch me, *Coronel*."

I spoke my last word with an air of contempt, departing before he could contradict me. Striding back toward our roadblock vehicle and, with it, the Venezuelan troops, I considered the situation.

It wasn't that I minded a good fight—under any other circumstances, shwacking some of the dirtbags responsible for keeping a scandalously corrupt administration in power would've been more recreation than work. Instead, the deep sense of anger welling up within me stemmed from the fact that by killing those men, I'd also be killing any hope of conducting our ambush against Sofia. We'd already been compromised, whether by fate or dumb luck, and now it was all a matter of surviving long enough to worry about the fallout. There was no time to consider how or if we'd be able to continue our mission afterward, so I didn't. What would be the point? I'd been in a hundred gunfights, and probably two had panned out even close to how I'd envisioned before the first shot.

And truth be told, I just wanted to get this thing over with.

By then I could see Herrera's men and Felix ahead, an icy silence hanging between them and the Venezuelans who were glancing up at the surrounding terrain on either side of the path. I couldn't tell if they heard Cancer repositioning the ambush or if they were merely trying to locate our people, and at this point I didn't care. I simply continued walking, preparing to stop between the Colombians to have a nice clear sector of fire to share the contents of my magazine with the army troops ahead. My right hand rested on the pistol grip of my slung M4, and I used my left to wave the money as if I were showing a tennis ball to a group of dogs.

"Two thousand," I said, tossing the roll of cash to the central leader in a long, high arc. As all three sets of eyes ticked upward to track the projectile, I began the adrenaline-soaked process of lifting my rifle, bringing my left palm to the handguard to stabilize the weapon for the first shots of a now-imminent gunfight.

The entire process only took a second, maybe less, my sights aligning with the left man's chest by the time any of them realized what was happening. A fleck of rain hit my cheek, and I ripped two subsonic rounds through his sternum.

Then I swung my aim to the rightmost man, delivering another double tap to center mass as he stumbled backward with his weapon half-raised.

I drove my sights to the leader just in time to see the wad of money strike him in the forehead, causing him to flinch—not that it would've made a difference. He was wildly unprepared for the sudden onslaught, still fumbling to get a grip on his rifle much less accurately employ it by the time I pumped three bullets through his chest, feeling the sting of a second raindrop as clearly as if it were shrapnel.

Now the engagement was a simple shooting drill, my lone objective to repeatedly engage the targets in the same order, left, right, and center, until all three were dead without a doubt. Thus far all had gone flawlessly—rage always brought out the best in me—and I was in the process of delivering a pair of follow-up shots to my original target when I detected a flash of movement on the right flank.

The second man I'd shot was lying on his side, trying to bring his weapon to bear but standing no chance against my reaction time, vantage point, and stable shooting position. I seamlessly transitioned my aim to him, delivering my next round just as a wild burst of unsuppressed gunfire broke out to my right and his body erupted with bullet impacts.

I looked over in horror to see Fabian, the ponytailed bastard who was supposed to drive the roadblock vehicle, training his M16 toward the man he'd just blown apart.

"God-fucking-damnit!" I shouted, my curse dwarfed by the echo of his gunshots. A low growl of thunder snarled overhead, and then the sky unleashed a torrent of rainfall.

"*Get ready*," Cancer transmitted, "*here they come*."

Reilly charged through the pouring rain, struggling to maintain his one-handed hold on the machinegun while his other hand clutched the heavy bag tethered by way of a belt of bullets leading to the weapon.

He followed Cancer, who raced ahead to identify a suitable vantage point for the chaos to come before pointing to a tree and, looking back to ensure the medic nodded in acknowledgement, darted off to find his own firing position.

Such combat theatrics were unfortunate but necessary, because in contrast to Hollywood's portrayal of single-handed machinegun employment by a bare-chested hero, actual reality was a motherfucker. Reilly's primary weapon was an M60, most likely supplied to the Colombian military by America when they upgraded their own forces to a more current variant of belt-fed machinegun.

The weapon constituted over 23 pounds of metal in an oblong mass, not counting the nearly thirty-pound bag of linked ammunition he carried in his left hand. Four hundred rounds seemed like a lot until you considered the fact that an M60 could discharge that load in somewhere around 40 seconds if he depressed the trigger carelessly—fine if he only had a single target, but wildly insufficient when a horde of at least semi-trained Venezuelan fighters were about to stream through the breach.

And since the vegetation was too high for Reilly to simply rest the bipod on the ground and alleviate himself of the machinegun's weight, he did the next best thing.

Absent an assistant gunner and in stark contrast to the Rambo movies, accurate shooting from the hip was nigh impossible even for a man of Stallone's build, while even a two-handed firing position—the stuff of *First Blood*—was of limited use when everything forward of the bolt reached liquid magma levels of heat with sustained fire.

In truth, controlling a machinegun from a kneeling firing position was about as easy as wielding a cannon but best managed by what Reilly did now, shifting his non-firing hand to the weapon's carrying handle and tucking the buttstock to his side with the opposite elbow.

The first Venezuelan Tiuna crested into view, accelerating furiously onto the side road. No matter, Reilly thought, because barring any semblance of armament, its means of propulsion would be severely limited when thirty rounds of 7.62mm bullets laced through it.

The massive weapon bucked wildly as he pulled the trigger, requiring him to appraise the sight of his bullet impacts and "walk" the stream of tracer rounds into his target, which hadn't changed since the objective had switched from a deliberate ambush to a hasty withdrawal. As the sole team member with a belt-fed machinegun, obliterating engine blocks was his bread and butter, and this lead truck was the first to go.

His fire was interspersed with blasts of thunder, visibility through the rain limited but sufficient for him to see that his opening salvo had been successful in obliterating the first vehicle's engine. The hood was a cratered, smoking hulk at this point, but the vehicle continued to roll forward regardless, its momentum carrying it further down the side road.

No matter, Reilly thought, David and his counterparts would make short work of any surviving occupants. He transitioned his aim to the second Venezuelan truck and repeated the process, this time in a far more expeditious manner.

The driver panicked, slamming on the brakes rather than trying to accelerate through the kill zone—a fortuitous turn of events, though Reilly had no visibility on the third truck and it probably didn't matter. The remaining men in the convoy would be bailing out of their vehicles and maneuvering on foot, he knew, and with precious little ammo remaining he turned his attention to thinning the enemy's ranks the only way he could.

Reilly's next burst was directed at the cab of the second vehicle, which withered under his fire in a cloud of metal fragments and exploding auto glass. Anyone who'd survived that onslaught was extremely unhappy and, as it turned out, still alive—his machinegun bolt thunked forward, and Reilly glanced down to see that his belt of ammo had evaporated into a pile of scattered links below.

Dropping the machinegun in place, he transitioned to his slung Galil and transmitted, "Two trucks down, road is blocked, machinegun's empty."

David replied in remarkably short order, his voice shrill over Reilly's earpiece.

"*Then get your ass to the trucks*," he began. "*They're flanking from the north.*"

~

Cancer led the way downhill, glancing back through the rain to see that the men of the recently displaced ambush line continued to pursue him. Shouted orders only did so much when managing a semi-literate partner force—it was far more effective to tell them to follow you, then move wherever you needed them to go.

He threaded his way down the jungled slope, transmitting as he moved, "Angel, how are we looking in the back?"

"*They're keeping up,*" Ian replied. "*We've got everyone but Doc.*"

Cancer had ordered the intelligence operative to bring up the rear, ensuring that none of Herrera's people got lost in the jungle. He wasn't about to leave anyone behind, whether mercenaries or Americans, and once they reached the stationary convoy they'd need every barrel they could get.

With side road access blocked by two downed Tiunas, it didn't take a tactical genius to know that the Venezuelans would abandon their attempts at a vehicle onslaught and transition to a dismounted assault over the hill to their north. David's confirmation that it was already occurring, however, put Cancer in a race against time; if he didn't get the ambush line into the fight asap, he risked arriving to find the convoy had already been overrun. He caught sight of the first Tiuna obliterated by Reilly's gunfire, its windows pockmarked from bullet holes when David and company had slaughtered any surviving occupants. No sign of movement, so apparently they'd been successful.

As the vegetation cleared out at the base of the hill, he saw that the Venezuelans hadn't yet overrun the parked convoy—though not because of the team's defensive effort, if you could even call it that.

David was hunkered behind the second truck's engine block, feverishly returning fire at the muzzle blasts flickering through the trees. Felix cowered beside him, utterly useless with or without a weapon, while the remaining two mercenaries were spraying bullets wildly into the trees with zero accuracy. He couldn't yet see Herrera, but knew it wasn't in the man's constitution to run away. Whether alive or dead, he was down there somewhere.

Struggling to maintain his footing through the rain-drenched undergrowth, Cancer transmitted, "Suicide, we're twenty seconds out."

He was almost to the road when one of the mercenaries below angled out from behind the second truck to get a better view and caught a bullet to the shoulder. He stumbled backward and sideways, and then it was all over for the kid with the ponytail—he got lit up like a Christmas tree, ventilated by a half-dozen shots and probably triple that number of near-misses as some unseen Venezuelan fighter dumped the remainder of his magazine in record time. Shit, Cancer realized, the enemy was close, and the only option now was to defend in place. Trying to lead the mercs behind him in a flanking maneuver against an enemy force of unknown size would be a disaster: half of them would be shot dead by the time they crossed the open ground of the side road, though it wasn't until Cancer had almost reached it that he finally located Herrera.

The former Colombian officer was beside a closely grouped trio of Venezuelan bodies, firing his IWI assault rifle in well-aimed bursts. That much was all well and good, save the fact that he was doing so while standing in the open despite the ready availability of vehicles to take cover behind. A military man should have known better than that, and Cancer sped toward him with an idle sense of curiosity as to whether the good colonel didn't care about surviving, or had an outright death wish. Either way, his loss would have grim consequences for the remainder of their mission, and minimizing that possibility became Cancer's sole focus in life.

He set foot on the side road and took off at a sprint, grabbing Herrera by the shoulder and pulling him along for the ride. No sooner had he released the man behind the comparative safety of the designated roadblock vehicle than the space where he'd been standing received a hailstorm of incoming rounds that chopped up the mud; someone had dialed him in and would've punched his ticket absent Cancer's intervention, and both men knew it.

"*Gracias*," Herrera said, assuming a far more sane firing position over the hood.

"*De nada*," Cancer replied, turning to see the men of the ambush line arriving at a jog.

Cancer ordered the first in their ranks to a firing position behind the rear truck, then began directing the remaining mercenaries to leapfrog to the remaining vehicles.

"Third truck...you, third truck...second truck..."

To their credit, they moved as if their lives depended on speed, racing toward their assigned positions without hesitation. One of them never made it—by appearances the oldest member of the mercenary force, the portly man with graying hair was halfway between the second and first vehicles when he caught a burst of gunfire and dropped screaming to the ground. None of the other mercs made a move to drag him to safety, and within two seconds it didn't matter; the Venezuelans finished him off and his body twitched spastically in the final moments of life.

Ian arrived last, huffing for breath with his suppressed M4 in hand. Cancer sent him to the third truck, which left only the lead vehicle without an American providing accurate fire. Cancer had been maintaining a running count as the mercenaries streamed onto the side road, and sent the last of their number to the head of the convoy with one man still unaccounted for—Reilly, still making his way down the hill.

"Doc," Cancer transmitted, "I want you at the lead truck when you get here."

Then he evaluated the outcome, looking down the length of the convoy to see the mercs in their assigned positions. He was doubtful any of them would achieve an enemy kill unless it was by luck or at point-blank range, but at least they were evenly distributed behind the trucks, returning fire and slowing down the enemy's advance. Now it was a fight to the death to defend their vehicles—no one was making it out of here on foot—until Worthy and that little mustached shit arrived.

The pointman came over the net a moment later, speaking between panted breaths.

"*We got another...Venezuelan convoy moving in...from the south...I'm two minutes out.*"

Cancer replied, "If you're not here in ninety seconds, we're all dead."

"*Copy.*"

After confirming that Herrera's men were all gainfully employed and no improvements could be made to the defensive line, Cancer dealt himself into the gunfight.

He took up a firing position at the rear truck, keenly aware that he'd be broadcasting muzzle flashes with his suppressor removed in anticipation of initiating the ambush rather than a hasty defense. Shifting his Galil barrel, he searched for targets at the convoy's left flank; that was where he'd try to penetrate if he were the enemy, and if their fighters managed to slip behind the team's trucks it would be game over.

Which was exactly what they were trying to do.

The first Venezuelan soldier he located was moving for a tree at the base of the road to his left, less than ten meters distant. Cancer instinctively knew he was the pointman for a larger element, which made putting him down all the more important. By the time he'd taken aim, his opponent had crouched beside the tree with only a fraction of one leg exposed. Cancer put his sights on the visible kneecap and fired a single shot that missed, as did his second attempt.

But the third round fired in as many seconds found its mark as evidenced when the man fell to the earth with an ear-splitting shriek of pain audible even amidst the rain and gunfire. Now his upper body was in view, ripe for a kill shot that Cancer didn't take; instead he held his fire, looking for other targets that might respond to the panicked screams and cries for help.

Two men came to the rescue, valorous but stupid, both appearing as little more than dark forms moving amidst the jungle backdrop. Cancer opened fire and saw one drop from view, while the other continued his Medal of Honor charge undaunted. This was too easy, he thought, letting the man proceed within a few feet of his friend before unleashing a double tap not for the chest but the stomach: if these people cared about saving their own, he'd get a lot further by racking up wounded instead of kills.

At least one of the rounds found its mark, the soldier now gut shot and completing a clumsy, stumbling fall to the wet undergrowth not far from where the first man was rolling around and clutching his knee. Both were screaming, the latest casualty flopping around like a fish out of water; this was fucking fantastic, Cancer thought, a delightful game of shithead whack-a-mole.

Reilly transmitted, "*In position at the lead truck.*"

More Venezuelan figures advanced toward Cancer, all of them part of some larger maneuver element trying to slip around the left flank. Cancer opened fire as he saw them, now engaging targets deeper in the jungle with three-round volleys. 7.62mm had a far better chance of penetrating than the lighter 5.56 rounds being fired by most of his teammates, but his visibility was limited by rain and vegetation, and he couldn't take any chances. If he passed up an opportunity to shoot at the fleeting figures while they were visible, he might not get another one.

Some reached the jungle's edges regardless of his efforts, their presence often apparent only with the flickers of muzzle flashes. Incoming rounds popped against the truck, one cracking straight through a window. Cancer returned fire at everything he could see: shadows, blasts of flame from an enemy's barrel, the occasional glimpse of a fatigue uniform in the brush. It was largely impossible to tell which shots were hits and which were misses, but the volume of Venezuelan fire seemed to be abating. As soon as he couldn't find an immediate target, he pivoted left and finished off the man with a shattered kneecap, firing his final round before ducking behind the truck and conducting an emergency reload.

His next scan revealed the gut-shot soldier had slowed his flailing, the onset of shock and blood loss setting in. Cancer held his fire, choosing to save the bullet for someone who could put up a fight and finding a suitable candidate blasting an AK-103 from the undergrowth.

Without time to take careful aim, Cancer engaged him almost reflexively and was pleased when one of the rounds struck the man in the face, a chance headshot that he hadn't intended. A puff of blood and brain matter and then he was gone, racing the raindrops to the earth below. The air was thick with gun oil and his Galil was hot with use in his grasp—was there anything better?

As it turned out, there was.

"*Coming in hot*," Worthy transmitted.

Cancer glanced back to see the pointman darting down the hill with his Colombian counterpart in tow. He transmitted, "Racegun, post at the second truck. If we don't get fire superiority and exfil in the next thirty seconds, that second convoy's going to hit us."

He wasn't exaggerating. The only reason they'd lasted this long against such a numerically superior force was that the Venezuelans were largely untrained, with no masters of fire and maneuver to be found, and Cancer took a momentary glance to the right before feeling the utter shock of what he saw there.

Herrera was still alive and shooting, as was the rest of Cancer's team.

The mercenary force had taken a heavy toll, though, their bodies strewn across the path, blood mixing with groundwater in puddles of sludge. Jesus, he thought, they'd lost at least four of them, and he directed his attention back to the jungle in time to see a particularly bold Venezuelan soldier charging forward and firing a Belgian FNC assault rifle from the hip, some real action-hero shit that was going to cost him his life.

Cancer took rapid-fire shots, fearful that this sprinter would score a random hit despite his seeming unwillingness to aim. The man's FNC went silent as he dropped to his knees, coughing a splurt of blood onto his chest before face-planting into the mud.

Worthy transmitted, "*In position.*"

The update, as it turned out, was largely unnecessary—the volume of incoming fire soon reduced to a trickle of popshots, any advantage held by the Venezuelans evaporating with Worthy's arrival. He was unmatched for split-second reaction time, and must have seeded his fair share of death in record time: before long, there was no gunfire at all, just the patter of rain until David's final transmission of the fight.

"*Exfil, exfil, exfil.*"

34

I braced myself against the seat as the Kia fishtailed around a curve, the slick mud causing the rear tires to lose traction even with four-wheel drive.

Once I was certain we weren't going to crash, I turned to address Herrera beside me, then quickly decided to leave him alone for the time being. He clenched his bottle in a trembling hand, blinking hard between sips and whispering unintelligibly to himself, face contorted with unspeakable rage. If I'd suspected him of being complicit before, now I was positively certain he was on our side if for no other reason than no professional actor could pull off this act so well after one drink, much less the six shots I'd seen him down since the attack.

We'd just lost two vehicles and nearly half of his fighters, to say nothing of burning through an ungodly amount of our ammunition, only to run for our lives and give Sofia every opportunity to carry out, well, whatever the hell it was she was doing in Michelena. Anything we accomplished after this point would be purely reactive, and while that much was nothing new for my team, I wondered when Vega would tire of financing the expedition and simply order his men home. Christ, I thought, at this point we were a team of CIA contractors who, unbeknownst to our boss, were beholden to a drug kingpin and lucky to have that much. We'd had some half-formed plans and psychotic improvisations before, but this mission was shaping up to be our biggest shitshow yet.

Nowhere was this more apparent than in my own internalized reaction —after getting accountability of my team I'd scarcely said a word, handling the change of plans with only slightly more composure than Herrera. I was furious about our discovery by the Venezuelans, furious at how poorly the mercenaries had responded even under the direction of my team, furious with myself for not somehow preventing that entire situation in the first place.

Finally I keyed my satellite radio and spoke.

"Raptor Nine One, Suicide Actual."

"*Send it,*" Duchess replied.

I hesitated before replying—part of my delay in reporting came down to struggling mightily with how to frame the next bit.

We couldn't have been any more certain as to the organizational identity of our attackers. They were wearing goddamn uniforms, after all, but slaughtering military servicemembers of a sovereign nation, even one as corrupt and rotted as Venezuela, was tantamount to an act of war. Given the Agency's limited intelligence reach here, I was banking on the fact that my team would have some degree of plausible deniability in the event that a report of a bunch of dead soldiers ended up on Duchess's desk. In the meantime there was no use getting everyone at Langley all hot and bothered about the dustup—we had bigger things to worry about.

"Our element was attacked at the ambush site by a superior enemy force, affiliation unknown." With that out of the way, I quickly continued, "Estimated twelve EKIA, six mercenary KIA, and we lost a couple trucks so we're down to two. 'Yellow' on ammo and trending toward 'red.' At this time we are evading east and prepared to move toward Michelena, but assess Sofia will change her route once she learns of the attack, if she hasn't already. We need another satphone ping to re-vector and establish a new ambush, over."

A pause before Duchess replied, "*Your men are okay?*"

"We're fine. Everyone who survived came away without a scratch. So where do we stand on SIGINT intercepts?"

Her tone turned somber.

"Our birds can't cross into Venezuelan airspace. We're running them along the border, but her future communications will likely be out of range."

I pressed my hands against my face, rubbing both eyes before responding with utterly false optimism.

"Then we're going to set up outside Michelena and try to pick up her trail there."

"*Good copy*," she said, with remarkable composure given the circumstances. "*I'll monitor source intelligence reporting and let you know if anything pops.*"

What both of us left unsaid was the obvious: absent any specific information that could pinpoint Sofia's new route, we didn't have a snowball's chance in hell of finding her. She wasn't going to miss that little slaughter just off the main road; she'd realize we were here, rightfully presume that we'd been trying to interdict her en route and therefore knew her destination, and adjust her plans accordingly. We could stake out Michelena all we wanted, but this last compromise was our mission fucked, and both Duchess and I knew it.

That wouldn't stop us from trying, of course, though banking on luck was a dangerous proposition when down to six mercs and Herrera, who was well on his way to being dead drunk and probably better for it.

Our small convoy cleared the storm then, rain giving way to a sky mottled with clouds broken by rays of sun. We came alongside a small, barren field, and for reasons unknown to me, Herrera suddenly shouted at the driver.

"Pull over. Everyone out."

"We've got to keep moving," I said, but the driver braked regardless.

Herrera was adamant. "The army will not pursue us this far off the highway."

"Yeah? You were also sure they could be paid off, and look how that turned out."

Every other vehicle occupant was already bailing out of the truck as he grabbed my shirt, pulling my face toward his and whispering a shockwave of booze toward me.

"They were paid off, *pirobo*. Just not by us."

Ian exited his truck and looked for David, desperate for any explanation of why they'd done something so devastating to their prospects of survival as stopping here.

This was lunacy in its most basic form—for all Ian knew, the second Venezuelan convoy had cleared the side road and was now speeding along the muddy paths his team had just traveled, easily following their fresh vehicle tracks.

Herrera pointed a finger at the field and yelled, "Line up."

His men did so in remarkably quick fashion, standing shoulder to shoulder as they awaited the next order—which, as it turned out, was directed not to them but to Ian's team.

"Kill anyone who does not drop their weapon."

David was the first to take aim at the small mercenary force, a move that bore horrifying implications. These men had just lost six of their own, abandoning the bodies in the race to flee the objective, and now, the very same American team leader who'd led them into this mess was training his gun upon them at Herrera's order.

Ian followed suit, feeling sick to his stomach as he took aim on the terrified Colombians who were throwing their rifles to the ground and raising their hands in surrender. Worthy and Cancer joined the impromptu firing line, leaving Reilly on rear security.

Felix tried to join his American counterparts, his feeble attempt cut short when David said, "You go, too."

The sub driver responded with a look of shocked betrayal and a stuttered excuse that ended as David continued, "Get your ass over there or die right here. Your choice."

That served as all the convincing Felix required to fall in on the Colombians' left flank, after which Herrera shouted, "Five steps backward."

His men did so, taking shaky steps away from their weapons on the rocky ground.

David advanced and the rest of the firing line moved beside him, looking for all the world like they were about to summarily execute these poor bastards. Only then did the team leader transmit the first, and only, explanation Ian had for what was about to transpire.

"*It's a shakedown.*"

Then Herrera yelled again, his voice quavering with anger.

"I have been working in Venezuela for years. The army did not accidentally stumble upon us. We have a *sapo* in our midst. And if he is not lying dead at the target area then he is going to wish he was. Phones!"

One man amongst their ranks responded quicker than the rest. Nikolai, the mustached fighter who'd accompanied Worthy on left-side security, produced his cell phone and held it out while the others were still reaching in their pockets.

Herrera descended upon him with fury, delivering a vicious blow to his face.

Nikolai fell like a puppet with the strings cut as his commander dropped to his knees before patting him down.

Herrera withdrew a hand from Nikolai's pocket, victoriously thrusting a second cell phone skyward. Then he grabbed the man's shirt, lifting him in an almost superhuman display of strength before shoving him backward, where he stumbled and fell.

"Who else was with this little rat? *Who?!*"

No response from the dumbfounded remnants of his mercenary team, who were met with significantly better treatment—Herrera checked their phones, then patted them down in turn. Several of them were already looking at Nikolai's collapsed figure with murder in their eyes, and why wouldn't they? The man had, apparently, waited comfortably outside the ambush line with the full knowledge that death was about to descend on their ranks. And Herrera had been right to stop, Ian realized. To continue would allow the traitor to send another message in due time, leading to an attack that only Nikolai would survive.

Herrera finished his search and dismissed them to recover their weapons, a move that made Ian uneasy: would they turn on the Americans who'd just held them at gunpoint? He glanced left to see his teammates lowering their barrels but spreading out, keeping a discreet vigil on the newly liberated fighters in anticipation of an all-out gunfight. For three nauseating seconds it appeared as if that was about to occur, the Colombians racing to their rifles and taking aim—but only at Nikolai, who was now sitting up and blubbering in Spanish, blood streaming from both nostrils.

The mercenaries were shouting at Herrera, competing to be heard in their overlapping requests to kill the traitor until their commander silenced them with a shrill whistle.

Then and only then did Herrera actually examine Nikolai's second phone, laughing triumphantly as he shouted two words.

"*Un minuto.*"

Any confusion as to what the colonel meant was settled by the reaction of the surviving mercenaries.

They descended upon Nikolai like a pack of rabid dogs, delivering savage kicks, punches, blows with the buttstocks of their rifles that were met with shrieking cries for mercy. Herrera watched the scene with delight, a mad king surveying his subjects, and Ian closed the distance with David and spoke quietly.

"If I can talk to him—"

"Let it happen," David cut him off. "If they don't take it out on him, they're going to take it out on us."

"*Coronel,*" Ian called, "the phone please, sir."

Herrera carelessly flung the device at him, and he lunged forward to catch it amid the sounds of Nikolai being beaten to death. Ian began a hasty examination of the device's contents, which didn't take long—only one programmed number, and a single text exchange consisting of two messages. The first was outgoing, and even Ian's relatively sparse abilities in Spanish told him it held an approximate location for the ambush with a notation to look for the side road. It was sent at 5:33 that morning, when they were en route from the DC-3 airfield to their ambush position and, quite clearly, passing through an area of cellular coverage. Ian hadn't seen Herrera brief his men on the tactical plan and knew for a fact that David had told him not to; and yet, he must have disregarded their advice and done so at some point.

Equally telling was the response to this text, sent 33 minutes later. Two words, *muchas gracias*, that told Ian everything he needed to know about what followed. With limited routes to reach Michelena, Sofia had sent the

Venezuelan military in from the highway for no other purpose than to keep it clear for her convoy's safe passage and timely arrival. If she'd had the Venezuelans attack from the east, it would have flushed the team toward her; she didn't care about killing his team, he realized, only preventing their disruption to her plan. That meant she was on a fixed timeline and, he suspected, planning on leaving the country in relatively short order.

Regrettably, her convoy must have already been well past the ambush position on the way to Michelena. To what specific location in the town or why, he had no idea, but the device in his hand would ultimately provide the answers to both.

Herrera shouted something to his men and Ian looked up, returning his focus to the horrific sight: the mercenaries getting in their final blows on Nikolai, whose body beneath his fatigues was a misshapen mass of broken bones, one arm folded back at the elbow, odd lumps in his torso indicating a series of fractured ribs that had surely induced a fatal degree of internal bleeding that wouldn't kill him soon enough.

He was still conscious though not screaming, having lost the ability to protest and instead gasping for air through a blood-smeared grin of missing teeth. The face was unrecognizable, completely overtaken by swelling, bruised flesh that rendered both eyes into narrow slits, one of which wept a stream of tears tinged with scarlet.

Herrera unholstered his pistol, a 1911 that was likely provided by the US along with everything else his merry band of trafficker muscle carried for the purposes of dispatching their opposition.

He stood over the fallen man, firing two rounds into his groin. This restored Nikolai's screams to now-deafening levels of pain, eliciting a gleeful cackle from Herrera, who straddled the flailing body, jabbing the pistol barrel as far into the gaping mouth as it could go. Nikolai's cries ended amid the cracking pops of shattered teeth, after which he was reduced to emitting a gagging whimper.

Finally Herrera pulled the trigger a third time, ending the gruesome display once and for all.

He stood and shouted, "Get in the trucks. We ride to Michelena."

Ian allowed himself one last glance at Nikolai in his final resting place, his open-mouthed grimace facing a sky whose clouds were parting to allow blazing sunlight, as if the very weather in this place reveled in the narco justice that had just prevailed.

As David turned to join the mercenaries on their way back to the trucks, Ian grabbed his arm to stop him.

"Get Duchess on the line."

"We'll have time on the way—"

"Right fucking now," Ian demanded. "Don't you get it? This phone is the missing link. It takes a SIGINT plane and a hell of a lot of equipment to trace a satphone call. But analyzing a cellular network? Shit, David, the Agency can do that remotely and in their sleep. Nikolai almost got us all killed, yeah. But this"—he waved the cell in front of the team leader's face—"will give us Sofia."

35

Worthy watched the phone in his hand, monitoring the icon of his lead truck as it glided across the map display.

He transmitted, "Well, boys, we've officially reached the outskirts of Michelena. Suicide, I recommend we follow this main road to the north side of town. If we haven't run into Sofia's convoy by then, we can start running parallels on the side streets and hope to catch sight of her while we wait for Duchess to get a cellular hit."

Cancer responded from the rear truck, where he rode with Reilly.

"If *she gets a cellular hit. Big 'if.'*"

Beside Worthy, Ian groaned with contempt and responded over the net.

"She will," he said defensively. "Even if Sofia knows we're in Michelena, it's not going to stop her from doing whatever she came here for."

Now Reilly chimed in, "*Let's hope so. Because shooting it out with her would be a whole lot better than staring at this town all day. I mean, am I the only one who's getting depressed?*"

No, Worthy thought, you most definitely are not.

To call this area bleak was to do the word a disservice—in reality, it was a vision of the soul-crushing poverty that marked a majority of Venezuela.

The dirt roads were lined with abandoned, rusted-out car hulks, the buildings to either side of the road decrepit. To his right, a group of four shirtless boys took turns hurling bricks through the remaining windows of what looked to be a former grocery store, its exterior bearing the chipped paint of what had once been a mural depicting fruit, meat, and vegetables.

The boys looked at the trucks as they passed, their reaction to the vehicles—plastered with bullet holes, wind streaming through broken glass—one of momentary interest before they snatched up another volley of bricks and resumed their efforts against the building, then were gone from his view.

Then the trucks glided past a mountain of trash piled twenty feet high in an open area beside the road, a town landfill kept at the outskirts due to the smell. The stench was overpowering even within the confines of the truck, and his driver muttered a curse before accelerating to get past it. Yet there among the trash heap were a half dozen adults, mostly women, picking through the detritus, presumably in the hopes of finding something that was at least semi-edible to feed their families.

Worthy had been prepared for checkpoints, military patrols, and police that needed to be either bribed or killed. He hadn't been prepared to take in the sheer despair of these surroundings, and realized that without coca fields or any value as a cocaine smuggling corridor, the government had simply abandoned this area as insignificant.

Now he felt like he was back in Nigeria—the oil supply of both countries should have filled the surroundings with thriving population centers teeming with economic potential. Instead, political corruption had gutted the landscapes completely. Greed left unchecked, it seemed to him, was an evil almost tantamount to the very extremist groups that sprang up under such conditions.

Still, even the dismal view was almost a welcome reprieve from the thought of Nikolai.

His death hadn't been an easy thing to watch for any of them, but Worthy was the only team member who'd had close contact with the man—time spent, as it turned out, being lied to. He cringed at the memory, releasing a pained sigh that must have been overheard by Ian beside him.

"What's wrong?" he asked.

"Nothing," Worthy replied. "Just thinking about some stuff Nikolai said."

"Well, what did he say?"

Worthy looked over at Ian, his presence in the lead vehicle a quite unusual change of pace—normally he and David were joined at the hip while on a mission. But given that a chance sighting of some seemingly insignificant detail could help illuminate Sofia's intentions, David had insisted on putting the intelligence operative up front. And Ian, for his part, was taking the job seriously. His gaze darted from the windshield to both side windows, scrutinizing their surroundings as they proceeded.

Worthy looked back outside the vehicle, then admitted the truth.

"I feel like an idiot, man. Nikolai gave me some sob story about the US government spraying poison on his family's crops. I took him at face value—now, I know he was lying."

"He wasn't," Ian said matter-of-factly. "Aerial eradication under Plan Colombia. We sprayed glyphosate, the same chemical used in Roundup, produced by a company called Monsanto. It was supposed to be safe, of course, and Monsanto had plenty of scientists putting their names on ghostwritten research papers to make it appear that way. All that didn't come out until after Bayer acquired them for sixty billion. Within a few years Bayer paid out over ten billion in damages to US customers who sued for major medical complications. Mostly cancers of various kinds, namely non-Hodgkin's lymphoma."

"Could that stuff cause birth defects?"

"Absolutely. And you think any of those local farmers like Nikolai's family will ever see a dime from the US? Or get any medical support for the children who are fucked for life from ingesting poison in their drinking water?"

Worthy was speechless, reduced to shaking his head in disgust.

"Nope," Ian concluded, "they're left on their asses while the US and Colombian governments declared the effort a success despite the fact that cocaine production is higher than ever. Just another day in the War on Drugs, and if you think that's bad, consider the environmental implications—"

But his sermon ended when their mercenary driver rebuked them both with a firm, "No, this is wrong."

Ian looked taken aback. "I think I have my facts straight, Juan Carlos."

"You do not."

"About Plan Colombia, or the glyphosate?"

"About Nikolai," the driver replied. "His family did not grow crops. He is from the barrios of Medellín. We came up together in the same combo, the same gang. He told you what you wanted to hear, because you Americans love your stories about everywhere else in the world. Nikolai played you, like he played all of us."

The revelation left Worthy speechless. He'd felt such pity for the man, an emotion Nikolai had probably cultivated for an extra split second to get the drop on him if everything went to shit during the firefight.

Before he could mentally chastise himself for the oversight, however, David transmitted with breathless urgency.

"*We're in business—cell phone analysis came back. She called a number in Michelena less than an hour ago.*"

"Send the grid," Worthy replied, eyes fixed on his phone.

"*It's not a grid*," David replied, "*it's an address. The call was to a landline—this has got to be her destination.*"

Worthy entered the address that followed, feeling his eyebrows shoot up at the result.

To the driver, he said, "One kilometer straight ahead, I'll tell you when to turn. Floor it, fast as you can."

The mercenary at the wheel didn't hesitate, swerving around a man pushing a wheelbarrow stacked high with sheets of scrap metal before accelerating forward.

Worthy transmitted, "It's less than four miles away—we'll be there in ten minutes. Looks like a secluded property with a gated entrance, and a long driveway leading to a single house."

David replied, "*Whatever it is, we're hitting it. Ram the gate and take us straight to the X. Everything past that will be me calling audibles. I'm going to put Herrera's men outside to deal with any squirters. We're doing a unilateral assault.*"

A wise choice, Worthy thought. After seeing Herrera's crew in action, taking them inside the house would put the American team at risk of friendly fire that was probably equal to the chances of getting shot by Sofia's people.

David continued, "*I want us to clear fast and make contact as quickly as possible. If we're lucky, Sofia will still be inside.*"

36

Reilly's passenger side window was open, Galil propped over the doorframe as air whipped inside the cab.

Worthy transmitted, "*Thirty seconds out.*"

The convoy sped through the town's northeastern outskirts now, tires rumbling over a gravel road as the jungle passed in a blur, punctuated by gates marking driveways to unseen residences. This must have been where Michelena's wealthy lived, or used to, and Reilly felt a pang of regret that he wasn't in the lead vehicle. There were precious few opportunities in life to ram a gate, and he was about to miss out on a big one.

"*Ten seconds*," Worthy said. He followed the transmission almost immediately with the words, "*Gate's open.*"

Well that was anticlimactic, Reilly thought, though also noteworthy—not a single gate had been unsecured on the way here.

He felt his truck braking to make the turn, then accelerating up the winding driveway as Worthy spoke again.

"*House in sight, one vehicle parked outside.*"

No one responded over the net, keeping the frequency clear for Worthy's updates as the first set of eyes to arrive. But that didn't stop Cancer from shouting his prediction at Reilly from the opposite side of the Kia.

"She ain't here."

He was probably right—Sofia was unlikely to part with the security of her three-vehicle convoy, and the fact that Worthy hadn't specified which vehicle was outside meant that it wasn't one of hers. Whoever they were about to kill in the next minute or two probably wasn't going to be their primary target.

"*Front door is ajar*," Worthy transmitted, which was only slightly less unbelievable than what Reilly saw next.

The black Ford Explorer with a trailer hooked up to its hitch made him do a double-take—it was as out of place in Michelena as the house behind it, a two-story, apricot-colored structure with peaked roofs of red clay roof tiles. Thank God they hadn't attempted a stealthy assault: the house had so many windows it was a miracle they weren't getting shot up already.

His truck screeched to a halt behind the other two, and Reilly flung open his door and stepped into the blazing sunlight.

Worthy was already running toward the front door, with Ian struggling to keep pace behind him. The mercenaries were flooding out of the vehicles now, racing to surround the house and presenting a moving obstacle course that Reilly and Cancer had to shove their way through in their pursuit of David as the number three man.

By the time they finally broke free of the mess, his team leader was already clearing the front door.

Reilly arrived seconds later with Cancer at his heels and, unable to determine which direction David had gone, broke left. The move almost caused him to trip over the staircase he found there, rising upward to a balcony overlooking the open foyer that David had already crossed. Instinctively, Reilly mounted the stairs and swept his aim across the balcony—the first teammates inside had to clear the ground floor for immediate threats come hell or high water, leaving it to the final men inside to worry about more peripheral risks.

And the balcony he scanned now was most certainly that; Reilly now held the only vantage point on the elevated area, which could be filled by enemy fighters at any moment. All they'd have to do was huck a grenade or two onto the ground floor to make an assault up the stairs a costly proposition.

Apparently Cancer shared that assessment, because he fell in next to Reilly and gave him a quick shoulder squeeze.

Reilly methodically ascended the stairs, as concerned with his footing as he was with the ability to accurately engage targets as they appeared. But by the time he reached the top, none had; save the thundering footsteps of his teammates on the first floor, the house was silent.

Coming to a stop at a corner near the top stair, Reilly felt Cancer's hand alight on his shoulder and awaited his second-in-command's judgment call —five men were far too few to clear a house of this size, but the risks of involving Herrera's men in close-quarters combat were far greater. Given the circumstances, they could either press the initiative on the second floor with two men or maintain their position until Worthy, David, and Ian finished at the ground level and joined them. It wasn't a matter of a right or wrong answer; it was a matter of two already wrong answers, and either could prove worse than the alternative depending on how the enemy reacted to the intrusion.

Cancer's response was predictably in line with his temperament: he squeezed Reilly's shoulder, and the medic advanced onto the second floor, cutting left to clear the corner and immediately thinking, *oh fuck*.

The small landing was ringed by doors, a veritable death trap if any bad guys were up here. Reilly charged toward a corner entrance and shouted, "*Manos arriba*."

The Spanish term for *hands up* would irritate Cancer to no end, he knew. It wasn't intended for Sofia's people, who were highly unlikely to comply, but instead for any innocent civilians who may have been present. Just because a violent trafficker had passed through didn't mean a family wasn't living here, as with any country where the population didn't have the option to isolate themselves from the violence swirling around them. Given how dead quiet the house had been so far, Reilly thought his odds of stumbling upon a cowering child were higher than those of getting shot at. No self-respecting gunslinger would simply wait and allow themselves to be cornered—unless, of course, they were waiting in ambush to take out some of their attackers.

That thought hung heavy on his mind as he flung open the first door and pivoted right, flowing along a bedroom wall and sweeping his rifle toward the center of the room while Cancer did the same on the opposite side. The bed was made, the smell of dust in the air, no targets and no complications beyond a closet door that Cancer stopped beside, getting a nod from Reilly before he pulled it open.

Empty.

Reilly knelt to peer under the bed, then rose in time to fall in behind Cancer as he exited through the door with his weapon up. They moved back to the landing and slipped inside the next door of their counterclockwise clearance effort—another small bedroom, comforter neatly arranged over the bed, closet empty. All these details indicated this was no full-time residence; it was far too neat and orderly, the interior too barren of personal possessions.

Cancer was the first out, and Reilly watched him duck into a room on their left before calling out, "Short."

He'd just entered a bathroom, Reilly knew without bothering to look inside. Instead he flowed past, closing with the final main door to his front. It was slightly open, and Reilly pushed past it to see the master bedroom. He flowed along the wall, allowing Cancer to cut left as they converged their aim to the center of the room. A rumpled bedspread was the first indication of life they'd detected so far, and from the looks of it, may well be the last: a dead man was lying on his stomach at the foot of the bed, a gaping exit wound in the center of his spine. Reilly needed no close examination to know that the injury was inflicted by a 12-gauge shotgun. Sawed-off Sofia had struck again, though why she'd chosen this man in a seemingly random town, he had no idea.

Cancer and Reilly quickly cleared the master bathroom and walk-in closet, both devoid of luggage or indications that the dead man had planned on staying.

They approached the body as David transmitted, "*Ground floor clear, no joy.*"

"Second floor clear," Cancer replied. "We got a dead guy in the master bedroom. Send Angel up."

"*Copy.*"

Reilly took up a position against the wall, then lowered himself to the ground as Cancer rounded the man's opposite side and lay down next to the body.

"Ready?" he asked.

"Yep," Reilly replied, staring at the dead man's side with an intense focus.

Cancer took hold of the corpse and said, "One. Two. *Three*."

Then he rolled the body partially sideways, exposing the floor beneath him to Reilly's view.

One of two things would occur at this point. The first was that there would be a grenade or some other boobytrap beneath the body, and upon Reilly's command, Cancer would release the dead man in the hopes that his body weight would either prevent the device from exploding, or at least absorb the blast to the extent that it could with a 12-gauge hole in its center mass.

The second option was what occurred now—the carpet beneath the body was an oozing mess of blood flecked with bits of flesh and bone that had drained out of the entry wound, but there were no explosive charges to be found.

"Clear," Reilly said. "Roll him."

Cancer flipped the body onto its back as Reilly stood, examining the corpse with a quizzical expression and muttering, "What the hell? What do you make of that?"

"No fuckin' clue."

"Me neither. I mean, he should be—"

"Should be," Cancer agreed. "But he ain't."

They heard footsteps on the stairs, followed by Ian calling out, "Coming up."

"Over here," Reilly replied, then listened as Ian moved toward the sound of his voice.

The intelligence operative entered and stopped dead in his tracks, jaw falling open as his gaze locked on the dead man's face.

Ian went pale then, looking like he'd been the one to get shot instead of the dead son of a bitch lying on the floor. Reilly put a hand on his shoulder and said, "Hey man, you okay? You look like you're going to be sick."

But Ian didn't respond, and Reilly followed his gaze to the corpse in an attempt to figure out the problem. This was confusing, sure, but no cause for speechlessness.

Or at least, Reilly hoped not.

The dead man's face was not Venezuelan, or even Colombian—instead he bore remarkable similarity to any number of friends and foes they'd seen after their last border crossing through the mountains of the Wakhan Corridor.

Cancer slapped Ian on the back and said angrily, "Snap out of it, dick-wad. You saw plenty of dead Chinamen when we were in China."

Ian swallowed, blinked twice, and said breathlessly, "Doc, you were right—Weisz didn't pay Sofia 25 million for cocaine." He nodded toward the body. "And he...he's not Chinese."

Reilly shrugged. "Okay, so then...what is he?"

37

Duchess found herself holding her breath as Lucios stood, turned to face her, and announced, "Facial recognition software has confirmed 97 percent fidelity– the deceased is on our watch list."

The entire OPCEN fell silent. The only thing to go through Duchess's mind before she spoke again were Ian's words after he reported the outcome of the raid in Michelena, the fear in his voice palpable even over satellite communications.

I hope to God I'm wrong, but if not we're in some deep shit.

"Identity?" Duchess asked.

Lucios continued, "Mai-Chin Byeon, one of the head scientists at the Pyongyang Bio-technical Institute. North Korea claims it's used to produce agricultural pesticides, but corroborated intelligence and satellite imagery indicate an operational biological and chemical weapons facility."

Duchess tried to swallow the lump forming in her throat. "And what is Byeon's area of expertise?"

"Venomous agent X, more commonly known as—"

"VX," Duchess interrupted. "This is the same nerve agent used to assassinate Kim Jong-un's half-brother in Kuala Lumpur?"

"Yes, ma'am," he confirmed. "It's tasteless, odorless, and can be deployed in liquid or aerosol form, which means skin contact, inhalation, or ingestion through contaminated food or water are all lethal."

"What's the fatal dose for an adult?"

"A fraction of a drop. VX is a weapon of mass destruction, banned under the Chemical Weapons Convention. Given Venezuela has an embassy in Pyongyang, we can infer that—"

"The Supreme Leader," Duchess cut him off a second time, "saw fit to help them jumpstart their own chemical weapons program by providing a scientist on loan."

Lucios nodded solemnly. "Given the facts, our worst-case and most likely scenarios are one and the same: the $25 million payment from Erik Weisz to Sofia was, at least in part, for her to obtain and transport VX for use in an unspecified attack. My assessment is that she's trying to get the VX out of the country as quickly as possible, particularly after repeated attacks by Project Longwing. With the New Panamax vessel headed east on a trajectory to skirt the Venezuelan coast, that means she'll push the VX offshore sometime in the next two days. Whatever Weisz's ultimate target, the attack is now imminent."

Duchess considered those facts, which were, regrettably, not nearly enough to compensate for what they *didn't* know—namely, what quantity of VX Sofia now possessed. But a rogue WMD of any kind was sufficient to warrant the highest levels of operational support, and her ground team was about to get the kind of assistance they previously only dreamed of.

At least, Duchess thought, if she could manage this properly.

She cut her gaze to Project Longwing's Joint Terminal Attack Controller and asked, "Brian, what's the status of our aerial SIGINT platforms?"

Sutherland responded, "We've got one U-28 up on the Colombian side of the border with three hours of station time remaining, and a second fully fueled for the next shift."

"Both are now authorized and ordered to enter Venezuelan airspace. Vector the first bird toward Michelena and within range of Sofia's cell phone. I want the second U-28 airborne as soon as possible with the same instructions, and once that's done, get every possible UAV and ISR asset routed to scan the road networks between Michelena and the coast to locate Sofia's convoy. Gregory, you stay at his side and work out the legal justification—I don't care how you do it, just get it done."

Without waiting for a response from either man, she turned her attention to the J3.

"Wes, what DoD assets are in the vicinity of Venezuela?"

The bearded former Marine directed his gaze to his computer. "Marine Raiders are already staged at Curaçao with their rotary wing support for the ship takedown, but if we're looking at VX they'll need a few WMD specialists from DEVGRU. Naval assets: Joint Interagency Task Force South has two Legend-class Coast Guard cutters a couple weeks into their ninety-day counternarcotics rotation, and Southern Command has a Navy Freedom-class combat ship, the USS *Wichita*, with an MH-60 Romeo helicopter. All three are close enough to stage off the coast within 12 to 18 hours if they start hauling ass now."

"Excellent," she said with a crisp nod. "I want those JIATF and SOUTHCOM ships to immediately reroute as close as they can to Venezuela while remaining in international waters. Notify the WMD specialists, and if there are any other Coast Guard, Navy, or Marine vessels that can deploy quickly enough to reinforce within the next 48 hours, I want them set in motion now. We'll need a full-scale naval blockade."

Jamieson turned to face her, one eyebrow cocked in confusion.

"Understood, ma'am, but we're going to need Pentagon approval before any of those commanders can lift a finger."

"You give them the heads-up, and I'll deal with the Pentagon. The commanders will receive official orders within the hour."

Then she addressed the OPCEN. "Wes will remain in place as deputy OPCEN director. I'll be departing to set up a forward-deployed command post aboard one of the vessels in the Caribbean. When that container ship gets taken down, I'm going to board along with the site exploitation teams and transmit all further guidance."

Summoning a breath, she concluded, "Make no mistake, ladies and gentlemen. We've just discovered Sofia's plan. A WMD-grade chemical warfare agent will be departing the Venezuelan coast in the next 48 hours unless we stop it. And as long as I'm at the helm of Project Longwing, that's exactly what we're going to do."

38

Ian sat at the dining room table in the house formerly occupied by the man he now knew as Mai-Chin Byeon. His conferral with Duchess confirmed what he'd feared upon seeing the corpse: a collaboration with North Korea, who, like Venezuela, was one of those peculiar nations that prioritized military armament over any semblance of functional infrastructure for its people.

He flinched at the sound of a loud crash from upstairs—his team was in the process of tearing the house apart, searching for anything of intelligence value while they still had the chance. But that effort was unlikely to bear fruit, Ian knew.

Byeon had surely transported the VX in his trailer and possibly even the vehicle cargo area as well, both of which were now empty; they totaled 450 cubic feet of storage space. Together with the late-breaking realization that Weisz had paid Sofia 25 million dollars for VX, that meant she was now in possession of a potentially astronomical quantity of almost certainly pure liquid VX, a substance banned by the UN in any amount over four ounces per year, per nation.

Anything else of value had long since been removed by Sofia and her people, and yet the team's search continued due to the lack of any meaningful alternatives.

It wasn't that the Americans and their mercenary partner force were reluctant to pursue Sofia, whose head start increased with each passing second; rather, they simply didn't know where to go, and wouldn't until Ian received an update from the radio he now monitored.

David burst into the dining room, the disparity between his full military kit and the otherwise domestic surroundings comical.

He asked, "Can we move yet?"

"No," Ian replied. "Find anything good?"

"So far, just this." David held up a Ford key fob. "So we're up to three trucks, at least. How'd it go with Duchess?"

"Things are finally, *finally*, starting to look up for us. Sofia was here to pick up VX, and a lot of it. Basically the king cobra of nerve agents."

The team leader frowned.

"Was that...supposed to be good news?"

"Of course not."

"We really need to work on your transitions."

Ian leaned forward in his seat and explained, "The good news is that stopping WMD is a top priority for everyone. Whatever assets Duchess couldn't get for us before, she is now. The SIGINT birds that have been wasting fuel along the border just got clearance to cross into Venezuela. The first is headed this way as we speak."

But David seemed unimpressed by that pivotal development, giving an indifferent shrug and asking, "So, what, we're just supposed to hope Sofia uses her phone again?"

"No," Ian said. "We're going to ensure it."

He picked up Nikolai's cell phone from the table and held it up. "The Agency reviewed Nikolai's previous text and screened it for safe words. They sent me a prepared message stating that we're headed south into San Cristobal to refit."

"Why south?"

David should have known damn well why they were feigning a movement south, Ian thought, but rather than chastise him about it, he explained, "Because based on what we know, Sofia is moving the VX toward the coast for maritime transfer to the New Panamax container ship. That means she'll either move north on Highway 6 toward Maracaibo, or northeast along the Andes using Highways 1 or 7. So my mock update from Nikolai, may he rest in peace, is meant to put her at ease and, more importantly, get her to acknowledge with a return text. Once that happens, we'll know her route and can get moving."

He concluded, "And by this time tomorrow, Duchess will have so many assets working the coast to find her that it won't matter whether Sofia uses her phone or not—we'll have her dead to rights. Believe me, our odds of locating our target just went up tenfold."

David was squinting at him now, looking perturbed.

"Locating our target...with VX."

"Right," Ian said. "I thought I was pretty clear on that point."

Clearing his throat, David began, "Maybe I'm being overly risk averse, Ian, but—"

"But what?" he responded impatiently.

The team leader threw up his hands.

"What if she uses it on us, dumbass? I mean, we don't even have gas masks."

Ian laughed, draping an arm over the back of his chair. "Relax, David. No way it's been converted to an aerosol yet. I guarantee Sofia purchased the pure form, which is an amber-colored liquid. All she has to do is put a drop on someone's skin to kill them, so what does it matter if we have masks or not?"

"Oh," David said, feigning relief. "Thanks, Ian. This is all extremely comforting."

"Always a pleasure keeping you up to speed."

"I was kidding, jerkoff."

"So was I," Ian snapped. "You know how painful my job is? Half the time I feel like a substitute teacher with a classful of kids who don't give a shit. But hey, maybe we should deal with WMD more often. At least you guys would start paying attention."

Before he could respond, one of Herrera's mercenaries entered the room and spoke urgently to David.

"The *coronel* needs to see you—now."

Nodding, the team leader looked at Ian and said, "Let me know as soon as you have anything."

Ian shot him a thumbs up as he departed with the Colombian man—just a moment too soon, as it turned out, because he'd barely left before Duchess's voice came over his earpiece.

"Angel, this is Raptor Nine One."

"Go ahead," Ian replied, lifting Nikolai's phone and double-checking the prepared message to ensure he hadn't accidentally added a character while showing it to David. Something as insignificant as a spare punctuation mark could warn Sofia that the message was sent by an imposter, and at this point the entire mission hinged on the device in Ian's hands.

Duchess continued, *"Our SIGINT bird is in position over Michelena. Need you to send that text asap."*

Ian hit send and replied, "It's done."

"Stand by."

A moment later the phone vibrated in his hand, sending a rush of chills up his spine. He was communicating directly with his team's primary target, although the return message wasn't exactly a landmark of espionage material.

The text showed the same two words that Nikolai's previous text had elicited: *muchas gracias*. Ian quickly transmitted to Duchess.

"Just got a response, looks like she bought it."

"We've got her," came the response, spoken with mere seconds of delay. *"Route 1, past El Vigía. Get moving."*

"On it. I'll have Suicide check in from the road."

Ian pocketed the phone and reached for his transmit switch to notify his team of the development—after a seemingly endless wait, they could finally continue their pursuit.

But the sound of someone entering the room caused him to look up, expecting to see David.

Instead one of Herrera's men was striding toward him with a gleeful expression. Had they actually found something of significance in the house?

Before he could ask, the mercenary lifted his M16 rifle upward on its sling and, reversing the motion with blinding speed, brought the buttstock down across Ian's skull.

39

Cancer ripped a final drawer out of the dresser and, finding it empty like the rest, tossed it aside. Then he reached upward and flung the entire dresser to the floor, where it landed with a crash.

No false backing, he saw, nor was there a compartment in the wall behind it. A waste of time and effort, just like everything else in this search.

He was moving to the nightstand when he heard Herrera yell from downstairs.

"The army is coming! Get in the trucks!"

Cancer bolted for the door, hurdling the dead Korean's body with the minor irritation that David hadn't yet transmitted the only suitable order for such a development. He did so himself on the way to the stairs, keying his radio and saying, "Exfil, exfil, exfil," on the passing chance that anyone had missed the announcement. Reilly and Worthy emerged from the guest bedrooms, following Cancer as he took the stairs two at a time on his way to the first floor. Once there he glanced into the dining room for Ian—already gone—and took his Galil in both hands before leading the way to the front door. Herrera stood beside it, waving them out with the words, "Go, *go!*"

The sun was waning as Cancer stepped outside, moving for the convoy that had already been staged for departure. Each vehicle faced out in the designated order of movement, with the addition of the black Ford Explorer that would be coming with them. Cancer fled past the now-detached trailer, though it wasn't until he rounded it that he saw what awaited beyond.

He skidded to a halt, realizing he had a half-second to either open fire or put up his hands in surrender.

The mercenaries were all here, though not to depart the objective. He saw the bound and gagged form of David, who was either unconscious or dead, and Ian, who looked completely incoherent, at best managing a bleary gaze through half-closed eyelids. Felix lay on the ground beside them, unrestrained and awake—the bastard hadn't even sounded the alarm when he had the chance.

Over them stood two mercenaries with barrels pointed down, ready to execute their hostages given the slightest wayward response.

The remaining fighters had their weapons aimed at Cancer before he came to a full stop, a few of them shifting their barrels to cover Reilly and Worthy behind him. Cancer saw all this in an instant, a two-part calculation unfolding in his mind. One, that David and Ian were dead no matter how the rest of his team reacted. Two, that even with himself, Reilly, and Worthy engaging targets as quickly as they could, they had no chance of killing all these men without being cut down themselves. Which wasn't to say they couldn't make one hell of a go at it, but that wouldn't help to stop Sofia and the payload of VX she was speeding out of the country.

Cancer released his grip on the Galil, throwing up his hands and turning to face the house to locate the only decision maker left.

Herrera had exited the front door and was taking a circuitous route to join his men, remaining clear of their fields of fire with his 1911 in one hand. Reilly and Worthy had followed Cancer's lead, thank Christ, and had their hands up as well.

Cancer called out, "*Coronel*, let's talk. It's not in either of our interests to piss off Vega."

Herrera rounded the trio of Americans, joining his men as Cancer rotated to keep him in sight, to gain any comprehension of why this was happening and how he could counter it.

And, as Herrera came to a stop three meters away, the answer became clear.

"Vega is dead."

Those three words induced the kind of *oh shit* reaction that was almost alien to Cancer at this point in his career, and he felt a knot forming in his gut as Herrera continued, "The men on motorcycles got him a few hours ago. He was shot 37 times. Someone just took over his operation, and if I do not pledge my allegiance now, I will be killed."

"Then pledge your allegiance, sir," Cancer said, "but leave my men out of it."

Herrera laughed.

"And leave five witnesses with knowledge of our airfields, the tail number of one of our planes? Did you honestly think Vega would let you leave Venezuela alive after learning his routes? He was certainly crazy, but he did not care about you bringing him Sofia's head. Vega only wanted revenge for his friend. After that you were to die, and now you will."

"If Vega is dead," Cancer said, "then you don't have to carry out his order."

"Ah, *sí*," Herrera conceded, laughing, "but I will not have the CIA coming after the people that feed my family."

This was combat negotiation at its most critical, and Cancer's moment-by-moment analysis of the colonel's concerns needed to be on point and to the letter if he was to secure any chance of survival for his team.

Lowering his hands, Cancer threw back his head and responded with a laugh of his own.

"*Coronel*, you think we're CIA? Congratulations, sir, you're right. And no other organization in the US government has worked so closely with drug traffickers."

Herrera's face flashed a quizzical expression, and Cancer readily seized on the opportunity to delay by way of confusion. No one on the team was a student of history as much as Cancer—maybe Ian, but he wasn't able to intervene at the moment and would probably fuck it up even if he could. Hell, half the team had wanted to shoot him in the midst of any number of his geopolitical rants.

"The CIA," Cancer went on, "equipped Golden Triangle opium cartels in exchange for intelligence in the Korean War, not to mention flying opium for the Hmongs to build a private army in Laos during our involvement in Vietnam. You know more than I do about the Contras and Sandinistas in Nicaragua, not to mention letting Noriega run drugs in exchange for his support right up until he sided with the Soviets and threatened our access to the Panama Canal. Then we paid opium warlords in Afghanistan to fight the Soviets. We don't give a shit about drugs coming into the States, only about fighting our enemies."

He was telling the truth now not out of any moral obligation to the man who was about to kill them all, but rather because Herrera struck him as something of a human lie detector. The speed with which he'd attacked Nikolai based on his reaction to the no-notice shakedown was something Cancer wouldn't soon forget, and he wasn't about to provide any additional incentive that would hasten his team's demise.

With a good-natured shrug, Cancer pointed out, "*Coronel*, the CIA and narco networks have been working together for a long time. You might not be high enough in the food chain to realize that, but check it out: when somebody crosses the Agency, we go to the ends of the earth to terminate that person. That's what Sofia did and that's why we're after her—and by the way, your name is the one that we vetted. If you take us down, you're looking over your shoulder for the rest of your life. Or we can part ways as friends. Believe me, sir, you don't want to see what lengths our people will go to in order to settle scores with anyone who stabs them in the back. So let us go, and no one will ever threaten your profit or your family. You have my word."

The former lieutenant colonel didn't back down, nor was he unmoved—though not, as Cancer could see at once, by any detailing of historical trivia or threats of retaliation. His bloodshot eyes were flooding with tears, and Cancer realized for the first time what had driven this man to such a state of despair.

Eberardo Herrera had spent a lifetime at war, first on behalf of the Colombian Army and then on behalf of the traffickers. He'd almost certainly been a corrupt military officer, but age and the steady approach of death had increasingly confirmed that this was what his life had amounted to, all the money suddenly meaningless in the wake of his atrocities. There was no going back and, unless Cancer provided some recourse in the next thirty seconds tops, nothing to disincentivize him from committing one more.

So rather than provide any additional data, Cancer exploited the emotional component and slowly, carefully dipped one hand into his pocket to recover a pack of cigarettes and his lighter.

"*Coronel*, with your permission, sir."

"Yes," Herrera said with a sniffle. "Smoke, all of you. Smoke one last time."

Cancer lit a cigarette, drawing a breath to ensure the ember was lit. Then he turned it in his fingers and approached Herrera, keeping his other hand aloft under the watchful eyes of the mercenaries keeping aim as he moved.

"For you, sir. For taking us all this way. I understand you must go, but you don't have to kill us before you depart."

Herrera snatched the cigarette and sucked at it greedily, trying to summon some level of control as Cancer took slow, steady steps backward and came to a stop.

"We're all old soldiers." He cut his gaze to David on the ground and said, "Well, some older than others. But soldiers, just the same. Just like you, sir."

"Not like me," Herrera replied without malice. The statement had the tone not of an insult but a compliment—he was emotionally distancing himself from the men he was about to kill, and in the process ceding the moral high ground to his victims.

"Just like you," Cancer repeated firmly. "We've all done horrible shit for our country, for our egos. But we can part ways now as comrades, and not enemies. My team might get Sofia or we might be killed, but we're either leaving Venezuela or getting buried here. Right now your name is clean in the eyes of the Agency, and we intend to keep it that way."

It was a precipitous moment, and Cancer readied himself for the inevitable shootout. Given the numbers and lack of covered and concealed positions for which to dart, his team would be annihilated to a man; but if this was going to be a throw-down, they'd sure as hell make the most of it, and Herrera would be the first to go.

But Herrera relented at last, cutting his gaze to the absolute last person Cancer cared about.

"Felix, get your gear."

Cancer looked over at the little dirtbag, who rose from the ground and dusted himself off.

Then, idiot that he was, Felix sneered defiantly.

"No," he declared, quite unexpectedly to Cancer and, judging by the soured expressions before him, everyone else as well. He walked through the line of fire to stand beside Cancer, Worthy, and Reilly. "I stay with the Americans, and I will not go until Sofia is dead. If you have a problem with this, you may shoot me now."

Herrera did have a problem with that, though he elected not to pursue Felix's foolishly suggested recourse.

Instead, the disgraced former colonel ripped the cigarette from his lips and threw it to the ground in disgust.

"Load their gear," he instructed his mercenaries, "all of it."

"*Coronel*," Cancer cautioned, "since you have spared us, I must notify you that our equipment and uniforms have embedded tracking devices. If we don't report in, the Agency will assume we're captured and launch an airstrike."

It was, of course, total bullshit. No paramilitary element in the world wanted to keep their location hidden from their employers quite so badly and consistently as his Project Longwing team, but whether Herrera actually bought it or merely wasn't willing to risk the consequences of calling Cancer's bluff, the ruse seemed to work.

Herrera corrected himself, "Get the money. Leave the gear."

What ensued would have been painful to watch under the best of circumstances, much less with a WMD in the hands of a diabolical woman speeding away from Michelena.

The designated executioners remained in place to dispatch David and Ian, while two others kept their weapons trained on the remaining team members. The rest descended on the rucksacks, upending them to deposit the contents that were then kicked around in the desperate search for cash.

One by one, the banded packets of US and Colombian currency were found and delivered to Herrera, who flipped through and pocketed them in sequence. This was bad, Cancer thought, perhaps only slightly preferable to being killed. Sure, each team member had some cash on their person, and the colonel wasn't dumb enough to compromise his overwhelming security advantage by ordering a pat-down of three armed men. But they didn't have enough to last any amount of time in Venezuela.

As the final packet of cash was found and delivered, Herrera wheeled around and kicked David's motionless figure in the ribs, shouting, "Only 10,000 dollars, ey, *pirobo?*"

"*Coronel,*" Cancer said, trying to conceal the obvious implications of begging, "leave us one vehicle. That's all I ask."

Herrera said something to one of his men, a short exchange that Cancer couldn't hear. The mercenary nodded before striding toward the Americans—or, more accurately, he realized, toward Felix.

There was no word of warning, much less a formal request. The fighter slung a fist into Felix's nose, an audible *pop* confirming a nasal fracture had been inflicted in the process. The sub driver simply collapsed, clearly a stranger to hand-to-hand combat, and the mercenary knelt to strip the gold Rolex from his wrist before delivering it to Herrera.

Felix thrashed about on the ground, shouting Spanish profanities until Cancer hissed, "Stay down, and shut the fuck up."

Herrera grinned at the sight of the Rolex in his hand, and he pocketed it before fixing his gaze on Cancer with a look that said, *defy me now and see what happens.*

Then he shouted, "Turn around."

Cancer didn't do so immediately, instead conferring a nod of respectful deference before he slowly turned in place, keeping his hands up.

Worthy and Reilly weren't so quick to acquiesce, glancing at Cancer as if he were mad for agreeing.

"Do it," Cancer said, looking at them with feigned confidence to convey that everything would work out. Both were too young and inexperienced, at least relative to himself, to understand that this was both a security and a face-saving measure for Herrera.

Warily, they both followed suit.

The fear of getting shot in the back was certainly present, though Cancer rationalized that if Herrera truly wanted them dead he'd have no problem making it happen no matter which direction they were oriented. Instead he silently willed this hollowed-out husk of a man whose life he'd saved, thank you very much, to honor Cancer's one and only request at the end of their brief negotiations.

He heard vehicle doors slamming, ignitions cranking, then the roar of engines speeding away down the long driveway—please, Cancer thought, *please* let there be a truck left behind, just one truck—and he whirled back around to appraise the outcome of his plea.

Every single vehicle was gone, the last one in the convoy visible for a split second before it vanished around the trees.

"Cock*sucker*!" he shouted, anger overcoming all else. Herrera and his men had overpowered two team members as hostages so he could lure the remaining three into an inescapable trap, and more infuriating still was the fact that Cancer had taken the bait and led two teammates into the fray. Hook, line, sinker. Fuck.

Worthy and Reilly ran past him, dropping to their knees beside David. Reilly peeled one of the team leader's eyelids open.

"He's alive," the medic called, pinching David's trapezius to try and rouse him to consciousness and, when that failed, resorting to a sternum rub.

But the team leader's survival was precious little consolation, Cancer thought, given that Herrera had handed them all a death sentence by abandoning them in the middle of this godforsaken nation. He didn't move an inch, his thoughts darting between the particulars of their current circumstance with such intensity that he didn't hear Felix rushing to his side, breathless.

"That was incredible."

"Shut up, fuckface," Cancer snapped, turning to face the sub driver and nearly jolting at the sight.

Gruesome streaks of dark blood ran from both nostrils all the way down his chin, where they converged into a single stream that drizzled onto his shirt.

"Gah," Cancer sputtered, "I thought you were ugly without a broken nose. Why didn't you get out of this when you had the chance?"

With a remorseful shrug, Felix said, "Your words, *mi amigo*. I too have done some terrible things. I cannot take them back, but if I help you get Sofia, this will be a form of penance, no?"

"No," Cancer said flatly. "You stupid, ugly bastard. Still, that was some gangster shit you said."

Then he set a hand on Felix's shoulder, gave it hard shake, and leaned in to continue in a whisper, "You may have an abnormally small cock, but you got some balls, my friend."

Cancer shoved Felix away from him, seeking to restore order to the universe of his team. Events like this fragmented the reality of a soldier to moment-by-moment fear for survival, he knew from experience, and unless the leadership swiftly filled that void with guidance, everything could quickly go to shit even more than it already had.

"Reilly, how long until those two scumbags are functional?"

"Thirty minutes to an hour."

"Worthy," Cancer shouted, "get your inbred cousin-fucking Billy Bob slack-jawed cross-eyed ass over here."

The pointman abandoned his current effort of trying to cut Ian free and ran over.

"What's up, boss?"

Cancer jerked a thumb toward Felix.

"Take this vagina-drying eyesore to the nearest property. Don't come back until you have a vehicle. They don't give it to you, then take it. This isn't the time to grow a conscience, son, you get me?"

"Got it, Cancer. But that whole thing was...I mean, *trackers*? In our equipment? Did you actually say 'airstrike?'"

Cancer sneered, responding with his favorite law of war.

"If it's stupid but it works, it isn't stupid. Now go."

40

Worthy took up a position beside the front door, directing his suppressed M4 toward the space a foot and a half above the handle.

With his body situated between the nearest window and the door that the first bullets would likely puncture if this home's occupant decided he didn't particularly care to sell his vehicle to an unknown solicitor, he glanced rearward to see Felix standing tentatively behind him.

Darkness was falling now, and Worthy kept his night vision flipped upward in anticipation of an entry into the lit home, the plot of land adjacent to the one where Cancer and Reilly currently managed David and Ian's recovery. Unlike the house bearing the cold body of a North Korean scientist, however, this one appeared to possess one or more living occupants—while a 360 exterior sweep had revealed no movement, the lights were on and a late-model Hyundai SUV sat in the driveway. Probably too new for him to hotwire with any degree of efficiency, and even if he wanted to give it a go, the red light blinking inside the vehicle assured him he'd set off the car alarm in the process. Uninterested in being surprised by a gun-wielding homeowner, Worthy decided to initiate contact on his own terms instead.

He waved Felix forward, resuming the grip on his rifle as the sub driver moved to the opposite side of the doorway as instructed and then knocked three times.

A small dog began yapping incessantly, though no one answered the particularly hideous gentleman caller in the form of Felix, who merely shrugged in response.

Worthy let the situation develop, not wanting Felix to appear overly aggressive in eliciting the homeowner's attention. But he couldn't deny that the events of the past hour had taken their toll on him, both mentally and emotionally.

He was the only one with the close quarters shooting reflexes to even consider opening fire on the mercenaries after they'd turned against his team, and even he would have been taken out long before he could have saved anyone. Then again, what did he expect? Worthy was one of five men whose country wanted them to commit sanctioned murder against the deserving without admitting she was doing so for fear of how she'd be perceived on the world stage. Hypocrisy at its finest, which he didn't particularly care about from an ethical standpoint. After all, combating terrorism justified almost anything short of resorting to the same tactics.

But from a practical and tactical standpoint, Worthy cared deeply. How many times had his team been sent to near-certain death and then left to cobble together some semblance of a plan by improvising on the fly? There were never enough people, never enough resources. They'd only gotten this far in the mission against Sofia by violating every maxim of their operational restrictions. If they somehow succeeded, the Agency would take credit for a job well done. In the far more likely event that they failed, that same organization would happily write Project Longwing off as a failed experiment in targeted killing, if not prosecute the team for any number of transgressions that had thus far remained undiscovered.

Either way, Worthy could rely on no one but his teammates, and at present not even them; only Felix, who, despite his sudden and unexpected loyalty in the wake of Herrera's betrayal, could just as easily decide he was better off on his own and sabotage their efforts at any and every conceivable juncture.

When there was still no response to Felix's knock, Worthy nodded back to the door, instructing him to repeat the process.

This time Worthy heard footsteps approaching the door, though there was a significant pause before a gruff male voice finally called, "*¿Quién es?*"

Felix replied in English as instructed, repeating Worthy's orders more or less verbatim.

"Good evening. I would like to pay you two thousand dollars for your car. In cash."

It was an astronomical sum given the team's only funds consisted of what they'd carried in their uniforms, and an audible snort preceded the homeowner's response.

"Then slide it under the door."

Worthy flashed an index finger to Felix. The sub driver peeled a hundred-dollar bill off the wad in his pocket and slid it beneath the door as instructed, then said, "I have the rest. Just open the door, and hand me the key."

In truth they were taking the car and paying for the privilege whether the homeowner consented or not; the only question was whether doing so would involve a cordial cash transaction or raiding the house to find the keys, and Worthy desperately hoped for the latter. There had been little means of assessing police presence in Venezuela thus far, but the last thing they needed was an APB for the one vehicle that could put them on Sofia's tail once more.

The man unlocked the bolt, a promising development whose potential ended when he cracked the door an inch, casting a beam of light outside.

He spoke in Spanish, sounding incredibly suspicious—understandable, Worthy thought, given that Felix looked like a tattooed bag of shit under the best of circumstances. With a freshly broken nose, the very sight of him was particularly difficult to stomach, and the tone of the ensuing conversation turned increasingly skeptical as both parties communicated in Spanish.

Worthy was hard-pressed to determine what was going on here. Felix was waving the cash, which didn't seem to convince the man, whose responses took on an ever more confrontational tone. Meanwhile the dog continued to yap, which irritated Worthy to no end—he'd grown up with hunting dogs, and had no understanding of nor empathy for toy animals meant to sit in one's lap between outbursts at the slightest noise.

Meanwhile Felix and the man continued arguing in words that he couldn't understand, the conversation seeming to reach some imminent breaking point. Worthy's patience ran out after a few seconds that seemed like much longer. He'd finally had enough.

Pivoting on one heel to spin his back to the house, Worthy used the opposite foot to mule kick the door as hard as he could.

The door popped inward with incredible force and ricocheted back into his boot sole in a fraction of a second, and he could tell by the vibration that a human body had been displaced in the interim.

Spinning to face the entryway, he drove a forward kick into the door and then shouldered through it to enter the home.

There was a prostrate man clutching his face, flanked by a pump-action shotgun he'd dropped in the course of his fall. Worthy kicked the weapon away and swept his suppressed M4 across the house interior to scan for anyone who might seek to intervene in what was about to happen.

All he found was the dog, a flash of white fur scampering into a far room and out of sight.

Aiming downward, Worthy looked at the man—obese, hairy, wearing a sleeveless T-shirt, sweatpants, and flip flops, hands held up in a futile effort to defend himself. Initially pointing his rifle at the ground beside the man's head, Worthy thought better of it and instead found the space between his inner thighs before firing two rounds that splintered into the floorboard.

The expended brass from his cartridges was still rolling as he pressed the tip of his warm suppressor between the man's outstretched palms, planting it square on his forehead before speaking in a tone that was uncharacteristically violent.

"Keys, motherfucker, or I paint the floor with your brain."

Worthy expected the man to grab his barrel, which at this point was perfectly fine with him. He'd gone into this encounter expecting a family who'd receive the furthest possible extent of his team's meager remaining finances along with a sincere apology, and now he almost hoped that this fat shitbag would give him a reason to pull the trigger in self-defense. His team was in dire straits and facing a terrorist threat that he didn't trust his own country to be able to stop, and if Cancer's admonition not to "grow a conscience" had seemed absurd when he'd initially heard it, Worthy was now willing to make the sniper proud if not insecure in his role as the team's resident sociopath.

But no such outcome occurred; the man moved one hand amid the cries of his yapping dog, though only to point at the door behind Worthy.

He glanced over his shoulder to see a keyring dangling from a peg beside the entrance. Felix snatched it up and Worthy suddenly deflated, wondering what had caused him to swell with such immediate violence and what this job was turning him into.

"Pay him," he said to Felix.

And rather than do anything so trite as toss the bills on the ground, Felix instead advanced and dropped to his knees, stuffing the currency into the man's mouth like a mafioso hellbent on making a point. Worthy grabbed Felix's shoulder and wrenched him up, using one arm to drag the emboldened sub driver back to the doorway.

"*Muchas gracias*," Worthy called, "*hasta luego*."

Then he shoved Felix outside, hastening to follow and slam the door shut behind him before hearing the satisfying beep of the Hyundai unlocking.

41

Cancer braked at the edge of the driveway, wheeling the Hyundai Santa Fe left and aligning its headlights on the long stretch of gravel road before accelerating amid Worthy's narration from the passenger seat.

"One mile to right turn."

"Got it," Cancer replied, taking a glance in the rearview mirror before asking, "Boss, you gonna report we're back on the move or what?"

I checked the phone in my hand, appraising our location—no easy task given that I was wedged between a door on one side and Reilly's massive form in the center seat. Ian was equally uncomfortable on the medic's opposite side, our seating arrangement dictated by his incessant checks for TBI and brain bleed. No dice on either so far, and aside from a dull headache and an incredibly tender mass of swollen flesh on my scalp, I felt remarkably coherent.

Then I replied, "Duchess is going to be pissed enough to find out we're unaccompanied, and I don't want to drop that bomb until we're at least on the highway."

It was partially true, at least. Though to be honest I wasn't in any rush to inform the CIA that my entire team had very nearly been wiped out by our own partner force; equally significant in my delay was the very real factor that I didn't remember, well, any of it. A mercenary told me that Herrera sought my counsel, I'd exited the dining room and stepped outside into the sunshine, and then I'd awoken on the ground, gagged and with my hands tied, with Reilly rubbing my sternum to restore consciousness. Our convoy was nowhere to be seen, and Worthy and Felix were moving off into the wood line.

So what the hell had happened?

Only Cancer and Reilly's explanation filled me in, the events they detailed sounding so ludicrous that for a moment I thought my entire element, American and Colombian alike, was playing one elaborate practical joke.

Part of that was my own initial nausea and disorientation, to be sure, followed in short order by the sight of Ian beside me. The knot on his head combined with the fearful return to his senses assured me that this was no joke, and that reality brought me to full consciousness with a surge of adrenaline quickly hampered by the sluggishness of my physical responses.

Reilly said to no one in particular, "Well, let's look at the bright side: at least we don't have to cut off Sofia's head anymore."

"This is true," Felix replied behind me, "though perhaps we should anyway."

I'd almost forgotten the sub driver was with us, crammed in the far back along with our rucksacks.

"Yeah?" Ian asked. "Who's going to do that, Felix, you?"

"I thought you were going to."

Looking over from the passenger seat, Worthy called back, "No, Felix, I think you're the right man for the job." He chuckled and added, "You guys should have seen him stuffing money down the throat of whatever poor bastard owned this truck. Felix turned into a regular Pablo Escobar."

"Thank you," Felix replied.

"It's not a compliment."

Ian said thoughtfully, "It kind of is, though. Pablo Escobar had an affair with the country's hottest news anchor. That would be like Reilly becoming a drug kingpin in the States and sleeping with Robin Meade."

Worthy countered, "Whoa, whoa—I think you mean Megyn Kelly."

"Wrong," Reilly said adamantly. "Did you even consider Erin Andrews?"

Cancer snickered.

"ESPN doesn't count as news, asshole. And you're all wrong—take the whole picture into account, and the only proper comparison is Vivian Brown."

"Who's that?" Worthy asked.

"Weather Channel, you hick. The confidence, the smooth delivery...and if we're gonna be so shallow as to discuss looks, then frankly there's no comparison."

"My God," Reilly gasped, apparently recognizing the name, "he's right."

Then, sounding troubled, the medic added, "But the weather isn't really news, either."

Cancer shook his head. "Better pick up a dictionary: 'noteworthy information about current events.' The weather affects us all, so you're goddamn right it's news."

I said, "Cancer off the top rope, guys. Discussion over."

"Discussion over," Worthy agreed, "because we got a right turn coming up. Town outskirts coming up on our left."

Judging by my glance out the window, it was hard to tell if he was right —the only illumination outside of our headlights was a few scattered fires. Electricity was apparently at a premium here, along with everything else. But I could make out vehicle headlights to our right, moving swiftly along Route 1.

Within two turns we were on the highway, swiftly accelerating northeast, bypassing the Venezuelan Andes on our way toward the coast.

The mountain contours on my map imagery looked positively heinous, and I was immeasurably grateful we didn't have to traverse on foot. Most of our operations had involved negotiating steeply elevated terrain—a hallmark of insurgency strongholds for good reason—and I much preferred the comfort of vehicle passage to hauling a rucksack over that kind of landscape. When we did our next mission, if there was a next mission at all, the odds were against us being this lucky.

But for now we were on our way. Nightfall worked to our advantage for the time being—we'd all changed into a set of civilian hiking clothes packed for the purpose, tactical vests tucked between our feet to withstand passing observation in urban areas—but the longer we remained unseen by the outside world, the better.

"Boss," Cancer said, breaking my train of thought.

"Yeah?"

He drove in silence, as if I'd deduce his meaning without being told. When I offered no further response, however, he clarified.

"Call Duchess and explain we're fucked."

"Right," I said. "Yeah, it's probably time to let that cat out of the bag."

Then I transmitted, "Raptor Nine One, this is Suicide Actual."

I was confused upon hearing the response—it was routine as could be, though the speaker was most certainly not the woman I was used to communicating with on our excursions.

"*Suicide Actual, this is Raptor Nine One. Send it.*"

Whoever it was, she sounded like she'd been dragged out of a Wisconsin hunting lodge, and I instinctively replied, "Who is this? Where's Duchess?"

"*Duchess is moving to a forward-staged location at this time. I'm filling in on comms.*"

That was interesting, I thought. The Agency must have been particularly concerned about the VX for Duchess to leave the confines of CIA headquarters. I'd met with her exactly once outside of that venue since the beginning of Project Longwing, namely when she surprised me in my hometown, and the sight of her had been something akin to a bear in the suburbs.

"Whatever," I replied. "Be advised, we just lost our entire mercenary force."

"*Gunfight?*"

We should be so lucky, I thought. I'd have certainly preferred if Herrera and his band of shitheads were all dead. Better still if I'd been the one to make it happen.

"Negative," I said. "They had a loss of morale from previous casualties, and assessed the risk of continuing the mission too great. Herrera jumped ship on us and took everyone with him."

Felix said, "Not everyone."

"Shut up, douchebag," I yelled back, then transmitted, "Except Felix, he's still with us. Moral of the story is that we're looking down the barrel of an unassisted exfil unless you can line something up for us."

"That won't be a problem. Likely Maritime Department pickup along the coast, given the way things are unfolding, but we'll get working on options. What's your current status?"

And that was the million-dollar question, one whose truthful answer would lead me ever closer to realities I didn't want to face.

"All men and equipment accounted for, no injuries," I began, fully realizing the irony of that last statement given that Ian and I had been clubbed over the head and Felix had a shattered nose. "However, we faced a significant delay in acquiring alternate transportation. Currently on Route 1 just outside of Michelena, down to one vehicle and about five grand of operational funds. Hurting on ammo; if we get in another good scrape we'll be down to what we can find in battlefield resupply. Please advise on Sofia's location and how far we are behind her, over."

"Last ping put her on Route 1, in vicinity of Caja Seca. About a four-and-a-half-hour head start on you."

I felt my shoulders sag—this was an insurmountable advantage in time and distance, and even with the entire US military and intelligence machine now seeking to stop her, there was zero chance my team would be pulling the trigger. Herrera had fucked us, and in doing so removed us from any relevance whatsoever in the proceedings ahead. At this point, we'd be lucky just to make it out of Venezuela.

For a moment I considered muttering a curse to myself, thought better of it, and keyed my mic.

"Shit."

"Don't be so hard on yourself," the woman replied. *"Sofia's nearest coastal access will be in either Coro or Puerto Cabello, depending on which route she takes after clearing Lake Maracaibo. That means a ten-to-thirteen-hour trip minimum, which won't put her next to the Caribbean until just before sunrise at the earliest. She still needs time to load the VX onto a boat and send it toward the New Panamax, which won't be off the coast of Venezuela until tomorrow night."*

"Bottom line," I asked, "where do we stand?"

A brief pause before she answered, *"Bottom line is that all available intelli-*

gence indicates we have approximately 22 hours before Sofia takes to sea with the VX, by which time we'll have a naval blockade off the coast and every conceivable ISR asset in place to find a pinpoint location before she's able to get underway. Unless our intelligence assessment is grievously wrong, your team is still in the fight."

42

Reilly stared out the open window of the safehouse, letting the salty warm air wash over him in an attempt to quell his mounting anger.

It was hard to believe they were still in Venezuela. With no indications of oppressive poverty or criminally inept political leadership, it was difficult to reconcile the crumbling infrastructure and desperate refugees on the country's west side with what he saw now.

Across the street was an undeveloped field of low bushes the size of a city block, beyond which bicyclists in sandals glided along a paved walkway. Past them was a strip of golden sand, the beach traversed by bikini-clad women who, even at this distance, he could tell had bodies that would rival Isabella's.

But the main feature was calm Caribbean water spreading endlessly below the sapphire sky, a sight of such beauty that Reilly could almost forget he was on a mission at all—at least, if he'd had any half-decent food to calm him.

But hungry or no, he should have appreciated the situation far more than he did. His team had made it all the way to Sofia's last known location in Puerto Cabello without incident, no small feat for a cross-country road trip that stretched through the night and well into the following morning. After their missions in the Philippines, Syria, China, and Nigeria, the simple act of traveling that far without enemy contact was inconceivable; and yet they'd not only reached Puerto Cabello uncontested, but waltzed directly into an Agency-procured safehouse that Reilly would gladly visit for vacation, much less stage at for an imminent raid using whatever bullets they had left.

Now, all they could do was wait.

He glanced left and right at the buildings flanking the safehouse, a series of perfectly ordinary homes, hotels, and restaurants lining the beach as they would in any civilized nation.

The city was remarkable for how unremarkable it was—the only notable installations included a major shipping port, state-owned shipyard, small naval base, railway terminal, and a regional airport. There were only two commercial marinas, but no way to tell which boat was Sofia's or if it was even present at all; the odds were just as good that a vessel would be arriving tonight to pick her up along with the VX. Other than that, unless anyone on his team had a burning interest to visit eighteenth-century colonial fortifications, there simply weren't many tourist attractions to speak of in Puerto Cabello, whose name made absolutely no sense to Reilly in the first place.

He heard someone enter the room behind him and whirled around to see Ian looking tentative, fearful.

Reilly asked, "They find her yet?"

"No," Ian replied, adding in a soothing tone, "but the Agency is running a full-court press of ISR and SIGINT over the city. It's only a matter of time before they find a pinpoint location."

Reilly shot back, "You said that when we got here, which is why David wouldn't let anyone leave for food until twenty minutes ago. And I'm hungry, Ian, because I gave most of my food to refugees."

"I told you, buddy, you could have one of my field rations—"

"I don't *want* one of your field rations, *buddy*," Reilly snapped. "I want my goddamn pork and nuts, like we got in Colombia. You can't spoil a high performance athlete like myself with premium foodstuffs and suddenly expect me to go back to prison-grade slop."

Ian held up his palms, trying to calm the medic.

"We talked about this. You're getting hangry, that's all—"

"And another thing," Reilly cut him off. "*Cabello* means hair, right?"

"Yeah. It does."

"So you brought me here, and then you made sure David wouldn't let anyone leave the safehouse because Sofia would pop up any second, and now everyone's hungry and pissed off while we wait for some real food to arrive to our little slice of paradise in Port-fucking-Hair."

Ian grinned, but the expression quickly faded under Reilly's smoldering glare.

Then he replied, "The name is from the Spanish colonials. They said the water was so tranquil they could use a single hair to tie their ships to the dock. Pretty smart for Sofia, if you think about it. She's got one shot to make the linkup with the New Panamax, which is going to be off the Venezuelan coast tonight. A single storm could ruin her chances, so she picked the one spot where a weather event was least likely to occur."

"If I don't get some food real quick, there's going to be a weather event, all right. It's called my fist, your face, and—"

He went silent at the knock on the door, then threw back his head and gasped, "Oh, thank God."

They moved to the front room, where Cancer opened the door to allow Felix and Worthy to enter. Both men carried plastic bags loaded to the breaking point, the intoxicating aroma of fresh bread and exquisitely cooked meat wafting into the room.

Whisking their payload into the dining room, Worthy announced, "We got tamales, beef stew, plantain filled with beef, cheese rolls, yucca balls. We got corn bread, we got seafood soup, and we got this." He set his takeout on the table and rifled through it to produce two bulging brown paper bags, one soaked with grease.

Reilly held his breath, feeling his bottom lip tremble as Worthy held out the bags to him. "Some Scooby snacks for our honored medic. Just like they make them in Colombia."

The medic released a groan of ecstasy, snatching the bags and retreating to a chair to let the feast commence.

He was so enraptured by the sight inside the bags that he barely noticed David sauntering in from a side room, joining the team as they took their seats and began digging in. Worthy hadn't been joking, Reilly saw—one bag had his roasted nuts, and the other was stuffed to capacity with the pork that had become an obsession if not an addiction during their time in Medellín.

Reilly ate greedily, stuffing a meat strip into his mouth and following it up with a handful of nuts before chewing with delirious happiness.

Felix was unimpressed, however, his first bite of a tamale causing him to ruefully shake his head and comment, "This tastes much better in Colombia."

Lifting another meat strip and waving it at the sub driver, Reilly declared, "I don't want to hear a single complaint from you. You're the one person here who had a chance to get out of this mess."

Recoiling at the outburst, Felix looked to David, who explained, "He's hangry."

"What?"

"Hungry-angry. He'll calm down soon, just give him a minute."

"Oh," Felix replied. Then he looked at Reilly. "But what else would I do, if not come with?"

Reilly swallowed another mouthful and said, "Hmmm, let's see. Enjoy your freedom with Isabella, maybe even your wife."

"Wife? What wife?"

The medic deposited a handful of nuts in his mouth and chewed them slowly while glaring at Felix.

"You told me on the way to our ambush site that you started running drugs because you were getting married. Or was that all bullshit?"

"Ah, that." Felix nodded. "I am from Buenaventura. Very poor town, much of it slums. You know who had the biggest houses, the finest cars? Fishermen who had gotten a single load across and been 'crowned.' To do this once is to be set for life. Do you know why I did not run one load and retire?"

Reilly shook his head.

"My wife wanted more. And more, and more. So I kept running across the sea, and one time when I returned to my home, a stranger answered the door. She had taken everything and left."

"Woof," Cancer grunted. "Where is she now?"

"You may as well tell me, *mi amigo*, but the bastard who is porking her landed on quite a stack of pesos, I can tell you that much."

David picked through a container of beef stew with his plastic fork. "You never went looking for her?"

"I made inquiries, for a time. But she hid well, knowing what waited for her and her *marica* if I found her."

Reilly raised his eyebrows.

Felix held up his right hand in response, the pinky and ring fingers extended.

"This many bullets, *mi amigo*."

Sure, Reilly thought. Felix was a real tough guy right up until there was any opposition—during their fight to escape the ambush position, Reilly had seen him cowering behind a truck when there were plenty of weapons lying around next to the dead mercenaries.

But he said nothing, already beginning his transition back to his usual mild-mannered self. Instead Reilly continued shoveling food into his mouth, gradually noticing that the sub driver was watching him with a look of utter fascination. He was a hideous sight—crooked nose, two black eyes, and a fixed stare.

"Why are you looking at me like that?" Reilly asked with his mouth full.

Felix shrugged.

"I am impressed, that is all. Not many visitors will eat this."

"What, the pork?"

Cancer silenced Felix with a murderous glance, leaving Reilly to chew his food, looking from one team member to the next with an increasingly haunted expression.

"What?" he asked. "What is it?"

David said, "Reilly, are you still hangry?"

"No," he replied, gleefully chewing as he spoke. "I feel great. Why?"

David gave a subtle nod of consent to Felix, who explained.

"That is not pork, my friend. *Ponche* meat comes from the *chigüiro*, which is a...how do you say...like a hamster. No, bigger..."

"A guinea pig?"

"Much bigger."

Cancer intervened, "Surprise, you've been eating 120-pound rat."

Reilly swallowed.

"What?"

Felix snapped his fingers with an epiphany and said, "Capybara. The English word is capybara."

Ian supplied, "The world's largest rodent."

But Reilly was still in denial, now analyzing the meat for texture and consistency before insisting, "No, this is pork."

David sighed, taking on the role of a father trying to explain that Santa wasn't real to a child who was reluctant to face the truth. "Ever notice how no one else on the team has touched it?"

Cancer was smiling malevolently now. "They're like water pigs, Reilly, swimming in their own shit."

Pushing the meat aside, Reilly grabbed the other bag and said, "At least I've got my—wait, these are nuts, right?"

Felix shook his head. "No. We call these *homigas culonas.*"

"Ant asses," Cancer said.

"*Sí,*" Felix agreed, "it means 'big-ass ants.' After the wings and legs are pulled, we roast and salt them. They are delicious, yes?"

"I wouldn't know," Cancer replied, "because no one but Reilly has eaten those dirty motherfuckers."

Reilly felt sick to his stomach now, though whether from eating too much too fast or from the sheer betrayal of his teammates, he couldn't say. He teetered between rage and resignation, unable to determine how to react.

Finally he said the only words that came to mind, spoken in a breathless inquiry.

"But, I mean...*why*?"

David set a conciliatory hand on his shoulder.

"Because we could, Reilly. Because we could."

43

Duchess sat before her open laptop, shoulders crammed between the gunmetal gray walls on either side of her cramped workspace.

She tried to ignore the noise of the Navy personnel working in the combat information center behind her, along with the disquieting fact that she could actually feel the ship rocking in the waves, a slow, churning momentum that made her wonder if she was in any danger of losing her last meal.

Departing her OPCEN to forward-stage in the Caribbean was a calculated risk. Between the transit time and limited connectivity until she reached her destination, she'd had to temporarily compromise her usual God's-eye view of all things related to the mission at hand.

Ultimately, though, she simply couldn't outsource the split-second assessment and decision making that she anticipated the New Panamax takedown would require. Whatever was aboard that ship—and with Sofia's 216 containers in place, Duchess knew it held far more than storage space for the VX—it would dictate the purpose and guidance for a tremendous number of military and intelligence resources. Trying to make those decisions based on information being relayed to Langley was more than she could bear; instead she'd simply board the ship herself the moment the Marine Raiders deemed it secure, see the contents of Sofia's containers for herself, and orchestrate her nation's response with the reflexes of a hunter pursuing a wounded predator into the brush.

There were, of course, selfish reasons as well.

Duchess's career path had kept her confined to the halls of Langley for far too long, and the thought of being whisked to the front lines of a terrorist plot was too good to pass up. This was the Caribbean, after all, and if she got to take in breathtaking scenery and immaculate weather while stopping a WMD, so much the better.

So she felt more than a little dismayed when, after arranging an Operational Support Airlift flight, she'd been spirited via small jet to Guantanamo for transfer to a waiting CH-46 Sea Knight helicopter, then ended up here, aboard the USS *Wichita*, as expected. In the Caribbean, a shining jewel among paradise destinations, just as she'd hoped. All should have been well with the world, right up until she found her workstation to be a claustrophobic phone booth of a compartment in the ship's combat information center. The only reprieve from that was living accommodations consisting of triple bunking with two junior officers who were like twenty-something versions of Jo Ann—annoyingly upbeat and overly talkative.

So much for a thrilling adventure at sea, she thought. And the food—well, the food sucked, plain and simple. Why anyone would volunteer for repeated exposure to such conditions by joining the Navy, she had no idea. But whatever these sailors were getting paid, it wasn't nearly enough.

The sound of her phone ringing brought with it a tremendous wave of relief; finally, a distraction from the limited oxygen supply of this prison cell of an office.

Lifting the receiver on the first ring, she said, "Duchess."

The response was jittery, excited even, from a man who usually acted anything but.

"Ma'am, it's Wes. I think we've got something here. Will update when able, but this is developing quickly."

"Are the developments good or bad?"

"Good, ma'am." He chuckled. "Very good. I need to monitor this right now, but advise you to have the team stand by. Whether or not we initiate is up to you, but those men deserve all the notice we can provide them."

"Consider it done. Waiting to hear back."

She hung up and snatched the satellite radio mic, transmitting quickly.

"Suicide Actual, this is Duchess."

David replied, "*Go for Suicide Actual.*"

"Get your men kitted up and prepared to move. Something's happening; I'll tell you more when I have it."

"*Finally some good news. Kitting up and standing by.*"

She'd barely set the mic down before her phone rang again, and when she answered this time it was with a single word. "Go."

Wes replied, "Ma'am, we've got positive identification."

"What kind of PID are we talking?"

"In short?" he asked. "All of it. Eight minutes ago, MACE-X flagged satellite imagery depicting the Toyota Prado from her convoy out of Colombia parked beside the building. It bears the same light machinegun bipod scratch marks on the roof paint fore and aft of the sunroof as the center vehicle in her previous order of movement, therefore the most likely to have transported Sofia. By the time we vectored in ISR and SIGINT, there was a geolocated outgoing cell phone ping plus or minus ten meters of the truck. ISR was able to take real-time snaps during the call, and captured photos of an adult female in civilian clothes standing outside the building talking on the phone. Recording of that call has just been matched to radio intercepts from her FARC field communications, and we've confirmed a 92 percent match based on audio quality."

Her pulse was racing now. "Transcript of the call?"

A pause amid the sounds of a computer mouse clicking on the other line, and then Wes answered, "She spoke with an unknown party, new cell phone number that we're trying to run down. Here's the translated transcript verbatim. Sofia: Is the vessel underway? Recipient: Yes, everything is in motion. It has been a success. Sofia: Thank God. Recipient: I will see you on the other side. Best of luck, Commander. You are a champion. Sofia: Farewell, friend."

"Anything else?"

"That's it."

Duchess had to force herself to breathe. "Keep trying to run down the other cell phone, see where they were calling from because it sounds like they're sending a boat to pick up her and the VX and transport them to the

New Panamax. If we're lucky, the recipient's grid can give us the boat's point of origin and allow us to identify the vessel before it reaches her, not after."

"Will do, and concur."

"Now tell me about Sofia's current location."

"*Norteca Logística El Mazo*, about two miles from the team's safehouse. It's a cargo warehouse facility across the bay from the naval base, provides storage space for rent, and thus far we've seen no indications that the business is complicit; it appears to have been a standard contract on their part. The unit she's in has two offices on a second-floor balcony and a rolling door for moving cargo. Target packet is in the works, but she's got dock access to load the VX directly onto a boat. Due to the close proximity of the naval base, though, she might use one of the commercial marinas to the west."

She asked, "Is the local dock access sufficient for the Maritime Department pickup?"

"Absolutely. Our shooters can walk right out the building and onto the boat, and the crew is standing by to launch on order. Once they're underway with the team aboard, there's nothing in the Venezuelan naval arsenal that will be able to keep up. Hell, I'm not sure there's anything in the *American* naval arsenal that would be able to keep up."

Not necessarily wrong, she thought, though the capabilities of the team's exfil asset was the last thing on her mind.

"What about the other two vehicles?"

"What other two vehicles?"

With a frustrated sigh, she replied, "Sofia crossed the border in a three truck convoy. One is outside the building, so where are the other two?"

"Oh, right. So the storage unit is forty feet by forty feet, but we don't know what kind of storage provisions are on the ground floor in terms of shelving and shit like that. So there may not be sufficient room for all three. My guess is that the other two are parked inside, staged for a hasty exfil in the event of an attack."

The theory struck her as dubious, though she couldn't identify quite why; on the surface, it seemed the most plausible explanation by far.

"I want Lucios running MACE-X scans to search for them. Expand the country list from Colombia and Venezuela to all adjoining nations."

"You got it."

"We have continuous coverage over Sofia's current location?"

He cleared his throat and answered, "Brian's got birds lined up for the next 72 hours. Zero gaps. Wherever she goes, we'll be following."

God, Duchess thought, this should be a home run straight down the middle. But some lingering suspicion in her gut told her not to leap for joy just yet. "I want to speak with our ground team before I set anything else in motion."

"Um, sure. We'll be standing by, ma'am."

She ended the call, lifting the radio mic and hesitating before she transmitted. Wes sounded confused at the delay—after all, all the dominos were seemingly lined up.

But her job was nothing if not to be the cooler head prevailing no matter the circumstances, and while Sofia was undoubtedly present at the facility, Duchess wasn't yet convinced that a ground assault was necessary.

After all, doing so would require sending her team into harm's way more than she already had. If Sofia was going to send a boat loaded with VX north into the Caribbean sometime that night, it would be a remarkably simple interdiction for the Marine assets staged to stop her. A five-man assault into a surely well-defended site known to be loaded with nerve agent, by contrast, was a monumental risk for everyone involved.

Her instinct was telling her to send the ground team, while logic was telling her the opposite. In the past she'd almost universally sided with instinct, but the overwhelming array of factors told her that an assault was both a ludicrous and unnecessary proposition. For once she had every conceivable asset lined up to stop the VX, and Sofia along with it.

And maybe that's what the issue was—this seemed too easy, everything neatly packaged for the taking. With precious few exceptions, that ran counter to the entirety of her counterterrorism experience.

She murmured to herself, "Don't overthink this."

Then she transmitted, "Suicide Actual, Duchess."

"*Go ahead*," David replied at once.

"We have PID," she began. "Sighting of a vehicle from Sofia's convoy, corroborated by voice intercepts and visual image of a female outside the building during the call. She's hunkered down at a cargo warehouse facility two miles from your current safehouse."

"Then what are we waiting for?"

Duchess swallowed. "We know she's taking a boat out tonight. And since we have continuous aerial coverage and a full-scale naval blockade in place, there's no reason to send your men into danger right now. We can stop her at sea, then use your team to conduct site exploitation on her staging area once it's known to be free of VX. Then exfil as planned."

David seemed unconvinced. "*That assumes she'll do everything according to the intelligence assessments.*"

"Correct. Which, given the facts, has an extremely high probability of being accurate."

"I don't like it."

"Why not?"

He sounded exasperated as he explained, "*Are you listening to yourself? Duchess, how often has one of our targets ever done anything remotely close to what we thought they would? Sofia is sitting on a bunch of VX along with money provided by Erik Weisz. Both of them are lunatics, but neither is stupid. And if one thing we think we know turns out to be wrong, we could be looking at WMD in the wind. Do you really want to trust the naval blockade?*"

Duchess felt almost relieved at the verbal barrage, if for no other reason than David's gut instinct was aligned with her own.

"You're right," she said at last.

"I'm always right."

"Don't get ahead of yourself," she said, more harshly than she intended. Then she continued, "I have authorization for a coastal exfil for your team, and the Maritime Department boat is standing by. I do *not* have authorization to use DoD assets to conduct a raid in Venezuela or even reinforce your element with any additional shooters until the presence of VX is confirmed. You're the only Project Longwing team we've got, and thus the only ones who could attempt this if we choose to."

His reply was immediate. "*We're expendable—got it. So what else is new?*"

"You understand the risks of going in alone?"

"Duchess, I appreciate your concern. But we're wasting time that I could be

using to plan this thing with my guys. She's there right now. The longer we wait, the longer she has to throw us a curveball."

Duchess felt her shoulders relax as a message from Wes flashed on her computer screen, and she opened his secure email to find a target packet that she double-clicked to open.

Scanning over the aerial view of Sofia's location, she transmitted her response to David.

"Stand by for grid."

44

Cancer piloted the Hyundai Santa Fe north along *Avenida 1*.

Despite the fact that his entire team was packed like sardines into the SUV with all their equipment, Cancer considered this mission almost unsettlingly banal: daylight, with a positive ID on their target's exact location, and in a tropical paradise. After all the horrid locations they'd penetrated to snuff out terrorists, something about this gave him the heebie-jeebies.

He caught his first glimpse of the water ahead as Worthy spoke beside him.

"Right turn ahead, that's *Calle Zea* street. Short final."

As he made the turn, Cancer heard David transmitting to their headquarters, "Moving into final position."

This was the crux of conducting a hasty assault—they had a location, and the men and weapons to hit it. They had a vehicle, and the stakes of a WMD intended for use against civilians. Training and odds aside, this was go time. All that remained was to strike as hard and fast as possible, utilizing speed, surprise, and violence of action to bring the fight to Sofia and hopefully prevail. There were a million ways for this to go wrong and only one for it to go right, and at this point roughly thirty seconds remained to figure out which outcome would occur.

Cancer glanced left, seeing the crystal waters of the bay and beyond it, the Agustin Naval Base with its assortment of docked warships and security boats. They'd never hit a target so close to an enemy military installation, and hopefully never would again.

The view to his right was far more appetizing: long buildings dotted with the rolling doors and pedestrian entrances of a seemingly endless succession of cargo storage units, one of which held the woman they'd been sent here to dispatch.

"That's the Prado," Worthy said, indicating a black SUV parked against the side of the building, its front bumper facing out. "Sofia's unit is the rolling door just to the right of it."

"Got it," Cancer confirmed, continuing to glide the Hyundai forward with no change of speed. The odds were as good as not that Sofia had someone posted in an innocuous location to report incoming traffic, and considering what he was about to do, there wasn't much time remaining before his team's intentions would be clear enough.

That was to say nothing of the fun fact that they were assaulting a facility presumably containing an enormous quantity of liquid VX. To that end, they used the same contingency protocol they would if discovering that a building was rigged to blow—if anyone on the team transmitted "landslide," it was every man for himself in fleeing as quickly as possible, security be damned.

Cancer steered toward the Prado, calling back to Felix, "Hey shithead. This black truck up ahead is your only mission in life."

There was a clinking sound as Felix tapped his crowbar against the Hyundai's window, confirming his orders. "I break a window, unlock it, and search. Who could mess that up?"

Reilly replied, "Ideally, no one. But under the circumstances you're the most likely candidate."

By then Cancer was reversing to a stopping position thirty feet from the adjacent rolling door. "Felix, stay with Sofia's truck until we call you inside. Now beat it."

He heard the sub driver exiting the vehicle, then put the transmission into drive and eyed the pedestrian door to the cargo unit, located to the

Prado's left. That main door was a deathtrap—very likely boobytrapped, and if the church at Sofia's jungle camp was any indication, possibly the target area for a reinforced machinegun position somewhere inside the building. That kind of situation begged for a wall breach, preferably from one of the adjoining storage units, but they didn't have sufficient demolitions or, indeed, time to pull that kind of thing off without getting compromised.

Then there was the not-insignificant problem that only one of three trucks was parked outside the building, which pointed to the obvious probability that the remaining two were parked just inside the rolling door, facing out and prepared to haul ass in the event of an assault. Creating a roadblock to their egress was critical, and that, combined with the limited breaching options, had quickly narrowed the team's choices down to the maneuver that Cancer performed now with a considerable amount of childlike glee.

As soon as Felix was clear of the vehicle, David transmitted, "Initiating raid."

Cancer punched the gas, his Hyundai accelerating steadily toward the rolling door. Over the sound of the engine he heard Reilly quietly chant, "Shit, shit, shit," right up until the moment of impact, which transpired with predictable results.

The rolling door crumpled like a soda can under his truck's momentum, ripping free of its tracks and folding under his bumper in a split second. Cancer braced for the imminent impact with a parked vehicle beyond, only to find that *there was none*.

He wheeled the truck left, now intent on closing the distance with the stairs to deposit the second-floor assault team as close to them as possible without rupturing a container of liquid VX in the process. The concrete floor was barren, no tanks of amber liquid or 55-gallon drums in sight, which wasn't to say it was completely free of obstacles: as he'd suspected, a desk was positioned twenty feet from the main door with an M249 light machinegun propped over it.

The man standing behind the desk was wholly unprepared for the team's chosen method of incursion. He jumped like a marionette at the explosion of screeching metal, a look of horror on his face as he realized first that the rolling door had just been blasted by a vehicle, and then that the mobile battering ram was heading straight for him.

He had exactly two seconds to reconcile those circumstances and choose fight or flight, deciding on the former as he bolted for the M249 and desperately tried to reorient it away from the main door and toward the truck. By then it was far too late to save him—the front bumper knocked the desk aside before striking him in the pelvis, his face bouncing off the hood before he flew backward and lost control of his weapon.

Cancer slammed on the brakes, seeing his opponent's body mid-flight on its way to impact with the far wall as the M249 grew rapidly in his field of view, the weapon now a full-fledged projectile. Its barrel punched through the windshield directly in front of Cancer's face, sending a spray of glass dust into the cabin before the front sight post arrested its progress and the truck screeched to a full halt. Cancer faced a stunned moment of disbelief—the light machinegun was embedded in the windshield like Excalibur, buttstock fishtailing across the hood. If he'd been going any faster or braked any later, that fucking thing could have soared clean through the glass and decapitated him.

"Dismount," David shouted, and the second-floor assault team bailed out of the truck.

~

I scrambled out of the truck, making landfall on the concrete floor and moving toward the base of the stairs.

My intention had been for Worthy to be the first man up, backed by myself and then Ian. But Cancer's impromptu use of the truck to take out the M249 gunner positioned me closest to the stairway, an opportunity I couldn't afford to pass up—the initial moments of an assault were make-or-break time, with mere seconds often making the difference between gaining an effective foothold or being hopelessly outgunned.

The forward charge took on an air of hesitancy, however, as I caught sight of the untouched main door: it was rigged with blocks of demolition in what would have been a devastating boobytrap had we tried to breach it.

Cutting right toward the stairs, I took a final glance at the ground floor that revealed things were more or less going to plan.

The lone fighter may or may not have been dead, but he was most certainly out of the fight. His body had impacted the far wall as evidenced by a bloody smear, and he'd bounced a full meter before landing in a heap of shattered bones and grotesquely contorted limbs.

Reilly took up a position next to the engine block, preparing to guide Cancer backward until he'd attained a vantage point on the second-floor balcony from which both men could provide suppressing fire with their more powerful 7.62mm weapons.

Worthy was closing in on my rear while Ian, in a surprise wild card move, had mounted the truck's hood and was in the process of wrenching his prize free of the glass—the M249 light machinegun that he apparently intended to carry onto the second floor, where we now knew the VX to be located.

I moved up the stairs, aiming upward to locate the enemy fighters who were opening fire with an assortment of automatic weapons.

My line of sight had barely cleared the balcony when I saw an enemy fighter on the second floor, spraying an FN FAL rifle over the rail at our truck. The fact that he wasn't facing the stairs instead was the only reason I was still alive right now, and I opened fire at once, my rounds sparking off the rail with a few lancing into his side.

By then one of my teammates had found his mark as well, entry wounds blossoming on the man's chest as he jolted at the impacts of incoming fire from two angles and dropped dead—no stuntman fall over the rail, I noted with dismay—and I continued my ascent up the stairs.

The view over the dead fighter's body was a walkway spanning the cargo unit's back wall, where the doors to the two offices were open. I heard unsuppressed automatic gunfire and distinguished muzzle flashes from both, the remaining shooters wisely remaining far enough recessed from the entrances to be out of sight from both myself and, presumably, Reilly and Cancer on the floor level.

Sweeping to the first door and holding my position, I raised my non-firing hand in a fist over my shoulder, opening and closing my palm twice in rapid succession before resuming the grip on my weapon.

Worthy's response was so immediate I realized he probably didn't need me to signal at all: he rounded my side and hucked a flashbang through the doorway, then ducked back behind me.

We'd brought only one of the stun grenades from our Medellín stockpile into Venezuela, carried on the off-chance that we'd have to clear a room with innocent civilians.

But the gunfire from within the room stopped at once, ceding to a thump of the flashbang against the wall and the sounds of someone scrambling inside—for all he knew, we'd just chucked in a lethal fragmentation grenade. Whoever had been shooting was either going to take cover, flee the room into my sights, or, least preferably, manage to throw the flashbang back out at us.

I felt a surge of elation when it detonated within the room, emitting a deafening blast and a blazing flash of light. Proceeding immediately, I button-hooked left around the doorway.

The interior was a shadowy space where I collided almost immediately with a dark figure, our rifles clanging off each other as both barrels were forced down. Rather than retreat and block the doorway to Worthy and Ian, I lunged forward to tackle the fighter to the ground. His body landed on a desk and we toppled over it and onto a chair that flipped under our collective weight, sending us falling in a clumsy descent that ended with both of us on our sides.

By then taclights lit the room, illuminating a man's grimacing face inches from mine, his cheeks flecked with blood from the flashbang blast. We violently grappled with each other, trying to prevent the other from gaining sufficient standoff to employ a rifle.

The awkward wrestling match concluded when Worthy shouted, "Leave him," and I shoved the man, my back braced against the wall as I planted a boot against his stomach and kicked him away.

That maneuver provided all the standoff needed to end the fight once and for all—Worthy fired two rounds into his skull, the close-range headshots sending whiffs of pink mist into my face. I wiped my eyes and fought my way upward, stumbling over the office chair in an attempt to rejoin my teammates, who were already flowing back out the door and onto the balcony.

Ian stepped out from beside Worthy, following the pointman as they closed with the second and final upstairs door.

He angled his rifle around Worthy's side, the effort cumbersome with the weight of the captured M249 now slung across his back. Ian didn't know why he'd chosen to take the bulky weapon with him, only that a split-second calculation concluded he'd be able to do so in the time it took David and Worthy to fall into the number one and two positions on the stairway.

Whether his teammates would praise his ingenuity or ridicule him in the aftermath, he wasn't sure, nor did it matter at present—if they didn't put down whoever was in the final room, surely Sofia, there wouldn't be an aftermath to worry about.

The shooter was firing wildly from within the doorway, benefiting from superior cover, concealment, and what seemed to be an unlimited supply of ammunition.

Cancer transmitted, "*Hurry it up, we're getting eaten alive down here.*"

Worthy was halfway to the door when the shooting ended momentarily, and Ian saw a dark projectile fly forth from the door, soaring over the balcony and toward the shooters below.

"Frag!" Ian shouted, the only warning he had time to provide before a second grenade followed the first and the shooting resumed.

David grabbed him from behind, pulling him out of the stack and yelling, "Take that M249"—his message was punctuated by the splitting blast of a grenade detonation below—"start shooting at that door, and don't stop until you're out of ammo."

Ian transitioned weapons to the sound of a second blast on the ground floor, shifting his suppressed M4 to his side and lifting the far more cumbersome light machinegun into a two-handed firing position. He was thumbing the safety when Worthy stepped back and guided him into position a foot away from the wall as the number one man, by which time Ian hoisted the weapon to his shoulder, crouched down, and opened fire.

The first burst of automatic fire caused his barrel to climb, and Ian muscled the weapon back into position, blasting three- to five-second bursts to ensure the majority of his ammunition found its destination.

Worthy pushed him steadily forward from behind, controlling the pace of their three-man element as they closed with the doorway. Ian's footfalls occurred atop a surface of expended brass and metal links, the hot discharge spilling over his thighs as he stepped and fired, stepped and fired, increasing the length of his bursts as he gained control over the weapon.

He had completed a particularly long burst of unrelenting gunfire at the bullet-shattered doorway now four feet distant when he realized the light machinegun had nothing left to give; the trigger was reduced to an impotent scrap of metal against his index finger.

Ian started to say the words "I'm out" but didn't have the chance—Worthy's hand on his shoulder went from gently coaxing him forward to a superhuman thrust downward, flinging Ian to the floor.

~

Worthy leapt over Ian's now-prostrate body, soaring in a low arc as he wheeled his weapon sideways in anticipation of a baseball slide toward the doorway that was fast approaching.

It was a desperate, impulsive maneuver, but a calculated one nonetheless; by the time they readied a fragmentation grenade of their own, the shooter inside could lob one or more at Reilly and Cancer below, who were lucky to be alive, if they were at all. Worthy had the experience to risk pitting his considerable reflexes against Sofia, alleviating the threat to his team by assuming all the danger himself. If she managed to get the upper hand against him—not inconceivable given what he was attempting now—then David and Ian would put her down. Maybe Worthy would win and maybe he'd lose, but this fight would end in the next three seconds.

He was halfway through the leap, descending toward the rapidly approaching doorway, when a new thought entered his mind: the VX had to be in the room with her, and unless it had some unprecedented form of ballistic protection, they were about to face a torrent of liquid nerve agent spilling forth, a single drop more than enough to kill them.

Worthy impacted the ground on his right side and slid forward with his suppressed M4 angled upward, cresting past the doorway and coming to a stop dead-center to see Sofia Lozano at the end of his barrel.

She was a nightmarish sight—hair down in greasy tangles, face flushed with wrath, standing amid a graveyard of expended brass and discarded weapons. The shotgun was in her grasp, aimed from the waist just over his head as he opened fire, seeing that he'd be lucky to forestall his own death under the best of circumstances.

Worthy pulled the trigger with all the speed honed over his stint as a competitive shooter, discharging subsonic rounds with mere fractions of a second between shots. Sofia's abdomen and chest were dotted with a flurry of entry wounds that grew in number at a tremendous rate—he was emptying his magazine as fast as he could, unwilling to move out of her line of fire and unable to do so even if he'd wanted to. He was fully exposed on his side, and to retreat behind cover now was to allow Sofia to get off a shotgun blast that would make short work of his face.

His M4 bolt locked to the rear while Sofia was still standing, though not for lack of accuracy—a majority of his shots had found their mark and any number of them could prove fatal in seconds. The shotgun lowered in her grasp before ejecting a massive burst of flame. Worthy heard the shot as a low, distorted roar, felt a pelting scatter of buckshot ripping into his left arm as she fell dead, a ghoulish death grin marring her features below lifeless eyes that gazed at him hollowly.

Worthy gasped in pain and visually cleared the room behind her, looking for the now-perforated tanks or barrels spewing VX in his direction. He was already starting to call "landslide" to evacuate his team, the word forming on his lips before they parted in shock instead: the room was empty save the remnants of a gun stockpile she'd used to fight off their assault, the only object of interest was David's body as he vaulted Worthy and cleared the room, wheeling sideways to administer a double tap to Sofia's head before shouting, "Site exploitation."

Ian was all too eager to comply, abandoning the M249 for his rifle as he moved in to fingerprint the body and search for intelligence. David returned to the doorway, kneeling beside Worthy to assess his wounds.

"You took some buckshot, but you're good." Then he rephrased the final words as a question. "You good?"

"Yeah," Worthy grunted, sitting up and loading a fresh magazine. He looked at his left side, finding three bloody pockmarks that rippled with searing pain but were sufficiently far from major organs to present an imminent medical crisis.

But at the moment he realized this, his team faced a crisis of a different sort.

Cancer transmitted, "*We've got police closing in.*"

I retraced my path down the balcony at a run and transmitted over the team frequency, "Exfil, exfil, exfil."

"*Support*," Cancer replied.

"On my way," I said, then keyed my command radio to send Duchess my first update since the raid had commenced.

"Sofia's dead. Negative VX on site, I say again negative VX."

Duchess replied, "*Additional vehicles from her convoy?*"

The question struck me as odd, though I had no time to ponder why she'd chosen that particular line of inquiry amid the far more pressing issue that our goddamned WMD was unaccounted for. My concentration was occupied by grabbing the rail and pivoting onto the stairs, descending them two at a time as I replied, "Just the one truck. She had three men with her, all EKIA."

"*I'm authorizing the container ship takedown. Get out of there.*"

I was setting foot on the ground level when I received a different transmission over the same frequency, this one a man's voice speaking over the roar of wind in the background.

"*This is Mako Four Zero*," he said. Just the person I wanted to hear from, I thought. The callsign was for our Maritime Department exfil vessel, although my enthusiasm waned when he continued, "*Naval base is scrambling armed ships toward your location—we're not going to be able to access the bay.*"

"Bump to alternate," I replied.

Then I darted past the explosive-laden main door and entry vehicle with Felix standing beside it, still clutching his crowbar as he called out to me uneasily, "The Prado was empty."

I didn't waste my breath with a response, instead noting that Felix looked for all the world like a kid who'd just woken from a night terror. My footsteps took me over the blast sites of Sofia's grenades and shell casings strewn across the concrete. The rolling door was a crinkled sheet of twisted metal cast aside, and I skidded to a halt beside Cancer, slapping him on the arm to relieve him from security duties. I said, "Get the truck started," and then keyed my team radio to transmit, "Alternate exfil, alternate exfil."

Reilly stood at the far side of the doorway, angled in the opposite direction. He wasn't yet shooting, nor did I see any targets to my front.

Only then did I glance outside, peering across the bay at the peninsula to our north. Flat gray vessels were indeed taking to the water from the Venezuelan naval base situated there, and even if we made it to our exfil boat, odds were good that they'd blast us out of the water on our way out. And while the last thing I wanted to do right now was transit a full mile to the nearest commercial marina, we had absolutely zero say in the matter.

I shifted my position to look toward the sound of sirens approaching, seeing that the police Cancer referenced had yet to arrive. From the sound of it, though, they'd be here in remarkably short order.

My heart sank as I registered a new sound, audible even above the din of sirens and infinitely more terrifying.

Our truck's engine emitted a long, high-pitched whine before going dead, the process repeating once more before Cancer transmitted, "*Our vehicle is fucked.*"

"Keys," I transmitted in response, "search the bodies for keys. We're riding Sofia's truck out of here."

Worthy shouted back, echoing across the building's interior, "On it!"

I scanned for the enemy outside, hoping to God that we'd be able to locate the keys before needing to attempt a hotwire. The only alternative was to take one of those responding police vehicles by force, which would thrust our waning ammunition levels against a numerically superior force and likely leave one or more of us dead along with a trail of police bodies. Certainly not preferable, but if it came down to them or us, then that was exactly what would happen.

The sirens stopped short, the police exercising at least some level of tactical judgment in not screaming all the way into the site of recent gunfire and explosions. Instead I got my first glimpse of two dismounted men peeking around the corner of an outside building, finding they weren't police at all: both wore the navy uniforms of a port security force, and there was no opportunity to fire a warning shot—I'd scarcely taken aim before they scuttled out of sight.

Worthy shouted from the balcony, "I got keys!"

I transmitted, "Racegun, get Felix and cross-load the rucks. Everyone else in a security perimeter around Sofia's vehicle—Venezuelans get one warning shot, and then start smoking motherfuckers."

45

Ian whipped the Prado into a left turn, heading south and away from the bay now teeming with armed security ships from the Venezuelan naval base.

The view after his turn was far more preferable—a straight, two-lane stretch of *Avenida 1*—and Ian floored the gas.

Warm sea breeze whipped in through his missing driver's side window, reduced to sharp chunks of auto glass scattered on his seat and the floorboard after Felix smashed it apart with a crowbar to search the vehicle.

Worthy spoke from the passenger seat as he navigated the ride with the help of his phone.

"Seven blocks until your right turn. About a mile to go until the marina."

"Got it," Ian replied, weaving between sparse civilian traffic. The big SUV strained to complete the maneuvers, and he heard the rumble of rucksacks shifting in the vehicle's far rear, followed by a pained grunt and a complaint from the only man stuffed back there with the gear.

Felix cried, "*Jesucristo*, take it easy up there."

"Stop talking," David snapped before continuing, "Ian, if we get compromised, I want you to bail onto the side roads for evasion. We can't afford to lead anyone to our exfil."

The team leader was seated in the back between Reilly and Cancer; together with Ian, the four of them had pulled security during the remarkably fast transition from their decimated infil truck to the Prado, taking with them Sofia's shotgun for display in the team room if they made it that far. On the plus side, they hadn't even needed to fire a warning shot to convince the port security guards that coming any closer wasn't worth their lives; on the negative side was, well, everything else, starting with the fact that all those living witnesses had already transmitted their vehicle make and model to every cop in Puerto Cabello. With the city's police station roughly six blocks from the objective, the odds of them making an uncontested flight to the coast were close to zero.

Worthy said, "Four blocks to go."

Veering left, Ian accelerated past an old pickup before swinging back into the right lane seconds before a head-on collision with an oncoming van whose driver blasted the horn in protest. Storefronts and parked cars were a blur on either side of the road as Ian narrowed his focus down to identifying available gaps in traffic. If they were going to outpace police response, they'd need every possible second to access a suitable pickup point, which were in extremely short supply largely as a result of the vessel that would be picking them up.

In selecting a dedicated exfil boat to penetrate Venezuelan waters, they could have chosen one that could simply pull up to the beach to get them, or something with sufficient speed to outpace any naval pursuit. They couldn't have both, and given the fact that this escape was occurring in broad daylight, they'd sided with speed—all well and good, provided they could make it to a point with sufficient depth for the bastard to pull up in the first place.

They'd been able to make a full PACE plan—primary, alternate, contingency, and emergency—of four exfil locations, but just barely. The primary pickup was at the objective and that obviously wasn't going to happen; with the naval base across the bay from their target and extending east along the coast, their alternate and contingency locations were the only two commercial marinas in Puerto Cabello, both to the west, and the first of those two choices was fast approaching.

"Two blocks," Worthy announced, then, "one block...right turn, right turn."

Ian braked for the ninety-degree intersection, cutting the wheel and lining up on a short stretch of road as Worthy continued, "Take a right up ahead, then follow that road around to the left. Half a mile out from the marina."

Ian completed the next turn without issue, but following the route as it curved left proved considerably more difficult. He hadn't yet reached the first intersection along the stretch when a white police cruiser with its light bar flashing flew in from the north, braking to a full stop to block their progress.

Ian's response was instantaneous, not that there was time for any deep thought about the matter. He spun the wheel right, making an effort to bypass the cruiser's trunk and, assessing there wasn't sufficient clearance, instead drove the corner of his bumper into the car's rear quarter panel while punching the gas.

The Prado blasted through with ease, spinning the police car counterclockwise with its engine block serving as the fulcrum.

Then they cleared the intersection, though not before spotting two additional cruisers approaching from the side road to the right.

David asked, "Distance?"

".2 miles," Worthy replied.

Cancer muttered, "No way," voicing the obvious conclusion from being compromised this close to their alternate exfil site. Once they committed to the long one-way road leading into the marina there was no going back, and given the effort to transition men and equipment from truck to boat, they'd be overrun long before making it out alive.

David ordered, "Evade to the south."

Ian took the next left as Worthy began feeding him directions, striving to construct a circuitous route that would cut the police's line of sight as they threaded their way to the next available pickup point.

Behind them, David transmitted to the Maritime Department asset standing by at the now-useless marina.

"Alternate exfil is out, we're headed to contingency." Then he asked, "Distance?"

"1.2 miles," Worthy said. "Will run a bit longer with evasion. Ian, jam a left up here. That's *Avenida Bolivar* ahead."

Merging onto the southbound road was easier said than done. Ian made a split-second judgment that he could cut off an 18-wheeler with sufficiently drastic inputs to the steering and gas, and he whipped the Prado sideways into a fishtailing turn as the semi braked to avoid impact.

Worthy tensed in his seat and scolded Ian. "Try not to get us killed."

Cancer replied to the pointman, "Shut up, you fuckin' bullet magnet. Can you make it through more than one mission without getting shot?"

To this, Reilly added, "At least I didn't have to save his life—again. But after that little stunt with the rat meat, he can forget about pain meds this time."

Worthy ignored the banter, guiding Ian through a right turn onto a road that paralleled the coast westward.

Here the race to flee police pursuit took on a tinge of the surreal—the truckful of armed men who'd just emerged from the carnage of Sofia's last stand was passing through a veritable tourist paradise of hotels and restaurants, street cafes and beachwear stores. The people of Puerto Cabello froze at the sight of the truck, stopping to watch with stunned expressions as they carried shopping bags, pushed strollers, or pulled their bicycles over for a better look. This was about as incongruous a setting for a life-or-death flight from danger as Disney World, and it wasn't until Ian had turned onto the final straightaway before the marina road that he thought to check the fuel gauge.

"This thing's down to, like, an eighth of a tank." One final *fuck you* from Sofia to his team, he thought.

"If we need any more than that," Reilly commented, "we're screwed anyway—"

Felix interrupted, "Police! Behind us, coming up fast."

Ian checked his rearview, finding the image obscured by the scrawny Colombian man seated atop the rucks.

The sideview mirrors provided a clear enough picture, though—there were three of them, two cruisers and a pickup with light bars gleaming, their sirens barely audible over the roar of wind beside him.

David said, "Engines and tires. For God's sake, don't shoot anyone."

Ian heard the rear windows rolling down, followed by a whooshing sound as Reilly and Cancer shifted to lean outside, orienting the team's 7.62mm weapons rearward and opening fire with suppressed shots. He drove a perfectly straight line, holding his speed to provide the most stable shooting platform possible until he heard Cancer shout the results of their volley.

"We got one engine, the other two fell back a hundred meters."

"Distance?" David asked.

"Quarter mile to the second marina," Worthy answered as their two shooters retreated inside the vehicle.

"Flip to emergency, try to lose them. If they follow us all the way to the boat, we'll kill them all."

"Shit. Immediate left, immediate left." Worthy paused his commentary until Ian skidded through the intersection, then continued, "Then a right on *Avenida la Paz* up ahead. No use burning time evading if we're down to our last shot at getting out of here."

He was right about it being their last shot—the emergency exfil was considerably farther than the first three options, decidedly non-commercial in nature, and the only suitable coastal access before miles of swampy marshland that extended all the way to the next town. Now exposed, they didn't have the time or the gas for any more attempts.

David transmitted to the boat driver, "Contingency exfil is out. Move to emergency location."

Ian whipped a hard right onto *Avenida la Paz*, exposing a four-lane divided highway with far too many cars obeying the posted speed limit. He gunned the Prado forward, passing one car and sideswiping another when it wouldn't get out of the way quickly enough.

Driving aggressively wasn't a problem for Ian at the moment; instead it served as an almost cathartic means of dispelling the growing sense of dread whose cause he couldn't yet pinpoint.

He needed time to think, to process the latest developments in a mission that had taken them from the Colombian jungles to the Venezuelan coast; he was missing something, he just didn't know what. Had they even killed Sofia? Ian thought they had, although he wouldn't know for sure until he could transmit a digital image of the corpse's fingerprints to the Project Longwing OPCEN. But with all the convenience of her voice match on a surveilled phone, he was beginning to wonder if she'd sent a stand-in to play a voice recording. If Sofia realized she was being tracked, such a diversion certainly wasn't outside the realm of possibility.

David asked, "Why wasn't the VX on site?"

Ian shook his head, grunting as he rammed the fender of a pickup to convince it to speed up and overtake a vehicle in the slow lane. "She must have already loaded it onto a boat. Probably just waiting until nightfall to send it out to the New Panamax."

"Hang on," the team leader said, receiving some incoming transmission on his command frequency. Then he relayed, "Marine Raiders are taking down the ship right now. Duchess is about to go in with the search teams."

Reilly said, "Can you imagine Duchess with a gun? It'd be terrifying."

"Maybe for you pansies," Cancer replied. "Personally I wouldn't mind seeing that."

"You can't be serious. She's even older than you."

"I'm telling you, she's got that whole Vivian Brown thing going on. Sign me up."

Ian sped past an honest-to-God mini Walmart as Worthy announced, "Take the next right, four hundred meters."

It didn't take them long to arrive at the designated intersection, and Ian braked hard before cutting the wheel to arrive on a northbound road. There, the tourist and residential scenery fell away—to his right was an undeveloped strip of sandy scrubland; to his front, the Caribbean.

To the left, however, was a chain link fence surrounding a massive complex with long, low buildings interspersed by vast fields of industrial storage tanks lined in neat rows. This was Vopak Venezuela S.A., a state-owned metal industry supplier with exclusive access to the westernmost coastline of Puerto Cabello—and, if all went according to plan from here on out, the team would be capitalizing on that fact.

Worthy directed, "Half a mile straight ahead, then veer left at the Y-intersection."

Ian remembered the route well from their planning. It was remarkably simple, provided they could get inside; there simply weren't many routes remaining before reaching the sea.

"Veer left."

Ian did so, and was already flooring the gas pedal as Worthy continued, "Go, go."

The gate ahead was a chain-link barrier on a sliding track, flanking a guard post where a security guard emerged, waving his hands for them to stop. If he stepped into the road he was dead, and he started to do just that before reversing course and diving out of the way.

Ian steered the Prado through the gate, flinging it clear of the tracks. There was a tremendous screech of metal on metal as it flipped over the roof of the truck, vanishing from sight as Worthy called, "Right turn, follow the road."

Now they were speeding past parked flatbeds and tractor trailers on either side, and Ian had barely completed the turn before Worthy shouted, "Next left."

Around the bend, the road transitioned to an uphill grade with a ramp rising steeply off the passenger side.

"This is it—right, right, right."

Ian careened the truck up a long ramp, then steered onto a three-lane strip of unmarked, elevated pavement that extended in a perfectly straight path seven hundred meters northeast. He accelerated as the perimeter fence flashed beneath them, then a sandy strip of beach, and then they cleared the land altogether, racing down the pier as it stretched twenty feet over the Caribbean Sea.

"On the pier," David transmitted to their pickup crew, "ten seconds out."

Then, to his team, he continued, "Unless they interfere, let them be. We've already been spotted by half of Puerto Cabello."

He was referring to the crew of a small freighter docked off the left side. Ian caught glimpses of men on the deck, shielding their eyes from the sun as they tried to comprehend how or why a beat-up Toyota Prado was speeding down the pier at 70 mph. If they thought the appearance of the truck was noteworthy, he thought, then they were in for one hell of a surprise once they saw the occupants.

But he didn't have much time to observe them before focusing back on the pier, whose end rail was fast approaching. Ian mashed the brake, slowing the vehicle until it finally lurched to a halt, and his team bailed out to secure the perimeter.

Cancer leapt out of the truck, first scanning the crew aboard the freighter for any indication they'd intervene in what was about to occur—no dice, the five men scattered about the deck merely stopped and watched like the team was some zoo exhibit. Then he scanned down the pier in the hopes that a police cruiser would qualify for some well-earned attention from his Galil.

But the long slab of pavement was free of pursuers, and somewhat disappointed that he may well have already pulled a trigger for the last time on this mission, he approached the far rail while withdrawing a length of folded tubular nylon webbing. The olive drab coil was an item he rarely traveled without: it took up little space, weighed virtually nothing, and had innumerable uses. The reinforced double layer of one-inch-wide material could be hastily tied into myriad configurations for negotiating obstacles or hauling casualties or equipment up or downhill, though for its current use, Cancer had simply knotted a locking carabiner to each end.

Arriving at the rail, he looked over the edge to locate their exfil asset.

Maritime Department was the Special Activity Center's answer to waterborne operations—if a clandestine or covert mission required diving, driving a boat, or both, these CIA officers were the obvious choice. They maintained a diverse fleet of vessels for the purpose, and for this desperate exfil from the Venezuelan coast, they'd sent the very best.

Rocking in the gentle waves twenty feet below was the speedboat they'd arranged: a Nor-Tech 5200 Roadster, which was essentially a 52-foot-long bullet. It had seating for ten, though only two Maritime Department officers were aboard, both dressing the part of millionaire playboys in swim trunks, linen shirts, and designer sunglasses. While one remained at the controls, the other stood in the seating area to await Cancer's pass.

Looping one end of the tubular nylon around the rail, Cancer clipped it into place on itself to create a fixed end. Unfurling the remaining coil, he took hold of the opposite carabiner and hurled it at the boat below.

The length of tubular nylon whizzed down in pursuit until the carabiner thudded into a padded sun lounge at the rear of the boat. The Maritime Department officer scrambled to retrieve it, then attached it to a tie-down point and took out the remaining slack in the line with a hasty knot before shooting Cancer a thumbs up. He'd barely stepped aside before Worthy and Reilly clipped the first rucksack to the tubular nylon—Ian's ruck, he saw, with the pistol grip of Sofia's shotgun emerging from the top flap—and released it. The heavy bundle spiraled into a speeding freefall that ended when it smashed into the space between seats, the speedboat rocking under the force of impact.

Five more rucks followed in quick succession, the team forming an assembly line to get them over the side as quickly as possible as the boat drifted away from the pier, stretching the improvised nylon zipline taut. Combined with the sudden weight of the rucksacks, the speedboat tilted perilously to its port side—the CIA officer on deck produced a knife and flashed it at Cancer, who confirmed all the heavy gear was aboard by running a hand across his throat.

The man proceeded to slice the nylon tether as Cancer turned to his team and said, "Go."

David, Worthy, and Ian mounted the rail without hesitation, still clad in tactical vests with their rifles slung. Reilly hesitated before joining them with the comment, "I fucking hate swimming," and then all four jumped in near-unison, falling twenty feet before splashing into the Caribbean.

Cancer was about to follow when he noticed that Felix had failed to heed his order, instead choosing to shake his head with violent speed.

"I cannot jump," he gasped, "I am scared of heights—"

That was as far as Felix got into his confession before Cancer grabbed his shoulders and flung him over the rail. The scrawny Colombian turned into a cartwheeling display of flailing limbs as he fell, screaming, into the blue water.

By then Cancer had climbed over the rail and adjusted the Galil at his side, giving a final glance down the pier to see that no one was following. Behind him, the freighter's crew had settled in for the show: two of them were seated with their legs dangling over the side, eating sandwiches as they watched.

Cancer shouted at them, "*Adiós, muchachos.*"

Then he leapt, the view before him sky and sea, the water speeding upward as he gained velocity and looked up mid-fall to gauge his team's progress. Ian was already climbing the boarding ladder at the rear of the boat, while the remaining three were completing the short swim toward it. Felix was doggy-paddling behind them—Christ, Cancer thought, the man sucked at swimming along with everything else—and the warm air whipping over him turned to a whooshing roar before his boots slammed into the water.

Cancer plunged beneath the waves, waiting for his descent to slow before he kicked his way upward and broke the surface to take his first surging breath. He oriented himself to the boat before transitioning to a sidestroke, pulling hard to overcome the weight of his kit and weapon. There wasn't much distance to cover, but negotiating it took considerable effort.

Looking forward, he saw that Felix was finally ascending the boarding ladder while holding a flotation device that the Maritime Department officers had apparently tossed to him out of concern for his well-being. Cancer wasn't far behind, though he almost didn't want the swim to end. After nearly a month of scuttling across two countries in search of Sofia, the job was finally done and it felt like the warm seawater was cleansing him of the entire ordeal, of losing Maximo and nearly getting killed by his own partner force.

Finally he grasped the ladder, righting himself in the water and climbing the rungs as quickly as he could with his waterlogged gear. Even at idle, the speedboat's engine had a snarling grumble of an exhaust note that left little doubt as to its insane potential for power.

Cancer crossed over the padded sun deck toward two rows of triple helm seating. David, Ian, and Felix were seated across the first, and Cancer leapt into a chair beside Reilly, who was already digging through his aid bag to treat Worthy beside him. Everyone present and accounted for, including both CIA officers now at the cockpit, looking back for confirmation. Cancer's ass had barely landed in his chair before David yelled, "We're up."

That was all it took to confirm the vessel's potential for speed. The driver opened up the throttle, unleashing a throaty roar from the engine as the bow tilted upward and the speedboat catapulted forward across the waves, away from Venezuela.

46

Duchess climbed down the rope ladder with deliberate effort, keenly aware that she was essentially dangling midway between a hovering Seahawk helicopter and the now-halted New Panamax vessel below.

At least the view was great from up here, or would have been if she didn't have to maintain such focus on not falling to her death: deep blue Caribbean water on all sides of the ship, the horizon a 360 sweep beneath a cloudless sky, interrupted only by the ship's mast to her left. She glanced up to see the procession of people following her down the ladder. This first wave of follow-on personnel was limited to those with an immediate need to board: Navy explosive ordnance disposal, DEVGRU WMD experts, and herself as the lone intelligence specialist.

Then she looked down at the expanse of white metal below, the highest surface of the ship comprising a relatively narrow slab high above rows of multicolored containers stretching far to the front. Transitioning her hand and footholds quickly to narrow the distance, she finally set foot on the roof of the ship's bridge, a dizzyingly elevated pinnacle situated to provide the captain an unrestricted view of the sea over the seemingly endless cargo.

Duchess cleared the area to make room for the next man down, and was moving to link up with the single escort waiting to take them to Sofia's containers when she received a transmission from Wes.

"Duchess, the team just made it into international waters. And the fingerprint analysis came back positive: Sofia is dead."

She replied quickly, "Relay confirmation of Sofia's death to our guys. I just boarded the New Panamax."

Then she turned her attention back to her escort, suddenly insecure about his first impression of her. She was attired in a helmet and sterile fatigues, with a bulletproof vest bearing twin radios, camera and transmission equipment, and a holstered Glock pistol, the sum total of which paled in comparison to the man before her.

The Marine Raider was six-foot-two of solid muscle wrapped head to toe in tactical kit: body armor, primary and secondary weapons, high cut ballistic helmet with panoramic night vision device flipped up so the four monocles were facing skyward.

He looked unsettlingly calm for someone who'd just fast-roped from a helicopter flying twenty feet over a moving ship, then cleared for threats while moving toward a sister team that was doing the same from the opposite end. The man reminded her of Wes, in a way, and at present that gave her at least some degree of comfort.

He simply waved at her to follow, then moved out—there was no use trying to talk now, not with the Seahawk hovering overhead. She glanced behind her to see the file of site exploitation personnel following her before the rope ladder detached, falling limply as the helicopter increased throttle, its nose dipping under the sudden acceleration. Duchess crouched down as hot air thick with exhaust fumes washed over her, and then the bird thundered away, leaving her to inhale the first scent of clean seawater she'd had this entire trip.

The Marine led her to a stairwell on the side of the bridge and began his jogging descent, and Duchess struggled to keep pace amid the frequent switchbacks.

She called out to him, "What did you find?"

The Marine didn't break stride as he led the way down the metal stairs spanning the bridge and four stories of crew accommodations beneath it. He called over his shoulder, "You've got to see it. It's hard to explain."

Duchess felt almost slighted by the comment—what the hell was that supposed to mean? The least he could do was provide a brief synopsis of the containers' contents instead of a dismissive ambiguity.

But whatever was inside, she wouldn't have to wonder for long. They reached the deck at the rear of the ship, and with Sofia's containers comprising the last two rows, they'd arrive any moment now.

He moved swiftly along the narrow gap between the hull's edge and the containers, stopping just short of the stern to reach for a door and pull it open for her to enter.

And that was her first indication that she'd missed something critical; the door was on the side of a container, and twenty-foot units simply weren't built like that. Scrutinizing the wall of containers beside her, she saw that it was just that—a wall. Not a stack of individual containers, but rather the components were welded into a single sheet of metal siding that, to anything but an up-close examination, would appear identical to the cargo elsewhere on the ship. Rather than loading actual containers, someone had gone to great lengths to create a large and essentially invisible storage space for something much bigger—the question remained, what the hell was it?

Even the door blended into the facade, cut out of a sidewall panel and re-attached with internal hinges. She'd never seen anything like this, never even *heard* of it, and felt the giddy anticipation of learning at last why Sofia would go to such lengths to conceal her cargo.

As Duchess stepped through the doorway and into the cavernous interior, her heart sank.

There was nothing.

The entire space was empty aside from a few Marine Raiders sweeping their taclights over bare floors and walls made of container siding, looking for something, anything of significance. She looked up to see a solid top to the structure, nothing suspended or hanging, just the seams allowing light to pass through a series of parallel slats.

"Make way," someone called from behind her, and she stepped aside to allow the stream of site exploitation people to enter as she scanned the interior.

This all should have been a relief, a positive indication that Sofia hadn't yet emplaced her cargo, which would be interdicted at any moment by the array of US military resources standing by to do just that.

But Duchess knew that Sofia's true prize was VX, and no possible level of production that the Venezuelan government was capable of could account for this much room being required. Something in her gut told her that whatever the explanation for this disparity, it was going to have devastating consequences for the Agency, the US, and possibly the world.

But two events in the next thirty seconds convinced her there was still time to gain the upper hand.

The first was when one of the Marine Raiders called out, "Agency?"

"Here," she replied, striding forward to meet him.

He extended a hand containing something she couldn't make out in the dim light, explaining, "Crew's not talking yet, but we found this. It doesn't belong to anyone on board."

She took the item from him and found it to be a Colombian passport.

Flipping it open, Duchess examined the first page and then flipped through the booklet, looking for anything notable but reaching the end feeling far more perplexed than enlightened.

"Thank you," she said. "Anything else you locate needs to be brought to me immediately."

"Yes, ma'am," he replied, turning to depart.

No sooner had he left than she received an incoming radio transmission from Wes.

"*Duchess, J2 just got a MACE-X hit on the two missing vehicles from Sofia's convoy.*"

"Excellent," she replied. "Where are they?"

47

I continued to wince against the rush of wind that made breathing a deliberate effort, albeit one that I was growing accustomed to aboard the insanely fast speedboat—for the past ten minutes, we'd been blasting forward at full throttle, casting a tremendous spray of white foam in our wake. Between the earsplitting roar of the engine and the wind whipping in our faces, we'd barely been able to hear each other over radio communications, much less while trying to shout back and forth.

The Maritime Department officers manning this beast finally relented, easing off the power and allowing us to proceed forward while enjoying the warm sun on our faces, the salty air and view of idyllic blue water in all directions.

One of the drivers shouted back at us, "We just hit international waters."

To say I was relieved would be an understatement—it wasn't so much that I was worried about the Venezuelans catching up with our speedboat, particularly since ISR had confirmed they broke off pursuit within two miles of the coast.

Rather, the invisible line across the Caribbean signified that we'd made it out of Venezuela, a symbolic victory that had been nearly inconceivable at several points in the operation. Our mission was complete with Sofia's death, and we'd soon be able to link up with the US naval barricade and watch from the sidelines as the VX was located and interdicted by any number of forward-staged elements.

Cancer seemed considerably less concerned about us crossing into international waters than he was with more immediate necessities. As soon as the engine noise abated, he shouted at the CIA officers with urgency.

"Got any cigarettes? Mine are soaked."

One of them looked back with a broad smile, his response to a great joke dissipating upon sight of Cancer, who'd been dead serious.

I received a transmission from the OPCEN, then relayed the message's contents to my team.

"Raiders just took down the New Panamax."

From the center seat beside me, Ian asked, "What did they find?"

"Waiting to hear back, Duchess is boarding now. Good news, though: OPCEN just confirmed the fingerprints—that was Sofia in the last room."

Ian seemed to visibly relax, which I found odd. Had he ever suspected otherwise?

"God," Worthy drawled, "I certainly hope so. Otherwise we went to a hell of a lot of trouble for nothing."

I continued, "Case of beer to you for the kill."

Cancer responded, "And he fuckin' earned it, *Reilly*."

"What's that supposed to mean?" Reilly objected. "I earned it on our last mission, too."

"Sure, if you want to count a mortally wounded terrorist literally and figuratively landing at your feet after someone else did the actual work."

"Now, now," I countered, "the team rules are very clear on this point: beer award is for whoever puts the target's lights out, regardless of whether or not they've already been shot."

Reilly agreed, "Exactly."

"Although Worthy did in fact earn it, while you won on a technicality."

Before the medic could respond, Felix asked, "What about me?"

"I told you, *caremonda*—you'll get debriefed, paid, and repatriated to Colombia through diplomatic channels."

"Yes," he said impatiently, "I mean, how long will this take?"

"Who cares?"

He shrugged. "Isabella is waiting on me."

Cancer seized on this opportunity to reprimand Felix, nearly shouting at him, "Quit your whining, you fuckin' degenerate. You had a chance to bail on this and you blew it. If there's anyone here who shouldn't be complaining, it's your ugly ass."

Felix blinked. "I was trying to have some honor. Like you."

Cancer belted out a laugh. "You think we have honor? Pal, you're looking at five of the most maladjusted people on the face of the planet. Ian's the only one smart enough to hold down a real job, and he's so goddamn irritating he'd probably get beaten up in the break room."

I never heard Ian's response—Duchess transmitted over my earpiece.

"*Suicide, I'm sending you a data shot. Prepare to receive.*"

I pulled out my phone and replied, "Standing by. What did you find?"

"*The containers weren't containers at all—it was just the siding, welded together to create one large hidden cargo space. There was nothing inside. Dimensions in feet are 140 by 16 by 48.*"

To my team, I called out, "Sofia didn't load containers, she had the siding put together to create an empty room. One hundred and forty feet long, 16 feet wide, 48 feet high."

Then I transmitted back, "So if nothing was inside, what's in the data shot?"

"*A passport we found,*" Duchess said. "*It doesn't belong to anyone on the crew. The OPCEN has confirmed it's a false name but has zero facial recognition yet. I want Angel to take a look, because we're at a loss right now. And there's something else—the two missing vehicles from Sofia's convoy have just been found.*"

"Great," I replied. "Are they in Puerto Cabello?"

"*Cartagena.*"

For a moment I thought she was fucking with me.

"Cartagena, *Colombia*?"

"*Yes. Just tell Angel, and have him look at the passport.*"

I gave a frustrated sigh. If the Agency couldn't identify the face, then what was Ian supposed to do with it?

"All right," I said, "it's coming through now. Stand by."

Having only heard my outgoing transmissions, Ian surmised, "Sofia's missing trucks were in Cartagena?"

"Yeah. And they found a passport aboard the ship. Fake name, no facial ID. Duchess wants you to take a look."

Ian said nothing, which was about the most troubling thing in my world at that moment. He stared at his lap, then forward at the cockpit, and finally right and left at the Caribbean to our east and west.

As my phone uploaded the incoming file, and for reasons I couldn't explain, I wondered if the face would belong to Vega—maybe the trafficker had played us all along. Or perhaps it was Maximo. Had the asset meeting at the museum actually been his doing, for some reason I couldn't yet divine?

But when the snapshot of a Colombian passport finally uploaded, I saw the name Sebastian Oliveira paired with a face that belonged to neither man—nor, I realized, did it belong to anyone I'd ever seen.

He was in his fifties, clean-cut, with gray hair, tanned skin, a small scar on his right eyebrow, and facial features that appeared Latin American. The smiling and confident man in the snapshot appeared not only innocuous but trustworthy; I saw nothing suspicious about him in the least. If I passed him on the street, I wouldn't have thought to look twice.

Presenting the phone to Ian, I said, "Here's the passport picture."

Ian didn't take the phone immediately; his lips were parted, eyes gazing hollowly forward. He looked pale, like he was on the brink of throwing up.

Wagging the phone in front of his face, I said, "Hey bro, wake up. I said—"

Then he ripped the device from my hands, not even bothering to look at the screen. Instead he passed it to Felix and asked, "Who is this?"

Felix hesitantly accepted the phone, staring at the screen as his eyes flew open.

"*Capitán* de Zurara! I told you, the man had more passports than—"

"You're sure?" Ian asked.

"He trained me for years. Of course I am sure." His expression turned hopeful. "This means he was not killed in the airstrike?"

"No," Ian said, snatching the phone back. "He wasn't."

"De Zurara is alive?" Felix began excitedly, then proclaimed in an outburst, "He is alive!"

Ian turned to me. "This explains it all, David—the empty cargo space, the crane. How we didn't find Sofia during our first raid."

I was beginning to feel the onset of seasickness. It had never been a problem for me before, but this was a degree of nausea I couldn't ignore.

Frowning, I said, "I don't understand."

"Sofia had a sub."

"No shit," Cancer replied, "we found it and rode it down the river."

Ian shook his head. "Not a low-profile vessel. A fully submersible one, like they captured off the coast of Spain. Western Colombia has the most sophisticated clandestine shipyards in the world. Sofia built a true submarine, and when we did the raid with AFEUR she was right there, beneath the surface. But how do you get a sub to Venezuela? The Panama Canal is too shallow. So she loaded it onto the container ship and made sure we couldn't see it with aerial surveillance. Once the ship reached the Caribbean, they put it back in the water."

Reilly protested, "But we were tracking her phones the whole time—"

"It's because we were tracking her phones," Ian snapped, "that Sofia did what she did."

Cancer leaned forward and growled, "Keep talking, cocksucker."

Ian continued, "She knew we were onto her because she had a source in Herrera's outfit, right? She sent the Venezuelan military to knock out our ambush, then picked up the VX as planned. But she only used two trucks to send the VX back to Cartagena, which is a straight shot east of the Panama Canal. The ship's crew must have put the sub to sea as soon as the crossing was complete, before our drones were in place. Meanwhile Sofia went to the coast of Venezuela, leaving nice, juicy SIGINT hits for us to follow. She dragged every possible US asset away from the actual loading point, and sacrificed herself to safeguard her plan."

If my seasickness was bad before, now it was reaching new heights—I felt dizzy, my stomach knotted with tension.

Then Ian looked at Felix and asked, "What are the capabilities of a 40-meter sub?"

"It could not be that long—the largest are 36 meters in length. These are double hull, with ballast tanks in between, Russian design. Operating depth of thirty meters. They can carry 150, perhaps 200 tons."

"Range?"

"A diesel engine could travel no more than 4,000 kilometers. But if it has diesel-electric propulsion? Just under 7,000."

Ian gave a sickeningly insincere laugh. "How long would that take to build? How much would it cost?"

"To build? Two or three years. The cost, 15 or 20 million."

Looking skyward, Ian explained, "Weisz's first payment to Sofia wasn't to finance the July 4th attack. It was to build a sub. That means we're looking at a terrorist plan three years and 45 million dollars in the making. The naval blockade isn't going to see a boat leaving Venezuela because there isn't one—the VX was transferred in Cartagena onto a submarine piloted by de Zurara. It's already underway. And once the VX reaches its destination, it's going to be unleashed."

Grabbing his arm, I asked, "What's the destination—US? Europe?"

"Somewhere that's closer to access by the Atlantic than the Pacific."

"Christ, Ian, that's half the planet."

He met my gaze then, nodding absently.

"I know."

I looked north across the shimmering waters of the Caribbean and beyond it, the United States. Then I glanced east toward the Atlantic, filling the void between Africa and Europe...then I recalled Felix's statement about the fully submersible vessels used to traffic cocaine across the ocean.

Once they make it to sea...they are ghosts.

My nausea suddenly became overpowering.

I spun away from Ian, grabbed the hull with both hands, and retched over the side.

BEAST THREE SIX:
SHADOW STRIKE #5

David Rivers is used to his targets being chosen by the CIA.

But this time, the target has chosen him.

When a senator's daughter is kidnapped in Benghazi, a Filipino terrorist named Khalil Noureddin claims responsibility and demands to negotiate with only one man: the leader of a CIA team that tried and failed to kill him over a year ago.

David remembers the failure all too clearly. And while his team narrowly escaped a ruthless terrorist force, the attempt catapulted Khalil into international notoriety and caused him to vanish completely—until now.

With David surrendering himself to Khalil to facilitate hostage negotiations, and his team embarking on a harrowing infiltration across Libya to support the rescue effort, the clock is ticking with an innocent woman's life hanging in the balance.

But capturing a high-profile hostage is just one element of Khalil's plan.

To uncover a far more insidious plot unfolding in Libya, David's team will have to negotiate brutal militias, Russian mercenaries, and operatives of a mysterious terrorist syndicate...before it's too late.

ABOUT THE AUTHOR

Jason Kasper is the USA Today bestselling author of the Spider Heist, American Mercenary, and Shadow Strike thriller series. Before his writing career he served in the US Army, beginning as a Ranger private and ending as a Green Beret captain. Jason is a West Point graduate and a veteran of the Afghanistan and Iraq wars, and was an avid ultramarathon runner, skydiver, and BASE jumper, all of which inspire his fiction.

Sign up for Jason Kasper's reader list at
severnriverbooks.com/authors/jason-kasper

jasonkasper@severnriverbooks.com